Mother

Also by Belinda Brett

Dreaming of Water

Mother

Belinda Brett

PIATKUS

First published in Great Britain in 1998 by
Judy Piatkus (Publishers) Ltd of
5 Windmill Street, London W1

This edition published 1998

The moral right of the author has been asserted

*A catalogue record for this book is available
from the British Library*

ISBN 0 7499 0457 7

Set in Times by
Intype London Ltd

Printed and bound in Great Britain by
Biddles Ltd, Guildford and King's Lynn

For Nick and Henry with love and thanks

Acknowledgements

With special thanks to my mother, my brother Edward, and my godmother Pam, and to Brenda Chapman and Tom and Pam Stuttaford.

28 October 1996

Haze covered the sun on the day Hilda Maddison was buried. Shafts of smoky light hit the long black body of the hearse as it drew up at the lych gate. In the car park of the recently built supermarket, just beyond the stone-wall boundary of the thirteenth-century church, shoppers glanced up curiously as two funeral cars arrived behind the hearse. Some of the shoppers watched for a moment before turning away to set off purposefully for the automatic doors of the crowded emporium, or to offload their groceries from wire trolleys into their cars: the jumbo packets of high-fibre cereal, the prepacked chicken drumsticks, the ready meals, the cans of diet cola, the plastic bags of washed green salad.

At the lych gate the doors of the funeral cars were opened. One by one, Hilda's family stepped out, to be greeted by the priest.

Inside the church the flat white light struck coldly through the clear glass of the lancet windows and was warmed to a faint glow by the blue and red and gold of the stained-glass east window, which pictured Jesus with St Andrew and bore the message, 'Come with me and I will make you fishers of men'.

The organ played gently, a Bach fugue. Silently Hilda's surviving friends and relations waited to pay their last respects to her mortal remains. The heavy door creaked shut. There was a whispering of clerical vestments, the sound of muted footsteps and, foot on the soft pedal, the organist set out to render 'The Entrance of the Queen of Sheba' more solemn than triumphal, as the pall bearers, shouldering her narrow coffin

1

with its single spray of white roses, bore Hilda slowly up
the aisle along which, fifty-six years before, to the sound of
Mendelssohn's 'Wedding March', and on her father's arm, she
had moved radiantly towards Clive and her future.

'I am the resurrection and the life, saith the Lord.' The
congregation stood.

Hilda's son, David, and her daughter, Alice, walked side
by side behind their mother's body. Then came David's wife
Jonquil, and Alice's husband Ralph, followed by Hilda's
grandchildren. First, David's daughters, Louisa and Helen,
both weeping, and lastly Alice's children, Rosamund and
William.

Ralph lifted his eyes from Alice's bowed and black-clad
shoulders to the back of her head. She was wearing a black
felt hat with a brim. Her glossy hair curved down from under
the hat and rested on her collar. She would be weeping
behind those dark glasses. He wanted to touch her. But she
would accept no comfort from him. He switched his gaze to
the pale wooden coffin, and felt the familiar animosity. Why
couldn't you have died when you should have done, he
thought, beating back his anger. Ahead of him, Alice turned
awkwardly into the front pew. Beside him, Jonquil sniffed and
fumbled for her handkerchief. Ralph looked again at the
coffin and visualised what was inside it. I am not the only one,
he thought, who has reason to wish that Hilda's heart attack
in April had finished her off then.

At the rear of the cortège, William concentrated on
keeping back the tears. He tried counting his breaths. He'd
discovered that controlling his breathing helped at difficult
times. He first started doing it when he was quite young, to
stop being sick on the school bus. He'd used it in the exam
room to calm his nerves. But now, however hard he tried to
count 'one – in; two – out; three – in; four – out', and so on,
the feel of his grandmother's stick-like arm, and her hand
twitching in his as he helped her up the stairs that last time,
were more real to him than what was happening now. And yet
it was true. He was really here. Just as his grandmother,
except for her poor empty old body, was not. Through blurred
eyes William watched the pall bearers lay down their light
burden. Automatically, he followed Rosamund into the front

pew, behind his mother, his uncle and aunt, his stepfather and his cousins. He glimpsed his mother's white profile, Jonquil's black-gloved hand clasping a prayer book, Helen's round, tear-stained cheek, as they turned to face the coffin, all alone on its stand in front of the pulpit. The organist played the introductory bars of the first hymn. Rosamund cleared her throat and in a barely audible voice started to sing with the rest of the congregation. William's heart thumped as he thought; they're following a script. The prayers, the music, the hymns, everyone knows what to do. My family, all these people behind me, are behaving as if everything is right and proper. He felt his whole body sway backwards and the edge of the seat digging into his calves, as his mind shied away from the apparent normality of this ceremony. He gripped the insoles of his shoes with his toes to steady himself, and felt his suspicions strengthen. He fixed his eyes on the pure white flowers resting on the top of the coffin and he knew, with a terrible certainty, that his grandmother had not died naturally. Someone, quite close by, had played a part in her death.

> Goodness and mercy all my life
> Shall surely follow me;
> And in God's house for evermore
> My dwelling-place shall be.

Hilda had not been a regular churchgoer: Christmas and Easter, if ever. The priest, who was young and who had recently come to the parish, hardly knew her. Over a glass of sherry Alice and David had told him a little about their mother. Now, he spoke in a light, quick, unparson-like tenor of Hilda's war service in the Wrens, of her devotion to her family, her love of life, her wit and honesty. Her old-fashioned virtues.

Soon, they were standing to sing.

> Abide with me: fast falls the eventide:
> The darkness deepens: Lord with me abide.

Jonquil, who had doggedly chosen that hymn, was blowing her nose. Tears were rushing down Alice's cheeks, blindly, she

3

reached out to David. He took her hand and closed his fingers round it.

Where is death's sting? Where, grave, thy victory?
I triumph still, if thou abide with me.

Outside, the sky, a quilt of back-lit cloud, glared down on the open grave with its headstone inscribed with Clive's name, below which a space had been waiting for his wife's name to be similarly carved in the veined marble. Flowers, frivolous and bright, were banked by the fresh-dug earth. There were no wreaths and no lilies. Hilda had hated both.

The tolling of the single church bell had to compete with the revving of engines in the supermarket car park, as the family, sombrely clothed, gathered for the committal.

David took the gleaming spade from the priest and cast a dollop of damp soil onto the lid of the coffin. Then the spade was offered to Alice, who shrank away. 'I can't,' she whispered. Ralph, standing behind, took the implement from her hand and carried out the necessary ritual.

When it was all over, Jonquil stood for a moment, gazing at the great quantity of flowers, the chrysanthemums and dahlias, the carnations and roses, at the cards with their hand-written expressions of affection for Hilda. 'Mother would have appreciated this,' she said.

'She wouldn't,' William said. He was outraged. 'Granny didn't want to die.'

15 April 1996

Hilda

If parson lost his senses – and people came to theirs. Echoes in my head. Over and over. No room for thought. *If parson lost his senses.* Have I lost mine? Words twist and turn. I try to catch hold of them. To make sense of them. *Maimed and shabby tigers.* Why *'maimed and shabby tigers'*? And then again over and over, *If parson lost his senses – and people came to theirs.* Where am I? Blue curtains I do not recognise. Strange noises – separate from the one I hear in my head. Coughs, moans, shouting.

If parson lost his senses. A line of poetry. How odd it should sound in my head now. Now. Slowly it comes. A memory of unbearable pain. Cruel hands grabbing my chest, squeezing the life out of me. Am I dying? Am I dead?

I remember a light shining. A woman dressed all in white. A mouth filled with large teeth. 'Stop making all that noise,' she says. 'You must be quiet.' And then falling back into a black hole. Now. Surely it is not me making those terrible noises?

The unfamiliar curtains are flicked aside and the woman comes and stands over me. Her lips stretch wide over the long teeth. She looks into my eyes, touches my wrist. She tells me I have had a heart attack but I am doing fine. *A heart attack.* That must have been the strangling pain, and this alien place a hospital. She says I was brought here yesterday. I say I am cold. I want my electric blanket. She closes her lips and smooths the heavy blankets which do not warm me. 'Your daughter's on her way.'

5

Alice. Warmth floods up from inside and almost conquers the cold.

'Soon. Will she be here soon?'

'This afternoon.' It must be a smile, that stretching of the lips. She opens all the curtains that enclose my bed and disappears.

This afternoon. What time is it now? Where's my watch? How long must I wait? I search for a clock. But everything is blurred. Where are my spectacles? I strain my eyes and see I have fellow sufferers in this earthly hell. Without my spectacles, I cannot make them out clearly. But my hearing is too keen to block out their anguished cries. Opposite, someone is coughing – great bubbling, hawking, gut-wrenching spasms. Somewhere a thin, high voice is wailing, 'Will you rescue me?'

I cannot bear it. I am clothed in a strange gown of scratchy cloth. Stretched out on this hard mattress, my bones ache; my skin is cold and clammy. A rubber sheet? I will not remain here. I can just make out the open door of the ward. I watch and wait for Alice to come through it. Alice will take me home.

If parson lost his senses – and people came to theirs – and he and they together knelt down with angry prayers. . . . Knelt down with angry prayers. The next line. And then – *maimed and shabby tigers.* On the tip of my tongue, out of the corner of my eye – *little hunted hares.* Alice will look it up in *The Golden Treasury.* Why doesn't she come?

Opposite, next to the coughing, I make out a male figure hunched in a chair.

That voice again, very high pitched – a mewling kitten. 'It's all nasty and wet and cold down here.'

Clear and sharp as a diamond catching the light I see: *we're all dying in this place.* Where is Alice? I watch the door. I watch the door for a very long time. A gawky girl, my Alice. Brown hair in plaits; red ribbons – her favourite colour. Grey pleated skirt, lace-up shoes. Off to school. Anxious eyes. 'Shall I take my mac Mummy?'

My daughter. Bobbed hair, crow's feet round her eyes; anxious in a different way. At last: I know her shape so well: gawky girl, rangy woman. At last she comes swinging through that door. 'Mother.'

I am flooded with relief. 'Oh Alice: darling Alice; I thought you were never coming.'

She puts her arms round me and says she's here now and how do I feel and everything will be all right.

I say everything will be all right once I am home. There is a pause: the space of a heartbeat, and she says she will not take me home.

'The doctors won't allow it,' she says. 'You need more care than I can give you.'

'Oh bugger the doctors.' I am angry with my daughter. Afraid. I tell her I am perfectly all right. If she won't take me home I shall order a taxi myself, and just go.

Alice's eyes are not anxious. They are adamant. She will not take me home. The nurse with the long teeth appears and says, 'Come now Mrs Maddison: we won't keep you any longer than we need. We're short enough on beds.'

I want my electric blanket. I'm cold. Alice says something to the nurse and now I see that Alice is angry. The nurse goes. 'You see what it's like', I say. 'You can't leave me here.'

Alice says please be good and cooperate. Sister says this ward has only been open a week and they aren't stocked up. No electric blankets. No bedsocks. Hot water bottles are too dangerous. Alice says she will bring me bedsocks tomorrow. *Tomorrow*. That I can't go home until the doctor has seen me again. She is staying in my house and she will fetch me home just as soon as it's allowed. I do not know if I can believe her. *Am I going to die?* Alice says of course not, don't be silly. I've had a funny turn. She untucks the blankets and takes my foot in her hand and begins gently to rub warmth into my flesh, my bones. Suddenly I remember: *what about Pinky?* Alice says, don't worry: I'll look after Pinky. Pinky. I long to stroke his smooth black coat, touch his long whiskers. Hear his purr, like a little engine inside him. But wait. Alice has Emily. Emily is a large yellow Labrador dog and Pinky is afraid of her. *Where is Emily?* Alice is annoyed. She tells me of course she has brought Emily with her and there is no way Emily could possibly harm Pinky. More likely the other way round. When Alice goes it's like a cold grey fog closing in around my bed.

Alice

'It's your brother on the phone.' Ralph passes me the receiver. *Your* brother he says. It's always *your* brother, *your* mother, *your* children. Distancing himself as if they would contaminate him.

And then David *my* brother tells me calmly, our mother has been taken ill. 'It was a little heart attack,' he says in a consciously steady voice. 'Don't be alarmed.'

But I am – alarmed. I sit down on the bed, clutching the receiver. I try to take in what David is telling me. Chest pains in the night. Sick in the morning. A state of collapse by the time Mrs Curtis arrived at nine. Mrs Curtis called an ambulance. 'There's been some damage to the heart, but if she gets through the next few days she should make a good recovery. She's asking for you Alice. Can you come?'

'Of course,' I say immediately.

'You can always stay with us, but Mother would probably like you to sleep at her place – she's worrying about that wretched cat. And it's more convenient for the hospital.'

I put down the receiver. 'Mother's ill,' I say to Ralph who is putting on his trousers.

'Nothing trivial, I hope.'

Sometimes I really hate Ralph. 'She's had a heart attack. She might die.' I burst into tears. 'And if that was meant to be a joke, now's not the time.'

Buttoning his shirt, Ralph says, 'I'm sorry.'

I'm still crying.

Ralph puts his arms round me. 'So you're leaving me then; to go and look after her.'

'I have to.'

He wipes my eyes with his handkerchief. 'What about that smart-arse brother of yours and his wonder-wife? They're on the doorstep after all.'

'She wants *me*.'

'It's lucky you're free then. Able to drop everything and rush to the rescue.'

Free. He loads the word with irony. Who is ever free? He means I don't have a job at present because Billy went bust three months ago. I loved working for Billy. I felt at home in his dark little shop with its panelled walls and the beautiful antique furniture. But it seems his stuff – 'Early Oak' – is just not in demand.

Ralph strokes the hair away from my eyes. 'Don't stay away too long.' I am comforted by the tenderness in his fingers. And then he spoils it by saying, 'Don't forget you have a husband,' in such a way that I am made aware of duties, responsibilities, not love.

I go down to the kitchen, fill the kettle and put it on the hotplate, lay the breakfast table and try to plan for the next few days. Ralph appears, freshly shaved, uncommunicative. I know he is thinking about work; projecting himself into the day ahead. He is unconcerned with the problems, emotional and practical, that preoccupy me, except in so much as they affect him. Selfish bastard. And yet I sort of admire his single-mindedness.

Ralph shovels cornflakes into his mouth. I often wonder at his ability to move his jaw so rapidly. Crunch, crunch; crunch, crunch. The bowl is empty and I've only managed a couple of spoonfuls of mine.

'Let me know what the form is.' He jingles his car keys in one hand and lays the other briefly on my shoulder.

I'm near to tears.

'Bye then.'

I watch from the dining-room window as he backs his car out of the garage into the cul-de-sac, turns and heads for the road. I ring the hospital to tell them I'll be there by evening. They say my mother is comfortable.

How can you be comfortable after a heart attack? I hope they mean she's not in pain. I cannot bear to think of my mother in pain – losing her vitality. She is seventy-five. Not *really* old. Perhaps her heart is tired. And this is just a warning sign. I imagine my own heart, pumping blood unobtrusively round my arteries. And then I stop. I prefer not to think of what's going on inside my body.

I clear the breakfast table and load the washing machine. I go to the supermarket. When I come back, weighed down with bulging plastic bags, William is packing books into his rucksack, ready for afternoon college.

'I'm not eating that muck,' he says watching me unpack low-fat ready meals.

I tell him Granny's ill and I have to go and look after her.

'You're not going to leave me with *him*.' Guilt. Why do I have to feel guilt? For landing William with Ralph?

Even when we were married, William's father showed very little interest in either of his children. And now he is out in Tanzania building a hotel for tourists, Richard might just as well never have existed. I cannot believe I spent ten years of my life living with that man. What did we do? What did I feel, travelling through all those weeks and days and hours and minutes?

I tell William he and Ralph will both have to make an effort. Ralph often says he gets on better with my children when I'm not present. I pretend to us both that I believe this.

William fastens his rucksack and picks up his bicycle lock. 'I'll be out most of the time anyway,' he says. 'And I'll do my own cooking.'

I know what this means. William has a healthy appetite and he likes to cook, relying heavily on the frying pan. I sigh and remind him that he's plenty of studying to get on with. And don't stay out late, I plead. Ten-thirty on weekdays. I imagine him returning at midnight and disturbing a peacefully sleeping Ralph.

William is sixteen. All gangly limbs; an undisciplined bush of curly brown hair, which Ralph, whose own dark hair shows signs of thinning, is always binding on about. *Doesn't that boy ever wash his hair? Doesn't he own a hairbrush?* Even Mother says a rake would be of more service to William's hair than a comb. *Mother.*

William looks at me and his clear as water grey eyes seem

10

to register my concern. 'It'll be all right,' he says. 'I'm sorry about Granny.'

I stand in the porch and say goodbye to William as he sets off for college on his bike. Then, auto-pilot takes over and, while I worry about Mother, enables me to operate the tumble dryer, iron six of Ralph's pure cotton shirts and push the vacuum cleaner over the carpet in an attempt to eliminate yellow Labrador hairs. I dust the dining-room table: reproduction George III. And the Chippendale-style chairs.

Our house is furnished with the products of Ralph's factory. The date – 1835 – is set in the brickwork on our front wall, just below the slate roof. Our rooms are spacious with wide sash windows and high ceilings, and two of them have the original white marble fireplaces. They provide the ideal setting for Ralph's furniture, which he likes kept pristine, in case a visitor might want to buy something. Familiar with Billy's solid oak refectory tables and carved court cupboards, I've gone off Ralph's reproduction mahogany, which is unfortunate. I plump up the cushions of the saggy old sofa I refuse to get rid of, and I ignore the cobweb on the ceiling cornice. Then, I fling clothes into a suitcase, and retrieve six mugs containing mould at various stages of growth from William's attic bedroom. On the way down, I pass Rosamund's open bedroom door. Her room looks unnaturally clean and tidy. When Rosamund is home from university, her bed, her chair, the floor are littered with clothes and books, newspapers, magazines and plastic bags containing goodness knows what. It always surprises me that a person who can be so well organised when she wants to, chooses to live in such a muddle. But Rosamund says she always knows exactly where everything is, and she can find anything she wants straight away. I wish she were here now. Rosamund is one of those blessed people whose presence always makes you feel better. Tonight I must telephone her, far away in Edinburgh, and tell her about her grandmother. She'll be upset.

I bolt bread and cheese and gulp coffee. Emily regards me with anxious old eyes from her basket in the corner of the kitchen. Come along, I say. She thumps her tail and gets stiffly out of her basket. I add Pedigree Chum and a sack of dog biscuits to my small pile of luggage, load my old Peugeot and lock up the house. As I turn out of the cul-de-sac into the main road, a sudden gust of wind buffets the side of the car, and by the time I reach the A12, torrential rain is battering the roof and streaming down the windows.

The windscreen wipers swish ineffectively back and forth and Classic FM belts out its curious mixture of the sublime and the banal: I feel uneasy about my parting from Ralph. He does not understand my responsibility to my mother. I know how he sees it: *'ours is a primary relationship.'* He makes me feel guilty for abandoning him for lesser ties. I do not want to drive to Kent in a rainstorm to look after my mother, but at this moment it seems she has the prior claim. Perhaps I should feel important: being so needed. But I don't. I feel torn and guilty. I should have given him a hug and told him I loved him, instead of just accepting his cool 'Bye then'. One of my sister-in-law's little sayings is 'Never let the sun go down on your wrath'. And another of Jonquil's sayings is 'I always put my husband first'. But Jonquil makes sure David's needs concur with her own. Life is simple for Jonquil.

By the time I get to the M25, the rain is petering out and a feeble sun lights up the clouds. I wonder, what is it that makes Ralph and me a couple? For that's what we are, indubitably, a couple.

The first time I met him, one flash of those brilliant blue eyes and I was instantly captured. I marvel at it now: so blatant. We were both married to other people at the time. Something else to feel guilty about. I was bewitched by the strength of his passion for me. I am still awed by the power of his emotions. Delighted by his tenderness; astounded at his rage; distressed by his possessive jealousy. He wanted us to have a child, but I refused. I have Rosamund and William. I didn't want any more children. As recently as last week, he said, 'If we'd had a child he'd be about eight by now.' Sometimes I feel bad that I denied Ralph fatherhood. But it's too late now.

We still have good times together.

As I cross the Dartford bridge, the sun is strong enough to turn the flat waters of the Thames from rust brown to a dirty

silver. Waiting at the booth to pay the toll, I decide to telephone Ralph as soon as I arrive: to make things up with him.

My heart twists at the sight of of my mother, so diminished.
You are my mother, I think, a person of substance, a powerful
force, worthy of respect as well as love. I do not want to feel
sorry for you.

Her body hardly raises a mound beneath the coarse
blankets. The black pits that are her eyes flare eagerly when
they focus upon mine. Her thin hand is cold as ice. Sister
dismisses, piously, all my requests to warm her, baring teeth in
a grimace which exposes receding gums and doesn't even
pretend to be apologetic. She bustles away, her frizzy hair, the
colour of stewed tea, seeming to frizz more extremely at
the effrontery of anyone daring to ask for so many unavail-
able luxuries.

'*You're not going to die.*' I reassure, thinking: not yet; I'm
not ready to lose you. Please don't die. My eyes fill. I concentrate on rubbing warmth into my mother's small cold feet.
The skin is tissue-thin over the branching veins.

She expects me to take her home. When I refuse, I see
betrayal written all over her face.

The doctor has an ebony skin and a tall and commanding
presence. He says my mother will pick up gradually. In a few
days we'll notice the difference. She should make a good
recovery, bearing in mind her age. And then, provided at first
there is someone to care for her, she may go home.

I understand her distress. Even diminished, my mother
looks sane and youthful in this geriatric ward with its two
rows of iron beds, occupied by half-alive old women: scare-
crow hair, white as lint, knobbled, age-spotted hands plucking
at sheets, cracked voices mumbling nonsense. A brisk orderly
in a brown and white checked uniform sprays heavily floral
air freshener, which fights with the pungent odours of disin-
fectant, ancient flesh and urine, but fails to overpower them.

'Soon,' I say. 'You shall go home as soon as you are well
enough.' I take the hand, resting lightly on the sheet, and kiss
the thin, soft cheek.

'You'll stay?'

'Yes. Don't worry. I'll look after you.'

13

'Ah.' There is satisfaction in the monosyllable which is hardly more than a sigh. She closes her eyes.

I sit, holding my mother's frail cool hand, and try not to think that I don't want to be doing this. She sleeps, her breathing so light that it doesn't seem possible she is taking enough air into her lungs to stay alive. When Rosamund and William were babies, I used to bend close to their sleeping faces to confirm the existence of their shallow breaths. With Mother so pale and still, I am tempted to do the same. I sit there a long while. Eventually, I loosen my hand, and whisper, 'I should be going soon, Mother.' She tightens her grip. Gently, I pull away. Her eyes open: muddied brown. The expression they hold reminds me of other eyes, some other time. Young grey eyes. My son's eyes on his first day at school. But the look is the same: *don't leave me.*

I reclaim my hand. In the comfortless hospital bed, Mother's frail body does not stir. All her remaining vigour, all her power, is vested in her eyes. 'Goodbye Mother.' I kiss the flat cheek. 'I'll come back tomorrow.' I slip through the blue curtains surrounding her bed and walk out of the ward without a backward glance. I shall drive quickly to my mother's house and telephone Ralph.

April 1996

Hilda

I am waiting for Alice. She promised she would come at visiting time. Surely it is visiting time. While I wait, pictures and words roll around in my head. It's like watching a film, but the story keeps changing. I test myself. Try to visualise my house. My staircase. Does it run up in a straight flight to the landing? Or is there a curve at the top? *Straight.* My sitting room. Two wing chairs, two-seater sofa, blue flowered chintz. Curtains: Regency stripe, green and grey. No. I gave those curtains to Alice. I've given that girl too much. Spoilt her. Plain curtains. Blue the colour of the flowers on the sofa. Wallpaper. I see flowered wallpaper. White cabbage roses, green leaves, trellis. My bedroom. But, wait. A baby in a crib; a crib with pale lemon muslin skirts sweeping the floor. Baby Alice, or was it David?

Where is she? Where is Alice. Always late. Why can't she be on time? I look down at the notepad she brought me. I have my glasses now. My handwriting looks unfamiliar. I started with my name.

Hilda Maddison. Age 75.

Daughter – Alice Halliday. Telephone number 786511. I had trouble with that. Numbers dancing in my head. But I made myself wait and in the end they sorted themselves out. They look right now.

Son – David Maddison. Daughter-in-law – Jonquil Maddison. Telephone number 394821. Numbers are difficult.

Jonquil came. She said you're in the best place Mother. There's a bitter wind out there. She put her handkerchief to

15

her nose and looked only at me. She didn't stay long. She brought orange juice. It tastes dusty and I dislike drinking from a plastic beaker. Orange juice does not suit my bladder. I imagine a dry martini, pale, pale yellow with a twist of lemon. Clive used to make me a dry martini before dinner. Alice must bring gin in a plain bottle. I search for the biro, which has slipped between sheet and blanket and write: To bring please Alice: (You see I am not mad. I can make lists.)

Hair cream in tube. Nail scissors and file. Cotton wool. Liquid make-up (All in dressing table drawer.) Hand mirror.

I have not seen my face for days. Where are the looking glasses in hospitals? My lips are sore, wrinkling themselves ever thinner and drier.

Also, please, some lip salve.
And some cologne. 4711. A carrier bag; my green National Trust one if you can find it. To put everything in. I can't find the side combs for my hair. Thompsons on the High Street. Or Boots if you must. Something to read.

I shall ask Alice to find a book of short stories; nothing gloomy. Not modern depressing ones.

My other reading glasses. The ones with the horn frames. Used to belong to father.

Alice's father. My Clive. How long since he died? It seems a very long time, but I believe it is not. I do not want to think of his death.

I was so young when I married him. And so in love. The second of June 1940. No trouble remembering those numbers. That date. It was the most beautiful hot, English summer day. I could not believe this was me; the luckiest girl in the world. Marrying Clive. So handsome in his uniform. I thought I would burst with excitement, burst out of my cream crêpe dress with the bolero jacket. Flowers in my hair and a scrap of veil which blew round my face as we stood together outside

16

the church. The second of June 1940. Dunkirk. My wedding day. Locked in my memory for ever: in perfect focus, the colours unfaded. And the sounds.

The rumble of gunfire across the Channel.

In a dream, drifting down the aisle with Clive, my hand tightly held in his. Unconcerned by the tears pouring down the seamed face of my Uncle Herbert. He was waiting, like many of those people rising to their feet as the two of us passed among them, waiting to know whether his son had made it back from France. It came later. My understanding of all their fears.

We had one night for our honeymoon. The Bull Hotel in Rochester. There, I'm not dotty. I can remember that.

It's yesterday and the day before I can't be sure about.

We had the honeymoon suite. The drawers were full of confetti from other weddings. And, then, Clive went off to finish his training and I went back to work in the Bank. I stayed on in our little cottage in Loose. I remember a thatched roof and a stream. He came home whenever he had leave. And if he couldn't get back, then I went to him and we stayed in guest houses and bed and breakfast places. I can still smell that smell: boiled cabbage. Feel the soles of my feet shrink from the cold lumpiness of cracked linoleum.

Now, I am a prisoner in this horrible place. The woman in the bed opposite is at it again. A long bout of gut-wrenching, body-jerking coughs. Her lungs must be solid. Clive's lungs never recovered from his time in the army, sleeping on damp ground in a tent. Marching in all weathers. But he didn't cough like that. His was a short, dry, rasping cough. Bronchitis every winter, and he wouldn't give up smoking.

Hacking and spluttering. It makes me feel sick. I sip the orange juice, acid in my throat. And, suddenly, that poem again. *Maimed and shabby tigers.* Poor moth-eaten old tigers in zoos. The jungle faded from their eyes. I once took David and Alice to London zoo. Alice cried when she saw the giraffes: long graceful necks and sad eyes and so little space. Alice loves animals just like I do. But she is a dog person. I am a cat person. I long for my little cat. If I could feel the weight of him, curled on his blanket down by my feet, I would not

17

feel so alone. I trust Alice is looking after him properly: that she is not allowing that big dog to bully him.

Alice. Where are you Alice? Why have you abandoned me here?

I'm frightened. Suppose Alice never comes?

And now a tall black man and the nurse with the teeth are standing by my bed. She says here is Doctor. So very black. They speak in low voices to each other and loudly to me as if I am a deaf child. You are to have some tests, they shout. 'But my daughter's coming,' I say. 'Alice. Alice is coming to take me home.' 'When you've had your tests, dear,' they say.

'But she won't know where I am.'

'Don't worry,' they say. 'We will explain.'

I have a fluttery feeling inside my stomach. And a small pain in my chest.

The black doctor and the nurse go away. I shut my eyes.

Someone comes and stands beside my bed. With a rush of happiness, I know it is Clive, back from the army. His hair is shorn. He is thin and sunburned. I feel my whole face smile as he puts his hand over mine.

'Come along Luv.' It is not my Clive, but an unfamiliar young man in a white uniform. 'We're going for a ride,' he says. I plummet down a deep, echoing well. Another young man appears. I'm moving. Shoes squeak on the floor. They are trundling me along a hospital corridor. 'All right Luv?' I would prefer not to be called 'Luv', but they are jolly young men and they don't shout at me. I have not the strength to say, firm but pleasant, 'My name is Mrs Maddison'.

Alice

'You've been away a week.' Ralph's voice is tight and peevish. 'Isn't it about time you came home? You *have* got a husband you know.'

I listen while he complains that there is no food in the house. The phone crackles. Not true: what about the stack of ready meals in the freezer? But getting anything out of the freezer, defrosting it and putting it in the oven is too much trouble for Ralph. He says William has eaten all the bread and not replaced it. Ditto the cornflakes. 'And last night William and his friends came clomping in at eleven-thirty. Sat around in the kitchen, scraping the chairs across the floor and droning on to all hours. You can imagine what it was like in the morning. Dirty coffee mugs in the sink and crumbs and spilt milk all over the table. And he left the kitchen light on all night.'

'How are things at the factory?' I ask, to distract him. Ralph loves his factory; loves his work. I walk round with him sometimes, while he checks on progress. He's at home there. I can see how he savours the smell of fresh-cut wood, the air of concentrated activity. I watch him talk to the men. They are all good craftsmen he says. I can see they respect him. He can do everything they do. He's proud of his product. High-quality reproduction furniture. It's a job these days, he says, getting good apprentice carvers. Even the standard acanthus leaf carving on a chairback needs to flow and suggest movement. Hand finish.

The new router machine, says Ralph, after all those problems, is working well. The walnut bureau cabinet, a 'special'

19

for a Belgian customer, is on schedule. 'Remember the Cuban mahogany I got hold of last year,' he says, enthusiastic now, and I listen attentively while he tells me some planks are excellent with good figuring. Some full of knots and rather ordinary. They've started on the dining tables. Harry's slowing up, he says. Harry is the chief polisher. But he's getting on now. He has back trouble and his eyes aren't so good. I ask after Trudy. Trudy is Ralph's secretary. She has very bad skin and usually her over-anxious desire to please irritates Ralph. Now, he says with satisfaction, Trudy's being extremely helpful. Offered to do some shopping for him. I don't acknowledge this reproof, but ask, the absent but still dutifully interested wife, about his plans for the new range. Practical furniture, to fit in to both modern and old houses. Kind of pseudo Art Deco, I think he means. I just hope he isn't going to use bleached walnut. Yes, he says some woman's coming to see him tomorrow with new designs.

There's a pause and then he does actually ask after my mother. 'How's the Monster? Still enjoying ill health?' I tell him, icily, that Mother is a little better. 'Better enough to be released? Or only better enough to demand a pink gin?'

I remain silent and he asks again when am I coming home. To look after him, he means. Why can't he tell me he misses me? Instead of emphasising the inconvenience of my absence? I tell him I'm just off to have supper with David and Jonquil. 'Well don't pussy-foot around,' he says. 'Make them take over so you can come home.'

I say I'll try, and then I suggest he might come here for the weekend. 'Mother would like to see you,' I say, which we both know is untrue. I tell him I don't have to be at the hospital all day. We could go out somewhere. Take Emily for a walk. Have lunch in a pub. 'I'll see,' he says. 'I'd better go, there's someone at the door. It's probably William, forgotten his key again.' I tell him I'll hold on so I can speak to my son. When he comes back, he says it wasn't William after all. Just the Jehovah's Witnesses. 'Told them I was a Muslim.'

'Please give William my love,' I say. 'Tell him I'll give him a ring tomorrow.'

And then he starts up again. 'I don't know why you encourage William to cook, Alice. He's making an appalling mess of the cooker. And he's buggered up the waste disposal. God knows what he dropped down there; probably one of your Georgian tablespoons. You're good at training dogs, Alice, why can't you train your children?'

I feel a sob rising in my throat. He must have heard because there's a pause and suddenly he says, 'You left your blue shoes by the wardrobe. Toes pointing slightly in as if you'd just stepped out of them. And your pink cardigan's on the back of the chair. The sleeves look very empty.'

'Oh Ralph,' I say, 'I miss you too.'

I put down the telephone and set off to have supper with David and Jonquil, at Hunter's Moon. Hunter's Moon is our family house. David and Jonquil live there now. But they don't own it. Yet. Hunter's Moon still belongs to Mother. When Father died, Mother moved out of Hunter's Moon into this small modern house, just half an hour's drive from Hunter's Moon. For the convenience. I don't think she likes it much. But Hunter's Moon is far too big for her to manage on her own. David kept on his and Jonquil's flat in Pimlico, since David works in the City. But he seems to spend more and more time at Hunter's Moon. And of course, Jonquil is there, with Louisa and Helen. They act as if it belongs to them. I'm sure they expect it to – one day. But Jonquil shouldn't bank on it. I don't know what's in Mother's Will, but I've heard her say, 'Equal shares when I'm gone.'

The cherry blossom shines, pale as puffs of cloud in the half light as I drive past the orchards. They call Kent the Garden of England. This place is full of memories for me. Paul, my first boy friend, kissed me under a cherry tree in this orchard, on the way home from school. I pass the Wheat Sheaf Inn where we drank cider. Paul was Captain of Cricket. He had fair curly hair, and broad shoulders and tanned and muscular forearms. I thought he looked like a Greek god. I loved to watch him play cricket, but eventually I got bored listening to him talk about it afterwards.

I turn into the narrow road leading to the drive. Recently tarmacked, it used to be a sandy track. But the hawthorn still flowers in the tall hedges, like billows of sea-foam. My grandfather built Hunter's Moon in 1928. It's of warm red

21

brick, with a shingled roof and gabled windows with leaded glass. It has a timbered porch with an old-fashioned pink rose scrambling over it. I was born here. I grew up here. Now Jonquil has taken over. As I pass through the wide wooden gate that always stands open, along the drive to the broad, gravelled sweep that lies in front of the house, I fight nostalgia for the careless ease of my former self, for the safety of childhood. Rules for dealing with maudlin reminiscence mean I cannot allow myself to run my fingers over the date I scratched on the banister rail to mark my first period at the age of twelve, to investigate the loose floorboard in the bedroom that used to be mine; perfect hiding place for my running-away rations when I was ten, jealous of my brother and fighting with my mother, and later, for my first love letters from Paul.

If I was living at Hunter's Moon, its atmosphere of relaxed solidity, its unfussy elegance would have been preserved. There would be no high-tec kitchen, no double-glazing and no Spanish floor tiles. I often wonder at my Mother's forbearance in the face of this insensitive renovation of her home. But, there, David can do no wrong in her eyes. And Jonquil can do no wrong in David's eyes.

There was once a grass tennis court in the garden of Hunter's Moon. It was interestingly bumpy; we uscd to mark it out with a special white line-making machine. David and I had a lot of fun on that tennis court, with our friends. It's been converted to clay now. And there's a wire fence round it, instead of the tattered netting which didn't always stop stray balls from flying into the wild part of the garden. *That* looks more like a miniature municipal park now rather than The Wilderness, which is what I used to call it. It surprises me that David doesn't have more affection for our old grass tennis court, and that wild bit of garden we used to play Robin Hood in. It seems the girls needed a better surface for their tennis coaching. And Jonquil supervises the gardener. She gives him *carte blanche* with the axe. She's had most of the shrubs and trees hacked down out there, to make room for her studio: a Hansel-and-Gretel type wooden hut. She spends a lot of time in there painting flattering portraits of their friends.

They've invested heavily in comfort: gas-fired central

heating, thick wool carpets and sofas and armchairs with proper feather cushions. And they're the only people I know who have down-filled duvets and pillows in their guest bedroom. I would have thought, being an artist, the interior decoration might turn out a bit more interesting. But Jonquil has replaced all our old faded chintzes and the hand-blocked wallpapers my mother used to like, with pale bland colours – hardly a pattern anywhere. I suppose she thinks her portraits look better on a plain background. She does have a lot of ornaments – porcelain figurines of shepherdesses, harlequins and columbines, cherubs and some valuable Doulton vases. They stand around on the mantelpieces and on occasional tables: David and Jonquil *do* buy Ralph's furniture. 'Must support the family', Jonquil says, each time they have a new piece.

I park my car in front of the double garage, get out of it and walk towards the porch. There are buds on the pink rose. The door opens and Jonquil comes out. She's wearing a droopy blue smock dress and her long fair hair is tied back in a matching scarf. Her voice trembles, as she says, 'Oh Alice, we're so pleased you're here – it's all so dreadful.'

David, looking serious but collected, says 'Come and sit down', and presses a glass of white wine into my hand. We talk of our poor mother abandoned in her hospital bed. David says, 'we must all make the best of it. I believe she'll pull through.'

We drink our wine and talk some more, serious and rather stilted. And then David disappears into the kitchen. Jonquil and I resume our self-conscious conversation. I ask about the girls and she asks about William and Rosamund and then David comes back and tells us we're ready to eat. We go through to the dining room. 'He carves so beautifully,' says Jonquil. 'It's lamb, with rosemary and garlic. English lamb. Ridiculously expensive but New Zealand just doesn't taste the same.'

The meat is pink and thickly sliced. It lies in a white dish on the glossy dining table: Ralph's Georgian reproduction two pedestal mahogany (without the extending leaf on this occasion). I am sitting on one of his Chippendale-style dining chairs. I decide not to remark on this, to avoid being reminded

23

of my brother and sister-in-law's gracious patronage. But I'll tell Ralph when I talk to him next. The table is beautifully polished and the chair is comfortable. He'll be pleased. As usual, the silver cutlery is bright enough to see your face in. David serves the lamb and tells me to help myself to new potatoes and broccoli.

Jonquil says, in a wobbly voice, 'I've been working on a picture of Pinky, from some sketches I made last time I was there.'

David sits down and picks up his knife and fork.

I say the lamb looks delicious and help myself to mint sauce.

Jonquil's expression eases into solemn mournfulness and she says, 'It will be so sad if Mother never sees it.'

I wish Jonquil didn't call my mother 'Mother'. Why can't she call her Hilda like Ralph does?

Jonquil goes on talking in a dopy voice, 'Dear Mother. She did look a poor old thing when I saw her today. And someone died last night I believe.'

I knew about that. I only hope Mother didn't realise. When I arrived at the hospital this morning I heard the Sister with the teeth speaking quietly into a telephone: 'Olive Lennox has died.' And then, while I sat talking to Mother, a young nurse came and pulled the curtains round us. I'm ashamed to say, my curiosity overcame my appreciation of what is fitting. I parted the curtains a crack and peered through. I saw a metal trough on wheels, covered with a blanket, being pushed out from behind the closed curtains of the bed opposite. And I remembered the sad old man who had sat hunched by that bed, dabbing his eyes.

I don't know if Mother saw me looking. She said, 'It was dreadfully noisy last night. I can't imagine how they expect you to get any sleep. When can I come home?'

Jonquil says she finds it all so upsetting, she's not sure she is helping Mother by visiting.

Jonquil was very young, just graduated from art college, when David married her. He impressed upon my parents and me her special needs. He said she was very sensitive and not very strong. And it was because she was creative.

Being sensitive and not very strong has enabled Jonquil to

get out of doing boring, unpleasant things like carrying heavy shopping baskets and dealing with dirty nappies. But it hasn't impaired her organisational abilities. Over the years of their marriage, I've watched my brother gradually take over any domestic task not undertaken by the daily. Jonquil still manages a little cooking. But, then, cooking is creative. I'm awed by my sister-in-law's talent for conducting her life so exactly to suit herself. I envy her such gifts. What I don't know is this. Is David genuinely fooled by her alleged fragility? Or does he play along with it for reasons of his own?

Jonquil says, 'If you don't mind I'll give the visiting a rest for day or two. When I get back from that place I just can't work. It seems to block me.'

I think to myself, you're an artist Jonquil. Where's your artist's eye? I think of the wizened old lady in the bed at the far end of the ward. She has long white hair and a tiny triangular face with large puzzled faded blue eyes. This morning she was casting around with her hands and calling in her high childish voice. 'Is this my back door key? I want fish and chips for my dinner. I like dark chocolate; dark chocolate and bananas.'

What if my mother becomes like that? Disorientated. Infantile.

Jonquil's voice is trembling uncontrollably. 'I just can't bear it. I keep thinking of that picture I painted of Mother for her seventieth birthday and how her face has changed. All shrunk and wrinkled. Like a balloon that's been let down. I'm sorry; I'll have to go and find my handkerchief.' She pushes back her chair and rushes from the room.

I say, 'Oh dear,' and look down at my plate.

David says, 'It's all right for you. You're not as sensitive as she is.'

I control my indignation and say, icily restrained, 'If Jonquil can't cope with hospital visiting, I'd appreciate it very much if you could have Mother to stay for a while when she comes out. I really need to go home.'

'The trouble is,' says David, all seriousness, 'trouble is, of course we'd have her to stay with pleasure, but it's *you* she wants. It's *you* she wants to be with.'

25

I knows this to be true. I value it, for who does not value love? But I feel the weight of it too.

David gets to his feet and says he will make coffee. I tell him not to bother as I should be getting back.

He says, 'Oh Alice, won't you have coffee with me?'

My dog needs to be let out, I say, and there's Mother's cat. I thank him for supper and ask him to say goodbye to Jonquil for me.

My brother has lean cheeks and a careful smile. Once he had dimples and an impish grin. 'I'm sorry about all this Alice,' he says and for a brief tantalising moment, in his hazel eyes, I recognise the playmate of my childhood. Together we would make dens, deep inside the curtain of leaves formed by the huge old laurel bush, sacrificed in favour of Jonquil's studio. One day we cooked potato chips in candle grease on an old tin plate over another candle. They tasted rather strange and we'd been incredibly sick. But we never let on why. I wonder if he ever thinks about those carefree times.

He hugs me and says, conciliatory, 'I'll do what I can to help.'

I cannot quite disguise the sharp edge to my voice. 'I'm sure you will,' I say.

Driving away from Hunter's Moon, I think to myself that the chances of David and Jonquil taking Mother in when she comes out of hospital are nil. It will be up to me to look after her. I'll have to stay on. As I draw nearer to Mother's house I think, if you buy something just for the convenience of it, then that's exactly what you get. Mother's small square house was built in the sixties. It is set in a quiet crescent of houses of the same vintage. It has an L-shaped sitting/dining room with glazed doors opening into a long rectangular garden bounded by conifers, an all electric kitchen because Mother doesn't trust gas, and a downstairs cloakroom which houses Mother's collection of ancient coats and outdoor shoes and boots. Mother refused to consider the bungalow David and Jonquil found first for her. She said, it was good exercise going up and down stairs and in any case she wouldn't feel safe sleeping on the ground floor, and the bungalow's garden was too small.

Mother has the largest bedroom, at the front of the house. There are two other bedrooms and a bathroom and a box-room which Ralph says he'd have a job to swing Pinky around in. Convenient, yes. But it's a dull little house.

I park my Peugeot in front of the garage containing Mother's Rover, and I wonder, with a catch at my heart, will she ever drive it again?

I unlock the front door and go inside. Every house has a different smell. Hunter's Moon, beneath the clogging odour of soft furnishings, still retains a faint aroma of floor polish and the *pot-pourri* my mother used to make from rose petals out of the garden. This house smells of Mother: a hint of Elizabeth Arden's Blue Grass; the damp soapy flannel smell of Mother's lock-knit underwear which is usually hanging up to dry in the bathroom, having been washed in the bath with Mother, and, sharp little pulses of it here and there, the elusive but pungent whiff of tomcat.

In the kitchen Pinky has taken over Emily's basket. He opens a complacent green eye and closes it again. Emily, who has failed to hear the front door opening, is curled behind the sofa in the sitting room. She senses my approach and thumps her tail against the floor I kneel down and stroke her warm head and her cool silky ears. She struggles to her feet and lollops stiffly into the kitchen. She roots out her dish from beneath the kitchen table, picks it up in her mouth and brings it back to me, wagging her tail and making her special Labrador talking noise; a not unmusical rumble in the back of her throat, which always reminds me of a person humming a happy tune. Pinky remains in possession of Emily's basket and as she approaches, he opens his glass green eyes and growls; an unpleasant, gargling, increasing-in-volume growl. Emily stands stock-still, drops her head and stops wagging her tail.

I say, 'Come along Pinky: outside; you both have to go outside before bed.' Pinky just goes on glaring and growling. I open the back door and send Emily out into the dark garden. Then, I grit my teeth, grasp Pinky round his fat stomach and pick him up. He stops growling and begins to purr, draped over my arm. I stroke him gingerly. It seems churlish not to, but I don't much like the soft sinuous feel of him; as if he doesn't have a bone in his body. But he's Mother's cat. Mother loves him. Mother trusts me to to treat him kindly.

27

Emily gives a little woof at the back door. So, I let dog in, put cat out and lock the door. Pinky can come back in through the catflap. Emily sniffs her basket suspiciously. 'Go on', I say, 'get in while you have the chance'. And she steps into her basket and lies down with a sigh.

In the double bed in Mother's spare room, I miss Ralph. Alone, I wake several times during the night. I wish he was beside me, breathing steadily. I want his musky warmth. When we make love, I feel how deeply we care for each other. Our private world is so intense. I feel no-one could ever love me as he does.

At other times, our private world might never exist. I can't seem to please him. I feel him watching, waiting for me to slip up, to be caught out in unwifely behaviour. Like forgetting to collect his suit from the dry-cleaners and not taking enough trouble over his meals. He makes me feel guilty if I'm talking on the telephone when he comes home from work. Pointedly, he will switch off 'unnecessary' lights. He rages if I should stand a mug of coffee on *his* dining table without putting it on a mat first. I think he believes I do all these things on purpose to annoy him. Living with Ralph is not relaxing. And then there's his relationship with my family. From the first, Mother complained that Ralph didn't know how to behave. Didn't choose to, which was arguably worse. I sometimes think Ralph and Mother are like two boxers squaring up to each other: he so physically advantaged; she so fierce in spirit. And then there are my children. Rosamund calls Ralph 'Your horrible husband'. William, who is naturally quiet and self-contained, mostly avoids him.

Eventually, I fall asleep.

In the morning, I find Pinky flat out in Emily's basket and Emily again curled behind the sofa. Emily gets to her feet and follows me into the kitchen. I fill the kettle and plug it in. As I get out the milk, I resolve to defrost Mother's fridge, which is ice-bound and cluttered with a variety of little jars and jugs and basins and saucers and plastic bowls containing portions of leftover food. Mother cannot bring herself to throw food away. It's because of the War, she says: you young people are such terrible wasters of food. You never knew what it was like to live with rationing. I haven't had the heart

28

to throw away the few spoonfuls of congealed shepherd's pie, the tiny mound of cooked rice, the half tin of spam, the mashed potato sandwiched between two saucers, the mug of tomato soup covered with cling-film, the baked beans in the tin going black round the edges, the solidified gravy in the Pyrex jug. Once, when Ralph opened Mother's fridge in search of ice for a gin and tonic, he said he was surprised she hadn't died from food poisoning. I think he'd have been pleased if she had. I expect he's hoping she'll have another heart attack and die now. He's always disliked her.

Mother isn't going to die is she? Not yet? The doctor is beginning to talk of 'when you go home'. And at the mention of *home* I see Mother's spirit belie the frailty of her body. Her eyes spark, her eager hand rises to smoothe her hair, and her thin legs twitch beneath the heavy hospital blankets.

Mother's heart attack was such a shock. I have been plagued with horrible thoughts like: if Mother dies, what do we do about her house? Her car? Her cat? Hunter's Moon? *Hunter's Moon.*

Should Mother be buried, like Father? I've heard her say she doesn't want a grave. She'd prefer to be scattered. But where? And what about the space waiting for her beside Father? What hymns should we have? I remember Mother saying she'd like to be carried in to 'The Entrance of the Queen of Sheba'.

Why am I thinking these things? And not *how much I will miss her, how I will grieve for her*. But how can you grieve ahead of time? You cannot know how you will truly feel. Now that it's ten days since the heart attack and Mother is recovering, I am ashamed to find myself worrying about the inconvenience of looking after her. Suppose she has to be looked after for a very long time? By me? What will that do to Ralph? To our marriage? *Suppose she gets gradually worse instead of better?* I want to go home. I don't want to feel sad about the pathetic leftovers in Mother's fridge, about the single portions of chicken pie and roast-beef-dinner-for-one in the freezer, about the umpteen packets of tomato cuppa soup and the four tins of Spam and the two of corned beef and the packet of Garibaldi biscuits in the food cupboard along with the tins and tins of Whiskas.

29

The kettle is coming to the boil. I drop Earl Grey tea bags into Mother's minuscule tea-pot and pour boiling water on to them. I am reaching for the milk when suddenly there comes an ear-splitting burst of agonised yelping. A panic-stricken child screaming for its mother. I spin around and see that huge cat, black fur standing on end, bottle-brush tail high and straight as a flagpole, clamped to Emily's head. I shout and charge across the kitchen, arms out, fingers grabbing for the horrible animal. His emerald glare is feral. He hisses. But he withdraws his claws, drops to the ground and shoots out through the catflap.

I turn to my poor old dog. She crouches, tail between her legs, shocked, silent. Timorously, she peers up at me, bright blood pouring from one eye.

Hilda

I have remembered the first line of that poem. I even remembered it for long enough to tell it to Alice, when she was last here. She said she'd look it up for me.

''Twould ring the bells of Heaven.' And then comes the bit I heard first of all: 'If parson lost his senses and people came to theirs.' It's funny what goes through your mind.

The trolley arrives with what they call 'your dinner, dear'. It's plonked gracelessly down on the bed table in front of me. I concentrate on lifting the cover from the plate; trying to fight the sudden swirling in my head.

I suppose it's fish. It's a greyish colour and the right shape: swimming in a thin pale sauce. I wonder when it was last swimming in the sea? I take a mouthful. It's definitely fish. Very fishy fish. The mashed potato is the sort you get out of a packet. I recognise that taste. I don't think I'll tackle the sponge pudding and custard. Definitely stick-jaw.

''*Twould ring the bells of Heaven.*' I push the tray away and fumble for my pad and pencil. I feel almost warm from excitement as my slow but obedient hand copies down the words that trickle into my head.

Twould Ring
The Bells of Heaven
The wildest peal for
Years if
Parson lost his
Senses and the
People came to

31

Theirs and
He and they
Together knelt
down with
angry Prayers for
Maimed and shabby
Tigers
and Little Hunted
Hares.

I'm sure there is something about *'little blind pit ponies'*. But the steady stream of words has dribbled away to nothing. I am exhausted. And cold.

Where is Alice? Surely she will take me home soon? I shall not survive here. I cannot stay here. She said *soon*. I shall take you home *soon*. I want to go home *now*. I ring my bell and ask them to bring the telephone. In the end it comes, pushed along on its trolley. I pick up the receiver and find I cannot remember my own telephone number. Alice is there, isn't she? Staying in my house, looking after Pinky and coming to see me when it suits her. I get it right in the end, but there is no reply, although I leave it ringing for a long time. Perhaps she's gone back to Norwich? To that demanding husband of hers. She's always running round after him. I do not understand what Alice sees in Ralph. The man is barely couth.

I cannot blame Clive. I could blame the business. The family timber business that Clive worked so hard, so very hard, to rescue when he came back from the War. It was on its last legs in 1945, but slowly my Clive built it up into quite an empire. We were able to live very well. But if it hadn't been for the business; my Clive's business, Alice would never have met Ralph. A black day indeed, the day Clive started to supply Ralph with wood veneers.

Where is Alice? When Alice comes I will *make* her take me home. Once I am home I will grow strong again. I will be able to rest. Alice will care for me. Cook me tasty food, not too much of it. I will walk round my garden. Smell the sweet scent of the honeysuckle I brought from Hunter's Moon. Touch the petals of my roses. Feel the sun on my skin. Pinky will be overjoyed to see me. He'll jump on my lap and purr. How I

32

long to stroke his soft black fur and to feel the warmth of his body on my lap.

'I'll have some chocolate when you can bring some for me please.' The dotty woman down the other end has started up again. Poor old thing, she seems to be alone in the world. I've seen no visitors. Yesterday, a nice young man visiting the coughing woman, brought in some chocolate for her. I heard him say to that dragon of a sister, 'I've brought in some Bournville for the old lady at the end.' I don't know if she got it. Her voice is wavery, but she can make herself heard all right. 'I always have a hot-water bottle in the winter.' I know how she feels. I so long for my electric blanket.

I stare at the door. People come in and out. I search and search for my daughter. But she does not come. Perhaps she has indeed gone back to Norwich. The telephone still stands beside my bed. Do I have Alice's number written down somewhere? Yes. I manage to find it in my notebook. The number rings and someone answers. But it's not Alice. I say hello. And the voice says, 'Hello Granny. This is William.'

William. Darling William. I'm so pleased to hear his voice. He asks how I am, and I tell him I'm much better only his mother is making me cross because she won't take me home. And where is she? 'Is she there, with you?' I ask. 'No,' he sounds surprised. 'Isn't she with you?' When I tell him I've no idea where she is, he tells me not to worry, he knows she is somewhere nearby and soon she will come in to see me. I don't know if I can believe him. But William has always been a truthful boy.

William is my only grandson. The other three are girls. It's nice to have a boy. I remember how thrilled I was when David was born. There seems to be something rather clever about giving birth to a boy. Alice was just the same when William was born. Poor William, he has to put up with having Ralph as a stepfather. I don't know how my daughter could do that to him.

I ask William how he's getting on. He says fine. They always say 'fine' don't they and you really have no idea. I ask after Ralph and William says he's 'fine' too. William is very loyal to his mother, he wouldn't complain about Ralph to me. But his voice has a guarded tone. 'And how's school, William?' He

33

says, 'Actually it's college'. And he's just come home from his English lesson. He says they're doing *Great Expectations*. Dickens, you know.

Great Expectations. I have a calf-bound set of Dickens. Thin India paper. They're in the bookcase at Hunter's Moon. I can't remember which ones I have read. I ask him to tell me about it. He's says there's this boy called Pip. And right at the beginning he's in the churchyard when a terrifying man appears from nowhere. He's ravenously hungry. It turns out he's an escaped convict. *Pip*, I say, the convict is called *Magwitch* and there's a beautiful girl called *Estella* and a mad old woman called *Miss Haversham*. I'm so pleased to be able to remember that. William says he's only got up to page 118. I ask about his teacher and he says Mr Darnley always looks half asleep but of course he isn't and he has a nasty habit of springing questions on you.

'What questions did he ask today?'

'He was on about imagery,' says William. 'You know when something reminds you of something else.'

'Tell me.'

'Well, Pip's in this run-down garden and he's looking at all these overgrown plants and he thinks they look like old hats and boots and saucepans and puddings. Mr Darnley says it's because Pip's very young. And so Dickens uses childlike images on purpose.'

It's difficult, thinking about anything for long enough to understand. Specially when you realise it's something you knew anyway. But enlightenment comes, eventually. 'You know William', I say, 'that reminds me of when you were a little boy and someone gave you a football. You were very keen on your football. Everything round was a ball. Malteser sweets, peas.'

'Granny', he says, 'That's *right*.'

'I'm perfectly sane you know, William. I really do think it's about time your mother let me go home.'

'She's been worried about you Granny. We all have. And Tim sends his love.'

William's friend Tim is a bit of a mixed blessing in my opinion. Alice says he was the naughtiest child she ever knew. She thinks he's a bad influence but they've been friends since they were very small. William brought him to stay with me at Hunter's Moon one summer holiday, a long time ago. And they hid in the chestnut tree and hurled conkers down at Barratt, who used to garden for us. And then they climbed up so high, Tim got stuck. Clive had to call the Fire Brigade.

'Oh yes,' I say, 'And how is Tim?'

'He's all right. He and this girl Marion fool around together at lunchtime. The food's disgusting Granny. They have that stuff Mum calls bathroom floor. And horrible greasy mince. And the shepherd's pie's mostly potato and not proper potato either.'

'I know.' And I tell him about *my* lunch.

'You know Granny, I could cook something much better. I quite *like* cooking. But Tim and Marion don't believe me and neither does Catherine.'

'Catherine? Who's Catherine?'

'Oh, she's just a girl in our English class.'

'Is she pretty?'

'Quite.'

I suppose William is old enough to have a girlfriend. Sometimes I forget the age of my grandchildren. They were babies such a short time ago.

'I told her I could cook her a really good lunch.'

'That's a nice idea William,' I say. 'I wonder what you should cook?'

'She says she likes pasta.'

'Well, there you are then,' I say. *Pasta*. What is pasta? Yes, of course spaghetti, macaroni. Suddenly I feel very tired. It sweeps over me in a great dark wave. I'm finding it hard to breathe. But it's so lovely talking to William. I don't want to ring off. Perhaps I'll die, connected to the telephone.

Maybe I've gasped or something. William's voice is saying, 'Are you all right Granny?'

'I'm *fine*,' I say, adopting his language. 'But I think I'll just shut my eyes for a while.'

'All right Granny. Sorry if I've talked too much,' he says. 'See you soon.'

William is so lucky. William is young. And free. He can go anywhere. Do anything. Oh Alice, why don't you come? I want to go home. But now I'm faced with the truth of it. Until

Alice comes, I'm stuck here and there is nothing on earth I can do about it. And then it hits me, with the sudden, overwhelming blackness of a power failure. It's not my life any more.

Alice

I could hardly bear to look at Emily's eye. But I made myself. It was almost closed up and pouring with blood. I put salt in a bowl of warm water and bathed away the blood with cotton wool as gently as I could. I talked to her all the time. She was shivering, but she didn't snap or growl, just patiently gave herself up to what was being done to her. There's a veterinary surgery in an avenue off the High Street. So I put my battered old friend in the car and took her there. The receptionist said of course the vet would see my dog but I must wait my turn. The woman could see what a state I was in; she had kind blue eyes behind tinted spectacles.

Now I am sitting on a bench seat in the waiting room. Emily lies on the floor. Blood is still leaking from her eye. I look around me, away from Emily's poor eye which I can do nothing about.

A large notice requests that pets should be kept off the seats. Over the other side, a fair-haired boy shares his seat with a beady-eyed Corgi. The boy, who looks about twelve, plays unconcernedly with the dog's ears.

If Mother were here, she'd say, 'I suppose neither of them can read, dear.' My mother can be very entertaining. I promised I'd go and see her this morning. She'll be fretting for me.

Next to the boy and the Corgi, a nervous Alsatian whines and fidgets. Its owner, all in black leathers with tattoos on the back of his hands, jerks the dog's choke chain and orders it loudly to 'Shurrup you', which distresses two old ladies, neatly dressed in raincoats and lace-up shoes. They each have an aggressive small dog; one a Jack Russell terrier and the other a Scottie. The dogs bristle and growl at each other and the little old ladies take it in turns to say, 'He doesn't mean it, he's very sweet-tempered really.' They exchange meaningful looks regarding the loutish behaviour of the Alsatian owner.

There are three cats: two in wicker baskets, mewing monotonously. The third, a younger, slimmer version of Pinky glares balefully at me from its wire cage. I want to throw up. I hate cats. I hate them for their murderous instincts, their inscrutable self-posssssion, their insinuating ways, their lack of humbleness. I cannot stare it out, this feline killer. Its owner is a young woman with bottle-blonde hair, cut short at the back with a heavy fringe at the front. She is wearing a smart, tight navy suit and high-heeled shoes. She smiles at me 'Oh your poor dog,' she says. 'Whatever happened to it?' I tell her tersely that a cat tried to scratch her eyes out. She says, 'Oh dear,' and turns for support towards the cat owners. The dog owners murmur sympathetically.

The vet, in a white coat, appears with a sad-eyed spaniel on a lead. It's owner, a hefty young woman with bare red legs, gets to her feet, and dog and owner greet each other rapturously. The vet hands over the lead and says watch he doesn't pull out the stitches. Then, he glances at a card lying on the reception desk, says 'Potter' loudly and disappears into another room, followed by the lout dragging the trembling Alsatian.

One of the old ladies smiles at the spaniel and says to the hefty young woman, 'He's ever so pleased to see you.'

'I've just had him castrated,' says the young woman.

Nobody says a word until the spaniel, unsteadily, and its red-legged mistress have disappeared through the door. The blonde starts off. 'I think it's cruel.' One of the old ladies says it stops them from wandering, but of course she's never had any trouble with Sammy. The other old lady says, 'Poor little chap; he's so young. She might have let him have a bit of fun first.'

I stroke Emily's head and watch as, one by one, the patients are admitted. Soon there is nothing left to look at except posters reminding pet owners of the importance of keeping canine vaccinations up to date, of regular worming, of the essential requirements for the health of gerbils, guinea pigs, pet rabbits and goldfish. Obese dogs are urged to attend weight-watchers classes on Thursday evenings. Eventually, it's our turn to see Mr Baxter. He looks about my age. He is not very tall, but stockily built, with curly brown hair and freckles. When he examines Emily, I see that he has gentle hands. He talks to her in a slow, quiet voice. 'You poor old lady, what's been happening to you then?' I explain that she's been attacked by my mother's cat; that I'm currently staying in my mother's house. I find myself telling Mr Baxter about Mother's heart attack, and as I do so, tears rush into my eyes and one of them falls on to Emily's side as she lies on the bench being examined. I feel such an idiot but Mr Baxter takes no notice and waits a little before asking any more questions. And then, when I've told him Emily's always been a very fit dog but she is twelve years old, he says he'd like to keep her in overnight. He wants to avoid an anaesthetic if possible, but he might have to do a small operation on her eye. He hopes to save her sight, but he can't promise. I'm on the point of getting uncontrollably upset at the thought of exposing Emily to the risk of not recovering from the anaesthetic; leaving her here, possibly for ever and going back to Mother's empty house alone.

'I must be honest,' he says, 'her heart doesn't sound too bad for an old dog, but obviously there's a risk.'

'I know,' I manage to croak.

Mr Baxter says kindly. 'Try not to worry. I'll look after her for you. She's just the sort of old dog I really like.'

When I get back to Mother's house, Pinky is waiting for me. He wraps himself round my legs purring. I want to kick him. Instead I give him a bowl of his foul-smelling catfood and his cat biscuits. I tell him I hope it chokes him.

I drink some of Mother's gin and eat a slice of toast and marmite. I ought to go to the hospital. Mother is expecting me and I promised to take her some mineral water and a packet of digestive biscuits. There's something else she wants. Suddenly I remember; the poem. Mother has been haunted by some poem and now she has remembered the first line. I fumble in my bag and find the scrap of paper on which Mother has written in wobbly handwriting: ''Twould ring the bells of Heaven.'

39

Most of the family books are still at Hunter's Moon, but in her bureau bookcase in the sitting room I find Mother's *Golden Treasury*. I look among the index of first lines and find it. I turn to the correct page and see, 'The Bells of Heaven' by Ralph Hodgson. *Ralph* I think; how curious.

I compare Mother's scrap of paper with the printed page in the anthology and find she got it mainly right. Her shaky handwriting, the lines breaking in all the wrong places, makes the poem seem even sadder. She's missed out two lines near the end and she's written '*Maimed*' instead of '*tamed* and shabby tigers.'

It's nearly four by the time I reach the hospital. Eventually, I find a space in the congested car park and hurry into the hospital via the the maternity wing. A group of hugely pregnant women in dressing gowns and slippers lounge about in the porch, smoking cigarettes and gossiping. I go up a flight of concrete steps and walk briskly along the corridor which leads to the main hospital block. Poor Mother, she'll have had no visitors today, unless Jonquil has had a change of heart. I pass a frowsy looking woman in an overall, leaning on a mop. The corridor is being refloored, but there are no signs of any workmen. Just a stretch of bare concrete where the new tiles end, edged by many metres of unpainted skirting board.

As usual, I have to wait for one of the lifts to descend. On the walls of the foyer there are glass display cases containing what appear to be intestines and partially identifiable internal organs. In fact, from previous examination, I know these to be tubular sculptures by someone called Simon Fisk. He has given his works names like 'The Secret', and 'Over the Hills and Far Away.' They look disgustingly mortal, but I assume they are made out of some kind of plastic, and have been put there to distract people from worrying that the lifts have broken down. There are several of us waiting now, confronted by Simon Fisk's works of art: the twisting pinkness of them, the rounded forms that look capable of pulsation. When finally I board a lift, along with a young man cradling a sheaf of pink carnations and an old man dangling a bottle of Lucozade by its neck, it's ten past four. I get out at the sixth floor and pass quickly through the glass swing doors into the geriatric ward.

'Oh hello dear!' Mother's voice is frosty. She is sitting in the chair beside her bed. Over her nightdress, she is wearing the lacy pink bed jacket Jonquil gave her one Christmas. Her old face is sallow and unsmiling, framed by her thick, smoothly brushed silver hair.

'She's been expecting you since eleven o'clock,' whispers the young nurse, behind her hand.

Full of apologies, I kiss my mother's cool cheek, and produce the bottle of Perrier water, the digestive biscuits and the *Golden Treasury*. Mother says, 'You really needn't have brought those Alice; we'll only have take them home again. My things are all ready; I just need you to help me get dressed.'

I look towards the nurse for support and say gently. 'The doctor says you're getting on really well, but I'm afraid I can't take you home today, Mother. Not quite yet. Maybe next week.'

The nurse, who is young and pretty, smiles encouragingly. 'Yes,' she says, looking at me, 'Doctor says Mrs Maddison is doing ever so well.'

The next few minutes are really tricky. I'm not sure whether Mother actually believes she is leaving the hospital today, or whether she is cunningly trying to bamboozle me into taking her home. I try to distract her by pouring some Perrier and showing her the poem, which she barely glances at, though I know from the satisfied firming of her mouth, that she is pleased to see it. After a while, she asks how Pinky is, and have I remembered to get some more of his special biscuits? I reassure her that Pinky is in very good health. There is no point in upsetting both of us by telling her that the vile creature has done its best to blind and possibly put an end to my innocent old dog.

There are no more references to going home and I begin to relax. Mother even manages the hint of a smile. 'I had such a lovely conversation with darling William,' she says. 'He was telling me all about what he's doing at college. But he says the food is terrible; just like here.' She pauses, giving special weight to the next phrase. 'He wasn't very forthcoming about Ralph.'

She must be getting better, I think, to get in a subtle little

41

dig like that. I hope William will be home when I telephone this evening.

Mother's supper arrives and I watch her push a flabby wedge of cheese flan around her plate. I encourage her to eat a little. She lays down her knife and fork. There is a calculated look of derision in her muddy brown eyes. 'It's no good Alice, even if it was edible, I'm just not used to having my evening meal before eight o'clock.'

By the time I'm preparing to leave, her bravado is wearing thin. She grips my hand very tightly and now I cannot mistake the fear in her eyes. I do my best to rally her. 'See you tomorrow, Mother. Then it's the weekend and David will be here. And next week, I'm sure they'll let me take you home.'

Mother's house feels horribly empty without Emily. Pinky springs through his catflap and performs his usual two-faced writhe of satisfaction at my return. I consider putting him out again and locking his catflap. But, instead, I ignore him.

I telephone home, and to my delight, hear William's voice. I ask how he is and tell him I miss him and I hope he's getting on all right with Ralph. He says, carefully, well he's out quite a bit and so is Ralph. Then he says, 'Granny telephoned at lunchtime. She didn't know where you were. She sounded awfully confused. You ought to make sure she knows what you're doing Mum.' I remind William, quite sharply, that I don't need him to tell me what to do. That I'd been held up on account of an accident with Emily. 'What accident?' Now he's alarmed. William loves Emily. He was only five when we got her. William and Emily grew up together. I remember the two of them racing around in the garden; William in his short trousers, Emily looking just like the Labrador puppy in the Andrex ad. As soon as he came out of school, she'd rush to greet him. They were inseparable. Sometimes I would go into his room to tuck him up for the night and find both their heads on his pillow. But I let it go. It was a bad time for William just then, with his father and me splitting up.

I explain about Pinky and taking Emily to the vet. I play down the seriousness of it. 'He's a very good vet. I'm sure Emily will be all right.'

'She'd better be,' says William. 'When are you coming home?' I tell him Emily won't be fit to travel just yet and also

I need to visit Granny in hospital and that I was rather hoping he and Ralph might come and see me, and Granny, and Emily for the weekend. 'No Mum,' he says, rather too quickly. 'I'll just stay here.'

'All by yourself? I'm not sure.'

'Don't you trust me?' he asks in a pained voice. I tell him of course I trust him; I just thought he might be lonely. He says, 'I like being on my own.' And then he asks where is my Italian cookery book? I ask him why on earth he needs my Italian cookery book and he says he just does. And no, of course he's not thinking of having a party while he has the house to himself. Well if you're doing any cooking, I say, please clean up the cooker afterwards. And could I have a word with Ralph. William says Ralph isn't there and then he adds, in his consciously helpful voice, exactly the tone he's picked up from his devious friend Tim, 'He's probably in the pub.'

Ralph telephones just as I'm getting into the bath. He seems to think I'll be going home at the weekend. And, although I explain that I have to stay here not just because of Mother but because of Emily, he's not at all understanding. But, grudgingly, he agrees to drive down after work on Friday evening. I can tell from his voice, he's been drinking. We say good night stiffly to each other and then I get back into the bath and lie there, sniffling, until the water goes cold.

In the morning, sick with apprehension, I go along to the veterinary surgery. I've only been there five minutes when suddenly, everything changes. My heart reverses its downward plunge and shoots up into my chest as if it would burst my ribs, for a smiling Mr Baxter is leading Emily towards me. She is carrying her bandaged head slightly to one side, but she sees me all right, wags her tail and pulls at the lead, which I take from Mr Baxter. I bend down and stroke the unbandaged side of Emily's head and her silky ear. 'Thank you for looking after her for me.' I'm so happy, I could kiss Mr Baxter on his warmly coloured cheek.

'Let the old dog take it easy for a few days and bring her back in a week and we'll take the bandage off.'

I thank him again and he warns me there won't be much

sight left in the injured eye. 'But she'll be able to manage well enough with the other one.' And then he says, with a humorous smile, 'You won't have to remind her to keep away from the cat.'

He's absolutely right about that. When we get home, Emily squints at Pinky, shoots into her basket and covers her head with her paws.

I must have been in bed for an hour when Ralph bangs on the door, very late on Friday night. Half asleep, I stagger down the stairs in Mother's dressing gown to greet him. He looks tired and not particularly pleased to see me. Maybe he was expecting a three-course meal, and me in my best dress. The avocado pear and cottage cheese salad waiting on a tray for him, receives the briefest of glances before he heads for Mother's drinks cabinet. I put my arms round him and say how happy I am he's here, but I'm so tired, I can't sit with him; I have to crawl back to bed. It seems ages before he joins me. In the morning I have a vague memory of his hands stroking me the way he does, but I'm too deeply entwined in shadowy dreams, too far away to inhabit my body.

28 October 1996

The Living left Hilda behind in the graveyard with the Dead, climbed into their waiting cars and drove away. Half an hour later, the house where Hilda had spent the last years of her life reverberated with the steadily increasing sound of her funeral party.

William was dismayed by the concentration with which these old people, his grandmother's friends, were piling their plates and filling their glasses to the brim, unerringly focused, it seemed to him, upon the whisky and gin, the sandwiches and cakes, rather than the reason behind the provision of all this food and the drink. He felt sick; burdened with the frightening certainty that had settled down on him as he stared at the white flowers trembling on top of the pale wood coffin. Last night, he'd tried to talk to Rosamund about the unexpectedness of his grandmother's death, about his own unwelcome suspicions, but she wouldn't listen. Now, looking very pale in her black dress, he could see she'd been crying. I'm all alone he thought, standing here beside my sister, surrounded by my family and all these old people, Granny's friends. What I am thinking is unacceptable to everyone here: except for the person who did it.

'I'll miss Granny.' Rosamund's voice seemed to be coming from a great distance. 'She could be really funny. She didn't mind what she said or if she upset anyone. But you and me. Her family. We could do no wrong.'

'I suppose not,' said William, only half listening to Rosamund's pensive voice.

'Sometimes she played one of us off against another. Like I

45

was always hearing about Helen being junior tennis champion, when I can't hit a moving object, and Louisa always remembering Granny's birthday when I sometimes forgot, and getting nearly a hundred percent at GCSE maths when I only just scraped through. But Granny would never let anyone outside the family say a word against any of us.'

Alone in the farthest corner of the room, Ralph was steadily getting through the whisky. William glowered at him and said savagely, 'After what *he's* done, I'm surprised he's got the nerve to turn up. He hated Granny anyway.'

'I sometimes worry I'm not more affected by all that's happened,' said Rosamund. 'When Dad left I don't know if I really minded all that much. Isn't that awful! He never spent any time with us. Perhaps there's something wrong with me. Maybe I blanked it out.'

Stuck in his corner, Ralph cast round for someone to talk to. Perhaps the old buffer having a second go at lighting his cigar? Grown uncomfortably hot, he ran a finger under the edge of his damp collar and felt, rather than saw, William's eyes on him. Covertly, he glanced towards the place where he knew they were standing, side by side. William and Rosamund: Alice's self-centred children. He'd done his best, but she'd never taught them how to behave. William looked belligerent, Rosamund tearful. With sudden pain, Ralph mourned the non-existence of his own little brown-eyed boy. The child she'd denied them, because she didn't want to run the risk of upsetting William and Rosamund. As he slid his eyes away from his wife's over-indulged children, he felt, in this room of hers, the hostile presence of his old enemy: Alice's mother.

He sucked in a mouthful of numbing whisky. Bearing in mind all the circumstances, there was no reason to feel guilt. His actions were perfectly justifiable. When people are hurt, they're inclined to retaliate. Alice just doesn't understand what it is to be a wife, he thought resentfully. If anyone could be held responsible for what has happened, Alice must take a large slice of the blame.

He remembered, with sharp nostalgia, their first meeting, in her father's office. He'd come to discuss satinwood veneer –

46

and when she just appeared as they were arguing the price (Alice's father was a hard businessman) – it was a *coup de foudre*. She was wearing a red summer dress with short sleeves and a wide neck. Her skin was smooth as silk and lightly tanned. Her hair shone like a new conker and her brown eyes looked straight and questioningly into his. That was ten years ago.

If one overlooked the last six months, their subsequent years together, though not idyllic, were full of interest and often exciting. He had tried not to resent her preoccupation with her children, with her mother. They were good times: the best of his life. Despite the conflict caused by their differing approaches to life, and their dissimilar characters, he'd always believed there was innate empathy one for the other. The living cord that bound them together. But she had failed to protect it. Refuted his observations that she did not value his love. Is it unreasonable, he thought sadly, to expect to come first in this life with the one person *you* always put first?

Ralph gazed down into his empty glass and decided to abandon his corner. As he moved slowly towards the old buffer still trying to light his cigar, he caught a glimpse of Alice offering a sausage roll to the vicar. She looked white and strained. For a fraction of a second his eyes met hers. Then she turned away.

April 1996

Hilda

'Here's Ralph come to see you Mother.'

I don't understand why Alice bothers to pretend I've any desire to see Ralph. I can't think why she's dragged him along. He touches my hand, the one that isn't holding Alice's hand, and says, 'Hello dear, how are you feeling?'

I do my best to give him a smile. I say 'Hello my boy,' and I thank him for the bunch of large black grapes he's laid on the bedside table. Too many pips and tough skins. I dislike grapes. But no doubt the nurses will be happy enough to take them off my hands. One of them comes in now, the plump one with the pretty blue eyes. While she's taking my temperature, darling David arrives, without Jonquil; *he* understands it's only my own flesh and blood I'm interested in seeing at present. He's always had more sense than Alice. When the thermometer has been removed from my mouth, David kisses me, and the nurse smiles at my visitors. I feel proud of my handsome son and my beautiful daughter.

'I've a wonderful family,' I tell her.

I don't have to look at my son-in-law to know how his face will turn grim at the mention of families. Alice believes I ought to make allowances for Ralph, on account of his unhappy childhood. It seems his mother ran away with his father's business partner when Ralph was only eight. That makes Ralph feel excluded from our family, because we've always been so close. But it's not my fault Ralph has a thing about families, and particularly about mothers. I really cannot be expected to bend over backwards in order to accommo-date his complexes. He's extraordinarily lucky to have married into our family. Dear Alice has to put up with a lot from Ralph. Not only is he very demanding, he does like telling people what to do, particularly Alice's children. I would definitely advise anyone, in choosing a marriage partner, to make certain the intended person has had a normal, happy childhood. I did warn her, but, there, she chose him. And no stopping her. Lack of judgement, I suppose. That first husband of hers was a dull little man, but she'd have been much better off staying with him; I always got on rather well with Richard. At least, being properly brought up, he had very pleasant manners. Alice says he doesn't bother about the children at all now, but she's probably exaggerating.

Ralph's taken off his jacket. David is full of smiles for me, but his eyes are tired. He works so hard. He's brought me a present. 'Jonquil's special iced buns,' he says. 'She knows how much you like them.' He goes through the motions of apologising for Jonquil's absence: she's taking Louisa to her riding lesson. I do hope they don't go in for a pony for those girls; it's such a terribly dangerous sport. But I say nothing. Then he tells me Jonquil has a big commission for portraits of the three little girls of some advertising tycoon; Helen hasn't been well, tonsillitis again, but she's getting over it. The cherry blossom is all out in the orchards, he says, and the bluebells are like pools of blue water beneath the trees at Hunter's Moon. 'You'll be able to come and see them soon,' he says. If only he were right. Oh Hunter's Moon! How wonderful to be at Hunter's Moon!

Ralph doesn't say much. He looks hot and edgy. I don't expect he likes hospitals. I don't like hospitals. Alice chats away to make up for Ralph, and all the time I can hear that dotty woman. 'Will someone bring me some chocolate; dark chocolate, I like dark chocolate.'

'You've no idea what it's like at night,' I tell them. And then I describe the strange and scary noises that wake me, and keep me awake. I tell them how impossible it is to get any rest here. I tell them about the disgusting food, about the Sister with the horse teeth who is not gentle and kind like a horse, but a bully. I look hard at my son-in-law and I say, 'You know Ralph, I don't think I'm fit enough to survive another week here.' I can see him go tense and I wait for Alice to say, as I

49

know she will, 'We'll get you home Mum, just as soon as we can – won't we David.' David nods, and says, of course they will. I pay no attention when Alice adds something about waiting for the result of some tests and seeing the physiotherapist.

David says he has to get back home to cut the grass: the gardener couldn't come this week. I rather hope Ralph will clear off as well, and leave me alone with Alice. But, no, Alice says she has to see to the animals, and they both leave together, Ralph gripping Alice's hand in that possessive way of his. If only Alice could bring Pinky in to see me.

My son and daughter disappear through the swing doors and now I am alone. I could even wish Ralph back again, so overcome am I with desolation.

I imagine David going home to Hunter's Moon, to cut the grass and admire the bluebells. My Hunter's Moon, for it still is mine. Gently, David prompts me from time to time to 'make sure you leave your affairs as you would wish, Mother'. And he's right: I should think about updating my Will. As things stand, everything I have is divided between my two children. If David and Jonquil want to stay at Hunter's Moon they will have to buy Alice out. Suppose Alice wants Hunter's Moon? I know how she resents Jonquil living in her old home. Sometimes I wonder myself if I was wise to let them move in there: it seemed sensible at the time, the best way of keeping the house in the family. If Alice lived at Hunter's Moon, Ralph would be there with her. *Ralph in Hunter's Moon.* Ralph's business is in Norfolk, not in Kent. And always likely to be so? *Ralph in possession of Hunter's Moon.* I have to think this out very carefully. And when I get home, I suppose I should ask Alan Sheppard to come along and help me tidy things up: once I've decided what to do. The swirling starts in my head; I know I cannot think about my Will any more. I shut my eyes and doze until the coughing wakens me as usual.

I dread the night; and it's drawing closer. This evening, they give me a pill with my bedtime Ovaltine (*Ovaltine, ugh!*) 'to help you sleep, dear'. Soon, I drop into blackness but the merciful blackness does not last. Relentlessly, my head fills with flashing, luridly coloured lights. They press inside my skull as if they would burst it open. Grotesque shadows threaten me. Harsh and chiding voices batter my ears. I don't know where I am. Who I am. When finally I waken and gradually the light returns, and I see a thin hand gripping the bed sheets, I am quite drained.

I watch the door and wait for Alice. When, finally she comes, alone this time, thank God, I tell her what they've done. I tell her they're doping me down with powerful drugs, and I'm simply not having it. I tell her I am frightened. If they give me a pill tonight, I shall refuse it. She tries to soothe me, and promises to speak to the doctor. Gradually, I begin to feel more like myself, as she talks quietly of my little house, of Pinky, of when I come home. She drinks a cup of tea with me. And then, she kisses me and tells me not to get upset; everything will be all right.

What makes her think that? Then, she says Ralph will be driving back to Norwich, and she must go now and get him a meal before he leaves. On her way out, I watch her have a word with Sister; *what good does she think that will do?* Then, alone once more, I wait for David to come to my rescue. But by the time supper arrives, there is still no sign of him. I have no appetite for my thin tomato soup and dried-up ham sandwiches. In the end, I have to face up to it: David is not coming; Jonquil and the girls have claimed him today.

As I long for my family, I think of William. Of course, I will talk to darling William. I take a spoonful of soup and chew up one of the sandwiches and then I ask for the telephone. And William is there; William answers the phone. 'Hello Granny,' he says, and his voice sounds so grown up. He asks how I am and I tell him what a horrible time I'm having. I tell him they've been doping me down and I don't know what drug it was but it gave me the most frightening night of my life. And as I think about drugs I worry that William might take something. I believe drugs are everywhere these days. 'William, promise me,' I say, 'don't ever take any drugs. They will mess up your mind.' 'Granny, I'm not an idiot,' he says. I ask him about college and try to remember what book he said he was studying for English. It's just coming back to me when William says, 'We're still doing *Great Expectations* and Pip has met Estella. Her name means star, and there are all these images of cold and glittering stars, and so the feeling of

51

Estella is often in Pip's mind. I'm quite enjoying it really. But we've got to do *King Lear* next.' *King Lear*. I don't remember much about *King Lear*, except it all turns out badly in the end.

I tell him his mother has been to visit me, and so has Uncle David. And Ralph. 'Oh yes,' he says, in his careful voice, 'I've been staying with Tim'. 'And what did you do?' I ask. 'We went to the Arts Centre on Saturday night,' he says.

The Arts Centre. What is the Arts Centre? In my day we entertained our friends in our own houses. It seems to be pubs and clubs now. Surely William is too young to drink in a pub? 'And what goes on in the Arts Centre?' I ask. 'I hope they don't serve alcohol.'

'They had a band on Saturday night. A lot of our friends went along.'

'Do you dance to this band?' I ask. Clive and I loved to dance. My Clive was very neat on his feet. I met him at a dance: the Cricket Club dance. We danced to Noel Coward. Later, after the War, there were the Friday night dinner dances. We'd make up a party with our friends, and dress for the occasion. The ladies in long dresses; the men in dinner jackets. Do people do these things any more?

William says Tim and Marion kind of move around a bit, but he usually just listens to the music. 'What about that pretty girl you were telling me about last time,' I ask. But I can't remember her name. William says, 'What pretty girl?' I say, 'Come on, you told me about a pretty girl in your English class.' 'Oh you mean Catherine,' he says. 'Yes she was there.' 'You were going to ask her to lunch,' I say, so pleased I've remembered that. 'Was I?' says William. 'Go on,' I say, 'You know you were. Or are you too shy to ask her? What's she like anyway? Is she fair, or dark?' William says she has long fair hair. She's a bit like he imagines Estella to be. 'Lunch?' I say. 'Did you ask her to lunch?'

'I might have,' says William. And now I know I shouldn't pry into his life any more. But I so dread the night time, and being alone, I cannot bear to let him go. In the end, William says, 'I better say goodbye, Granny; Ralph's coming back tonight and I haven't washed up.'

And now, the bedtime hot drinks are coming along. I see the plump and pretty nurse pushing the trolley through the swing doors. As she approaches, I brace myself to tell her I won't take one of those pills. But she is smiling and there, she places on my bed table a small glass containing a golden liquid. Surely it can't be? I hardly dare to hope that it might be. I sniff the liquid. And it is. A very small one, certainly. But it is indeed a glass of whisky.

Alice

Ralph and I are not on the best of terms. Having driven 150 miles after a long working day, specially to see me, Ralph says he was looking forward to a warm welcome and a bit of comfort. I could at least have stayed up long enough to greet him. A bowl of hot soup might have been nice, and surely I remember he can't stand rabbit food.

Does he not realise how exhausted I am, how much in need of comfort myself?

When Emily struggles out of her basket at breakfast, he strokes her bandaged head, and then he looks me straight in the eye and he says, 'Do you really think this is fair on the poor dog?'

'I suppose you think I should have her put down, do you?' I am full of hurt and anger. He just replies mildly, 'There comes a time for us all to go, you know, and euthanasia is legal for dogs.'

I make Ralph come to the hospital with me, although he says there's no point because he's the last person Mother will want to see. We buy her some grapes from the fruit shop on the corner.

I watch him sitting there: the Outsider, deliberately feeling superfluous in our company – Mother and David and me. By his withdrawn expression, he emphasises the family bond between the three of us, and his own lack of desire to become part of it. I often point out that since Jonquil, in exactly the same position, copes perfectly, he could try a little harder to fit in. But there he sits, not even trying to pretend he isn't hating every minute of it. He has taken off his jacket and he shifts uncomfortably in this hothouse atmosphere, unable to avoid breathing in the undeniable scent of mortality, of listening to the piping calls of the demented old lady begging for chocolate. When I catch his eye, he flashes me a wry smile which says: '*I'm doing this for you.*'

On the way out, he says, 'Your mother doesn't look too bad really, but some of those other poor old things. Talk about God's waiting room. Let's go and have a drink to cheer ourselves up.'

We stop off at a pub swarming with young people: the antidote?

Ralph has a pint of beer and I have a vodka and tonic. We exchange a few disagreeable words when I discover he's made William go and stay with Tim for the weekend, in case he should take it into his head to throw some wild party while he has the house to himself. I say this would never happen. William is extremely responsible and Tim is a bad influence. William is much more likely to get into trouble staying with Tim, whose parents are never there anyway, than he is remaining quietly at home on his own.

Then, we have another drink each and begin to calm down. I ask Ralph to try and be patient and understanding. Mother needs me. The doctor is talking about letting her go home next week. I must see her over that. She may recover quite quickly, I say. Ralph doesn't reply; just gives me another of his wry smiles. But when I remember to ask him about the new range of furniture he's working on, he comes to life. His hands move expressively as if to carve the shapes of the furniture out of the air. 'I think I've found a good designer,' he says. 'She's come up with drawings for an octagonal coffee table and a dining table with shaped ends. And I asked her for a glazed cabinet and a writing table, and she's done some rather good-looking chairs with curved backs. I shall use burr oak.'

'I'm glad you're not thinking of bleaching a whole lot of walnut.'

'Kitsch, that's what you'd call that, wouldn't you Alice? Well I'm not an antique dealer, I'm a furniture maker. And I quite like the idea of making something Art Deco-ish. I'm pleased with the woman's designs. The shapes are good, though a touch plain, perhaps.'

I suggest adding interest with some inlay. And Ralph says yes, he's already asked her to design something along those lines, a decorative stringing perhaps, using a lighter or a darker wood, to complement the dappled effect of the burr oak. 'What she's like, this woman?' I ask, imagining an untidy, arty person of indeterminate age with no make-up and flat shoes. 'Quite young,' he says, 'very good references from the Furniture College where she graduated, though that was some years ago. Worked for a furniture maker in Brighton, but nothing since then. Probably been taking time off to produce babies. She seems very keen to have the work.' I ask her name. Ralph looks thoughtful. 'Judith something; or was it Jill? Do you want another drink?'

'No, let's go home,' I say, and we return to Mother's house where Emily and ghastly Pinky are waiting for us.

I get the Bolognese sauce I made this morning out of the fridge and a packet of spaghetti out of the cupboard. 'Oh God. Not your spaghetti Bolognese!' says Ralph.

I'm hurt. I made it specially, I say; I thought you liked spaghetti Bolognese. Ralph says it isn't that he doesn't like it, it's just it's my most repetitive dish and he doesn't fancy it this evening. 'What else is there?' he asks, as if I could magic roast sirloin and Yorkshire pudding.

'Mother's store cupboard is a little limited.' I open it up. 'I could do you corned beef hash or a spam salad.'

'Spam!!'

'Mother likes it. She even fries it for breakfast. She says it's just as good as bacon.'

'Spam's wartime food.'

'Quite appropriate then, isn't it,' I say. 'Since you and I seem constantly to be at war.'

'Well, whose fault is that?'

'Oh Ralph. Please don't let's fight all weekend. Can't we have a cease fire? Let's pronounce this a safety zone, and I'll make you spam fritters à la mother-in-law.'

'Ugh! You can do better than that.'

'Suggest something.'

56

Ralph taps his forehead. 'Spam à la King with courgettes and new potatoes.'

'Sorry, no courgettes and it'll have to be tinned potatoes.'

'Spam chasseur.'

'No chasseur.' I rummage around in Mother's store cupboard. 'Spam and sweetcorn rissoles, with Dundee marmalade sauce.' We're both giggling now. Ralph comes and rummages in Mother's store cupboard with me. He holds up a box of processed cheese. 'Spam au gratin with peanut butter croutons.'

'Medallions of spam with croquettes of Smash potato.' I skid a packet of instant potato across the table.

'Curried spam with banana coulis.' An ancient tin of curry powder lands on the floor, followed by an overripe banana.

'Spam and beetroot quiche with a side-dish of Whiskas.'

'Casserole of spam and mushy peas with apricots.'

'Braised spam with Garibaldi dumplings.' There goes a packet of Mother's favourite biscuits. In no time, there are tins of food all over the kitchen table, and some on the floor.

We're laughing so much, we're clutching our stomachs in pain; tears of laughter streaming down our faces. 'Oh Alice, it's good to see you laugh,' gasps Ralph. 'You too,' I gasp back. Then, he puts his arms round me and kisses my mouth and my eyes. 'Let's go to bed.' Holding hands, we run up the stairs and collapse on to the bed. And I find that it's still there: our private world.

We spend most of Sunday morning in bed, and then we get up and take Emily for a little walk along the crescent. I know she's enjoying it because she's wagging her tail. Then we go and have lunch in the Wheat Sheaf. They've built on a chintzy, dark oak dining room – quite cosy. I have made a conscious effort not to think about Mother, abandoned in that awful hospital. I tell myself David will probably be with her right now, and in any case, I shall go along later. I feel relaxed and happy as Ralph and I chat companionably and tuck in to very acceptable roast turkey with all the trimmings, followed by treacle tart and ice cream.

'It's nice to have you to myself.' Ralph leans across the table and smiles into my eyes. When he smiles at me like that, my stomach still turns somersaults.

'I'm enjoying it too.' I smile back at him, and reach for his hand. Then unfortunately, he adds, 'It's such a relief not to be surrounded by your bloody family.'

'Please don't talk about them in that unpleasant way,' I say. 'I love them.' He looks at me with a serious expression on his face, and his hand tightens on mine. 'Pair bonding doesn't just happen you know. We need to work at it.'

'Surely not to the exclusion of all other family ties. I mean, you're not a leopard.' I'm trying to lighten things up. 'Male leopards kill their own offspring in order to remain dominant. So the poor female has to take the cubs away from him and rear them on her own.'

Ralph says, 'I don't know much about leopards. But I know what Eskimos do. They put their old people out in the snow.' He watches my face as he says this, and then he adds, 'Only joking! Let's have some coffee.'

I leave him watching the television while I go and visit Mother. When I get back again, there's no point in trying to explain how bad I feel at leaving her there, frightened and alone. But at least the doctor, who looks about twenty-one, listened when I told him the sleeping pills they've been dosing Mother with are giving her nightmares. Surely they could find something else to calm her down.

I make Ralph a mushroom omelette and then it's time for him to drive back to Norwich. 'Husbands and wives are meant to live together,' he murmurs as we're saying goodbye. I feel tenderness in his warm arms and in the touch of his lips, but I know he doesn't understand. He thinks my loving my family diminishes my love for him. But all love is not the same – like a loaf of bread divided into portions.

Alice

The doctor is smiling. He tells me my mother will be fit enough to go home on Friday – as long as there is someone to take care of her. Mother is overjoyed. Today is Wednesday. As I manoeuvre my car out of the hospital car park, I am relieved that soon I won't have to feel guilty about abandoning Mother in that depressing geriatric ward. But now there is absolutely no chance of me getting home for a break. Of course I'm glad Mother is so much better. I just wish I could look forward to her homecoming as much as she does. I arrive back at Mother's house, park the car and walk in through Mother's front door and there is Emily, in the hall, waiting to greet me. She must have heard the car, or somehow sensed my return. I stroke her head; run my fingers over the bandage, which is due to be taken off tomorrow. I cannot believe how upset I have been over Emily. It ought not to, but it does, approach the depth of concern I feel for Mother.

How awful that I so longed to fetch Emily home from the vet's, and yet I cannot deny I feel a certain amount of dread at the thought of Mother's return. She'll be here all the time. She'll want to talk to me; be with me. I won't have any space of my own. I'll have to look after her. How much will she be able to do for herself? Will I need to help her dress? Wash her emaciated old body? Take her to the loo? I'm not good at illness. Illness irritates me. When I am ill myself, I don't want anyone fussing round; I want to be left alone. But Mother is not like that. Neither is Ralph for that matter. They crave conscious care and attention. But nursing skills do not come easily to me. I find it hard to be patient and kind and cheerful.

59

I can do it for Rosamund and William. Being a caring mother comes naturally. I nursed them tenderly through their childhood illnesses: the maternal bond instinct.

But, I remind myself sternly, Mother cared for me when I was little. So, now it's my turn to care for her. Role reversal, that's all it is. But it will not help my relationship with Ralph, who believes in *primary* relationships, i.e., Husbands Come First. And then there's Rosamund, whom I haven't had time to go and see, up in Edinburgh: not that she appears to mind in the least; busy socialising no doubt, instead of getting on with her studies. My poor William is obviously having a horrible time being bossed about by Ralph.

But how do you deal with the conflicting demands of the people you love? Without sabotaging your own need for love? That's what's so special about dogs. I stroke the thick fur on Emily's chest and I tell her she's a very good dog. 'Whatever I do,' I say to her, 'you think I'm wonderful don't you! You don't put pressure on me, like Ralph, make me feel guilty like Mother, make me feel inadequate like William. You just let me be.' She licks my hand.

As I think of William, I wonder, is he at home? It's lunchtime and he doesn't go to college till the afternoon on Wednesdays. Suddenly wanting very much to hear my son's voice, I call my own number. William answers. 'Oh Hello Mum,' he says, 'What do you want?' I tell him I just rang up for a chat, and I ask him how he is. He says he's fine, but actually he's in a bit of a hurry. A little hurt by his offhand tone, I think sadly to myself, the time is coming when I shall need my children more than they need me. 'I thought you might like to know how Emily is; and your grandmother.'

'How are they?' He's humouring me.

I tell him Emily's bandage is due to come off tomorrow, and there's nothing wrong with her appetite. I tell him his grandmother will probably be coming out of hospital on Friday, which means I won't be able to get home for the weekend. He says never mind, and really he has to go now. I say, 'Surely you don't need to be in such a rush do you William?' He says 'Hold on a minute', and puts down the receiver. When he comes back, he says, 'How do you stop lasagne sticking together in the saucepan?'

'Put a drop of oil in the water; and why are you making lasagne?' He says college lunches are disgusting, and anyway, he likes cooking. And then he says he could do with a bit more money. 'I went to that stall you go to on the market, you know the one with the gypsy-looking lady, and the vegetables didn't cost much, but the mince at the grumpy butcher's was quite expensive.'

'You're not cooking for a party, are you William?' I ask, suddenly reminded of Ralph's warnings about what William might get up to if left in the house on his own.

'Why would I be having a party? I told you Mum, I'm cooking lunch. And I have to go now.'

'O.K. darling,' I say 'I'll get you some money. Enjoy your lunch, but please clean up the cooker afterwards.'

Ralph phones quite late, and I can hear from his voice he's spent the evening in the pub. When I ask him to give William a bit more money, I get treated to the usual tirade about William's scruffiness, and the state of the kitchen. 'The whole place was lit up like a fucking lighthouse when I got in. And he's broken the butter dish, the white one we bought in Brittany. I wish you hadn't encouraged him to cook, Alice.'

My stomach clenches as I anticipate his reaction to the news that Mother is coming out of hospital on Friday. When I finally manage to tell him, he says, 'Put out more flags,' and 'don't forget the "Welcome Home" balloons.'

'Please try to understand,' I beg.

'Oh I understand all right,' he says. 'You've just buggered up another weekend.'

In the morning, I take Emily along to the vet: I have the first appointment, so we don't have to wait. While I stroke her neck, Mr Baxter carefully removes the bandage from Emily's eye, talking softly to her all the while. 'She's healed up pretty well,' he says. 'You won't know how much sight she has left in the eye; she'll compensate with the other one.' I thank him, and make myself examine the wound. There are stitches around her eye, which is not fully open, and watering.

'Don't worry,' he says. 'It'll look better in a day or two.' He's remembered about Mother being in hospital, and asks after her. I say Mother is coming home tomorrow, and I haven't yet told her about Pinky's misdemeanour. 'We both love animals you know, but I can't stand that cat of hers, and I don't think she much likes my dog.'

'It's the same with children, I suppose,' he says. 'Your own are marvellous: other people's often aren't.'

I thank him again and he says if I'm at all worried about Emily, to bring her in to the surgery.

Now it is Friday. Mother's coming-home day. I have arranged to pick her up from the hospital at three o'clock. There are clean sheets on her bed, and extra cushions and rugs on the sofa because Mother won't want to be upstairs all the time. There is cold chicken and salad in the fridge; a wedge of ripe Brie, a slab of cheddar and cartons of apple and orange juice. I buy fresh brown bread and a supply of fruit and vegetables. I'm just eating a bacon sandwich when Jonquil arrives with an armful of tulips and a small bunch of asparagus. 'From the garden,' she says. 'To welcome Mother home.' When I suggest she might like to be here in person, she gives me a sorrowful smile and says she's so fiendishly busy, she simply can't manage it. 'I have a contract to honour, you see Alice, so just at the moment, I'm afraid work must come first.'

Mother is sitting in the chair beside her bed. She is dressed in the clothes I brought her yesterday, a jumper of soft blue which compliments her white hair, and matching blue check trousers. She is wearing her frosty expression, and greets me with a cool 'Oh, hello dear'.

The pretty nurse hands me Mother's small case and her National Trust bag, packed with her belongings and says quietly, 'I told her you'd be here at three, but she insisted on getting ready this morning'.

Mother says goodbye, very graciously, to all the nurses. Although she protests, they install her in a wheelchair and I push her out of the ward, down in the lift, and into the fresh air.

Once manoeuvred into the car with the help of the porter, Mother sighs happily and says can we stop off at the shops. 'I need some witch-hazel; I banged my knee on that frightful

62

bedside thing, and you know how I bruise. And some lip salve for my sore lips. And I'd like to get a little treat for Pinky.

Taking Mother home feels like escorting the Queen into Buckingham Palace. As we enter the crescent, neighbours pop up in their front gardens, or appear at windows with smiles and waves. Mother raises a regal hand in acknowledgement.

Installed on the sofa, propped against the flowered cushions, her fragile, trousered legs tucked beneath a fringed travelling rug, Mother looks extremely pleased with herself. Pinky, smugly sharing the sofa with Mother, toys with one of the special biscuits, selected after discussion with the pet shop owner familiar with Pinky's tastes.

I begin to feel like a lady in waiting, running back and forth to the Queen's commands. 'Alice darling, just another pillow for my back, there's a dear; the little down one, you'll find it on my bed, and while you're up there perhaps you'd fetch my diary and my telephone book. They're on the bedside table.' They aren't, of course, and it takes several more trips up and down stairs, in and out of rooms, to locate them.

'And now, would you believe it, I can't seem to find my spectacles. I know I had them dear. They were round my neck. Maybe they dropped off in the car.' Eventually I find them lodged between two sofa cushions beneath Mother's narrow behind.

'I'm so sorry dear, to keep you running about like this; but you're young and strong.'

'Mother,' I say, 'I'm forty-five.'

Around six o'clock there is a knock on the door and I open it to Mother's next-door neighbour. June is a small, round woman aged, I would think, somewhere between sixty-five and seventy-five. She has a deferential expression and tightly permed grey hair. She has been following Mother's progress over the last weeks, in a concerned and friendly manner. Beaming, she bears a pie on a plate. 'I was just baking when I saw your car, and there was plenty of steak and kidney and I'd made double pastry, so I thought, well you won't want to cook on Hilda's first night home.'

I thank her and invite her in. She says, 'Well, just for a

63

minute or two. I'd love to have a word with your Mum, but I don't want to tire her.'

I lead June into the sitting room and say, 'Look who's come to see you Mother, and she's brought us this lovely pie for our supper.'

Mother leans her head back exhaustedly into the cushions, glances briefly at the pie which is deep gold and decorated with pastry leaves, and says, 'How very kind', in her queenly voice. I take the pie from June and offer her a drink. She says she'd love a sherry. In the oak corner cupboard where Mother keeps her alcohol, I can find only bottles of whisky and gin. Mother watches me delving about behind the Gordon's and says there might be half a bottle of Bristol Cream in the kitchen. She got it for the trifle she made at Christmas. 'I can't drink sherry you know,' she says to June. 'It makes me liverish.'

June says she's ever so sorry she doesn't want to put us to any trouble, and perhaps she'd better not stop.

'Well, I am rather tired,' says Mother, passing a hand over her forehead. 'Come another time.'

Embarrassed by Mother's cavalier treatment of this kindly and useful neighbour, I see June to the door, thank her effusively for the pie, and make excuses: Mother's not quite herself, it's been a busy time settling her in. She'll be fine in a day or two. June says of course she quite understands, presses my hand with a damp palm and beams the gallant smile of the rejected.

Back in the living room, Mother says a drink's not a bad idea and why don't we have one now. 'How about a gin and French, with ice and a twist of lemon? Do we have any lemons? If not, the corner shop stays open late most nights.'

I tell her I probably ought to have a word with Dr Robson first. She says, 'Oh come off it Alice; a spot of Mother's ruin will do me nothing but good. I had a whisky nightcap in hospital you know.'

I relent, and pour her a small gin with a lot of tonic. I say, it was very kind of June to bring the pie and we'll have it for supper with a salad.

'Her pies are very stodgy,' says Mother. 'I gave most of the last one to Pinky.'

'Poor June. And you sent her off without even a drink.'

'I know dear. I'm sure she's very worthy, but she's an awfully dull little person.'

Sometimes Mother's snobbery makes me curl up inside.

It takes two hours to get Mother to bed. She says she's been so longing for a nice hot bath, and it will help her sleep. Mother wears clothes like onion layers. I help divest her of, first, the fluffy blue jumper and the blue check trousers, then the thin blue botany wool jumper, the knitted cotton shirt, the long-sleeved silk vest, the short-sleeved silk vest, the bra which is too baggy for her withered breasts, the tights (two pairs), the rayon knickers with legs, and finally, the stretch cotton pants. I sit on a stool and watch Mother very slowly soap herself and squeeze a sponge over her bony ribs. 'It's so lovely. I can't tell you how lovely it is to get into a nice hot bath. You don't have to stay: I'm quite all right you know,' she says, missing the hot tap by a mile as she reaches for it.

Eventually, I persuade Mother out of the bath and into a towel, held at the ready, and finally into her long, winceyette nightdress.

Then Mother needs her early morning tea tray: 'I'm quite capable of boiling a kettle. If you could just fill it for me, there's a dear, and plug it in, by the bed. And then if you could bring up the pot and a cup, with an extra saucer for Pinky. I've tea bags here. Oh, and some milk in that pretty blue jug, and two digestive biscuits please dear.'

By the time Mother's snores are issuing from behind her bedroom door, I am almost weeping with exhaustion. Ralph hasn't rung. Perhaps he is afraid of disturbing Mother. I pick up the telephone and it rings for a long time. Eventually, William answers. 'I was asleep Mum,' he says. 'Ralph's out.' I say, 'Never mind', and I ask him how he is and he says he's fine, which is what he usually says. But he doesn't sound fine, and it's not just that he's half asleep. He sounds miserable. I tell him Emily is doing well and his grandmother is safely installed, which seems to cheer him a little. I tell him I'm sorry I'm not at home. It would be nice if he said he was sorry too,

65

but he doesn't. 'You're not being very communicative, William,' I say.

'Actually Mum,' he says, 'I'm rather tired. You did wake me up.'

June 1996

Hilda

I'm a little hazy about time. Some days seem never-ending; others, although apparently not without incident, I can hardly recall. But I believe I had my heart attack in April: the date on today's *Telegraph* is 14 June.

I am not hazy about what happened in that hospital. Alone at night, I am still haunted by the horror of the geriatric ward. I cannot flush from my soul the black terror that enveloped me there: the drug-induced nightmares, the unearthly cries of my fellow prisoners, the chill pebble eyes and tombstone teeth of my jailer. My fear is that I shall have another heart attack, or a stroke, and helpless to prevent it, find myself readmitted. What can I do to ensure that I die in my own bed; in my own home? These are my torments as I lie awake in the dark reaches of the night.

Everyone says I have made a remarkable recovery. How lucky I am, they say. Lucky! to have a heart attack? And how blessed to have the support of a loving family. I ought to feel grateful. But I don't. I wonder if the heart attack has damaged me mentally as well as physically. I grow tired more quickly, but worse than that, I feel resentful. I resent their youth and health, the fullness of their lives. I ought not to, but I do.

When I first came out of hospital, Alice was here to look after me, which was lovely. But then she had to go away and look after Ralph and William. She has her own life, and I mustn't intrude on it.

She's always pressing me to go and stay, but that would mean putting up with Ralph. I can't even talk to Alice on the telephone without hearing him grumbling away in the background. Darling Alice, far away in Norwich, she comes when she can, and always stays a few days. It's quite restful for her really – a nice little break.

My son works so hard, I hardly see him, and Jonquil is busy with her art. But sometimes on Sundays, they ask me to lunch. They are very kind, and my granddaughters chatter away cheerfully. These days, Hunter's Moon is smart enough to feature in *House and Garden*. David and Jonquil must have spent a fortune on it. It's too smart, too formal, in my view; though I wouldn't say so to Alice. But I have said goodbye to Hunter's Moon. My Hunter's Moon. David and Jonquil have made it theirs. And I cannot deny them the right to keep it. At my request, Alan Sheppard came last week and helped me update my Will. I have told my children what I have done. Alice will get this house, and a larger proportion of my invest-ments, to compensate, but I know she feels deprived. She's always been jealous of David, and she and Jonquil have a prickly relationship. It's right that my son should inherit from his father. In any case, I could not risk Ralph taking over Hunter's Moon.

Mrs Curtis comes in every morning now, to bang the Hoover about, and do the shopping and prepare unexcep-tional meals for me to heat up in the microwave oven. But she's hardly stimulating company.

Not only am I lonely, I am bored: bored rigid, bored out of my mind; *bored, bored, bored*. There are so many things I can no longer do, and nothing to look forward to.

I expected to be a widow, because Clive, being six years older than me and not particularly robust, always told me I would be. At first it wasn't too bad. Of course I missed him. I never loved anyone else. But we'd led fairly separate lives. He was always preoccupied with the business, so I'd had to develop my own interests, and after he died, I carried on much as before, with my charity work, for the NSPCC, and the Cheshire Homes. I played golf, and social bridge, with my widow friends. But then I moved out of Hunter's Moon and came here. Now I am further away from my friends, who are also getting older and don't like to travel, even the short distance, to see me. Some of them have died anyway. For some time it has been an effort to get out and do things; meet new people. And the neighbours are really not my sort. But since my heart attack, everything has become a hundred times worse.

My family must be worried about me. Alice certainly knows I'm depressed because, suddenly, she has allowed Rosamund, who is on holiday from university, to come and stay for a few days.

Rosamund is such a darling. She is my eldest grandchild, the prettiest of the girls with her delicate bones and fair curly hair. She has been blessed with a sunny nature which, I have to admit, she inherits from her father. I believe she has a talent for languages. At any rate, she's doing modern languages at Edinburgh. Alice complains she spends all her time going to parties; probably that's only what Ralph says.

Having Rosamund to stay works out rather well. Our routines fit nicely together. We get up late. And we like the same kind of snacky food. After lunch, Pinky and I rest on my bed, and Rosamund reads and sunbathes in the garden. Then she takes me out in the car. Sometimes we find a country lane to walk along: the wild roses are so fragile and pretty at this time of year.

Sometimes we go into Maidstone, where we try on clothes in one of the department stores. Rosamund helps me with the zips and buttons, and laughs when I put on a dress back to front. I'm a size smaller than she is. We have a cup of tea and a cake in the cafeteria on the top floor. On the way home we buy something simple for supper. There's a programme Rosamund likes to watch in the early evening, but when it's over, we turn off the television because it's more fun to talk.

Fortunately, Rosamund isn't in the least stuffy about pouring me a decent drink. 'Gin Granny?' she says, 'Water and a touch of angostura?' She has tonic with hers. We have lovely evenings together. My granddaughter tells me about her friends in Edinburgh. There's a boy called Jake she mentions quite a bit. He's also doing languages, and they plan to travel around on trains in Europe later in the summer, which sounds extremely uncomfortable to me, but they are young.

We chat about all sorts of things This evening we are talking about the family, and I tell her what lovely conver-

69

sations William and I had on the telephone when I was in hospital, and how he cheered me up during that dreary time. But I haven't spoken with him much since then. I tell her we talked about his English lessons, and I was so pleased to be able to remember *Great Expectations*. It made me realise I wasn't going dotty. And then, I say, 'Tell me Rosamund, has William got a girlfriend? I don't like to ask him how it went, but I believe he was planning to cook lunch for a girl. I can't remember her name, but he seemed very taken with her.'

'Oh Granny,' says Rosamund. 'That horrible girl! She's called Catherine and she's very pretty, but totally selfish and unpredictable. William cooked this beautiful lasagne for her, and she never turned up. He's very cut up about it.'

I am shocked. 'Poor William. What a horrid thing to do.' I feel deeply hurt for my generous-hearted grandson, and am filled with rage towards this cruel and thoughtless girl.

'Whatever you do, Granny, don't mention Catherine to William.'

All too soon, Rosamund says she has to go back to Norwich. I try to persuade her to stay a day or two longer. I know how difficult things are for her at home: Ralph can be very unpleasant. Alice says it's because he's jealous of her relationship with Rosamund. And because he was deprived of his own mother, he can't stand Alice to be one: a mother, that is. Which is no excuse in my view.

When Rosamund goes, I shall be alone again. Stuck in this house. Rosamund, free as a bird, can fly anywhere. I look at her smooth young face and her eager eyes. 'You won't like it you know,' I say to her. 'Getting old is horrible.' Rosamund giggles in that infectious way of hers, but can't raise a laugh from me.

'It happens to all of us, if we're lucky,' she says, and adds more soberly, 'And there's not much we can do about it; come on, I'll pour you a spot more gin.'

She's trying to jolly the poor old soul along.

'I'm not afraid of dying, you know.' I tell her, and am touched and chastened by the look of compassion that washes over her pink and white face.

70

'You're not to talk about dying. It isn't allowed,' she says, and comes over and gives me a kiss.

It is true, I'm not afraid of death: of the nothingness of being dead. I'm afraid of the process of dying, of half dying. I've told Alice and David I don't want to be revived if I have another heart attack. I've said the same thing to Dr Robson.

Dr Robson is a charming young man, very attentive and understanding. He pops in for a cup of tea on his way home sometimes. But I'm a bit fed up with Dr Robson. I always give him a bottle of whisky at Christmas, and chocolates for his children. But he won't agree to sign the form from the people at Swansea confirming I'm fit to drive: unfortunately, his wife works for an insurance company. I bought my first driving licence when I was seventeen. I've had my own car since I was newly married. And now the Rover sits idle in the garage and I'm forced to get someone else, usually Alice, who is only available when it suits her, to take me around. I feel just like a parcel.

With each day that passes, I miss Clive more. I think about our time together and I remember moments of happiness which slipped away so fast. My loneliness stretches out ahead of me like an empty railway track. During the long rights, I listen to Mozart on my tape recorder and sometimes, to pass the time and because I haven't bothered to eat much during the day, I get up and make porridge for myself and Pinky. I carry my plate upstairs and eat the porridge in bed. Pinky has his in a saucer on the floor. I don't know what I'd do without Pinky.

If I look out of the window, I see lights on in other houses, and I know I am not the only sleepless person in the crescent, but it brings me little comfort.

But now, I must cheer up: Alice is coming to stay. She will take me to the specialist at the hospital for my check-up. She promises not to leave me there.

Mr Hilman looks rather young and insubstantial to be a specialist. He examines me in his little cell of a room at the hospital, while Alice sits on a chair nearby. Mr Hilman says he is very pleased with me. My blood pressure is lower than his and I'll probably make ninety. When I don't look absolutely delighted at this prospect, he smiles gently and says of course it's hard adjusting to one's limitations, but there are still plenty of interesting things to do. I tell him I'd find it much easier to adjust to my limitations if I was able to drive my car. He says it's not really up to him, it's up to the insurance company and it would be wrong to withhold information from them. He looks at Alice and then back at me, drawing a circle round the two of us with his gentle, irritating smile. He doesn't say it in words. His perceptive eyes and the curve of his shrewd lips spell it out to me: '*You're a lucky old woman.*' I know it, with my rational mind, but I do not feel it with my damaged heart.

Alice is not herself. Sometimes when I am talking to her, I don't believe she's listening. She is not so much fun to have in the house as Rosamund, and she makes a real performance over getting the meals. I tell her, as she well knows, I have a small appetite and I never have liked being faced with a plateload of food. She just says, in her bossy way, 'Mother, if you're going to build up your strength, you must eat protein.'

She fusses round that dog all the time, which is extremely irritating. And the poor old creature smells. She's got it in for Pinky, but as I told her, it's *his* house, he was only defending *his* territory.

Still, I mustn't complain, it's lovely to have her company and mothers and daughters can't be expected to get along well together all the time. Alice is very helpful to me. One day, we go into Maidstone and buy my summer shoes – canvas ones with laces, which support my foot nicely. And on another day she drops me off at dear Doris's bungalow in Loose to make up a four with fat Audrey, and poor little Ruth. Beryl's away, visiting her son in Washington, otherwise they wouldn't have asked me to play. I gave up on the bridge circuit a while ago. They all take it so seriously, and while I enjoy a social game, I prefer not to make it a commitment. They get very angry if you don't turn up. But poor Ruth's memory is so bad now, I don't know how they manage. After all, you need to remember what cards have been played and poor Ruth has to be reminded which ones are trumps.

On another day we go to the garden centre and Alice helps me choose a reclining chair. I like to sit outside when the sun is shining. We find a white plastic 'lounger' with a flowery cover: not exactly stylish but easily managed. While it's being packed, I notice a sign saying 'Shrub Sale' and so we buy a cut-price eleagnus, a rather small mahonia and a couple of hebes.

I am sitting in the 'lounger', which I must say is a great success. The afternoon sun is warm on my face, and I could almost forget the terror of my dark nights, were it not for the fact that Alice will soon go away, and I shall be alone again. But I must try not to think about that. Alice is planting the shrubs in the positions I selected. I watch as she digs a hole, sprinkles in a mixture of peat and John Innes No. 2, waters the hole, turns the eleagnus out of its pot, puts it in the hole, and gently firms the loose soil round its roots. I think of the pleasure I will get watching the miracle of its growth, the yellow and green of its leaves, the height and the width of its developing shape. I watch Alice preparing another hole. She cuts into the dark earth with the metal spade, and I find myself thinking, *when they put me in the ground, my bones can only decay.*

Someone is calling, 'Hello, anyone at home?' and here is Jonquil, looking very pretty in a pink dress. She is carrying a cake tin and a bunch of pink roses. 'I've brought you some butterfly cakes,' she says, 'I've been having a cooking day: it's really strange, I've been baking like a mad thing; I've just finished a commission and the creative side of me simply can't wind down. Come and have tea tomorrow and help eat some of my cakes. Alice might like a game of tennis.'

Alice puts down the spade and comes over. She says she was just making tea and why doesn't Jonquil stay and have some with us. But Jonquil says she's already late for her appointment with the hairdresser.

We are sitting in what Jonquil calls her 'bower'. I feel Alice wince every time Jonquil says 'my bower'. Once a vine grew here. Its grapes were hard and sour, but its dappled shade was alluring. Jonquil has replaced it with red climbing roses and a purple clematis. We have lapsang souchong in the silver teapot and artistically shaped shortbread biscuits. There is a shiny chocolate cake and a lemon sponge, decorated with lemon fondant icing and half moons of crystallised lemon. Alice is touchy, which I suppose is understandable. Not only must she feel sore about Hunter's Moon, there are other tensions between my daughter and my daughter-in-law. Poor Alice has been through a divorce, and David and Jonquil, apart from having a stable marriage, are rather an exceptional couple: David so successful and Jonquil making a name for herself in the art world. Alice should try to look interested: Jonquil is telling us how pleased the advertising person is with the portraits of his three little daughters. Unfortunately, we can't see them because they're away being framed.

Such busy lives you all have, I say to them; and my life is so dreary. Alice says, 'Come now Mother, you've made a wonderful recovery and you have a loving family.'

'Just don't tell me how lucky I am,' I say. Alice looks hurt.

Jonquil seems to understand. 'Poor Mother,' she says. 'It must be horrid. How can we cheer you up? You need something to look forward to. Everyone needs something to look forward to.' She pours more tea, thoughtfully, and then she says, 'What about a party for your seventy-sixth birthday? We haven't had a party at Hunter's Moon since my fortieth.'

A party! I love parties: the dressing up, the small talk, the fun. There is the smallest trickle of anticipation in the pit of my stomach. But if I am to have a birthday party I want it in my own home. They can't take me over completely. I will be the hostess at *my* party. That is what I tell them. Jonquil understands immediately. She says David will organise the drinks and she will make some canapes.

Alice is twiddling a strand of hair round her finger, a habit she had as a child.

'And you'll come and stay, won't you darling? Help me with my party. But first we must make a list and send out invitations.' Something to look forward to, I think and the trickle of anticipation speeds into a surge of excitement.

74

Alice looks doubtful and says, 'As long as you don't think it will be too much for you.' Of course, I realise at once, my party wasn't *her* idea. But Jonquil stops her putting a damper on things: 'We can't wrap Mother up in cotton wool you know,' she says, giving me a cheerful smile.

Jonquil starts to load the tea things onto a tray. Alice helps. I shut my eyes for a moment. They are talking in low voices. I strain my ears. Alice's voice sounds intense, worried. And then I hear Jonquil say firmly and clearly, 'We mustn't take away her independence.'

I shall have my party.

I am alone again, but now there is my birthday party to look forward to. Alice bought the At Home cards and we made a list: old friends from the golf club, my widow friends and of course all the family. I suppose Ralph will have to come. 20 July. Drinks 6.30 to 8.30. There was just time for us to write out the invitations and sent them off before Alice went back to Norwich. She made me ask June from next door, and that dreary husband, whatever his name is. I told her they won't fit in.

During the long nights, I listen to Mozart and plan my party. It's good to make plans. It blunts my loneliness. The trouble with my loneliness is that it cannot be relieved by the company of just anyone. It's the people I love, I need to have around me: my family. My party will bring my family together. Alice will come in good time, so we can get everything ready, and she'll bring William with her. I long to see my grandson.

This square box of a house is short on ambience, but I shall do my best with it; I have my standards, and my birthday party deserves waxed furniture, vases of flowers, polished silver, my best cut glass, and plenty to drink.

Hunter's Moon was the perfect setting. We had wonderful parties in the old days. In winter, the long drawing room would glow with soft light from our table lamps, and there would be a log fire burning in the fireplace. In summer I would open the French windows leading into the garden; night-scented stock in the nearby flower bed. Always a vase of fresh flowers on the hall table: the parquet floor smelling of lavender polish (it's covered with beige Axminster now).

Parties: pretty clothes; smiling faces. The gleam of silver, the glint of my lead crystal wine glasses. Everything shining. That party sound: a low hum to begin with, increasing to a jolly roar, as the drink flows. And Clive; my darling Clive. I always thought him the most handsome man in the room; as did most of the other women. But he chose me. He was mine. I didn't look too bad myself, in those days. I've never had a problem with my weight, like poor Audrey. I've always loved clothes and been prepared to take trouble with them. My little dress maker and some really good fabric, and people would mistake my home-grown dresses for designer gowns. Now my hair is white. Once it was dark brown, like Alice's; for parties I'd fold it into a chignon in the nape of my neck.

What shall I wear for my seventy-sixth birthday party? The lilac dress with the pleated skirt? But I don't much like the white collar. Since my little dressmaker died, I've had to rely on ready-made. The pink and grey two-piece is soft and comfortable and I can get my vest on underneath without it showing. I can cheer it up with my pearl choker. My pearl choker has a diamond clasp and the pearls are natural, not cultured. It's very beautiful, and I love it. I believe it's worth a lot of money, but Clive would never tell me how much. I've not had it valued myself, because it was a special present. I keep it in my little home safe.

Who shall I leave my pearl choker to? At present, jewellery forms part of my estate, to be divided between David and Alice. But Alan Sheppard tells me this can cause trouble. It would be best to allocate items of special value to a particular person. I do have three granddaughters as well as a daughter and daughter-in-law, he says. Why not make things easier for them?

I know that I want Alice to have my ruby engagement ring. The sapphire eternity ring is the right colour for Jonquil. Rosamund, with her fair hair and green eyes, must have the emerald necklet and matching earrings, Louisa the garnet brooch, and little Helen the gold bangles. But who shall wear my pearl choker when I am gone? I do not see Alice adorning

76

herself with it; but it would look well on Jonquil, who has always admired it. I'm afraid any one of my granddaughters is likely to sell my precious pearl choker.

When Clive fastened it round my neck on the morning of my fiftieth birthday, he kissed the top of my head and said, 'We've done all right together, you and I. It's been a good marriage.'

28 October 1996

William went on glowering at Ralph, alone in the far corner of the room, where Hilda's funeral party continued unabated, and he thought to himself, it's not surprising he's on his own. Who would want to talk to *Ralph*? He watched Ralph's eyes skip quickly over himself and Rosamund and he considered what Rosamund had just said about not much minding when their father left. 'I minded,' he said, reliving for a moment the incomprehensible distress of his five-year-old self. The anger and confusion. 'Lots of times I nearly ran away. I used to miss Dad. But now he never even remembers my birthday, so I've stopped. What I really hated was *him* coming.'

'I know,' said Rosamund. 'Mum could find someone better than Ralph. She's not bad looking for her age.'

'People are so selfish. If they want to be selfish they shouldn't have children. I'm never going to get married.' William switched his glare from Ralph to Jonquil, who was wearing a doleful expression and touching a small handker-chief to her eyes. 'They all wanted Granny dead you know.'

'You don't really think that do you?' said Rosamund in a startled voice.

'Think what?' said Helen, blundering up to Rosamund. Flushed and tear-stained, she was clutching her sister's hand.

'Oh nothing much,' said Rosamund.

'Isn't it awful,' said Helen, 'Granny being in the ground. I can't stop thinking about it.'

'It's only her body,' Louisa said. 'I don't believe in heaven, but I feel she's around, in her spirit, in the air.'

William moved away, threading his way through the press

of people. Mrs Curtis, who did housework for his grandmother, was standing near the kitchen door looking small and
forlorn. When she spotted William coming in her direction,
she smiled feebly and said, 'Oh William, I do miss your Gran.'
Her eyes had tears in them. She pushed wisps of orange hair
away from her face and sniffed. 'You haven't seen Pinky have
you? I've been looking all over. And I'm afraid of him getting
knocked down, with all these cars about.'

'He's probably hiding away,' said William. 'It's very noisy.'

'So long as that Mrs Lister hasn't shut him in anywhere.
She's very careless.' Mrs Curtis cast a black look at Mrs Lister.
Mrs Lister, who had been helping to look after his grandmother, was talking to Jonquil over the other side of the
room.

'I worked for your Gran eight years, William. Ever since
she first came here. Never missed a day. It just won't be the
same without her. A fat tear slipped slowly down Mrs Curtis's
pink cheek. 'I'll go and see if I can find Pinky for you,' said
William, backing away.

'And how are *you* William? I hoped we'd see you on this
sad occasion. Have you tried my Mississippi mud cake?'
Granny's next-door neighbour, whose name he had forgotten,
pushed a plateload of soggy brown cake beneath William's
nose.

'No thanks,' he said stiffly, 'I'm not hungry.'

'You could do with a drink dear. Arthur, fetch the boy a
drop of whisky. Your Mum wouldn't mind today of all days,
would she now.'

Arthur drained his glass and disappeared in the direction of
the drinks table. William remembered that the neighbour's
name was June. She was dressed in something dark and tightly
fitting. She looked very solid, as if she'd been filled with a
particularly firm kind of stuffing. Her husband returned with
two full glasses and pressed one of them into William's hand.
He took a mouthful, swallowed, felt immediately warmed and
gulped some more.

'It's a shame your Gran couldn't have had a bit longer,' said
June. 'You could have struck me down with a feather when
your Mum told me she'd gone. But then she was ever so
lonely you know. Arthur and me did our best, but we aren't

79

family. And family's what you need when you get near the end. We had Arthur's mum living with us for ten years before she passed on. Didn't we Arthur? It wasn't easy, mind, but there, it's your own flesh and blood. And we couldn't see her put in a home.'

'Granny didn't want to come and live with us,' said William. 'She wanted to stay here.'

'Well, that's independence for you. You know dear, Arthur and me regret not having seen more of your Gran recently, but I'm afraid we didn't hit it off too well with that Mrs Lister.' She nodded over to where Mrs Lister was talking to Jonquil, and dropped her voice to a confidential whisper. 'I never told your mum, but one evening I popped round with one of my pies; your Gran used to love my pies, and there they were, sat on the sofa, a bottle of gin between them, laughing and joking and, well, if you want to know, they were, in my opinion, rather too well away.' William looked at June's pursed lips and her hair, like a brand-new wig, and wondered if there was anyone he didn't hate.

'Pissed out of their minds, you mean,' said Arthur.

'Come now Arthur, don't upset the boy,' June dabbed a pudgy hand at William's arm.

'I'll have to go. I've got to find my grandmother's cat.' William slid out of her grip. He stopped off at the drinks table, tipped some more whisky into his glass, and set off towards Rosamund, but his path was blocked by Jonquil who was still talking to Mrs Lister. William always thought of Mrs Lister as the grey woman. Today, she had exchanged her grey track suit for something smarter, but it still seemed to be basically grey.

Jonquil was all in black and there was tear-smudged black round her eyes. She was saying in what sounded to William like an exaggeratedly sorrowful voice, 'Mother often stayed with us at Hunter's Moon. She got on so well with our girls, and their friends. She loved talking to the young people and hearing their opinions. I believe she was genuinely fascinated by their world. She was a very forward-thinking lady, you know. I always counted it a real pleasure to have her in our home, though I'm afraid David found Pinky a little trying, but dear Mother adored that cat and putting up with it was the least we could do.' Jonquil paused and touched her eyes with her small white handkerchief. 'Not all of the family realised quite how much she hated the idea of being dependent on us, and until recently she looked after herself pretty well, though it has to be said, she was never keen on cooking. After Father died and until you came to help, Mrs Lister, I'm afraid she virtually lived on packet soup and tinned ham. We watched her grow thinner and thinner. I used to stock her up with fresh food, but I suspect she'd give it to Pinky or throw it away. So then, I'd cook extra and take it round for her to heat up. But I'm not sure she even bothered with my Meals on Wheels. She said she just hated sitting down by herself to eat. Of course we invited her to Sunday lunch when were at home, and she certainly appreciated my food when she came to stay. Ate like a horse at Hunter's Moon. And always keen to try unusual tastes, even if, sadly, her tummy was sometimes not quite up to it.' Jonquil paused again to touch her handkerchief to her eyes. 'But I did enjoy making surprises for her. I get a lot of fun out of cooking. Do you like cooking Mrs Lister?'

'Oh indeed I do,' said Mrs Lister. 'But I'm a very plain cook.'

'When I've been painting all day, I find cooking relaxes me. Standing at an easel and concentrating the mind is quite tense-making. You won't have seen my studio, Mrs Lister. Dear Mother loved to come along and watch. She was so interested in my work. It was really rather flattering. Actually, I did have a little secret from her. I was working on a new painting of Louisa and Helen. For a surprise present. I was really looking forward to seeing her face when I gave it to her. Oh dear, it's very true, isn't it, that old saying about it being more satisfying to give than to receive.'

'Oh indeed it is.' Mrs Lister nodded her iron-grey head.

'And you know, Mrs Lister, some would disagree, but I always understood how much Mother valued her independence. If she overdid things a little towards the end, well it was what she wanted after all. I used to tell David, we can't wrap Mother up in cotton wool. I just knew it was cruel to hold her back. Too demeaning. She had a very open mind, if you know what I mean, Mrs Lister.'

William had suffered this for long enough. He swallowed some more whisky and stared hard at Jonquil and Mrs Lister.

'I want to know,' he said, more loudly than he had intended, 'I want to know about Granny's last hours.'

He had shocked her into silence. He saw Jonquil's fingers jerk on her glass. 'What do you mean?' she said finally, in a choked voice. 'Your darling grandmother is at rest and that's *all* we need to know. We shall miss her dreadfully.' She made a little noise in her throat and tears began to roll down her cheeks. She didn't bother with the small handkerchief clutched in her other hand. She just stood there in her long black dress, swaying, with her straggly fair hair and her pale face, looking like a white witch. David rushed over and laid an arm round her shoulders. He patted her wet face with his own large handkerchief, and said 'She was *so* fond of my mother.'

July 1996

Alice

I am at home but things are no easier between Ralph and me. Our volatile relationship gives rise to the usual arguments concerning my mother, my children, his expectations, my expectations. Must we be so often in combat to prove we are living; that we care?

Since the conflict between us over priorities is irreconcilable, perhaps this is why gradually I notice Ralph switching to sniping at me for what I consider trivialities. My so-called 'slapdash housekeeping' and my 'extravagant attitude'.

'Alice are you planning to grow mustard and cress?' running a distasteful finger through the dust on the dining table. 'Alice do you want to bring us all down with food poisoning?' handing back a less than spotless saucepan in a rare gesture towards helping with the washing up. 'Alice we do not live in a lighthouse,' snapping off lights.

He is clearly expressing dissatisfaction with his present way of life. With me. And I am sad. Eventually, in an effort to put an end to this cycle of pointless squabbling, I fail to respond to his predictable grumbling. Sometimes, I catch him looking at me in a speculative manner: a bitter little smile flickers over his face when I ask him what he's thinking. 'I'm surprised you're interested,' he says, and picks up the newspaper, or switches on the television.

On the spur of the moment, in order to demonstrate my concern for my husband and show him I value his dedication and commitment to his furniture, I pay him a visit at work. Trudy, whose complexion is much improved, seems pleased to see me and asks kindly after my mother.

Ralph doesn't look up when I enter his office. He is studying a large sheet of paper spread out on his desk, and he is not alone. A small woman with bubbly blonde hair stands beside him. Their concentration is total. I say hello and they both look up in surprise.

'Alice! hello darling. Everything O.K.?' Ralph manages to redirect his attention towards me.

'Just thought I'd call in to see how you're getting on', I say. Ralph introduces me to the woman. Her name is Judith Page and she is young. She has china-blue eyes and a white skin, and she is wearing a blue linen suit with a short skirt and a fitted jacket, beneath which is a flowery blouse with a bow at her throat. The blue flowers in the blouse are of the same blue as the suit and Judith Page's eyes. Her face is flattish, with a small mouth. She is the designer of Ralph's new range of furniture, and does not look in the least like the untidy arty person I have imagined.

'Look,' says Ralph. 'We're adding an end table to the burr oak range.' And he shows me the drawing they have been studying. 'Pedestal base,' he says. 'See the nice curve of the splayed feet. And we're putting in a small drawer. We'll offer it with a natural waxed finish or a deeper stain on the timber. Alice, Judith and I are just going down to look at the proto-types. Come with us and see how they're getting on.'

I always feel awkward walking round the factory, so vital, so familiar to Ralph, who laboured so hard to expand his father's small furniture repair business into the lively manu-facturing company it is today. The men glance up quickly from their work as we pass. Now and then Ralph stops to have word with one of them; he checks the easy sliding of a drawer with a cabinet maker, the hand carving on the cornice of a bookcase. In my ears is the steady noise of the wood cutting machines, the muted roar of the dust extractor. I smell the peppery scent of the wood, the astringent odour of polish and the warm reek of active men. Ralph is easy with his craftsmen, most of whom have worked here for years; many have sons working here too.

Judith Page is perfectly at home, demonstrating her knowl-edge by the confidence with which she relates to the men, asking questions of them, examining their work.

We inspect the burr oak dining table with its shaped ends and the writing table and a cabinet which will have glazed doors. They look practical and, I have to admit, classy, the outlines strong, the dappled wood appealing. They tell me they will use ebony and sycamore inlay in a Greek key-ring design to add decorative interest.

'Your husband has some wonderful craftsmen,' says Judith Page when we get back to Ralph's office. 'It was mass production at Cranshaws where I used to work. Your product makes me think of the difference between a Rolls Royce and a Ford Escort. And there's a good atmosphere on the factory floor.'

Ralph's pleasure is palpable.

I ask Judith Page what made her go in for furniture design. She tells me in her faint West country burr that she's always liked art, that she can draw and she enjoys working with her hands. After art school she went to furniture college because she didn't see a future for herself in fine art. 'I like the idea of designing something that people can use and get pleasure out of using.'

I find I've had enough of Judith Page. I gulp down the cup of tea Trudy has brought in for us, say goodbye to Ralph and his female designer and then I go home.

That evening I ask Ralph to tell me a bit more about Judith Page. 'What do you what to know?' he says. I say I can see she's a good designer. Where does she come from? Is she married? Does she have children?

Ralph says he thinks she lives somewhere outside Ipswich, and she has one little girl. When I ask what her husband does, Ralph says, 'Poor Judith's a widow. It's really sad. Her husband was killed three years ago in a road accident when the little girl was only a few months old. This is the first job she's had in all that time. It's very important to her.'

'Well I'm glad you've come to her rescue, dear,' I say nastily, echoing my mother's tone.

'Don't be so superior, Alice. Judith's not had it easy, like you. She's a gallant little thing and she needs every bit of help she can get.' Ralph's voice is self-righteous.

I look daggers at him. Ralph stares levelly back at me out of his brilliant blue eyes and he says, 'Come on Alice, you mustn't be grudging. You have so much more than she has.'

I think quite a bit about Judith Page and Ralph. In the ten years of our marriage, it has never crossed my mind that Ralph might be unfaithful. He is so possessive of me, so adamant that fidelity is paramount in marriage; even now that we are squabbling, still so ardent, I cannot believe he would betray me. I tell myself that Judith Page is a sorrowing widow, not an evil temptress. Also, I am at home most of the time now. Mother is managing quite well, with Mrs Curtis and a bit of propping up from me and Rosamund, who is on vacation, and nobly went to stay with her for a few days. I must behave in a mature manner and trust my husband.

Rosamund is here now, which is lovely, even if she is out most of the time catching up with old schoolfriends, and I can't sleep for worrying that something might have happened to her, as I wait for the sound of the front door to signal her return late at night. And then tense myself against the probable sound of the door closing with a bang which will waken Ralph.

I wonder if you ever stop worrying about your children? I sometimes think it was easier when they were little and I could protect them. William bothers me just now. He and his devious friend Tim went off on a cycling trip round the North Norfolk coast. They took a tent, but I think they mostly stayed in youth hostels. It rained, and I get the impression William is rather fed up with Tim, which is no bad thing, but I don't like to see him looking miserable. He's got himself a job washing up at a trendy restaurant in the city, which tires him out, and when he's home he retreats to his attic and listens to his tapes. He doesn't seem to want to talk, which upsets me. When he was a little boy we were such good companions. I suppose you have to accept your children need to grow away from you, like plants climbing towards the burning sun, out from the sheltering shade.

Rosamund and William and I are going to Mother's birthday party. To be precise, I am going a couple of days in advance of the party to organise it for her, and Rosamund and William are accompanying me. Ralph has promised to come in time for the party, and stay for the rest of the weekend.

I am not in favour of this party; not just because it will be a lot of work for me, but because I think the excitement will be too much for Mother. I have been overruled by David and Jonquil. They say it will do her good, that she needs some fun in her life, and she's always loved parties. Ralph is cynical. He says it's in their interest if this party is too much for my mother. Since she has decided to leave Hunter's Moon to them, from their point of view, the sooner she pops off the better, before she changes her mind.

Can I believe this to be true? I can believe it of Jonquil, whose emotional exterior conceals a nerve of steel, but not of my benign brother.

When Mother told me what she had done about her Will, I felt a terrible sense of loss. I have so loved Hunter's Moon. I feel as if I have given into custody the whole of my childhood to a woman who does not value it. Mother knows how I feel. But she's old-fashioned enough to believe in primogeniture and, anyway, she wouldn't want Ralph living in Hunter's Moon, I know that. In her eyes, she's done the right thing. It's logical. Inevitable, I suppose. But I am hurt.

Mother greets us with delight, and seeing her pleasure, I regret my mean-minded reservations about the work involved organising her party. She makes a particular fuss of Rosamund and William, anxious that they will find their beds comfortable; that they have enough blankets, reading lights, et cetera.

Rosamund teases Mother, rallies her with jokes. William is quietly solicitous, like an under-age uncle.

After supper on the eve of her birthday, I make sure that Mother has an early night. I hover upstairs while she has her bath, and when she is finally in bed, I go and say goodnight to her. While I'm sitting on her bed listening to her chatting away about who will be coming to her party, what she plans to wear, how pleased she is Rosamund and William are here, she suddenly says, 'Poor William, it's so sad that wretched girl let him down. He's very miserable, but I expect he'll get over it soon. We all went through it didn't we, dear? What was that

87

song Maurice Chevalier used to sing? "I'm glad I'm not young any more".'

William and a girl? I do not admit this is news to me. Another thing to feel hurt about. Why does my mother know this and I do not? My mother who is taking too much of my attention is now the confidante of my son, who has had too little of it. I cannot press William to confide. I must respect his privacy, but I wish he would to talk to me. I have hardly talked to William about girls and sex, having been more concerned with Rosamund risking early and disturbing sexual encounters. When William was little I tried to explain how babies are born, but since then I've not tackled the subject of his sexuality. Do I assume this to be his father's territory, or even Ralph's?

I need to talk to my son; and not just about sex, about human relationships: love and respect, romance and illusion. Not being able to stay married to his father hasn't helped. Don't do as I did. Do as I say.

I do not settle well in Mother's second bedroom. Along the landing, in the third bedroom, relaxed, unconcerned, Rosamund is catching up on lost sleep. In the little box room, William wrestles with the problems of growing up, and I cannot help him.

Mother's birthday morning is bright and warm. We watch her open her presents: a miniature rose in a terracotta pot, her favourite Bendicks bitter-mints, Floris bath essence, Blue Grass perfume, a caddy of China tea, a bottle of malt whisky from Ralph. ('No point giving your mother anything other than consumables.')

If she is a little flushed with over-excitement, there is nothing I can do about it now.

We have all day to prepare for Mother's guests. Mrs Curtis has spent weeks polishing the furniture and washing the china and glass. Because Mother keeps changing her mind about how the furniture should be arranged, William and I humour her by trying the dining table in different positions and moving the chairs around. At Mother's insistence, I polish the already shining silver table candelabra and replace the white cloth on the table destined for the drinks, with a blue one which I have to iron. Rosamund helps Mother decide what to wear. With everything out of the wardrobe, Mother's bedroom looks like a second-hand clothes shop.

David phones: can we collect the drink and the ice, he simply doesn't have time. William points out we don't have much time either. 'Just tell him, Mum,' he says. Nevertheless, William patiently accompanies me to the wine warehouse and we collect the red and white wine, the whisky and gin, the mixers and fruit juice, the plastic bags of ice cubes ordered by David. By the time we've done all that, it's lunchtime. Rosamund says I should stop being a martyr and sit down and relax. William offers to cook mushroom omelettes, and I let him even though I know it will mess up the kitchen. Mother's eyes are shining and her conversation is becoming disjointed. After lunch she goes to rest on her bed. Rosamund slides out into the garden to sunbathe and William and I take Emily for a little walk.

All efforts to coax William to confide fail. He assures me he is fine; everything is fine. Emily ambles along in her stiff way, tail swinging, head on one side, stopping to sniff at the base of trees, at clumps of grass beneath the wooden seats on the playing field, where she scavenges the end of someone's sandwich. 'She's all right, is she Mum?' My son's face tells me he cannot bear to see her painfully slow, half blind progress, and I know that he is remembering the lively puppy, the energetic young dog.

I tell him I've found a nice vet who says Emily is not in pain. I tell him about the injections and pills she has for her arthritis, and that the vet says a little exercise, just pottering around, keeps the joints mobile. I point out that she's wagging her tail, that she still enjoys her food. William looks at me doubtfully and I know he is thinking it's not much of a life for his childhood friend.

When we get back we put the wine to cool in the ice and lay out the glasses. Rosamund helps Mother get ready while William and I spread different kinds of pâté on cocktail biscuits, arrange prawns in vol-au-vent cases, tip nuts and crisps into dishes, and cut carrots and celery and red peppers into strips to eat with the dips I made yesterday. Jonquil's canapés,

I know from experience, will be high on artistry but low on quantity.

Rosamund calls for me to help Mother with her hair, while she gets changed herself. Mother is wearing her pink and grey skirt and jacket. The pink is a clear, jewel pink, the grey is soft as a dove's wing and the material supple. It drapes her body, disguising its thinness. With her silver hair framing her face, pink on her lips, blusher on her cheeks and a touch of grey eye shadow, she looks marvellous. I tell her so, and she smiles happily and asks me to fasten her pearl choker. Mother's pearl choker is magnificent. I lay it gently round her withered neck and fasten the diamond clasp. The pearls are lustrous, the diamonds sparkle. Mother looks confident, queenly. I am wary of those high heels, but I say nothing. She utterly refuses to wear her glasses. 'I can see better without them, dear.' Her voice has its imperious tone.

I change into my red and navy polka-dot silk dress, slap on some make-up and brush my hair. Rosamund is wearing an alarmingly short, black, thin garment that I haven't seen before. William, in clean jeans and white tee-shirt, has been persuaded to brush his hair. At six-fifteen we are all ready. Mother, bright-eyed, restless, sips a small whisky.

At six twenty, Jonquil floats through the door, draped in one of her pale, gauzy outfits. Ralph calls them 'Your sister-in-law's *Midsummer Night's Dream* gear'. Her long hair is loose and she looks pleased in an unpleasantly secretive way. David, in a light linen jacket, follows carrying the canapés very carefully. He says Jonquil has been hard at it all day creating them for us all and don't they look good! They are decoratively arranged on two flat silver trays: little triangles and squares of biscuit and toast set with glazed smoked salmon, olives, lump-fish roe, scraps of ham; pastry shells filled with tiny shrimps and differently coloured creamy mousses. William and I have not laboured needlessly.

David and Jonquil kiss Mother and wish her happy birthday. Then Jonquil, all smiles, presents Mother with something square and gift wrapped which turns out to be a portrait of Pinky. 'Just finished in time for your birthday, Mother,' she glows. Somehow, she's managed to make the vile creature look positively genial. Mother, of course, is enchanted and insists on David hanging it up immediately. Then we all have to stand and worship.

Jonquil's slightly bulgy eyes scan the room. 'Ralph not here?' she says ... I tell her Ralph is coming later, and ask where are Helen and Louisa? Jonquil says, it's so sad, but we had this tennis coaching course booked for the girls such a long time ago and how sorry they are to miss their grandmother's party. Somewhere near my left ear, Rosamund murmurs, 'How convenient for them'.

Six-thirty exactly. Ralph *promised* to come. Surely he will not let me down? Despite the traffic, he ought to be here by now.

The bell rings and as Rosamund opens the door, Mother says, not quite quietly enough, 'Oh dear it's June, and I think he's called Arthur. I was afraid they'd be the first to arrive and he's such a cracking bore.'

June and Arthur advance beamingly into the room carrying between them a basket piled with fruit. 'Happy Birthday, Hilda,' they say in unison. Arthur is wearing a blazer with shiny brass buttons. His thin dark hair is slicked down flat against his scalp. June is neat in yellow box pleats and short jacket.

The cars roll up. Soon the crescent is lined with elderly Mercedes and BMWs, and Mother is greeting her friends, most of whom I've known for a long time. They are pleased to see me and my children, whose names they do not always remember correctly. They have put on their party clothes and there are smiles on their wrinkled faces. Elderly men seem to be either short, paunchy and bald, or lanky and hollow-chested with thatches of white hair. The women, likewise, are either fat with wobbly white arms, disguising their girth in shapeless tents, or scrawny as ancient birds of paradise, tottering on skinny legs in their bright clothes. Pearls and gold encircle their necks; closely on the fat ones, loosely on the withered ones. Diamond, ruby and emerald rings hang beneath the enlarged knuckles on their age-spotted hands. How will it be for me, I wonder? Scrawny in all probability, provided I make it of course. And there is something touching and gallant about the way these elderly people are entering into the party spirit. Drinking in The Last Chance Saloon, I think to myself.

William takes round the wine, but no-one is drinking it apart from David and Jonquil and me. The old-stagers are knocking back the whisky and gin. Soon they are all shouting at each other and their intrepid laughter is reverberating around the crowded room.

William says, 'Perhaps they don't mind being old'. Rosamund giggles as we notice an old chap with a glowing complexion and a large stomach pinch the ample blue- and white-striped bottom of a woman who is definitely not his wife. 'God, Mum, you have to keep out of *his* way. These lecherous old men don't seem to have got the message they're past it! They won't keep their hands to themselves and I can't bear to look at their teeth.'

'I'm fed up of hearing about their clever grandchildren being solicitors or doctors,' says William. 'And they all ask me the same thing. "Where do you go to school? And what will you do when you leave?"'

Rosamund is drinking gin and tonic and I notice William has sneaked a whisky, but I say nothing.

Mother is flirting with Harry Garnham. Harry is younger than some and has close-cut curly grey hair that is receding rather than retreating altogether. He is wearing a rather dashing magenta bow tie and is smoking a large cigar. Mother is laughing at something he has just said. Jonquil, standing next to her, passes over what looks like a glass of almost neat whisky. I remember Ralph's cynical remarks. Seven o'clock: he should be here by now.

William and Rosamund drift away to hand round the snacks and I am cornered by Dickie Clarke, who used to play golf with my father. He is tall and thin with a flaming hook nose. He stoops over me, slopping whisky onto the floor, and tells me about his recently fitted pace-maker. He can play eighteen holes now without getting out of breath. 'It's a wonderful thing,' he says, 'Modern surgery. I keep telling Buffy he should have his hips done. Give the old bugger a new lease of life: get him back on the course. But I doubt he's got the guts. He's not been the same, you know, since dear old Madeline dropped off the perch. And mean! Well, we know he lost a packet with Lloyds, but he's still a wealthy man. Thought he wouldn't turn up this evening: won't go to parties in case he has to ask people back. Getting Buffy to spend money these days is like getting shit out of a rocking horse.'

I smile and laugh and consider how modern surgery extends people's lives, and I think that's fine, as long as it also improves them.

Mother is smiling up at Harry Garnham: her whisky three-quarters drunk. Jonquil is still by her side, uncharacteristically animated. I move over to them.

'Yes,' Harry says, 'Old Shorty Harmer's still above ground. Drinks like a fish these days; carries a hip flask in his golf bag. And Connie! Of course, I remember Connie: stunning looking girl. Lost her first husband during the War: married again, that swine Dickie Howlett. 'Sowlett', they used to call him. She married him, silly girl, but not before he'd had two of her sisters and the mother as well; or so they say!'

Jonquil slips away. Harry greets me and Mother says, 'I'm having such a lovely time darling.' William appears with a silver tray upon which cower the remains of Jonquil's canapés. They can certainly eat and drink, these old people. Harry takes the last pastry shell of shrimps and Mother says, 'Harry, this is William, my grandson; my only grandson.'

'Hello William,' says Harry. 'And where do you go to school?'

I notice June and Arthur, looking a little lost, standing together by the window, and I go over to talk to them. Arthur points at Mother's lawn and says he's got a sack of weed and feed in the shed which will get rid of the moss and the daisies. I thank him and he says what that lawn really needs is a feature: something like a rose pergola or a bird bath. June and Arthur have a pond with a fountain and a stone heron standing on one leg. I tell them I've been admiring their water-lilies. Rosamund appears and offers them a platter of cocktail snacks. They help themselves to one of our dips, and then Arthur leers at Rosamund, takes a gulp of whisky and burps fruitily. Rosamund giggles and June looks embarrassed. Arthur's veined nose is purple and his formerly slicked down hair is rising off his head as if lifted by the heat of his scalp.

93

'I think your Granny's been a bit too generous with the spirits,' June remarks to Rosamund and, turning to me, adds, 'It was ever so nice of her to ask us to her special party and it's a treat to meet her friends.'

'Snobby old lot if you ask me,' says Arthur staring malevolently across the room. June looks helplessly at Rosamund and me and says of course he doesn't mean it. It's just the whisky talking. Arthur says he certainly does mean it. He was telling the stuck-up cow in the nipple pink about his coy carp and, 'Oh she says, we had to get rid of ours when we drained the pond to build the swimming pool.' Arthur drains his glass and reaches out for the whisky bottle. June says, 'Don't you think you've had enough Arthur? You won't be able to lift your head from the pillow in the morning.'

'Thinks I can't hold my liquor.' Arthur winks at Rosamund and slops whisky into his glass. Rosamund says, 'I must go and find my brother,' and shoots off. I excuse myself and head away from June and Arthur.

It's eight o'clock and the party is reaching its zenith. The noise from these old people's lungs is deafening. Jonquil's canapés have all been guzzled and only my partially consumed dips and a few plates of nuts and crisps remain. The gin and whisky bottles are almost empty. The air is heavily scented and hazed with cigar smoke. Mother, incandescent with the overwhelming success of her party smiles and laughs by the settee with Roddie Bartram. Her colour is a shade hectic, I think, and is it my imagination, or do I see her sway a little as she reaches for a crisp?

Roddie Bartram is a bluff, portly old gent. He flew Lancaster bombers in the Second World War. He won't go in an aeroplane now. Slowly, I wend my way over and say hello. Roddie smiles and says, 'Just been talking to your son. Charming boy. Tells me he plans to be an airline pilot.' I'm just recovering from this piece of misinformation when Jonquil, colour high, eyes glowing, materialises beside me like Titania.

'Darling Jonquil,' says Mother. 'Such a lovely party: it was Jonquil's idea, you know, Roddie. Such a lot of work for the family, but I'm so enjoying seeing all my friends. And some of them are even older than me!'

Roddie smiles at Jonquil and Mother says, 'My daughter-in-law paints the most beautiful portraits. You *must* let her do your grandchildren.' Jonquil shakes back her hair, which is beginning to look a little straggly, and smiles coyly at Roddy. Roddy strokes his thick grey moustache. I can see he's quite taken with Jonquil.

Ten past eight. And where is Ralph?

David beckons me over. He and William are talking to Marge Coppice. Marge is draped in a brownish embroidered tent which has an African look about it. She is laughing, probably at one of David's funny stories. Her jowls wobble and there are red blotches on her face. Her scalp glows pink through sketchy white hair. She peers at me with eyes that are bleary, but sharp underneath, like a fish underwater. 'Your son says he doesn't play golf. Shame. All the time in the world to groove his swing. I've been telling him what a lot of fun I used to have with his grandmother. Oh I do hope my old sparring partner will soon get back on the course. Nice little player: straight down the middle and deadly round the greens. Me, I can't keep out of the rough ha ha ha!' Marge Coppice laughs wheezily and tells us how she'd whack the ball 200 yards off the tee miles past Mother's lady-like shot. How Mother would doddle her ball along a couple of times and just as Marge was thinking 'I've got you now' she'd slice her approach into a bush and by the time she'd hacked it out, Mother would be two foot from the pin, sink the putt for a par and Marge would be struggling to avoid a seven. 'Hardly play now,' she says. 'Dodgy back. Geriatric foursome once a month with three pals.'

'Would you like some wine?' William holds out the bottle.

'White wine's too acid for me, thank you dear, never touch it. Stick to the hard stuff.' She turns to me and says. 'William has just been telling me he plans to become a chef.'

'Really!' David raises his eyebrows. William avoids my eye. Marge says she's been enjoying David's funny stories, and how about another one. 'O.K.,' says David. 'What's the definition of a geriatric golfer?'

'Tell me,' says Marge.

'Someone who asks you what the score is on the odd holes and what your name is on the evens.'

95

Marge Coppice laughs and her jowls shake and her eyes water. 'Oh,' she says, 'It's terrible getting old. I hate it. You know what I suffer from?'

We all say, 'No, what do you suffer from?'

'CRAFT,' says Marge.

'And what's CRAFT?'

'Can't Remember A Fucking Thing,' she shouts triumphantly, squinting at David who bursts into startled laughter. Marge almost collapses with mirth. Her jowls quiver and her face turns puce.

William and I join in with the laughter and William asks, in a surprised whisper, 'Are old people's parties always like this?'

At eight-thirty, the atmosphere abruptly changes. As if a whistle has been blown to call Time at the end of a football match, with one accord, Mother's friends drain their glasses, extinguish their cigars, retrieve their handbags, fumble for their car keys and head for the front door. 'Wonderful party: thank you Hilda; you look in terrific form.' The general exodus is followed by the banging of car doors in the crescent, a revving of engines, a screech of tyres, some tooting on horns and off they roar in convoy.

'It's like bloody Brands Hatch.' Arthur is being coaxed towards the door by June. 'And they'll not pass a breathalyser – any of them!' He throws this parting shot triumphantly over his shoulder and lurches down the path, clutching June's embarrassed arm.

In the sudden silence the room, emptied of people, looks forlorn. Some of Jonquil's canapés had been ground into the carpet, the ash trays are full, the glasses empty.

When I start to to collect up the glasses and empty the ash trays, Jonquil says, 'Oh do leave that Alice. We all deserve to sit down and have a rest. I'm absolutely exhausted.' Then she tells Mother what a fantastic success her birthday party has been and how everyone remarked on how well she is looking.

'I thought Ralph was supposed to be coming,' says David.

'He phoned to say he's been held up,' I lie, and decide to call the bastard as soon as possible.

Rosamund disappears into the garden with a cigarette.

96

Mother, upright among the wreckage of her party, taut with nervous energy, suddenly looks very white. 'It *was* a good party, wasn't it?' she says appealingly. 'It *did* go well didn't it!'

I tell her it was a great party and try to get her to sit down and relax.

But Mother remains on her feet in the middle of the room, reliving her party. 'I'm so glad dear Humphrey was able to come. He's just back from South Africa, you know, playing for the Seniors. But did you talk to poor Archie. His cataract operation went wrong. Says he sees double now. He's very brave about it.'

I continue to try to get Mother to come and sit down, but she's like a clockwork toy set to perform. 'Hal's been having gold injections for his arthritis. He says they're marvellous, but Moira – and I do believe she's fatter than ever poor dear – Moira says he's a sick man. Oh well, none of us get any younger do we?'

Jonquil says, 'Beryl's still a wonderful-looking woman, isn't she Mother? Such good bone structure: perfect oval face, and her hair, so daring to wear it pulled back like that. I should love to paint her.' She yawns dramatically and lowers herself into a chair. 'David darling, pour me a glass of mineral water, there's a sweetheart. I've got that funny floaty feeling, as if I'm not really here, just dreaming it all. And could you bring over that little stool for my feet. I think if you don't mind, everyone, I'll do my meditation now.'

William says he's hungry. Rosamund, who has just returned from the garden says she's hungry too and there's some fruit and salad in the kitchen, and a pie that the next-door neighbours brought.

Mother says she can't face one of June's pies and she'd rather have a spam sandwich and some cuppa soup. 'We should never have asked them, you know,' she says to me. 'Whatsisname got embarrassingly tiddly: and they didn't fit in at all. I think I'll just go and put on something a bit warmer.' Before I can stop her she's tottering out of the door. I start across the room after her. Just as I reach the hall, there is a sharp yelp, a cut-off scream and the thud of a falling body. I

97

break into a run. Mother lies face down on the floor. From beneath Mother's buckled legs, a dazed expression on her battered face, Emily struggles to her feet.

Alice

Mother's face is white as chalk beneath the party make-up. I take her thin, unresisting wrist in my hand and feel for her pulse. I tell Rosamund to telephone the doctor.

'An ambulance surely,' says David.

Mother doesn't want to go to hospital ever again, I tell him sharply, and leaning close, I put my ear to Mother's open mouth.

David says, stolidly, stupidly, 'She might *have* to go to hospital.'

Rosamund says, 'Shouldn't you hold up a mirror: to see if she's breathing?'

I tell her to do as she's been told and telephone Doctor Robson. The number is on the pad by the phone.

David says, 'Bloody dog! How did it get down here? I thought you'd shut it in the bedroom.'

I want to lash out at them all: just standing there, uselessly, looking. I try to calm myself, to call upon that reserve of cool common sense that I believe exists within me, like a deep, tideless lake: that tough, emotionless core which takes over in a crisis. Mother's inert form looks so fragile, so defenceless. What is the right thing to do? I press the tips of my fingers gently into the translucent skin protecting Mother's raised blue veins and concentrate upon feeling for evidence of the pumping of her heart.

William says it wasn't Emily's fault, and leads her into the kitchen.

Jonquil appears in the hall and looks sadly down at my Mother lying there. 'Oh I can't bear it. Poor Mother, and it was such a lovely party: Her Swan Song. But she *did* so enjoy herself.' Tears are rolling down Jonquil's cheeks. She sways and grabs David's arm. 'Oh I think I might faint.'

Rosamund reports that the doctor is coming. He says not to move Mother. Just cover her up and keep her warm.

I tell David to take Jonquil upstairs to lie down. Rosamund fetches a duvet and we cover Mother's still, small form with it. I sit on the floor and rub Mother's cold hands. Do I feel the flutter of a pulse beneath that fragile skin? Is the heart beating too slowly, too infrequently to maintain life in the limbs, in the internal organs? In the brain? Is my mother dying?

'Shouldn't you give her some brandy?' William's eyes are huge with alarm in his colourless face, despite the level tone of his voice.

I tell him we'd better not do anything until the doctor comes, and wish I'd attended first-aid classes. Rosamund says we could give Mother the kiss of life. She once watched a video about how to do it at school. She kneels down beside me and says she thinks you pinch the nose between your thumb and forefinger and breathe into the mouth. And you have to press down on the chest, but it must be in the right place. 'Poor Granny,' she says, shakily. 'Is she going to die?'

'No.' I am suddenly filled with the certain knowledge that this is not to be the end. That Mother's heart is still beating, that life pulses, albeit slowly, through that indomitable circulatory system. And I am right, for now Mother draws a shuddering breath and begins to cough. Filled with relief, carefully, gently, Rosamund and I raise her head a fraction. Her lips are blue and trembling but she is able to articulate in a slurred mumble something that sounds like Alice. I say, 'I'm here Mother.' I tell her she had a little fall, she must lie still and Doctor Robson is coming. Rosamund reaches for my hand and together, hands clasped, we watch while Mother's face begins gradually to look less like a mask of marble. By the time Doctor Robson arrives, my mother is turning her head feebly from side to side and struggling to get into a sitting position. Hoarsely, but distinctly, she is mumbling, 'No hospital'.

Doctor Robson is cheerful and reassuring, even if he does

treat my mother like a recalcitrant child. He examines her thoroughly all over, takes her blood pressure, listens to her heart and finally he says she is a lucky lady. No broken bones, just a badly sprained ankle and a nasty bump on the head. He makes a point of asking her, quite sternly, if she's been remembering to take her pills. He tells me she needs plenty of rest. No excitement. He won't prescribe a tranquilliser because of the concussion. She'll have a headache for a day or two, he says, and I must let him know immediately if her condition deteriorates: if she starts to ramble or if she loses consciousness. I'm to keep an eye on her and he'll look in tomorrow morning.

Between us, we manage to get Mother upstairs and settled into bed. She relaxes against the pillows and closes her eyes.

David and Jonquil follow us slowly, as we go back down the stairs and into the sitting room, strewn with the relics of Mother's birthday party. David has his arm round a drooping Jonquil. He says, 'Shouldn't my mother be in hospital, Doctor?'

Doctor Robson is brisk and friendly. He says his patients do well to survive the geriatric ward. He doesn't send them there unless it's absolutely necessary. I think, what a sensible man. I thank Doctor Robson and see him to the door.

Back in the living room, David, his arm still protecting a wilting Jonquil, says, 'I'm taking her home: she's all in.'

Jonquil raises her head and looks at me. The tremble of her lips, the sorrow in her brimming eyes cannot quite camouflage what is truly genuine in her face. I can tell that she is bitterly disappointed. Jonquil wants my mother dead.

David strokes the long fair hair which is straggling over his wife's cheek. Ralph does not care for me like this, I think. As if my welfare is the only thing that matters. And Jonquil is not worth it. Envy and disgust twist my stomach so it hurts. Ralph should be here. I look at my brother, who has no thought for anyone but my sister-in-law, and I say that Mother can't be left on her own; she needs looking after. I tell him I had intended to go home tomorrow, but in the circumstances I'm prepared to stay a couple of extra days, but he and Jonquil will have to take over for the rest of the week.

David's face assumes an expression of abject apology. He

101

says, quickly, rushing to get it over with, 'Oh dear, Alice I know it isn't fair on you, but Jonks and I are taking the girls to Spain for a fortnight. The chap at the office is lending us his villa in Marbella. Flights are all booked. I can't disappoint Louisa and Helen, and Jonks has been working so hard, she really does need a break. We'll do our whack when we get back. Promise.'

There is triumph now in Jonquil's face. She says, 'Alice dear, if you don't mind me saying so, we all know it's you your mother wants. I realise it's hard, but if you could manage a little while longer, just while she's really poorly, I'm sure you'll find it very rewarding. And then I think we should consider getting her some professional help.' She manufactures a little forward sway and says, oh dear! she still feels rather odd. It must be the shock.

Rosamund reminds Jonquil curtly of the considerable quantity of red wine she was consuming. I say there's an awful lot of clearing up to do. Jonquil says she's sure Rosamund and William will give me a hand and why don't we get Mrs Curtis to come in in the morning? She'd probably be glad of the extra cash.

Consumed with anger and frustration and self-pity, I'm finding it hard not to burst into tears. I dig my nails into the palms of my hands and, fighting to keep my voice under control, I say that I understand the situation perfectly and David and Jonquil might as well get along to Hunter's Moon.

There is no reply when I telephone home, quite late at night. Next morning, as I'm picking the Sunday papers off the mat at around nine, an apologetic Ralph rings to say he's terribly sorry to let me down, but there was a crisis at the factory, and he couldn't get away. When I ask him angrily why he didn't phone yesterday, he says by the time everything was sorted out, it was so late, he was afraid of waking Mother. Then he asks, gently, 'Are you all right darling? You sound fraught.'

I say I'm not all right, and explain about Mother's accident. He says he's sorry to hear it, and goes silent when I tell him I won't be able to come home tomorrow after all, that I must stay here and look after Mother. 'What about the Golden Couple?' he asks. 'Can't they do something for a change?' I tell him they're going to Spain for a fortnight, 'Surprise, sur-prise!' he says.

I'm near to tears now. 'I'd much rather be at home. Please, you must understand, darling. I have to look after my mother.'

'Shouldn't she be in hospital?'

'She utterly refuses.'

'Make her.'

I tell my husband he'll be old and frightened himself one day, and anyway, Dr Robson says it isn't necessary.

'For whom?' says Ralph.

'Ralph, you promised to come to Mother's party. I'm sure you could have made it if you'd really tried. I could have done with your support.'

'I told you darling. I had a problem with the finish on a special. And Herb Lurie in New York is playing up. By the time I'd sorted all that out I didn't feel up to the drive.'

'I still think you could have phoned.'

'I can't tell you how hectic it's been.'

'Your priorities are clear to me.' Like a sour aftertaste, the picture of David, protective arm around Jonquil, lingers in my mind's eye.

'As yours are to me,' says Ralph.

Rosamund and William stay on with Mother and me for a couple of days. And then it's time for Rosamund to go off to Turkey with her university friends, although she offers to keep us company for a little longer, and catch up with her friends later. But that seems too risky to me. Rosamund, who is much more practical than I am, tidies Mother's bedroom and organ-ises her underwear drawer, sorting into neat piles the lock-knit vests (with sleeves and sleeveless), the knickers (thick ones, thin ones, with legs and without), the rayon bloomers (pink ones, white ones), and the brassières (cotton ones, nylon ones, front-fastening, back-fastening). And she transfers Mother's battery of pills into clearly labelled, easy-to-open bottles.

When Rosamund goes, she takes with her a light-hearted steadfast atmosphere of hope.

William stays for two more days. He has clearly been very upset by his grandmother's accident, and is subdued and uncommunicative with me. He doesn't want to talk about going back to college in September, or about his friends, or about whether he wants to go to university like his sister. He looks after Emily, whose condition has not been improved by being flattened. He feeds her and takes her out for short walks. William is very sweet with his grandmother. He sets up a day camp for her on the large sofa in the sitting room, carefully helps her down the stairs, tucks a rug around her, and collects together all the things she cannot bear to be without: her reading glasses, her diary, her telephone book, her portable radio cum tape recorder, the *TV Times*, the remote control for the television, Pinky's special biscuits, and he sits and talks with her while I'm busy shopping and cooking. I miss him badly when he goes back to Norwich to resume his washing-up job.

Dr Robson says Mother is a lot tougher than you might think. 'She's a great lady, your mother,' he says. 'I always enjoy coming to see her.'

Mother certainly perks up in young Dr Robson's presence, becoming quite flirtatious.

Physically she is more frail than when she came out of hospital three months ago. Mentally she is quite sharp: less confused than she was then, but troubled, dissatisfied. She is admirably brave about the plum-coloured bruises peppering her frail old body. When I rub liniment into her ribs and her shins and her thighs, I am wrenched by the feel of Mother's small bones beneath my hands, fragile as a bird's light frame. Taking her arm to help her upstairs, feeling the thinness of her cheek as I kiss her good night, I think, *how little of her there is!*

It is amazing how much time and energy can be expended on one old lady. I am kept active from seven in the morning when Mother and Pinky have their early morning tea until midnight, because it seems impossible to get Mother to bed any earlier. After our supper on trays in the sitting room, Mother likes to talk. She finds the television either boring or upsetting and refuses to read her library book because 'I'm so enjoying your company dear'. She catnaps during the day, but any movement by me will waken her, stimulating a request for a cup of coffee, help with buttoning her cardigan, the search for her book, my presence to discuss the forward engagements in her diary. Even given the opportunity, I have never been able to catnap during the day. Slowly I feel my physical energy ebbing away. My thoughts give me no rest. I miss my home. I miss Ralph, who telephones dutifully every evening, but is curt and businesslike. No warmth flows along the wires from Ralph to me. He denies it when I accuse him of never intending to come to Mother's party in the first place. And not having the decency to tell me. Priorities, I think. *My* family. *His* business.

He ought to have put on a good front. For my sake. To please me. I am not a demanding woman. Ralph is selfish. He doesn't see it like that of course. He'll twist it round so I am the one who is selfish. Perhaps I am? If being selfish means doing what you believe to be the right thing, because you feel bad if you don't. I'd much rather be at home with Ralph, but I'd feel guilty, and worry about Mother. And that state of mind would ruin my well-being and take away all the pleasure of being at home. So, if my state of mind and well-being are more important than Ralph's state of mind and well-being (unimproved by my absence), then perhaps I am selfish. It's easy for him: he sees things in black and white. As far as Ralph is concerned, some things are carved in tablets of stone: '*Thou shalt put thy husband first at all times.*'

Fatigue makes me irritable and intolerant. I worry about Emily who limps behind me wherever I go, turning her scarred face away from him, should Pinky be near. I cannot resist giving that evil creature's fat stomach a vicious squeeze when I pick him up to throw him outside while Emily eats her food in the kitchen. And I lock his catflap.

How can my mother possibly manage on her own? I cannot get her to wear her spectacles. Since her accident, she shuffles around apprehensively, arms held before her to ward off unseen objects. Fresh bruises appear daily. She regularly falls asleep in the bath. Although I do not sit with Mother while she has her bath, I make sure the door is unlocked and I hang around upstairs. Often her snores alert me to the fact she has drifted off. When I suggest she might have her bath earlier in the day when she isn't tired, she says, 'You will allow me to know when I wish to have my bath,' and denies falling asleep in it.

Mother talks to herself. I hear her monotone from behind her bedroom door, and through the open door of the sitting room as I work in the kitchen. I remind myself that people who customarily live alone *do* talk to themselves. Frequently, however, Mother's one-sided conversations are intended for my ears. Tottering along the hall, pointedly within my earshot, Mother will remind herself to be careful not to fall over that 'wretched dog' again. This morning I heard her say, 'Poor Pinky, there's none of your fish left. Greedy old Emily must have gobbled it all up.' While I'm washing up our lunch, she tells Pinky he's the best little cat in all the world. 'Let's go and have a cosy rest on my bed,' she says quite distinctly, 'and get out of everyone's way'.

I pull up the sink plug and watch the dirty water draining away and I find myself thinking: *what a long time it takes – dying.*

Sometimes Mother will take my hand, gaze at me out of dark, deep-set eyes and say, 'Darling Alice, you're so good to me. You're a dear kind girl.' And I am ashamed of my wicked thoughts.

Slowly, the days pass and here, in Mother's house, caring for Mother, I am oppressed by the relentless weight of my responsibilities. Estranged from my husband, I am anxious and homesick. My individuality is being extinguished, my life taken over, I think, as I unload Mother's nightdresses and blouses from the washing machine. Emily struggles up to follow me into the garden as I carry the basket of wet clothes outside to Mother's rotary clothes line. I watch the old dog more or less fall down the step onto the grass and I decide it's time I took her along to see that kind vet again. When we arrive at the surgery, Mr Baxter's friendly receptionist has been replaced by a stringy girl with lank mousy hair. I'm starting to tell her we have an appointment at ten o'clock, when we are interrupted by the telephone, which she answers immediately, making a performance over arranging an operation for someone's guinea pig. I'm always annoyed by this assumption that responding to the telephone takes precedence over attending to an actual person. It happens in doctor's surgeries, at travel agents, even at the butcher's if someone should ring up to order two pounds of sausages when you want to buy a piece of fillet steak on the spot.

I finally get in to see Mr Baxter. Dressed in his white coat, he greets us as pleasantly as ever. He and I lift Emily onto the table. I watch him examine her and I think, what a deal of information they must gain through their hands. How skilled and sensitive doctors and vets must be to learn such a lot by touch alone. I remember the gentleness with which Dr Robson examined Mother and the unfamiliar feel of Mother's light body beneath my own unskilled fingers. Mr Baxter's broad hands are swift and confident, moving over Emily's flanks and her back legs. His fingernails, cut short, are very clean. Well scrubbed hands. A safe pair of hands.

Emily stands, quiet and patient, with hanging head and drooping tail. And then we lay her on her side and he examines her stomach and the underside of her legs.

When he looks up, I read In Mr Baxter's face that which I do not wish to see. Hastily, I say I know her back legs almost let her down yesterday, but she seems so much better today. Please could she have another injection: it really seems to help.

Mr Baxter is washing his hands at the basin in the corner of the room.

'She's still enjoying her food,' I continue, hearing the desperation in my voice.

Impassively, Mr Baxter finishes drying his hands and looks down at Emily. Then, he looks up at me and says, 'Another injection will help for a while'. He produces a plastic syringe. 'Just hold her head.' He takes a fold of loose skin below Emily's neck and inserts the needle. 'It's in her spine – the arthritis – affects her hind legs. She's losing control, and sensation. She may become incontinent.'

I tell him Emily's always been a very clean dog. Still is. And she recovered so well from the operation. Together, we lift Emily down from the table and set her on the floor.

'Yes she did. She made a very good recovery for an old dog. Brain's all right. She's got the brain of a younger dog, but her body's beginning to pack up.'

107

'I know. I understand. But I don't think the time has come quite yet,' I say, possessive hand on Emily's head.

'Wait till you're ready,' says Mr Baxter, and looks at me so kindly, I'm afraid I might cry.

After supper, we have a telephone call from David in Spain, He talks to Mother, who assures him she is absolutely fine and darling Alice is being very sweet and kind, and she hopes they're all having a happy time in Malaga. Marbella, I say under my breath and listen to Mother's side of the conversation, from which I gather the weather out there is glorious, they've been exploring the countryside in a hired car, the girls have made lots of friends on the beach, and tomorrow they might all go to a bull fight. At this point, Mother hands the receiver over to me and I tell my brother I don't know how he can allow himself to support such a callous display of barbarity. He murmurs something about the corrida being an art form and Jonquil's keen to make sketches, and tells me about the wonderful drawings she did of the Flamenco dancers they saw last night. He says well done for looking after Mother and I remind him tactfully, aware of Mother's sharp ears, of his promise to do his share when he returns from Spain. He says of course he'll do what he can but he does have to go to work and it's not fair to put too much on to Jonquil, who has her own work to do, as well as running Hunter's Moon and looking after the girls. I do not suggest, over the telephone, with Mother nearby, that it would be easy enough for them to have her to stay (*or even to live with them – eventually*). I shall wait until I can talk to my brother in person. David is saying, rather pompously, that he and Jonquil have been having long talks about the problem and clearly Mother needs someone to keep an eye on her. It might be possible to find a well-educated woman who has time on her hands and could do with the money. She could organise the food and be company for our mother. I don't bother to tell him lady companions didn't survive the Edwardian era. He says, 'Look Alice, of course you have your own life to lead, and you can't expect Ralph to put up with you being away all the time. I really think you should contact an agency and get someone in. Then you can go home.'

When I put down the telephone, Mother looks me in the eye and says, 'I'm perfectly all right you know Alice: you really don't have to stay any longer. I'm quite able to manage by myself. Mrs Curtis can always do a bit extra.'

All night I worry about Mother trying to manage on her own, with only Mrs Curtis to help.

Mrs Curtis comes for three hours every morning. She arrives on her bicycle at nine o'clock. As usual, the first thing she does, after dismounting and securing her Raleigh, is settle herself with a cup of coffee at the kitchen table and tell me about her life. If I try to avoid this, Mrs Curtis gets huffy. I am constantly reminded of my great debt to Mrs Curtis, for it was she who called the ambulance on discovering Mother on the bedroom floor 'blue in the face and cold as death', following her heart attack. 'If it hadn't been for me,' Mrs Curtis says to me, 'your mum wouldn't be here today.' Mrs Curtis is a widow. Mostly I have to listen to her complaints about the man she lives with: a seemingly taciturn Polish painter and decorator, referred to as 'my friend'. Although she says he would like her to, she won't marry him because it would mean losing her widow's pension. This morning, Mrs Curtis tells me, with heavy drama, that she has developed a 'frozen shoulder'. This, as she demonstrates, means she can't raise her right arm any higher than parallel to the ground. I sympathise and suggest that cleaning for Mother might not be very good for the frozen shoulder and maybe she should take a break for a while. Mrs Curtis looks at me with misty eyes and says, 'I couldn't let your mum down, and It does me good to get out.' She drains her coffee cup, gets up slowly and wanders off in the direction of the cupboard where the Hoover is kept.

I cannot bear to watch Mrs Curtis crashing the Hoover into Mother's furniture. I pick up the yellow pages telephone book and take it upstairs.

August 1996

Hilda

It's a pity Alice isn't more sensible about that dog. It shouldn't be allowed to follow her around all day. It's a death-trap for me and, anyway, the poor old creature's worn out. She'd be much happier settled down comfortably in her basket in one place. Sometimes I look at Emily, hobbling about, confused as to where she is and what's happening, and I think 'Snap'. She and I are in the same decrepit condition.

Alice explained about my accident. And I do remember going out into the hall and tripping over something bulky, which turned out to be Emily. I went down with a terrible wallop and then I remember struggling up from some dark echoing space. My brain seemed to be pressing against the inside of my skull, every bone in my body ached, and there was a tap-tapping in my ears. Alice was there. She said, 'Rest now Mother,' and placed cool hands on my forehead. Now, gradually things are coming back to me, like early mist clearing from marshes, and I find my birthday party, still safe in my mind. I see the smiling faces of my friends, hear their laughter, feel the happy atmosphere. What a wonderful party it was! I so enjoyed the company of so many old friends. It was a tonic to be among my own kind: the greatest pleasure not to feel old and useless as I often do in the company of my children.

I know how lucky I am to have a daughter like Alice. She looks after me with great kindness, but ever since Rosamund and William went, I cannot help being aware of her desire to get away as well, back to that husband of hers. It's a terrible thing to feel you're being nothing but an old nuisance to

110

everyone. On the other hand, they owe me something, my children. And time is short. I don't say it, but I dread the thought of my daughter going home.

The days pass quickly; too quickly. I relish the comfort of knowing Alice is near. I see her and hear her moving round the house. Even when I'm asleep, I feel her calm presence. She does the shopping and organises tasty meals for us both. There's no housework, because Mrs Curtis takes care of that. Soon I shall be well enough to go out in the car, and visit my friends in the afternoons. At present I get a little exercise walking round my garden in the late afternoon, when the colours seem brightest. My Albertine rose is flowering, a mass of scented pinkish gold blooms scrambling along the wooden fence and covering the shed at the bottom of the garden. I planted the Albertine rose when I first came here, to remind me of the one growing over the porch at Hunter's Moon.

After our supper, on trays in the sitting room, Alice insists on the BBC News. I try not to look. I do not want to see children dying of starvation in Africa: I cannot bear the anguish of families torn apart by unnecessary wars. I don't need to know about the destruction of the Amazon rain forest, or witness sea birds floundering in oil slicks. Sometimes Alice suggests watching a film, but it seems such a waste. I tell her how much I'm enjoying her company, and can't we just talk. So that is what we do. There are certain topics it is safer not to mention. Ever since I told Alice what I'd decided to do about my Will, it has been impossible to talk about anything connected with Hunter's Moon, though she must realise it's right for David to inherit the family home. The problem of course is Jonquil. I wish Alice could be a little more generous-hearted. Nobody is perfect. Certainly not Jonquil, but she can be unusually understanding at times, and really quite endearing. And she makes my son happy. So, we talk about safe things, like the grandchildren, and sometimes Alice asks to hear about my young days, and we get out the photograph albums and the piles of loose photographs. There's no doubt, as you grow older, the past seems more real than the present. You dare not imagine the future.

I look at those black and white photographs of a girl in a striped swimming costume, poised on the end of a diving board: the same girl in a pleated tennis dress, racket in hand. Here she is again, wearing a low-waisted evening dress, a rope of beads around her neck, straight, dark hair, fashionably shingled, standing shyly beside a fair-haired young man wearing a dinner jacket. I think, this is me. This is how I was. I believe I can remember the naked feel of the back of my neck, the forward swing of my newly shingled hair, the roughness of my cousin Robert's dinner-jacketed sleeve brushing my bare arm. Poor cousin Robert: charming, happy-go-lucky cousin Robert was shot down over Germany at the beginning of the War.

Here are my first photographs of Clive. One pictures him astride a motor-bike. He is wearing leather gauntlets and long, laced boots. My mother would not allow me to ride pillion on that bike. Here is Clive at the wheel of a motor launch, handsome as a film-star in his Panama hat. The girl beside him, dark hair tied in a spotted scarf, smiling happily, is me.

I tell Alice what a wonderful time we had before the War. There were so many parties, lots of dancing. It was a romantic time. We read poetry, wrote letters to each other. I had beautiful love letters. Alice says she doesn't think young people write letters these days. I tell her I feel sorry for the young now, I really do. There's no mystery left. It can't be a good thing – this fixation with sex.

We had romance. We flirted, we danced; I still love those old romantic songs. And as I think of them, melody and words float into my head. My old voice is husky, but it tries to follow the tune and the words I am hearing: 'Some day I'll find you – moonlight behind you. As I draw near you – you'll smile a little smile – in a little while – we shall stand – hand in hand – I'll leave you never – love you for ever – all our past sorrows behind us.' There are tears in my eyes.

Alice smiles and tells me I sing beautifully. Songs are so dreary now, I say. They have no melody, no wit. Where are the Noël Cowards of today? 'The fountain of youth is a mixture of gin and vermouth.' That was Noël Coward. Almost as good as Oscar Wilde, don't you think Alice? 'Dance, dance, dance little lady'; I manage a snatch of another song. 'Oh yes,' I tell her. 'We danced well together, your father and I.'

112

'I know.' Alice loves to hear how Clive and I met at the Cricket Club dance. So I tell her again how I was very young and I drank too much fruit cup and Clive looked after me. He took me outside and we sat on a bench and talked until I felt better. Everyone was shocked when we went back inside. I was so very young, and I suppose they thought I was a bit giddy. And had allowed myself to be taken advantage of. But he didn't lay a finger on me. He was older than me, sophisticated and so handsome. I'd had my eye on him for some time. All the girls were after him. I couldn't believe it when he started to take notice of me.

Alice has my wedding photograph in her hand. 'How young you both look,' she says.

Smiling, we stand arm in arm, outside the church. The wind is lifting the short veil from my face. Clive, so handsome in his Service Dress. Dunkirk. The guns will boom for ever in my memory. Of course, we couldn't know how significant that day would turn out to be. Even in wartime, you plan a wedding in advance.

'We wanted to get married in May, but your great grand-mother wouldn't hear of it. She said May was an unlucky month. 'Marry in May and rue the day!' And so it turned out to be 2 June 1940. All leave was cancelled of course. But since your father was at training camp, he got special dispensation.

' "We shall defend our island whatever the cost may be." What would have become of us without Churchill?! I've always been against that wretched channel tunnel you know.'

'You both look very happy,' says Alice.

'I was completely happy to be marrying your father. But I wish we'd had more time together at the beginning. Of course, the War changed everything.'

Clive was posted overseas in 1942. From Sicily he went to the Middle East, where he was wounded badly in the leg. He spent months in hospital, and when he came out he was no longer fit for active service, so the army gave him a desk job, and didn't release him until the War was over.

I think, with sudden longing, of the many, many letters we wrote to each other: one, two, three a week for three years. When he came home after the War, we put them all together in a tin box with C.J. MADDISON printed on it in white paint. I found them when I was going through a lifetime of possessions, preparing to move out of Hunter's Moon. But I had to stop reading them; I cried so much. How sad, we never read them again, together. Not once did we think of it, in all the years that came after.

Alice picks up a photograph of me in navy blue with my sailor cap and collar and tie. 'You looked very good in your uniform.'

I remember how I loved wearing my uniform, apart from the lisle stockings and the thick bloomers. 'Black-outs' they were called, 'Passion killers'. Cami-knickers were in vogue.

'How strange,' says Alice, 'All the time Father was away in the army, you were in the Wrens. It must have been difficult, being married but leading different lives.'

I tell Alice, quite sharply, I didn't sleep around while her father and I were apart, though plenty did.

No-one knew what was going to happen; how long they'd got. Awareness of their own mortality cancelled inhibitions for many. I was faithful to Clive. I loved him. But I remember a 'subbie' with eyes like treacle toffee and a musical voice. We'd walked across the fields in our Wellington boots to a hop in a village hall. Still wearing my Wellington boots, I danced with him to the sounds of Glenn Miller. He held me tight and I was tempted. Poor boy, I heard later, he was lost at sea, when his ship went down.

Alice says, 'And it must have been equally strange for both of you when Father came back from his army life and you came out of the Wrens.'

'It took us a while to settle down,' I say, briskly, and try to push back the wave of sorrow, as I tell my daughter that of course it was wonderful to be together again. We'd both looked forward to it for so long, but life usually turns out differently from how you imagined it might be.

Clive threw all his energy into getting the business going again, and there didn't seem to be time for us to do things together. I admit to Alice that I missed the comradeship and excitement of service life, that I was bored and lonely. I begged her father to let me help him, but he didn't want me in the business. 'I started looking for a job, you know, but then I got pregnant with David, and of course we did want a family. But I don't think I was ever cut out for domestic life.'

Alice laughs, and says who is?

'I thought about going back to work, once the two of you were at school, but, as you know, your father had a very old-fashioned attitude towards women. He wanted his wife at home.'

'Some men try to get away with that even now,' says Alice.

'Well, maybe it was for the best, in the long run,' I tell her. I half believe this. 'And your father was a very good provider.'

'Poor Mother! Did you find it very tedious staying at home with David and me?' She picks up a photograph of herself and David building a sandcastle on the beach. 'I always envied David his blond curls, and look at those dimples! I'm such a plain child.'

I tell her she was a dear little girl, but David was a particularly attractive and outgoing little boy. Alice remarks nastily that he's certainly changed quite a bit since then.

I ignore this and say I wonder why *she* didn't have a proper career, knowing how keen she is on Women's Rights. 'You had more chance of it than I did.'

She rather unfairly says I didn't give her much encouragement. But I remind her it was I who suggested the secretarial course when her father wanted her to do domestic science.

Alice says she hated being a secretary and when she was young what she really wanted to do was be a vet. I point out that you need more than a love of animals to become a vet, and she wasn't good enough at maths and science.

Alice says, quite sharply, that it's lucky she hasn't got a high-powered job now or she wouldn't be able to look after me She might have been jet-setting all over the world or working in the family business, if Clive hadn't sold up when he retired.

I remind her that David didn't want to leave the law to run the business and perhaps if she'd been a boy she might have taken it on.

Alice takes umbrage at this. 'After what you just said about me not having a proper career when I had the opportunity for

115

it, that's a pretty sexist remark, Mother,' she says. 'Don't you think a woman could run a timber business?'

'Did you want to?' I return her challenge. 'You showed no sign of it.'

Alice backs down and says she supposes she's not very ambitious really. She gets sidetracked by people, and relationships.

'Well dear,' I say, 'Divorce and remarriage must take a lot of energy. And I don't suppose Ralph is very easy to live with.'

'He's like Father,' Alice retorts. 'Thinks a woman's place ought to be in the home. It's not like that any more, thank God. It'll be better for Rosamund.'

'I wonder!'

'Of course it will. You must know that from what you were saying about how you felt after the War. Women are liberated now.'

'But are they any happier? Is anyone any happier?' I often wonder about this. How we all want to be happy. But you can't hunt for happiness as if it's some hidden treasure, a Holy Grail, and once discovered, it's yours to keep safe. Happiness is a kind of by-product. Something makes you happy: achieving a goal, loving someone, being loved. I think of the good times I've had. It's been an interesting era to have lived through. But everything has changed so much and most of it not for the better. That's what Clive used to say. He used to say, 'It'll just about last my time out.'

I gaze at my daughter, and I wonder if she is happy. Her eyes look creased, as if she has been rubbing them, and there are glints of silver among the rich brown of her hair, a frown line between her brows. Ralph is not good to her.

'I adored your father,' I say to Alice. 'Maybe we didn't give each other all that we could have. But I miss him. I miss him more and more. I'm lonely. And I'm bored.' And then I tell her what I cannot help thinking. I tell her that I don't want to go on too long. I cannot face years of dependence.

Alice looks hurt and says, 'Mother, I wish you wouldn't talk like that.'

I tell her I have made my wishes known to Dr Robson. If I should have another heart attack, or a stroke, I don't want to

116

be revived. Although I strain to control it, my voice is unsteady, as I tell my daughter I will not return to hospital. And she is *not* to put me in a home.

Alice says soothingly, 'I promise we won't put you in a home, Mother.' And then she adds, in a serious voice, 'But if you are to stay here, we will have to get some extra help for you.'

Extra help? A stranger, in my house! I do not reply.

'Unless', says Alice, 'you would like to come and live with us.'

With Ralph's overbearing presence hanging between us, Alice is perfectly safe in making this offer. We both know that Ralph and I could not live under the same roof.

I thank her and say I prefer to remain in my own home. Alice says, again, that if that is the case, then she really does feel I need someone to look after me, for the time being anyway. She says she worries about me bumping into things because I don't wear my glasses. And she worries about me falling asleep in the bath. She is always going on about this. I say, quite firmly, 'Alice dear, do you actually know of someone who has *drowned* in the bath?' She doesn't reply. Her face takes on that stubborn look she had as a little girl. She says, 'You see, Mother, I can't be here all the time.'

'Well of course I know that,' I say. 'You can't help it. You have your life to lead.'

The reality of Alice going home and leaving me alone is looming terrifyingly near. But I must not let her sense my fear. I brace myself. I got through the War, didn't I!

'Alice, dear,' I say as firmly as I can manage. 'You must not worry about me. I'm perfectly all right. And I definitely do not need a keeper.'

But Alice has won. My keeper is here. Her name is Ann Lister. She is a big woman with a Yorkshire accent. She stands beside me, like a watchful bodyguard as Alice drives away.

28 October 1996

'Here's to you, Hilda, wherever you are!' Dickie Clarke pointed his ruddy hook nose upwards and raised his glass. 'God bless you!'

Roddy Bartram who was wearing the black armband specially purchased for attending the funerals of his friends raised his own glass in salutation. 'Well said, Dickie my friend. God bless you Hilda, dear old girl. I never thought you'd be harping before me.' The two men clinked glasses and drank deeply of Hilda's penultimate bottle of Glenmorangie:

'Birthday last time, wasn't it,' said Roddy, wiping his moustache with the back of his hand.

'Only her seventy-sixth. July.'

'Vicar did all right.' They both glanced over at the pink-faced young vicar, a cup of tea in one hand and a glass of sherry in the other.

'Nice service. Pretty church. Went to a crematorium job last week.'

They looked at each other speculatively.

'Wouldn't want that myself.' Roddy felt in his pocket to check the presence of the Havana cigar he was planning to treat himself to later on.

'Oh I don't know. I've asked the old squaw to scatter me out at the ninth.'

Dickie helped himself to a smoked salmon sandwich from a tray being carried round by Rosamund. 'Dudley doesn't look too good.'

'No. Poor old chap.'

'I can't tell you how much Arthur and me will miss your

mum,' said June to David. 'She had such a sense of humour. You never knew what she was going to say next. Oh dear, it only seems five minutes since we were all here celebrating her birthday. What a wonderful party. We did so enjoy ourselves It's nice to look back on isn't it.'

'Same snobby old lot here again, I see,' I said Arthur.

'Now Arthur! He doesn't really mean it, you know.' June gave David an embarrassed smile. 'Arthur's always had a bit of a chip.' David started to edge away, but June was too quick for him. 'I still can't believe Hilda's gone, you know. It was all so sudden. She was out in the garden with the secateurs the day before. I waved to her over the fence. Your sister looks very cut up. Of course she was very close to her mum, and it's always a shock when it happens. Poor Alice, she was white as a ghost when she came and told us. I do hope she was there to say goodbye.'

'How long since Clive went?'

'Must be seven or eight years now,' said Dickie thoughtfully.

'Weren't you playing with him that day?'

'Never forget it. The usual Thursday club foursome with Archie and Humphrey. I was actually partnering Clive. We were two up with five to play. Clive had just splashed out of the big sleeper bunker on the fourteenth. Grabbed his chest and keeled over, just like that.'

'What a way to go eh!'

'Easier for us all if he'd done it on the eighteenth, dear old chap.'

'Ha! Ha!' Roddy took a good mouthful of whisky, swallowed slowly and said, 'Poor Hilda took it very hard, I believe.'

'She did. I went and fetched her in my car myself. They phoned ahead from the club to warn her something had happened. But it was me had to break the news.'

'You poor fellow.'

'It wasn't easy.'

With another upward glance, they each drained their glasses. 'Feel sorry for the family today,' said Roddy. 'Seem a very pleasant lot. That attractive daughter-in-law is a painter,

119

I believe. Good-looking youngsters. Nice manners. Don't believe any of them play golf, though.'

They walked over to the drinks table and helped themselves to more whisky. Dickie said, 'Have you heard the one about Jesus and St Peter driving over the lake at the tenth?'

Rosamund said, 'Do you really think they *all* wanted Granny dead?'

'Well,' said William, 'she was being a lot of trouble. I've just been listening to Jonquil going on about how much she did for our Grandmother. You know how devious *Jonquil* is. And David's a bit of an arsehole really. Mum's been in a state about horrible Ralph. Horrible Ralph's always had it in for Granny, and he hated her taking Mum away from *him* to go and look after *her*. I once saw the bastard with his woman.'

'No! When? Where?'

'It was when Mum was with Granny. I'd just finished at Dominics. I was walking home. And I saw them coming out of Blacks.'

'What was she like?'

'Much younger than him. Blonde.'

'*Carpe diem.*' Harry Garnham materialised beside them. He rocked gently back and forth on his heels. 'Know what that means young William?'

'No,' said William, remembering the man from his grandmother's birthday party. 'It means,' said the man, savouring a large mouthful of whisky before continuing, 'it means you should bloody well live it up while you've got the chance. A literal translation would be "seize the day". Of course, that won't have a lot of impact on a young feller like you. But, believe you me my lad, it's cracking good advice.'

'Thank you,' said William politely. He turned to follow Rosamund, but found his path blocked by Marge Coppice. 'Ah, Dudley, I'm afraid your words of wisdom will fall on stony ground. We all know that youth is wasted on the young.' Her jowly face was familiar to William and then he remembered it was she who made David laugh at Granny's birthday party, with some joke about getting old. Did they spend all their time telling jokes? 'Excuse me,' he said, 'I have to find my sister.' Pushing his way through the crowd, he noticed his

120

mother talking to June. She looked upset by whatever June was saying, and more upset when she saw Ralph approaching them. William heard her say, 'I must speak to the Vicar,' and she sped away before Ralph could reach her. 'Bloody Ralph,' he said under his breath, following his mother with his eyes. Materialising beside him, Rosamund said, 'Don't worry about Mum and Ralph. They'll have to sort things out.'

'It's all right for you. You're not here. You don't know what it's been like.'

'Never mind, you'll be able to go away soon. William, I've been thinking about what you just said. Maybe you're letting your imagination get a bit out of control. You can't really believe they *seriously* wanted Granny to die.'

'I think someone might have made her her think she ought to die. They might even have *killed* her. Any of them could have done it you know.'

'That's a *terrible* thing to say!'

Marge Coppice barged up to them. The red blotches on her heavy face were beginning to meet up. She looked sentimentally at the brother and sister and said, 'Dear little Rosamund, and William, how are you bearing up, you poor loves? You'll miss your grandmother, I daresay – she was a force to be reckoned with. Didn't expect her to kick the bucket just like that. Terrible shock.' She sighed and helped herself absentmindedly to an egg sandwich from the plate Rosamund was holding. William waited for Rosamund to make some sort of response, but she didn't. Mrs Coppice finished her sandwich, squinted blearily up at William, and said, 'Taken up golf yet?'

'No,' said William.

'Well you know what they say, "Golf is like sex – you can enjoy it without being any good at it".' And she collapsed into wheezy laughter.

William and Rosamund pulled glum faces at each other. Nearby, David was talking to a short soft-bodied man with a round bald head bald fringed with the remains of his dark hair. 'That's Alan Sheppard,' said Rosamund. 'Louisa just told me. He's Granny's solicitor. Louisa says Granny's Will hasn't been read yet. Her parents don't know who will be inheriting Hunter's Moon. She heard them talking about it. They're worried Granny might have left Hunter's Moon to Mum!'

121

August 1996

Alice

Mother's hand is cold and unresponsive. Beneath my arm, her thin shoulders are hunched and unyielding. Her cheek quivers at the touch of my lips, and her brimming eyes, when she lifts them to mine, cry 'Traitor'!

Mother's delaying tactics have put back my departure from eleven o'clock, which would have avoided the traffic, till two which means I'll hit the East Anglian rush hour. Hardening my heart, I say 'Goodbye Mother. Take care, see you soon,' in my cheerful voice, raise my hand to Mrs Lister, get into the car and drive away from Laburnum Crescent, temporarily freed from daughterly responsibilities. In the rear-view mirror, I see Mother staring sadly after me. Beside her, Mrs Lister has taken hold of that fragile, unrelenting arm. No doubt she is accustomed to being needed where she is not really wanted.

I found Mrs Lister through a domestic employment agency. She provided excellent references from the son and daughter-in-law of her last employer. Mrs Lister is a tall well-upholstered woman in her late fifties. She has a passive, statuesque quality about her, as if she is planted very securely upon the ground. Her grey hair is stiffly coiffed, rising from her brow like a frozen North Sea wave. Her eyes are of a very pale blue and they hold a quiet, unfussed expression.

I interviewed her in Mother's sitting room, with Mother safely out of the way upstairs. Over a cup of coffee, I learned that she was a qualified nurse (retired) and for the last five years has specialised in private care for the elderly. She

122

stroked the silver locket around her neck and told me, in her pleasantly low voice, that it was a gift, and one of her most valued possessions. 'I was with Mrs Bunting four years,' she said. 'Lovely lady. Crippled with arthritis poor soul. Racked with pain; I can't tell you how she suffered. But it was peaceful in the end.'

Then, without prompting, she launched into further details about herself. 'As you can tell, I'm from Yorkshire and, we Northerners like to know where we stand with people. If I do anything wrong I prefer to be told. My husband is much older than me; a very quiet man who likes his own company. We haven't been blessed with children, so I have no ties. I can come as many days as you want and I can sleep in. But I always go to the hairdresser on Thursday afternoon. I have no other job at the moment, and could fit in with whatever you need. But I should tell you I shall be going on a fortnight's holiday the week after next. We're touring Scotland in our car. My husband enjoys driving and I like the lochs and the mountain scenery. We'll stay with relatives in Leeds on the way there and on the way back, which will break the journey nicely.'

I persuaded Mother downstairs and after a sticky ten minutes during which Mrs Lister warded off Mother's slit-eyed stare with a quiet smile, and I poured coffee and offered biscuits and kept up some kind of inane chatter, Mother put on her haughty, social expression and asked Mrs Lister if she liked cats. 'Indeed I do,' said Mrs Lister, putting out a hand to Pinky who had just sidled into the room. 'You *are* a beautiful pussy,' she said, stroking his back as he pressed himself ingratiatingly against her legs. 'What's your name then?'

When Mrs Lister had gone, Mother said grudgingly, 'I suppose she'd better come.' So, I arranged for Mrs Lister to look after Mother for one week, after which she would have her holiday and then we would work out some kind of regular agreement, depending upon Mother's progress.

Mrs Lister arrived at nine o'clock this morning, bringing with her a large suitcase, a portable television set and a Walkman. I settled her into the second spare bedroom and conducted her round the house, explaining where everything was. I showed

123

her Mother's pills in their separate bottles and I said Mother needed a little fattening up, as she hadn't been bothering to cook for herself. It is a relief to hand over my responsibilities to a woman well qualified to take them on.

The further I drive from Maidstone, the lighter my burden becomes. It's a bit like worrying about one's children. Before Rosamund went off to university, her evenings out were a nightmare for me. If she was late back, I'd be unable to sleep for imagining all the dreadful things that might have happened to her. Once she'd gone up to Edinburgh, apart from praying she would heed my early training, there was nothing I could do to keep her out of danger. I wouldn't know, if she'd gone joy-riding with some lunatic, or put herself at risk by walking alone in the dark. Now, I am unable to protect Mother from all the death-traps lying in wait for her around the house. It won't be my fault if the old girl falls asleep in the bath and drowns, or tumbles down the stairs and breaks a hip.

Driving briskly along the A12, I look forward to getting home: to seeing Ralph and William. I feel starved of my husband's company. I resolve to try very hard not to have a row with him, and to make an effort to see things from his point of view. The hurt and anger I felt when he failed to turn up at Mother's party has abated. A basinful of Mother is enough reason for understanding why Ralph might choose to make himself scarce.

There should be time to go to Sainsburys, to buy something special for supper. Salmon, perhaps? Wrapped in buttered foil and baked. New potatoes and sugar-snap peas. Raspberries and cream. If I manage to do everything right, perhaps Ralph will say he's pleased I'm back, instead of grinding on about being deserted.

My home looks sad and neglected, which is not surprising since I have been away from it for a fortnight. I put away the Sainsburys shopping and rush round with the Hoover. Fussy though Ralph is about 'his' furniture being kept pristine, he hasn't bothered to dust any of it. Neither has he cleaned the bath.

I go out into the garden to cut roses for the dining room table. The grass is calf high, and full of daisies. William arrives home on his bike and seems as pleased to see me as I am to see him. He says, 'Glad you're back Mum,' and even returns my hug. He says hello to Emily and gives her a pat. We have a cup of tea together and then I offer him a couple of pounds to cut the grass. So, he tears round with the electric mower and then treads grass cuttings over the hall carpet. I just Hoover them up. I make him a bacon sandwich and off he goes to his washing-up job at Dominics.

The salmon is in the oven, the new potatoes wait in their saucepan with a sprig of mint from the overgrown clump in the garden, the sugar-snap peas lie in a colander, the raspberries are looking pretty in a glass bowl, the cream and a bottle of Chardonnay are in the fridge. I wait for Ralph and feel a rush of pleasure when I hear the front door opening. I go into the hall to greet him. He is wearing his linen jacket and light-coloured trousers and is carrying the brown leather attaché case that belonged to his father. He looks heavy round the eyes and is in need of a shave. His dark hair seems to be longer than usual, as if in the last fortnight we've been apart, it has put on a growth spurt; the extra weight is making it flop over his forehead.

I am incredibly pleased to see him: I wish he didn't look so tired. I move quickly towards him and fling my arms round his neck. As my lips approach his, I feel him withdraw. It is almost a flinch. Never, in all our ten years together, has Ralph's familiar body felt like this. He is stiff and unresponsive. It is like laying hands on a stranger. I expected the comfort of his enclosing arms, the reciprocal touch of his lips, to relax against the intimate scent of him: a mixture of the dusty woody factory smell and the spicy aroma of warm male flesh. Stunned, I back away. It's like rebounding off an invisible barrier of unbreakable glass. Ralph looks different. He is thinner and there is something alien in his shadowed eyes.

'Steady on,' he says. laying down his attaché case. 'You made it home then.'

'Traffic wasn't too bad,' I reply automatically, trying to hold his eyes. 'Is anything wrong? You don't seem very pleased to see me.'

'I've got pretty used to you being away.' He takes off his

jacket, hangs it in the hall cupboard and follows me into the kitchen.

He's punishing me, I think, feeling cold and strange inside. I tell him there's some white wine in the fridge. But he is already pouring himself a glass of red from an opened bottle on the dresser. 'How is your mother?' he asks.

Not 'The Monster' which is his joky name for her, but '*Your* mother': *nothing to do with me.*

I tell him she's frail but fighting hard, and ask him acidly how is the new range of furniture that has been taking up such a lot of his time? He says it's coming along fine; he plans to show it at the Cologne fair and expects to do well with it. I tell him I'm *so* glad in my best ironic Mother tone. Then, recalling my resolution to try and avoid a row, I go to the other extreme and say obsequiously that I've made a special supper and it will be ready in quarter of an hour. He brushes my offering aside as casually as he'd flick away a fly. 'I need a shower,' he says and disappears with his glass of wine.

Involuntarily, my hand flies up to my chest, to still my heart which is jumping around as if it's received an electric shock. How can he be so changed? Ralph, whom I know so well? Paralysed, I stand in the middle of the kitchen. Then, I shake myself, go to the fridge, take out the bottle of Chardonnay, open it, pour myself a full glass and gulp it down like medicine. I check the salmon. It's ready, so I take it out of the oven, put the vegetables on to cook, and pour myself more wine.

Emily watches from her basket with her one seeing eye. I bend down and stroke her head. I tell her I don't know what I'd do without her. 'You love me don't you,' I say. 'And that nice vet has made you better. You'll stay a little longer won't you? To keep me company.'

Emily thumps her tail and licks my hand.

Ralph appears, looking younger and fresher, in jeans and a lavender cotton shirt I haven't seen before. His wet hair is combed back, and he has shaved. He sits down at the table and pours himself more wine.

We pick at our food. Mindful of my resolve to avoid a row, nevertheless, I can't believe Ralph and I are capable of this stilted, colourless, pointless dialogue which sprouts thinly among the acres of silence, and touches on the dualling of the

126

A11, the lack of rain, and the construction of out-of-town supermarkets. It feels as if the Ralph I know, eat with, sleep with, argue with is no longer here. As if this man, with whom I have shared the last ten years of my life in the most intimate if embattled way, has died, and in his place, looking out at me from those sheathed eyes, is some cold and alien spirit.

After we've finished playing with our food, Ralph says since he's driving to Manchester first thing in the morning, he'll go and fill up the car now. By the time I hear him return, I've done the washing up and am lying miserably in the bath. He does not come upstairs. I get out of the bath, dry myself, put on my white cotton nightdress and go down to see what he's doing. He is sitting in front of the television finishing off the bottle of red wine. I stand behind him for a moment or two before asking him quietly when he is coming to bed.

'Soon,' he says, without taking his eyes off the television.

I go up to bed and wait tensely for the opportunity to make everything all right.

When finally he slips in beside me, I roll towards him, curl my arm round his waist and rest my head against his chest. Usually he lifts his own arm, and slides it beneath my shoulder, pulling me against him so I can fit my head against his neck in the hollow beneath his chin. He does not move. I slide my hand slowly down his stomach and feel the muscles tense against me.

'It's very late,' he says, 'and I've an early start in the morning.'

I take away my hand and stare through the dark at the ceiling. Ralph turns over and soon his body goes slack and he falls into a heavy, fumy, red-wine-induced slumber.

Tears spring like hot coals into my eyes. I have sacrificed my marriage for my mother. Ralph doesn't love me any more because he thinks I don't put him first. I want to punch the pillows, punch Ralph, goad him into a living response. But instead I scrub my burning eyes with one of his large handkerchiefs and stare into the darkness. Is it really all my fault?

William comes in around twelve and goes up the stairs to his attic. It feels as if I do not sleep all the long night. At six o'clock the radio switches itself on. I know Ralph is awake, though he lies motionless beside me.

127

The unacknowledged resolution to avoid a row, the one-way effort to communicate, the sleepless night have generated a pure, hot swell of righteous indignation. I am being unfairly treated. 'Ralph,' I say, quietly. 'Please will you tell me what the matter is.'

'Nothing's the matter.'

'You know that's not true. Ralph, I don't deserve this.'

'I suppose I've just got used to you not being around.'

'What was I to do? I couldn't just go away and leave my mother.'

'Alice, this will go on and on.'

'How can it?' I say. 'Mother won't live for ever. 'I have to do what I can for her while she's here. She's been a good and loving mother to me. I love her.'

'What I mean is,' says Ralph, and his voice takes on a special intensity as if he's dredging up the words from the depths of his insides, 'this will go on, the way you feel about me. I just don't come first with you. I'm not sure if I can face that for the rest of our lives together. It's not just your mother, it's your children. Even your handicapped old dog. Everyone comes before me.'

We are lying side by side in the same bed, not touching each other. Trying not to cry, with the unfairness of it all, I tell him that's not true and he knows I love him but surely he understands I have other responsibilities which I can't just abandon to suit him. 'If you love me,' I say, and now I am crying, 'you ought to be able to see things from my point of view.'

'When did you ever see things from *my* point of view?' he says, exploding with sudden rage. 'Alice, you make me feel like a second-class citizen. And now you don't like it because all of a sudden I'm doing the same thing to you.'

I tell him how unfair this is. Just because there are other people in my life doesn't change or dilute my feelings for him. I feel the same way I always have. Still he lies motionless without touching me. Disbelief at what is happening vanishes, and is replaced by a desolate comprehension: I cannot reach him; it's as if he's switched off a light inside. Tears gush from my eyes.

Ralph does not touch me; gives me no word of comfort.

'Don't you care for me any more?' I pummel my fists into his chest. 'Answer me.'

At last, he catches hold of my hands and holds them captive. 'Stop it Alice. Stop this. You're getting hysterical.'

'Is it surprising?' I pull away from him. I scrabble for the tear-soaked handkerchief, scrub my eyes and blow my nose. 'You've got to tell me Ralph. I have to know. Don't you love me any more?'

He does not answer. I cannot guess what might be going on in his mind, in his heart. 'Tell me how you feel, Ralph.'

'I don't know,' he says eventually. 'I don't know how I feel.'

'You *must* know how you feel,' I yell. '*Everyone* knows how they feel.'

'They might know *how* they feel. But *what* is it they feel? Can you put a label on complex feelings?'

'Are you just telling me you're *confused?*' I'm suddenly a little stronger.

'If you like. All right, I'm confused. Alice, I can't take any more of this. I have to get up and drive to Manchester.'

He slides out of bed and goes off into the bathroom. Watching his resolute back view, I think how I have neglected Ralph for my mother. I've brought this upon myself. But does neglect truly account for his lack of empathy, his unkindness to me? I pull the sheet over my face and my concussed brain stirs into health and starts to think logically.

Ralph has a shower, shaves, and gets dressed. 'I'll bring you a cup of tea,' he says in a deliberately normal voice, and goes down to the kitchen.

While he is there, my obedient brain processes information: sorts happenings, words, people, searching for a deeper understanding of my husband's behaviour, until it reaches the obvious conclusion. I am stunned by the glaring simplicity of it. By taking him for granted, I've provided Ralph with the opportunity, the justification to look elsewhere for the devotion he needs. Ralph must be having an affair.

Hilda

I watch Alice drive away, in a rush to get back to Ralph. Life is so full of goodbyes. Time is running out. And now, this precious time left to me is likely to be spent in the company of strangers, instead of with the people I love; with my family. I feel Mrs Lister's fingers gripping my arm, and I fume that against my better judgement, I have allowed Alice to push me into having a keeper. The wretched woman is supposed to stay for a week, on trial. After that, says Alice, '*We* (but of course she means 'I') will decide how much help is needed.' Alice is mistaken. I shall make clear to Mrs Lister from the start, that my family have insisted on engaging her services; that I'm going along with it for the sake of peace and quiet, but, as she will soon realise, I am perfectly capable of managing by myself.

Alice's familiar red car rolls down the crescent and turns left, out of sight. We go back into the house. I call Pinky and I tell Mrs Lister it's time for my rest and that I'm perfectly capable of climbing the stairs on my own.

Once in my bedroom, I take off my skirt and my shoes, and lie down on my bed. Pinky curls himself up on his blanket in his usual place, down by my feet. I close my eyes and fall into darkness.

Clive's arms are holding me tight: my face presses against the rough cloth of his uniform; a button digs into my eye. I hear a small cry. Clive is gone. My eyes are streaming with tears.

A pale figure stands nearby. Who is it? Where am I? I blink to squeeze the tears from my eyes, to clear my head, slowly to separate the past from the present, and eventually I realise that the pale figure is Mrs Lister and she has a cup of tea in her hand.

Mrs Lister tells me she is fifty-eight, and she looks all of that, with her pasty skin and colourless hair. She wears a grey track suit, which does nothing for her homely appearance. But, for a heavy woman, she does her best to be unobtrusive, gliding silently round the house. She has a prickly relationship with Mrs Curtis. Mrs Curtis accuses her (quite rightly) of slowness. Mrs Lister is critical (quite rightly) of Mrs Curtis's sketchy cleaning. 'Dirty tea cloths harbour millions of germs,' she tells me, and brings back a giant bottle of Dettol from the super-market, and stands it in the bathroom.

Alice is always going on about me not eating enough and she's obviously told Mrs Lister to produce enormous meals. I feel like a fowl being fattened up for Christmas. She brings me breakfast in bed: orange juice, shredded wheat, which I don't touch, hard-boiled egg and toast soldiers. Lunch is tough old meat and two soggy veg, followed by stick-jaw pudding. For supper, on trays in front of the television, there is soup a spoon could stand up in, followed by something very substantial in the flan line. Mrs Lister, who has no small appetite, chomps away rapidly and watches me like a hawk. 'Aren't you going to finish up that little piece of meat then?'

Don't treat me like a child! I give her a look and lay down my knife and fork.

Something has to be done, so I brave up to it and tactfully put the woman right on one or two points. I tell her I have always been thin and I dislike being faced with plateloads of food. I tell her where to buy fresh fish and properly hung meat. I suggest grilled Dover sole and fillet steak, which I like served rare. I tell her boiled cabbage reminds me of the War. It was worth the effort, for I have put an end to greasy mince and lumpy mashed potato, rubbery stew and leaden dump-lings. Mrs Lister has made friends with my butcher and managed to find some quite nice cream cheese and honey-roast ham at the new delicatessen.

Despite my initial misgivings, I'm beginning to think it isn't so bad after all having someone like Mrs Lister moving

131

quietly about the place, not bossing me around. Also, she is turning out to be a pleasant person to chat with. After supper, we have a night-cap together. Whisky mostly (My Clive used to say whisky was the cleanest drink of all), but sometimes gin: Mrs Lister says there's no harm in a drop of alcohol and it's better than a sleeping pill. We talk, quite intimately about our lives. 'Please call me Ann,' she says, but does not dream of addressing me as anything other than Mrs Maddison.

Ann does not have a very easy relationship with her husband. She says he's rather a cold kind of man and since they have no children, she has to find a focus for her natural caring instincts outside the home. She's always loved old people, ever since she first came into nursing. 'It's dreadful how some poor souls are abandoned in hospitals, never visited by their families,' she says, 'Out of sight, out of mind, just wearing out their days.' And she tells me how once, when she was very young and on night duty, a sick old lady begged her to stay by her side. 'Please hold my hand,' she said. 'I don't want to die alone.' The old lady's son had visited that day and been told his mother wouldn't last the night, but he'd gone home anyway. 'So I stayed with her,' Ann says, 'holding her hand, and talking quietly: I don't know what I said. I just wanted to remind her I was there. Until she passed over. But do you know, I got taken to task by Sister for neglecting my other duties.'

'What a sad story!' I say and I tell Ann about the horror of the geriatric ward and about the abandoned old lady, crying for chocolate. 'Of course, I know I'm very lucky, I have a wonderful family, and they look after me quite well really, but they all have such busy lives.' And I tell her that my son has a big job in the city, and my daughter-in-law is a portrait painter, making quite a name for herself. 'I ask very little of them, you know. I'd hate to think I was becoming a burden. That's what we all say, isn't it. We don't want to be a burden on our families. My daughter is very kind but she has a demanding husband. There never seems to be time to sit and talk. Darling Alice is always rushing off somewhere.'

It seems a very long time since I was rushing off anywhere, I think to myself.

* * *

One evening, I bring out the photograph albums. Ann loves them and wants to know who everyone is.' She thinks my Clive very handsome, specially in his uniform.

'I was only a child in the War,' she tells me. 'My father was in the Home Guard. I remember him going out in his tin hat and my mother would worry. Our house had a cellar. Well, it was a coalhole really, and he used to make us go down there when the warning sounded. The house at the end of our street was bombed out. But someone up there must have been looking after them because they were with friends when it happened. They lost everything though, and the poor dog.'

She admires the photograph of me in my uniform and asks me in a voice full of respect what it was like being in the Wrens.

I tell her that when we were training we had to do our stint of square bashing and listen to some rather boring lectures on naval traditions and I once got a rocket from the Chief Petty Officer for being late. ' "Naval time is five minutes before time and not five minutes after", that's what he said to me. But it was so much more exciting than working in the Bank. I didn't have to join up you know Ann; I was in a reserved occupation. But when my husband was posted overseas I couldn't bear to stay at home alone.'

I pause for a minute and reflect that if I hadn't had the miscarriage, I would never have become a Wren. I lost our first child six days after I said goodbye to Clive. I started to bleed and that was it. The doctor said it was probably due to the strain I was under, and there was no reason to suppose it would happen like that again. Poor little lost baby. I was distraught, not knowing if I'd ever see Clive again, and maybe nothing of him to keep. The cottage full of reminders of what had been and what might have been. I needed to do something positive. So I joined up.

I tell Ann I was proud to be in the Wrens. I tell her I never remember being really frightened for myself. 'I was so young and you never think it's going to happen to you. Three on a mattress in a basement, hearing the doodle-bugs going over and listening for the engine to cut out. But it was terrible when the marine barracks got hit. They moved us out of

London then. I went to Felixstowe. We were billeted in a big old hotel on the sea front.'

Ann wants to hear more. So I tell her that I was a 'Writer', which is what they called the clerical workers. Not glamorous, but very responsible. I tell her how we shared the semi-underground communication boxes with the 'sparks', which is what we called the electricians. They used to give us tots of rum. And pretend it was cough mixture. 'I was tapping out weather reports, all in code of course, and issuing life-saving packs to the crews, and typing out sailing orders for the MTBs – half the time with no idea what they meant.' Ann makes awed exclamations and I tell her that the sailing orders were typed on rice paper, for easy disposal. 'You needed to be accurate because you couldn't rub out. The rice paper used to crack and had to be stored between sheets of greaseproof.'

'And I was just a little girl then,' she says, 'not understanding. I used to take my dolly down the cellar with me. And one night I forgot her. I cried when my mother wouldn't let me go back up to fetch her. I remember the sound of the sirens, but I'd be hard put now to tell you the difference between the warning and the all clear. I do remember carrying my gas mask to school. Goodness, I haven't thought about that for years.'

'One of the things I remember most is the secrecy. Everything was "hush-hush". And that was all part of the excitement. People didn't talk about what they were doing: they just got on with their jobs. Of course it was awful when anything happened. Hard to accept that someone you knew had been killed.'

'Fate,' says Ann. 'If it's meant to be it's meant to be.'

I tell her that just at the moment I'm thinking quite a lot about Fate. About what might be in store for me. But I try to keep it to myself. 'It's hard to discuss this kind of thing with the people you're close to. They get embarrassed or upset. Alice won't talk about dying.'

'It's the one sure and certain thing that will come to us all,' says Ann solemnly.

I look at her straight and say, 'I'm not afraid of death. I'm afraid off being carted off to hospital again: gaga. And I don't know how to prevent it.'

Behind her spectacles, Ann's pale eyes are full of understanding. I pour us another tot of whisky and tell her I wish I could be sure of dying at home.

Ann smiles gently and says, 'Mrs Bunting was able to remain at home, as was her wish. Towards the end, I did everything for her. We became very close. Lovely lady: always thinking of others. She suffered the most terrible pain you know: arthritis in every joint of the body. I used to push her round the garden in her wheelchair. She so loved her garden, but it gave her great distress to see it let go. A young lad came once a week, but he'd only cut the grass. I used to pull out a few weeds when I had the time. You should have seen Mrs Bunting's poor hands; the fingers all curled up and knobbly. And she'd been the most beautiful needle-woman. The house was full of her work: embroidered tablecloths and bed covers. Tapestry. They were exquisite. She could still manage a little tapestry. She made a beautiful set of chair covers for her daughter in Tasmania. It took her three years. She was working on the fourth one right up to the last. And do you know, she just completed it in time. I sometimes think wanting to finish those chair covers for her daughter was what kept her going. Poor lady. It broke your heart to watch. She could only manage a few stitches at a time. It tired her out so. But she said it was good to use her hands, despite the pain. It was a great sadness for her to have Sarah so very far away. George and Carol, the son and daughter-in-law, were very nice but not close if you know what I mean. They asked Sarah to come when things got really bad, but she got here too late to say goodbye. Poor Sarah. She *was* upset. But I was able to put her mind at rest. It was a comfort to know her mother had been released from her pain. She passed away quietly in her sleep.'

Ann strokes the silver locket she always wears round her neck and says, 'She was a brave and generous-hearted woman, Mrs Bunting. It was a privilege to be there for her at the end.'

'She was fortunate to be able to die in her own bed,' I say. 'I want that for myself. But it is a privilege not granted to us all I'm afraid. My poor husband was away from home when it happened. I didn't have a chance to say goodbye. And I regret

135

it bitterly.' The whisky scalds my throat as I think of that terrible day.

Ann says softly, 'It's hard for those left behind. But best for our loved ones to go quickly. I'm sure he was thinking of you when he passed over.'

'It was a heart attack. And I fear he had dreadful pain.'

'But not for long my dear.'

'He collapsed on the fourteenth. They called from the Club. Dickie Clarke came and fetched me, but I got there too late.'

Our last kiss. Dry lips brushing together. For some reason I noticed the buds on the Albertine rose, just beginning to open. I watched him load his clubs into the car. I called 'Goodbye love; hope you win.' He called to me in return and waved his hand.

We finish our whisky in silence and then Ann says, 'You will be united with him again: one of these days.'

'You believe in an afterlife do you Ann? You're a Christian.'

'I attend a Spiritualist Church,' Ann says in her quiet voice and lays a hand on my knee. 'We think of death as a crossing over. The other side, you see, is near us all the time. There's nothing to fear.'

Suddenly, I am very tired. I have talked too long. Swallowed enough whisky.

Ann notices, for she gets to her feet and says, 'Time for bed, Mrs Maddison, I'll just pop up and turn the taps on.'

Ann holds the towel ready as I step out of the bath, wraps it round me, pats me dry and dabs witch hazel on my most recent bruises. She seems to get genuine pleasure out of doing things for me. She turns down the bedclothes, plumps up the pillows and helps me into bed. Then, she brings me a glass of water and doles out my pills. It's a bit like having a lady's maid. I like it.

I sink my head into the pillows and fall asleep. It's still dark when I wake. I switch on the light; my watch tells me it's three a.m. I must have been dreaming of Clive. He is so strongly in my mind. Dearest Clive. I miss him. We had a good life

136

together. But oh, we could have given each other so much more.

I am too wide awake to go back to sleep. I turn on my radio, and set a tape running. Mozart will soothe me. My poor Clive. He did not have enough time to enjoy his retirement. His army service and the hard post-war years of driving the business forward took their toll. But, as Mozart's divine music washes over me, it is not the recent past that occupies my mind, but haunting glimpses of long ago. I see us so clearly, radiant, hopeful, and I yearn for my young love. I mourn the Clive who did not come back to me after the War.

Our wartime letters lie in their tin box down in the hall cupboard. I remember how I could not bear to go on reading those poignant evocations of our lives, undisturbed until, not long after he died, I took them from where we had lain them more than forty years before. Chronological order: 1942 to 1945. Mine to him, his to me. Some had whole sentences cut out by the censor. (We had to take care we wrote nothing that could reveal our positions, disclose our actions). 'I think we're off somewhere but I can't tell you where,' he would write. Much later I learned he was in Sicily, where he felt safe sleeping in a trench, although they were kept awake by German planes coming over every night, seeking out the shipping at Augusta.

'I've just shelled a lot of almonds for you and they are now drying in the sun,' he wrote. 'They come off the tree I have been sleeping under for the last three weeks, so that should give them quite a romantic appeal.' When he could find something suitable to put them in, he would post them to me; he hoped they wouldn't get pinched *en route*. I imagined my Clive lying on the hard ground and thinking of me. By the time the almonds arrived, they had grown dry and shrivelled, but they tasted sweet.

In spite of the censor, we wrote of our love, our ambitions, our hopes, our longing. Through chains of subtle words, marks made by a pen on airmail paper, I would catch the sound of his voice, feel the touch of his lips, know his thoughts. I believe we were closer, more intimate, more tender with each other during those three short years of separation, which

137

seemed so long at the time, than was ever possible during our long years of living together, which passed in a flash.

Perhaps we expected too much: a nirvana with the end of the war. If we felt disappointment, resentment, we concealed it. There were so many things I should have said to him: so many truths we could have explored.

The tape has come to an end. I turn it over, and put out a hand to stroke Pinky's soft coat. Soon, his purring accompanies Mozart's horn concerto.

Will I see Clive again? In an afterlife? In some insubstantial other world I cannot imagine? Ann believes the other world is very close; that crossing over, as she calls it, is natural, easy, certain.

When I am ready to go, if Ann is right, perhaps I will join Clive out there in the hereafter: to have another chance. On the other hand, death may be nothing. An end to being – anywhere.

I have made my Will, but it is not irrevocable. I know Alice is still upset about Hunter's Moon, and it worries me. Also, I have not yet decided who shall have my precious pearl choker.

Mozart's horn concerto is coming to an end. Curled by my feet, Pinky is silent. I believe I shall sleep now.

It is time for Ann to leave me and go off on her holiday. I find it hard to understand her choosing to spend two weeks driving about in the Scottish rain, but she seems to be looking forward to it. Nowadays everyone is very keen on holidays. I believe even exotic places are full of quite ordinary people on packages. Clive loved to travel, but I never got to choose where we were going. He would just announce one day, 'I've booked our holiday dear', usually the Caribbean, or Madeira – South Africa once – to get away from the English winter. We never went abroad in summer because of his golf.

'I hope you have a lovely time,' I tell Ann, who is bumping her case down the stairs. She says she certainly will and her husband will enjoy himself too, once they've got away. 'He doesn't say much but I know he likes it really. And we usually meet some interesting people. We stay in small hotels and

138

country pubs – sometimes we take a bed and breakfast – and people are very friendly.'

The thought of an empty house stretching around me is unnerving. I did not realise how comforting even an unfamiliar presence can be. And after a week of her company, Ann is becoming a friend. We stand by the front door, waiting for Ann's husband to come and collect her, and I thank her for looking after me. She says it's been a pleasure and as a dark green saloon car draws up outside, I find myself asking her if she will come and stay with me when she gets back from holiday. I tell her I enjoy her company and I don't feel ready to be left on my own.

Ann says, 'I'd be pleased to come Mrs Maddison. We get along quite well don't we: the three of us.' And she bends down and strokes Pinky who is lying in a patch of sun in the hall. She opens the front door as her husband walks up the path. He looks younger than I expected; a tall slim man with a straight back and thin grey hair. Ann introduces us and he shakes me by the hand and says he's pleased to meet me. He has a North Country accent, like Ann, but he is surprisingly soft spoken. He picks up her case and loads it into the back of their car, which is well polished and quite new-looking. Ann says goodbye and she's looking forward to seeing me again soon. It is amazing how bereft I feel as the green car draws away with Ann smiling and waving from the passenger seat. Looking back through the front door at my too empty house, I consider dropping in to see Arthur and June, and then I remember they are also on holiday. I believe they've gone somewhere peculiar like Lanzarote.

There are two days to get through before David and Jonquil return from Spain and then David has promised to come and fetch me. I am to have Alice's old bedroom, now the guest room, with its own new bathroom. Jonquil has agreed that Pinky may sleep in the room with me, provided he's in his basket and not on the bed covers.

I do not enjoy the two days without Ann to look after me. Mrs Curtis grumbles about what has not been done by 'your nurse'. They really don't get on, those two. I suppose Mrs Curtis, having been here so much longer, feels a bit displaced by Ann. But I can't help that.

139

My sleeping pills don't work, so I take two more in the middle of the night and wake with a headache.

It is a relief when David arrives in the Mercedes. Smiling and sun-tanned, he tells me my 'quarters' are ready and Jonquil and the girls are looking forward to seeing me. He loads my case, kindly packed by Ann, into the car; puts Pinky into his travelling basket a little roughly and, not surprisingly, gets himself scratched.

Standing on the porch at Hunter's Moon, Jonquil greets me charmingly. She kisses me on both cheeks and tells me I'm looking much better. Her pale skin has acquired a light, biscuity tan and the sun has put blonde streaks into her fair hair. Louisa and Helen come up to say hello and give me a kiss. Louisa is a very pretty girl, but she's gained rather too much weight and I'm sorry to see poor little Helen still has that hideous wire contraption clamped to her front teeth.

Carrying my case, David leads me up to the bedroom which used to be Alice's. The pink rosebud wallpaper has been replaced by yellow and white stripes and there are heavily draped curtains to match, which, in my view, block out too much light and air.

Helen follows us up and stays to help me unpack, chattering away about Spain. She says they saw some fabulous Flamenco dancing and she and Louisa did lots of swimming and wind-surfing. They drank sangria which was 'yummy' and the discos kept going all night, but Mum and Dad wouldn't let them stay later than midnight.

Lunch is paella. Jonquil says she always likes to try out ethnic dishes when she gets home; it prolongs the holiday atmosphere. She says Mediterranean food is very healthy and she's hoping to organise something called tapas for tomorrow.

The paella is full of rather tough mussels, and rice is the very worst thing: it gets under my top plate.

David strokes Jonquil's hair and says, 'Doesn't she look well?' She'd been working so hard, she really needed a break. I suppose it's quite touching really, to see how attached they are to each other. Jonquil puts her hand over David's and says they all had such a lovely time together and Spain was incredibly stimulating. The depth of colour is breathtaking, she says, and the Spanish a fine-looking race. She gets quite carried away describing it all, 'The old women (excuse me Mother!) look dramatic in their black clothes, with those wise weather-beaten faces, every centimetre wrinkled; it's the fierceness of the sun of course. And the men have fine muscular bodies, like polished mahogany; and shiny black eyes and hair. Poor David, I think he got fed up with me sketching away; didn't you, darling. I can't wait to get at my paints.'

After lunch, I rinse the rice grains from my top plate and Pinky and I go up to my bedroom for a nap. I carefully place his blanket by my feet, to protect the bed covers. It's no good expecting Pinky to stay in his basket.

When we come down for a cup of tea, David is in his study catching up on some work, and Jonquil is out in her studio. Louisa and Helen have set up the video machine, ready to show me their holiday. It takes ages and it's hard keeping my eyes open, but they've obviously had a happy time, though hot beaches and noisy water sports aren't my scene.

For supper, we finish up the paella because Jonquil found her work so absorbing, she forgot about cooking and there wasn't time to make anything else.

I'm a lucky woman. My family are all very sweet and kind to me.

The weather is beautiful and my granddaughters set up a comfortable chair for me outside, so I can watch them play tennis with their friends. I can't help agreeing with Alice that the old grass court was more attractive than this hard one, which is a nasty reddish colour. But David says grass takes a lot of looking after and the girls need a good-quality court to justify the money he's spending on their tennis coaching.

I do find pop music a bit of a trial. The girls have it on all day: a monotonous kind of thumping with a bit of moaning and droning thrown in. I have to ask them to turn the volume down.

Unfortunately, I see very little of my son at Hunter's Moon. He leaves for London early each morning and comes home just in time for supper. Jonquil is busy working on what she calls her 'Spanish Project'.

It is tiring watching my granddaughters and their enthusiastic friends playing tennis, so I walk down the garden to

141

Jonquil's studio. I call, 'Can I come in?' and push open the door. Jonquil is standing at her easel, mixing paint with a palette knife. On the easel is what looks like a half completed painting of a bull fight. It is mostly red and black, but I can just make out a patch of brown, which must be the bull, with his head down, and lances sticking into his neck. Jonquil greets me abstractedly, gives me a chair to sit on and dabs red paint onto the canvas. I sit quietly. My daughter-in-law's absorbed expression tells me she does not like being interrupted. After a bit more dabbing of the red paint, she stands back from the easel. 'What do you think?' she asks. 'I'm experimenting with a more impressionistic style.'

I tell her I think she's very clever but I'm not keen on her subject matter. She says of course she realises this painting is very different from the portrait of Pinky she did specially for me, and not just on account of the subject matter, more to do with the kind of treatment she knew I'd appreciate. She knows how much I love Pinky, and she tried to make that feeling live in his portrait. But, you see Mother, an artist must develop new ideas, even if they don't always come off. She tells me the corrida is a true artistic tableau, and bull fighters are very brave. I tell her I've heard that before, and I feel sorry for the bull. She says the bull is killed quickly and cleanly with a sword: it's a noble death. But, I point out, the poor bull is provoked and tortured. How heroically he fights for his life, she says. And does that make his death noble? I ask, becoming upset. Jonquil realises she has gone too far. 'I'm sorry Mother,' she says, 'I get out of control when I'm involved in a painting. I'll just finish this bit and then I'll put my things away and we'll go inside and have a drink.' While she dabs more red paint on the canvas and then cleans her brushes, I look round at the many canvases stacked against the wall, at a work table laden with jars and bottles and cleaning rags and brushes of every size. The air seems hot and heavy, and I breathe in the pungent smell of oil paint and linseed oil. Jonquil spends an awful lot of time out here, I think. I hope it's worth it.

We walk back to the house together and Jonquil tells me to go and sit down in the family room while she gets us a drink. It was called the drawing room in my day. I stretch out on the gold silk sofa. The French windows are wide open. If I half close my eyes, I can see the garden as it used to be: the herbaceous border a riot of summer colour.

Jonquil arrives with a tray holding our drinks and a dish of nuts, and sits down in an armchair. The gin is satisfyingly short on tonic. I look at my daughter-in-law's feminine shape, her pretty blue eyes, her slender fingers and I can't help thinking about the poor bull in her painting. I wonder if she actually watched a bull being killed. Death is omnipresent. I see the sword plunged into the animal's heart; the gush of blood, the arrested charge, the staggering fall: the stillness. I swallow more gin. Animals are supposed not to have souls: no heaven for bulls. 'Jonquil,' I say. 'Do you believe in an afterlife?' Jonquil shows no surprise and answers that she finds Heaven hard to to imagine, but she feels certain this life is not all there is. When I say I suppose I'll find out soon enough, she pours me another gin and instead of telling me, as Alice would, not to mention dying, Jonquil looks at me steadily and says, 'Mother, if you need to talk about how you feel, I am here for you.'

I recover from my surprise at her perception. The gin has loosened my tongue.

I tell her I am frightened of the future: of losing control of what happens to me. If another heart attack or a stroke renders me totally incapacitated, can I rely on you, I ask, on my family to take responsibility for me? I tell her my deepest fear is of being trapped in a living death. Jonquil says she has similar fears and if there is anything she can do to prevent this happening to me, she will do it.

We sit in silence for a moment, not looking at each other, and then Jonquil says in her quiet voice that she believes in euthanasia, that she would like to see euthanasia become legal in this country, and that it is possible in Holland.

'But not in England,' I say. 'In this country, how can you avoid total senility? How can you avoid losing control of what happens to you?'

Jonquil's face is full of sympathy. It is an enormous relief to meet unchallenged comprehension from this unlikely quarter. It had not occurred to me I would be able to talk to my daughter-in-law with such candour: that she would be so receptive to my fears.

She looks briefly out at the sunny garden before turning back to me, and saying, 'I believe there are certain steps you can take, Mother, that would put your mind at rest.'

I look at her expectantly and she tells me there is something called a Living Will in which you can make your wishes known to your family and your doctor and the people caring for you. 'It's a legal document. You get your solicitor to witness it. It's specially designed to avoid what you are afraid of.'

I feel the twitch of a pulse in my temple and ask how do I find out about this.

Jonquil says, 'There's bound to be something in a bookshop, or the library. I have to go into town tomorrow: come with me, and we'll have a look round.'

I am sleepless once more. After an exhausting day walking round the shops in Maidstone, I am too physically tired, my brain too active to relax. I cannot rely on Mozart to soothe me, because I have left my little radio cassette player at home. Euthanasia. Even during that dreadful time in hospital, I never once considered the option of being helped to die. I was intent on getting out of the place alive as soon as possible. I wanted to go home. I looked forward to doing most of the things I'd been used to doing, driving the car, playing golf, enjoying my family, visiting my friends: having fun. But I realise now, this will not happen. Falling over that wretched dog has set me back, put paid to my chances of getting better. Not only must I accept my dull and limiting life, it will get worse.

Everyone hopes for a quick and easy death. As you grow older, you become more and more conscious of the proximity of the inevitable. But a natural death cannot be compared with a planned exit, on a selected day at a particular hour, when life becomes intolerable. If the law allowed it, which it doesn't, and if a compassionate doctor offered me a way out, would I take it?

I pick up the book Jonquil and I bought today. I open it and on its first page I read about something called an *Advance*

Directive. I feel my old heart beat faster in nervous antici-pation, as by the rather poor light of the yellow-shaded reading lamp I learn that an Advance Directive, or a Living Will, should contain written instructions from you about the medical care you want if you become too ill to tell people yourself. The book makes you address the question of what level of irreversible disability you are prepared to accept. You must be specific about how much medical intervention you want, because without guidance from patients, doctors must do everything possible to preserve life. It lists conditions you might find untenable. Things like having to live in an insti-tution because your family cannot care for you at home. Or if you become paralysed, or unable to communicate, or blind. Whether or not you want to be fed by tube, or intravenously, or be given electric shocks to start up your heart. What it boils down to is letting them know at which point you should be allowed to die: a decision you need to make in advance. This you put in writing in a Living Will which must be signed by your doctor and witnessed.

Dr Robson knows I do not want to be revived. Would he sign such a document? Your family are not allowed to sign: presumably because they might want you dead.

Do my family want me dead? David and Jonquil, Alice and Ralph. Ralph probably wants me dead. But the others? My dearest David? Jonquil who has surprised me with her under-standing? My darling Alice? I'm an awful old nuisance; I know that. But I'm damned if I'll die to suit them.

Does this document have the power to enable me to slip away when I am ready? Can it save me from involuntary compliance with the doctor's ethic to preserve life at all costs?

I stare down at the black letters in front of me. 'To save a man against his will is the same as killing him.' I close the book, and turn off the light.

Alice

Has Ralph betrayed me? Ralph, whose fidelity I have never doubted? Over the last few months, by my absence, I have given him plenty of opportunity. Opportunity is no justification. I sit miserably at the kitchen table drinking cups of coffee and wonder what on earth I should do. If I confront him, he'd deny it. Unless he wants to get rid of me. Would he leave me? Would I leave him? Ralph, my love? I am confused and worn out. I need comfort and warmth: to be cared for and valued: the basic human needs Ralph accuses *me* of denying *him*.

I stare at the dark knots in the smooth-grained pine table, and my recording eye reproduces in my head, a full-colour print of Ralph and a small woman with bubbly blonde hair. They are studying a large sheet of paper spread out on his desk. Their concentration is total. They do not even hear me opening the door. I see Judith Page's china-blue eyes and her white skin; I see that the blue flowers in her blouse exactly match the colour of her eyes. I see her small mouth. I hear her softly insistent voice with its West country burr. I see how young she is. A tragic little widow, *in need of comfort and warmth, to be cared for and valued.*

Ralph is on his way to Manchester, but he will be home tonight. I could have it out with him then.

I look towards Emily's basket. But Emily is not there. I drift disconnectedly round the house, but there is no sign of her. Eventually I decide she must be with William. Slowly, I climb the stairs to the attic, growing nearer to the sound of William's tapes: the steady drumbeat, the monotonous

146

rhythm, the words repeating and repeating: 'Gonna live for ever – live for ever.'

William is lying on his bed with his eyes closed. Emily lies beside him.

'William,' I say, 'You know I don't allow the dog on your bed. And you can't tell me she got there by herself: she can't even manage the stairs.'

Without opening his eyes, he says, 'I carried her Mum'.

I don't need to have a row with William. Emily wakes up and wags her tail gently. I touch her head, and look round William's attic bedroom, which he is supposed to keep clean and tidy himself. Posters cover the walls, which were once painted saffron yellow. Clothes and tapes and books and bits of bicycle clutter the floor. I look out of the dormer window and see cars and people passing by on the street below. I wonder if any of those people have the kind of problems I have, and what they are doing about them.

William says, 'Are you all right Mum?' Does he sense my misery?

I tell him I'm fine, just a bit tired. The tape finishes and to my relief he doesn't insert a new one. Beneath the dormer window, William's work table is piled with text books and note pads, biros and pencils, and objects William has picked up from various places: a whelk shell, white as a bone, a piece of driftwood shaped like a bird, a cracked pot lid. Beside a copy of *King Lear* lies a note pad, on which he has written, in his rounded, easily legible handwriting, 'King Lear starts with the excessive parental demand for love. By giving away his kingdom, Lear lost all his power. So he had to rely on his daughters to care for him out of love. And they all let him down.'

'Mum,' complains William sleepily, 'You shouldn't read that. It's mine.'

'Sorry,' I say, 'But it's interesting.' *Excessive demand for love.* 'From what I remember of *King Lear*, it's the two evil daughters who cast him out. How does Cordelia let him down? The good daughter?'

'She was too high-principled to humour him. That's what Mr Darnley says, anyhow.'

Mr Darnley seems to be doing a good job, I think to myself,

147

teaching sixteen-year-olds to come to terms with the tragedy of *King Lear*. With all those bodies piling up at the end.

'I don't see why Cordelia has to die,' says William, rubbing his eyes and yawning.

'Lear can't accept it. Doesn't he imagine her breath stirs a feather?' I pick up William's copy of *King Lear*, and open it near the end. 'Never, never, never, never, never.'

'Mum, let's not talk about dying,' says William, sitting up in bed, and I remember how white he looked, staring down at Mother lying in the hall. So I ask how is his friend Tim? William says Tim has gone to Spain with his parents. In fact, *all* his friends have gone on holiday somewhere. Lucky old Rosamund is in Turkey, and going off on his bike with Tim and staying in Youth Hostels wasn't a proper holiday. I tell William I'm sorry it's being rather a dreary summer, but with his grandmother being ill, it's not been possible to arrange anything. It's been a pretty dreary summer for us all, I say. For instance, I haven't wanted to be away from home so much.

'Away from *him* you mean.'

'Away from both of you,' I say. 'And how have you and Ralph been getting along?'

'I don't see him much. He goes to work before I get up and I go to Dominics before he gets home.'

'I don't know what you've both been eating,' I say. 'But the freezer still seems to be full of the meals I bought you.'

'You know I don't like ready meals Mum and I suppose Ralph goes to the pub.'

'What time does he get back?' I ask cautiously.

'I don't know, quite late I think. You needn't worry, we aren't having rows or anything. In fact, he's been a bit better lately.'

Why? Why has Ralph been a bit better? Preoccupation with something, with *someone* outside his home? Blunting his territorial nature, his need to control. As my mother says, 'Ralph *does* like telling people what to do'. My children have frequently been on the receiving end of Ralph's controlling nature: the focus of rows between Ralph and me. When we married, he said, 'I'll try to be a good father to your children'. And I believe he meant it. But how can you be father to children who already have one? Even if that father goes off to the other side of the world and never contacts them?

I seldom think of Richard now. We married very young: I sometimes wonder if I fell in love with his motorbike. Riding pillion, I adored the speed, the excitement and the freedom, which I mistakenly identified with Richard, who turned out to be full of short-term enthusiasms and not exciting but irresponsible. He was easy-going and laughed a lot, but not always at the things I laughed at. He never caused me pain the way Ralph does: we were not connected enough for that. But he fathered my children.

It must be hard, being a stepparent; harder being a stepchild. Ralph had a stepmother so he ought to know how it feels. Perhaps that's the trouble. Ralph's father was under the thumb of his stepmother, who was hard and unloving. Ralph had no mother to take his side, whatever the circumstances: no loving mother to stand up for him. Ralph maintains he only disciplines Rosamund and William when absolutely necessary, that nevertheless I always take their side against him whatever, which may be true. And that he cannot bear.

I remember Rosamund at eleven yelling 'You're not my father; you can't tell me what to do.'

William is never openly defiant. William has always withstood Ralph's tellings off in silence and simply gone his own way. I know that underneath my son's adamant self-control, anger often seethes. I know he missed his father and I felt guilty for it. But Ralph did try. He used to play football with William, and take the boy on the practice ground with a bag of old golf balls and a cut-down hickory shafted club. Once he bought William a little tool-set for his tenth birthday. He tried to interest him in the business: took him round the factory, and gave him some wooden off-cuts to play with. William was polite, but Ralph was rebuffed.

Ralph wanted a child, and I denied it to him.

Stop! Stop! What am I doing? Making excuses for Ralph? None of this, surely, is grounds for betraying your wife; for taking another woman into your bed.

'Can I Mum?' William's voice penetrates my tortuous thoughts.

'Can you what?'

149

'Can I can go skiing with the college after Christmas?'

Christmas. What will my life will be like after Christmas?

Nothing stays the same; time sees to that. We all must accept change. Remembering my life with Richard is like watching a blurred video of someone else's life. How can I have passed all those minutes and hours and days and weeks and months and years alongside someone I barely think of now: except to feel guilty about? Can I bear to imagine that, one day, I will find myself looking back on my life with Ralph? I grow hot behind the eyes. I blink.

'Mum! Is anything wrong Mum?'

'Sorry. I wasn't concentrating. Skiing. You want to go skiing after Christmas. Yes, William, you may go skiing after Christmas.'

As I move round the house trying to complete a few routine domestic tasks, I talk to Ralph in my head. But everything I make him say in answer to my questions is unsatisfactory. I always felt being with Ralph was right. I thought I knew that, despite our differences in temperament, our badly balanced sense of priorities, the instinctive bond between us was as tough as a steel hawser. I'm not sure I have the courage to risk being proved wrong.

I am in bed when Ralph gets back from Manchester at eleven-thirty. I have drunk three-quarters of a bottle of wine, and am no nearer deciding what action to take. I lie still in the dark and pretend to be asleep, as I hear him coming quietly up the stairs. He turns on his bedside light, undresses, and goes into the bathroom. When he comes back, he slides into bed, puts his arms round me and says 'Sorry I'm so late, the traffic was terrible'.

It seems I have opted for non-confrontation: for pretending everything is all right really. The days pass with a sluggish but sure momentum. Ralph appears to be making an effort to mend things between us. I do not allow myself to believe he is doing this out of guilt.

All seems to be going unusually well at Hunter's Moon. Over the telephone, Mother is nauseating in her praise of Jonquil, 'so sensitive and understanding dear'. Louisa and

Helen are 'such dear girls' and darling David is 'terribly sweet' to her but of course he's working far too hard as usual. Jonquil, at her most complacent, tells me Mother is having a whale of a time. And then, on about the fifth day of Mother's visit to Hunter's Moon, Ralph answers the telephone quite late one evening. 'Of course Hilda,' I hear him say. 'I quite understand. I'm sure Alice will be happy to help out.' He hands the receiver to me, and there is Mother's voice, a little shaky, but full of resolve. 'I'm sorry Alice, I must go home. I need to see Dr Robson. I'm not at all well, and neither is Pinky.' My heart does a steep dive. Mother is due to stay at Hunter's Moon until Mrs Lister comes back from holiday. I don't want to help out. I don't want to leave Ralph. Jonquil comes to the phone and says Mother has a mild tummy upset but honestly she's perfectly all right. There's absolutely no need for me to come rushing down to Kent to look after her.

There is enough concealed steel in Jonquil's voice to make me suddenly protective of my old nuisance of a mother. I tell Jonquil I'll give her a call in the morning and see how things are then.

Barely awake, I answer the telephone at seven to Mother's resolute voice announcing that she is 'quite ready to go home, dear'. In the background I hear Jonquil asking Mother not to ring off. There is a fumbling of the receiver and then Jonquil is telling me, under her breath, that my mother has got herself into a state about the cat. 'I've told her I'll take it to the vet. I really think she'll settle down, you know, Alice. She was having such a lovely time here.'

'Well?' says Ralph after I've put the phone down, having promised to ring back shortly. I touch his arm and tell him I don't know what to do. 'If your mother needs you,' he says, carefully, 'perhaps you should go to her'.

'This is a marked change from your usual attitude.' We regard each other cautiously, inches apart in our bed. His expression is bland. This is my opportunity to confront him. Our eyes lock. His are purposefully blank but wary. What does he see in mine? Confusion, distrust? Or am I as successful a dissembler as he? I open my mouth, and the accusing words are ready, piling up in my throat, capable of transforming the contrived blankness in his eyes. Quickly, before I

151

can give voice to them, Ralph says, 'Well you won't be gone long will you? Mrs Whats-er-name's coming back soon.' His eyes flicker away from mine. Curtly I remind him I'll be away over the weekend. 'Never mind,' says Ralph, sliding out of bed. 'I've got a lot going on at the factory just now and a customer to see on Saturday.' He cannot conceal the relief in his voice. Is he relieved because I have failed to confront him? Does he reassure simply because he wants me out of the way? He registers the confusion on my face, and adds, 'The old girl won't last for ever, Alice'.

Once more I'm heading down the A12 for Maidstone. Emily dozes in the back of the car. I am a shuttle strung on a pulley. The top line draws me on, straining against resistance from below. The further I drive, the stronger is the backward pull. Why am I doing this? Why don't I just turn round and drive home?

Hilda

Alice arrives at last, looking cross. I can't help being ill. But my daughter is not cut out to be a carer. I've certainly learned that. Jonquil is also cross. They talk together in low voices and then Alice and Jonquil have a cup of coffee. I'm impatient to get home, but Jonquil says Alice has driven a long way and deserves a bit of a rest. I suppose she's right. Alice won't let me have any coffee. She says it will make my tummy worse. Since it still feels as if vicious hands are tearing my guts apart, I don't insist on the coffee, but those two take an awful long time drinking theirs. Eventually, they load all my bits and pieces into the car. Pinky, safely in his travelling basket, goes in the back with Emily. The old dog's breath is pretty hard to take. Alice says it's her teeth, but she's too old to have them scraped. When we get home Alice rings the surgery and asks Dr Robson to come round and check me over. Then she makes me go upstairs to rest on my bed, and I do feel a bit wobbly. I tell her about Jonquil's indigestible Spanish food. I think it was probably the squid. And that's what upset Pinky as well.

I'm always pleased to see Dr Robson: such a charmer. It's a shame he only comes when I'm ill. He asks me in his teasing way what on earth I've been doing to get myself in this state and Alice, who is standing guard like a policewoman, looks sternly from me to Dr Robson and says 'too much'. He takes my pulse and my blood pressure, and he looks in my mouth and my eyes, and feels my sore tum, very gently. Then he writes out a prescription which he gives to Alice. 'When her tummy's settled, perhaps some clear soup. And then light

153

meals only, steamed fish, chicken.' He laughs when I say that sounds very boring.

Unfortunately Pinky has an accident on the bedroom carpet while Alice is seeing Dr Robson to the door. Alice makes a terrible fuss about clearing it up, and says Pinky ought to be starved for twenty-four hours, which I think is quite unnecessary.

The medicine and a good night's sleep make me feel a helluva lot better, and when dear Dr Robson calls in at lunchtime, I tell him I'm almost looking forward to the steamed plaice and new potatoes Alice is preparing for our supper.

Darling Alice is rather too quiet and looks strained around the eyes. I can't say I'm surprised: the poor girl has an awful lot to cope with. It's a great pleasure to have her back with me again, and I tell her so while we sip our pre-dinner drinks: vodka and tonic for Alice, only Perrier for me. 'And it will be a nice change for you, dear,' I add and repeat what Jonquil was saying about it being a good thing for everyone to get away from their own home for a while. 'It's very peaceful here.' Alice smiles and I think how marvellous if she could be with me all the time. Of course I know that's not possible and Ann whats-er-name seems a very pleasant person, but I resent having to be looked after by a stranger. I won't think about that now.

I nearly fell over that wretched dog again this morning. She was lying at the bottom of the stairs and I simply didn't see her. I've told Alice to shut her in the kitchen, but it's no good, she just won't. The poor old creature has grown very thin round the hindquarters. She's moulting again and her harsh coat comes away in my hands. I watch her stagger down the hall, head on one side. Because I'm afraid of falling, I've started to shuffle along in much the same way myself. Old age is horrible.

Pinky has another accident; behind the sofa. Alice says she thinks he jolly well ought to have got himself outside, and surely we'd decided to starve him for twenty-four hours? I do not admit to the saucer of milk and half a pilchard I gave him at lunchtime. Alice says perhaps after all she'd better ring the

154

vet and luckily she manages to get the last appointment of the day.

After tea, we settle him in his travelling basket and Alice puts him in the back of her car. 'What about Emily?' I say. 'She'll only whine if you leave her here, and I don't want her tripping me up again.' I rather hope the vet might be able to do something about the dog's bad breath, but I don't suggest it. Alice says of course she'll take Emily and they might go for a short walk. 'You won't shut Pinky in the hot car will you? Remember to lock the doors so no-one can steal him.' I kiss Pinky goodbye on his head, between his ears. 'Look after him for me. He's very precious.'

It doesn't feel like my house when they've gone. The rooms are strange and empty. Suppose Pinky never comes back? Suppose he has a terminal disease and it's not just the squid that's making him ill?

I run water into a jug and fill the kettle in two goes. With my stiff arm, that's easier than carrying the heavy kettle to the sink. When the water boils I pour it onto a tea bag in my little teapot, which holds enough for two cups. I take the cup and a Garibaldi biscuit into the sitting room and sit down on the sofa. Pinky's red rug is spread on the end cushion. What will I do? How will I manage if Pinky never comes back? The thought of it turns me sick and dizzy: acid burns my throat. All alone. I shall be all alone. I haul my legs up onto the sofa, lean back against the cushions and close my eyes against the blackness that sweeps over me.

Clive is standing in front of me; young Clive. Dressed in his army uniform, he is leaning on a pair of crutches. There is a beseeching expression in his eyes. I stretch out my arms and call his name.

'Don't cry dearest; it's only my legs.'

My fingers almost touch his cheeks, brush against his moustache. But he is too far away; I cannot reach him.

My face is wet with tears and I hear myself saying, 'His leg got better. It was badly broken, but not smashed up.' And I know I must have been dreaming. But my Clive was so real. Now I am awake and alone.

For months after Clive died, I dreamed he was alive. I saw

him smiling at me from the other side of the dining-room table at Hunter's Moon, hanging up his old tweed jacket in the hall, loading his clubs into the car; *coming back from the golf club.* Always my familiar Clive: the Clive I grew old with. Why, now, is my young husband so clear in my mind? I can still almost see him, as I get up from the sofa and walk carefully through to the kitchen.

When I reach the kitchen, I find I've forgotten why I came here. And then I remember it is to see what the time is. I look at my familiar old clock which used to hang in the kitchen at Hunter's Moon. It has a round mahogany frame, and the Roman numerals on its white face tell me the time is six-thirty. They must have left around four. Why aren't they home? I make my way back to the sitting room, open the drinks cupboard, manage to lift out the heavy bottle of gin, and pour myself a good shot. Then I take the glass to the kitchen tap and splash a little water in it. Back on the sofa in the sitting room, I stroke Pinky's empty blanket and feel a sharp little jab in my heart. The minutes drag by. I pour some more gin and look up the vet's telephone number. My eyes are playing me up, and I get a few wrong numbers before finally one of those awful answer-phones tells me the surgery is closed and will open again at eight-thirty in the morning. Could it be that something really bad has happened to Pinky? So bad that Alice daren't come home and face me? She could have had a car accident. Or has she selfishly decided to call on Jonquil, with no thought for me – all alone and going out of my mind with worry? When I get up to have another look at the clock, there is a singing in my head. I probably shouldn't have had that last gin.

Alice

I arrive at Hunter's Moon to find Mother lying on the sofa in the drawing room, with Pinky sprawled on her lap. When she turns to greet me, I see that her dark eyes have sunk right back into her head, and I am shocked by her pallor. She stretches out her arms, and I bend to kiss her thin cheek. 'Darling Alice, thank goodness you're here – you've been *such* a long time.' Though tremulous, my Mother's voice retains its underlying note of command. Jonquil, from just behind me, tells Mother, quite sharply, that Norwich isn't exactly round the corner. 'Poor Alice, you must be worn out. Why don't you sit down and relax while I make us some coffee, and would you like a ham sandwich?' I ignore Mother's weak but petulant sighs and collapse into the soft cushions of the easy chair beside the sofa. Mother complains that neither she nor Pinky can keep anything inside them and she feels absolutely terrible. From the evidence of my eyes, I cannot disbelieve her.

After the coffee and a ham sandwich for me, Jonquil and I collect up Mother's possessions, which are scattered around the house. Jonquil makes light of Mother's condition which, in her opinion, is caused by Mother's stomach being unaccustomed to proper food, since it usually receives light snacks and bland ready meals. I don't bother to point out that for several weeks now, either I or Mrs Lister have been responsible for feeding Mother, and certainly not on snacks and ready meals. Jonquil says she's very sorry indeed that Mother's stay has ended like this. They'd had a good time together, and she was really enjoying having her. She's par-

157

ticularly sorry I've allowed myself to be manipulated into taking her home, quite unnecessarily. 'You know, Alice, I think you should be a little firmer with Mother. She'll have you running around after her for ever.'

Mother looks alarmingly unwell, but she is so unpleasant about poor Emily, I'm finding it difficult to be sympathetic and tolerant. She has no idea how hard it is for me to leave Ralph. I will not let myself think about what Ralph might be doing. She darts me a calculated glance from her position, huddled and belted in the passenger seat. 'I'm nothing but an old nuisance to you, Alice.'

I tell her not to be so ridiculous. We all love her and are trying to do our best to keep her well and happy. But, underneath, viciously, guiltily, I think, you *are* an old nuisance and in my black moments I want you dead. For you are ruining my life.

When I get her out of the car and into her own home, I realise the extent of what Jonquil refers to as 'a little tummy trouble'. Something has severely debilitated my mother. Shakily she heads for the loo, but does not make it in time. Pinky does not make it to the garden in time. I do feel sorry for my poor mother as I clear up the mess, and help her upstairs and into bed. I telephone the surgery and ask for a visit, and Dr Robson comes in the afternoon and gives my Mother a thorough examination. She perks up immediately at the sight of good-looking, sympathetic Dr Robson.

'Food poisoning,' says Dr Robson when I get him downstairs. 'And exhaustion.' I tell him since she's been staying with my brother and sister-in-law, I have no idea what could have done it. He scribbles on his prescription pad. No solid food for twenty-four hours. I'm giving her some rehydration salts. Make them up with water. Directions are on the packet.' And then he adds, gently, 'Don't worry too much. Your Mother is tougher than you think. I'll call in tomorrow, but give me a ring if she gets any worse.'

Food poisoning. Suddenly, I remember the disappointment I detected in Jonquil's face when Mother came to life after her fall. It's not in Jonquil's interest to keep my Mother alive. As Ralph pointed out before the party, she doesn't want Mother

158

changing her mind about Hunter's Moon. What was it Mother said about not enjoying *all that Spanish food?*

Exhaustion. From Mother's description of her stay at Hunter's Moon, it's not surprising she is exhausted. Jonquil seems to have trailed her round most of the the shops in Maidstone on a very hot day. The whole thing has obviously been far too much for her, and certainly indicates, if not a deliberate act of aggression, a sinister lack of concern by Jonquil for the constitution of a frail old lady.

Whatever poisoned Mother has just as badly affected the bloody cat. When, after a couple of days, unlike Mother, Pinky shows no sign of improvement, and I've had enough of clearing up after him, I decide to ring the vet.

I sit at the telephone table and I watch Emily struggle along the hall towards me, leaning against the wall for support. This morning I had to lift her out of her basket. Yesterday, in the garden, her back legs buckled, and she needed my help to get up again. Emily reaches me and collapses on my feet. A small voice inside my head whispers, *you can't let her go on like this.* When, finally, the receptionist answers the telephone, I make an appointment for Pinky and ask to speak to Mr Baxter. I tell him I'm bringing my mother's cat to see him and I will be bringing Emily along as well.

Mother parts from Pinky with tears in her eyes, and begs me, pathetically, to take good care of him. My sympathy for her evaporates when, with her usual acidity, she complains about Emily's bad breath. Nevertheless, I calm her down and, fearing a fall while I'm out, suggest she rests quietly on the sofa until I return. 'Very well dear, if you say so,' she says. 'But I'm perfectly all right you know.'

It seems important to give Emily the chance to enjoy a last amble and sniff around upon this earth, so I stop the car at the park and lift her out. It has been a beautiful day, very warm with a few fluffy white clouds floating about in a pale blue sky. Now, the afternoon sun beams benignly on Emily as she limps about on the dusty grass, nose down, tail swaying from side to side. Rooting around in the undergrowth at the base of one of the wooden benches, she finds half a kit-kat. She's still enjoying her food, I think, and though unsteady on her feet, she doesn't fall over. Irresolute, I lift my dear old dog back into the car.

There is no-one in the waiting room when I arrive with Pinky in his travelling basket. A notice on the wall reads, 'Flea eggs represent up to 50% of the flea population'.

Mr Baxter appears in his white coat. 'Let's take a look at him,' he says and carries Pinky through to his consulting room. I explain that the doctor has diagnosed food poisoning in my mother and I wonder if the same thing could have upset her cat. Mr Baxter examines Pinky and confirms the diarrhoea is likely to have been caused by something he ate, and not by a virus. Then he informs me that Pinky is also suffering from water on the heart. He gives Pinky an injection for the diarrhoea; 'No solid food until tomorrow', and hands me a bottle of pills for the heart condition, 'two to be taken three times a day'. We manoeuvre the unpleasant creature back into his basket. 'I'll put him in the car,' I say, picking up the basket. 'Back in a minute.'

Once outside, I want to drive home again. I stroke Emily's head, and look into her misty old eyes. Can I keep her a little longer? Enjoy just a few more weeks of her company? My hands are shaking as I lift her down from the car and take her slowly in to Mr Baxter.

'I'm not sure it's really quite time.' I lay my hand protectively on Emily's chest.

Mr Baxter looks me steadily in the eye. 'You can't keep putting yourself through this,' he says gently.

'I know.'

'I'll give her something to relax her. Just hold her head and talk to her.' In a daze, I watch him prepare a hypodermic, bend down and inject Emily in the flank. Then, together we lift her onto the bench. She lies quietly. I bend over and stroke her head and tell her I'm here and she's quite safe. Mr Baxter shaves a patch of hair on her leg.

'Good dog. Good Emily. There's a good dog.' I don't watch the needle enter the vein, just go on stroking her head and talking to her. After a few seconds, Emily gives a big sigh and it sounds like a sigh of contentment. Then she becomes absolutely still.

160

The tears are rolling down my face and falling onto Emily's head and Mr Baxter's hands as he raises her eyelid. 'It's all over now,' he says. And then, gently, he adds, 'I can look after her for you – unless you want to take her with you.'

Emily has gone. How can I put her poor worn-out old body in the car and find a place to bury it? 'Please. You do it.' The tears that have been trickling down my cheeks race into a flood.

Mr Baxter says, quietly, 'You look as if you need a stiff drink. Surgery's finished. Why don't you go and wait in your car while I see to things here. I'll join you shortly, and we'll go to the pub.'

Like a sleep-walker, I pass through the door he has opened for me at the back of his consulting room, and go and sit in the car with Pinky, who is curled up in his travelling basket. I lean my arms on the steering wheel, lay my head on my arms and sob. I weep for Emily who is lost to me, for Mother who is old and infirm, for William who is unhappy. I weep for lack of the Ralph I loved, and I weep with regret for my inept, unappreciated self.

After a while, like a storm passing, my tears begin to peter out. I blow my nose and scrub at my eyes with my saturated handkerchief. 'God what a sight!' My blotchy face stares miserably back at me from the visor mirror. I comb my hair and put on some lipstick. 'I've done the right thing,' I assure my reflection. 'I'm glad I did it for you, Emily.' I shut my eyes, lean back against the seat and take some deep breaths.

There is a tap on the car window. Mr Baxter opens the door and I get out. 'There's a reasonable pub down the road. I usually call in for a quick one before I go home.'

'You're very kind.' The evening air feels cool on my hot face. 'It's nice to have some company.'

Inside the 'Coach and Horses' Mr Baxter says, 'How about a whisky?' I don't usually drink whisky, but now it seems appropriate so I say thanks I'd like that, and Mr Baxter says to the barman, 'Two Bells', please Gerry.'

We take our drinks and sit down at a circular wooden table littered with beer mats. What look like half a dozen 'regulars' are lounging at the bar exchanging pleasantries. A lad in a

161

white tee-shirt and tight jeans is throwing darts expertly at a dart board in the corner.

'My name's Jonathan,' says Mr Baxter. My friends call me Joe.'

'And I'm Alice.'

'That's a good old-fashioned name.'

We sit in silence watching the other people in the pub, and I'm grateful Joe doesn't feel obliged to start up a conversation. My heart feels bruised. I drink the whisky which warms my throat and my stomach and slowly the warmth spreads outwards and upwards, easing the ache in my heart. Emily is still so near to me, I cannot *not* talk about her. I manage to blurt out, 'What you just did for my dog, Joe, please tell me, she really didn't feel any pain, did she? It was so quick.'

'No,' he says and adds slowly, as if he's weighing the importance of what I am asking and knows that I trust him to tell the truth. 'She won't have felt any pain. It's very humane.' He takes a mouthful of whisky and then he says, 'You never quite get used to doing it you know, and it's a terrible thing to be asked to put down a young and healthy animal because, for various reasons, no-one wants to look after it. But with an old, well-cared-for dog, it's good to be able to spare them any more suffering. I often think it's a pity we can't do the same thing for humans.'

'You believe in euthanasia?'

'*Voluntary* euthanasia.'

'So do I. But there's something gruesome about a lethal injection, and it's a lot to ask of a doctor. Like you, he might never quite get used to doing it.'

'I don't think we'd want him to.'

'No, of course not.' I gulp my whisky, 'Emily is free of suffering now, but I'm not.' I have to dab at my eyes with my useless handkerchief. 'I'm sorry – I'm bad company.'

'Don't apologise. I must tell you, since I lost my old border collie, I missed her so much, I still haven't been able to decide to have another one and face putting myself through all that again in another thirteen or fourteen years' time.'

'They become friends don't they – not just dogs. I sometimes think animals are better than people. In the wild they're

162

not vicious for the sake of it. People are. Domestic animals are perfectly fine, so long as they have decent owners, aren't they? We don't value animals. We destroy their habitat so they die out, or they overwhelm the insufficient land they're allocated, and have to be culled, like African elephants. We factory-farm chickens; we're incredibly cruel to pigs which are supposed to be highly intelligent. And look what we've done to the poor cows! Stuffed them with sheep's brains – herbivorous animals! And then we're amazed when it gives them a horrifying brain disease, which they can pass on to us. So then it's mass slaughter. Poor cows. I feel really sorry for cows.'

'It's the drive for cheap food. I came out of a farming practice years ago, because I got fed up with treating animals made sick by the conditions they were forced to live under. But the farmer won't take kindly to me when I tell him it's bad practice to buy low-cost meal for his cows, and that they've had too many antibiotics, and his sheep have got foot rot because he keeps them on marshy ground, and the disease his pig is suffering from is caused by overcrowding. He needs to operate commercially.'

'Do you believe animals have rights?'

'When people talk about rights I get uneasy. Rights seem to me to be something we grant ourselves with the aid of laws. Nothing to do with ethics. We're granted the right to vote. Our children are given the opportunity to go to school. We earn the right to own a house. I'm not sure any of us are born with a right to anything. We have to fight to get the kind of life we want and, until we can do that on our own, we're dependent on other people who may or may not be able to give us what we need. Animals can't fight for any rights people might think they're due. It's up to us, *higher animals*, to protect their interests. We use animals for food, for work, for companionship. They are at our mercy. And if we treat them brutally, we ourselves become brutal.'

'I hate myself for liking to eat meat. What about you? Are you a vegetarian?'

'Not quite.'

'Fish and free-range chickens and sheep that have grazed on hillsides.'

'That's about it. I'm not against killing animals for food, so

163

long as they've had decent lives and are slaughtered humanely. We all have to die.'

'I know.' *Emily* – I blink back tears.

'Let me get you another drink.'

He has kind eyes, greenish brown, crinkling at the corners when he smiles.

'Thanks.' He goes off to the bar and, watching him standing there, I am reminded of an oak tree. Oaks are strongly rooted. They have sturdy trunks, leaves with crinkled edges, greenish brown acorns.

If Joe is an oak tree, what kind of tree is Ralph? I think of sharp-spined cactus, occasionally producing spectacular short-lived blooms. Mother would be a bent old hawthorn with white flowers in the spring. William would be a young copper beech, tall and straight with richly coloured leaves: Rosamund a flowering cherry, not the flamboyant pink kind, but a white one with a froth of delicate blossom. Jonquil? A well-established willow whose weeping branches conceal the rot in her trunk.

Joe returns with two more whiskies and two packets of salted peanuts. He splits open a packet of nuts and offers them to me. I take some and say, 'Animals are sentient beings, but do you think they have emotions?'

'Domestic animals do. You must know that from your own observations.'

'Yes.' When I used to go out without Emily, the expression in the dog's eyes was one of pained resignation. On my return, she would bound around me with joy. I gulp my whisky and tell Joe I always wanted to be a vet when I was young, but I wasn't clever enough. Joe says if he was a young person wanting to be a vet today, he probably wouldn't be clever enough either, and he asks me what I do now that I'm not a vet. I tell him I used to work for an antique dealer, who specialised in early oak furniture and medieval carvings.

I realise, as I talk of it, how much I miss my job. Billy was fun to work for and I loved the things he dealt in: the massive trestle tables, worn smooth by centuries of use, the heraldic lions, the unicorns, the carved fruit and flowers, the virgins and apostles, the grotesque heads. I would touch the knobs and grooves fashioned from the smooth wood by the inspired

164

chisel of some unknown carver, and breathe in the spicy scent of dust and beeswax and aromatic timber till it prickled the inside of my nostrils.

'But Billy went bust. When the bank called in his overdraft, he sent them the keys to his shop with a note to the bank manager which said, "You've always been telling me how to run my business. Well, it's all yours now!" And he went off to live in Belgium.'

'He sounds quite a character.'

'Oh yes. So, I've been out of a job now for six months. I suppose it's just as well really, with my mother needing my support.'

'I remember your mother. She's the sort of person you notice: a strong-minded old lady with a lot of charm. You said she has food poisoning.'

'And you never told me whether you thought the same thing could have caused Pinky's problem.'

'It's possible.'

'Hmmn. Mother and Pinky have been staying with my brother and sister-in-law.'

'And are they in the habit of poisoning people?'

I laugh and say, 'Well, my mother can be incredibly trying. I'm looking after her at the moment and I should know. It's ridiculous: she's a poor frail old woman but she wears me out. She can't help being ill and she's very brave, but she loses things all the time, her glasses, her handkerchief, her wallet, her book, the remote control for the television. I spend *hours* looking for them. She depends on me to organise everything and then complains if it doesn't turn out exactly how she wants. She's the sort of person you take trouble to choose a present for, and she gives it back to you the next week. She shuffles because she's afraid of falling. That gets on my nerves, and even worse, she's always bumping into things because she won't wear her glasses, and I'm sure it's out of vanity. She was brought up with the generation that believed "Men don't make passes at girls who wear glasses," and it's stuck. Meals take for ever, because she eats so slowly. She's lonely and I'm sorry and I understand, but when I'm there, she latches on like a leech. She talks all the time – pursues me round the house. She doesn't give me any space. I worry because she

165

falls asleep in the bath, and she's so obstinate she won't take a bath at any time other than last thing at night, which means I can't go to bed until she's finished. You know, sometimes I think, maybe I'll just let her *drown*. Isn't that awful!'

'Old people have no concept of other people's lives. They're all like that.'

'It was more rewarding looking after Emily. Dogs are grateful. Dogs don't criticise you. Dogs love you in spite of and not because of.'

'Have another drink.' He catches the barman's eye. 'Two more whiskies Gerry please.'

'She wants me to be here all the time, and gets angry when I go home. And then my husband gets angry when I'm not at home with *him*. I feel like a rugger ball being chucked back and forth between them. And I don't please either of them.'

'Why not just please yourself?'

'I'm so used to worrying about keeping other people happy, I've forgotten how to.'

'But that's a cop out. It's avoiding responsibility.'

'What do you mean?'

'If you always do what other people want, then it's not your fault if things go wrong.'

I am blinded with the light of reason. I have a disease. To please yourself by pleasing other people is unhealthy. I am dependent on the ego boost supplied by responding to other people's needs. Do I do it through fear of upsetting them? which is unavoidable anyway? Or is it because I lack not only the talent, but the courage and imagination to aim for self-fulfilment? But it's not so simple as that and I tell him so. I say, 'Maybe it's easier for men. You're more single-minded than we are. Women get side-tracked by husbands and babies and ageing parents. We are nurturers; it's natural to us, and it's habit-forming. If we try to break the habit, we suffer from guilt.'

'You don't think perhaps you might be turning yourself into a bit of a martyr?'

I am disconcerted, having expected sympathy, not criticism. But he's right. *What do I want* seems a harder question to answer than *what do they want*. What I do *not* want, and this is becoming progressively clearer, is the kind of life I am currently living. Something has to change. And it is *I* who must bring about that change.

'My turn to buy the drinks.' I go quickly to the bar and buy two more whiskies and a couple of packets of crisps. I put them down on the table and say I suppose we shouldn't be driving.

'Top them up with plenty of water.' Joe opens the crisp packets.

I tell him he knows an awful lot about me and and it's about time he told me something about him.

'I'm a pretty dull chap,' he says. 'I'm very involved in my work.'

'You must have some spare time. What do you do then?'

'I go walking. I like the countryside. I like mountains. When I can get away from the practice, I go North for a bit of hill-walking. And when I'm up there on my own, sometimes I imagine myself clearing off to a crofter's cottage in Scotland, or North Wales, where I'd grow vegetables and catch fish.'

'What about your wife? Would she like that kind of life?'

'I don't have a wife any more. She went off with the jumbo jet pilot who used to live next door.'

I am taken aback, not just by what he is telling me, but by the matter-of-fact manner of the telling. 'How awful. I'm sorry,' I say, inadequately. I was expecting him to be happily married. He seems such a caring, deep-thinking man and, despite his own words, not in the least dull. I jettison the sympathetic wife I imagined for him, dressed in practical denim, and bottle-feeding orphaned puppies. Only a trivial woman would choose to leave such an attractive man. Yes, he *is* attractive, I think with surprise. Imprinted with Ralph, I'm unused to looking at men in that way.

'I didn't realise what was going on. They always say the cuckolded partner is the last to know. I thought everything was all right between us. Then, suddenly it came to a head. And it was all too late. They're married now and live in Croydon. Claire, that's my daughter, lives with her mother, but she comes to see me.'

'I'm sorry. I was married before, so I know all about divorce. You don't put yourself through it unless you absolutely have to. And it's dreadful for the children. Mine don't get on with their stepfather, I'm afraid.'

'Sounds familiar.'

We lapse into silence and I think it's a long time since I've experienced such companionable empathy. But the pleasant sensation gradually begins to be eroded at the edges. By confiding so much in this man, who is, after all, a stranger, I am guilty of disloyalty to Ralph and to Mother. Guilt turns into consternation as I remember Mother. I look at my watch and see, to my horror, that it's nearly eight o'clock. Mother has been on her own for four hours.

'My God, I forgot all about my mother! I hope she's all right. I have to go now this minute. Thank you, Joe, for being so kind.'

'It was a pleasure. See you again, I hope.'

I get to my feet and he comes out to the car with me. He lays a hand briefly on my shoulder. 'I hope everything is all right. Drive carefully.'

Hilda

Someone has entered the room. 'Clive?' I call.

'Hello Mother, it's only me.'

When I hear her voice, I realise it's Alice and I must have been asleep. I was dreaming of Clive so vividly.

'I'm sorry I'm so late. Are you all right?'

'I'm *fine*, dear,' I tell her, and then I remember, Alice left me alone for far too long. *Pinky*. Alice took Pinky to the vet. My heart starts to thump.

'Don't worry, Mother; here he is.' Alice opens Pinky's travelling basket, and he walks slowly out, stretches and jumps onto my lap. I'm so relieved, I feel the tears come to my eyes. 'Darling Pinky.' I run my hands down the length of his soft back and he begins to purr.

Alice says Mr Baxter was very nice, and he gave Pinky an injection and some pills. The pills are because Pinky has a little water on his heart, but there's no need to worry because it's easily controlled with these pills.

'Oh Alice,' I say. 'Poor Pinky. Are you sure he'll be all right? I've been terribly worried. Sit down and talk to me. I've been alone such a long time.'

I wonder whether Mr Baxter managed to do anything about Emily's bad breath, but it doesn't do to ask. Alice says she'd better just go and sort something out for our supper and she'll be back in a minute. Off she goes and I hear her clattering about in the kitchen. I call and ask her to bring one of Pinky's special biscuits. But when she comes back she says, rather sharply, 'No solid food until tomorrow. I've crushed his pills in some milk. He'll have to make do with that for now.'

She starts to go back into the kitchen, but I tell her I wish she'd just come and sit down a minute and why doesn't she help herself to a gin. 'And where's Emily. You haven't left her in the car have you?'

'She's not in the car,' says Alice in a tight strange voice and when I look closely at her, I see she's been crying. Suddenly, I feel the significant absence of the old yellow dog. 'Oh my dear,' I say, 'I'm so sorry. But she wasn't having a very happy time was she! It's a blessing really.'

Alice gets out her handkerchief and blows her nose.

It's so easy for animals. Emily had a good life. And she has been granted a dignified and painless death. She's a lucky dog.

I am feeling so much better. My tummy has settled down, the swirling in my head has stopped and my legs are no longer wobbly. Dr Robson says I'm doing fine and I'm a tough old girl. It's very odd. I know I do not want to go on too long, but as soon as I feel the end might be coming, I push it back with all my might. I cannot avoid fighting to stay alive. I suppose it's human instinct. What I want is a dignified and painless death. But not yet.

Alice says she's knows she did the right thing: she was glad she was able to give Emily one final gift. But she misses her dreadfully. I do understand. Animals have such short lives. I hope Pinky doesn't go before me. No other cat would be quite the same.

Because of Emily, I am able to bring up the subject of voluntary euthanasia. Alice does not say, as usual, 'Please don't talk about dying, Mother,' and we both agree that, since we cannot be guaranteed a peaceful natural death, it would be a comfort to be helped to die when we'd had enough. 'Maybe they'll change the law,' she says. 'There's quite a lot of pressure to do so.' Once more, I impress upon her that my greatest fear is suffering the horror of losing my senses, of being admitted to hospital unable to avoid being subjected to the inhumanity of life-prolonging medical 'care'. She says, 'Don't worry, Mother, I won't let that happen.' But can I trust her? 'I want to stay at home,' I say, 'right up to the end'.

'I know,' she says.

170

I don't tell Alice of the conversation I had with Jonquil, or about the books she helped me buy. Remembering my little talk with Jonquil and now, as I discuss the same thing with Alice, and I see her looking at me thoughtfully, I begin to wonder, do they want me dead? I'm an awful old nuisance. Life would be a lot easier for them all if I wasn't around.

Unfortunately, Ann Lister is due back today, and once she's settled in, Alice will rush off back to Norwich. It has been such a treat having her here, but I suppose I've just got to get used, all over again, to living with a stranger in the house.

Alice makes omelettes for our lunch, but I have trouble getting mine down. I tell Alice it's no good, I just don't feel hungry, and she pours me a very small whisky, which helps a bit. Then, she makes me a cup of coffee and tells me to put my feet up on the sofa, while she goes to Waitrose to stock up on groceries for Mrs Lister.

My peaceful rest on the sofa is interrupted by Ann Lister arriving in a very noisy taxi. Unfortunately her husband couldn't bring her because he had to take their car to the garage. 'The clutch started to play up as we came down the A1. Are you all on your own Mrs Maddison? Don't get up, dear. I'll just put my case in the bedroom and then I'll make us a cup of tea.'

I hear her muddling about upstairs and then she comes down and goes into the kitchen. Eventually, she brings the tea in on a tray, nicely laid, with the pretty tray cloth embroidered with cornflowers, the tea-pot, covered by the oak leaf National Trust tea cosy, the blue Wedgewood cups and saucers, milk jug, silver sugar basin and a plate of fan-shaped shortbread biscuits. 'A present from Edinburgh,' she says. 'And I brought you a caddy of special tea from a lovely shop called "Betty's". I do hope you'll like it.'

'How very thoughtful of you.'

I must say it *is* rather nice to be so well looked after. Alice usually dumps my tea down in a mug. I believe she *makes* it in the mug with a tea bag. And she never puts enough milk in.

Ann says she had a lovely holiday. The scenery was beautiful and they went to Lochleven Castle where poor Mary Queen of Scots was imprisoned. It rained that day,

171

which made it seem even more sad. They had lots of nice food: delicious fresh Scottish salmon and once they had haggis which isn't too bad if you pour a drop of whisky over it. She asks me if I had a good time staying with my son and daughter-in-law, and she is very sympathetic when I tell her Jonquil's cooking gave me food poisoning. I also tell Ann about Emily. 'Darling Alice is very sad, but really it was the kindest thing. It's a pity people can't be helped in that way. When they've had enough.'

'Oh I do so agree. Some of these high-minded doctors seem to think they should preserve life at all costs. But then maybe they aren't believers. For those of us who have knowledge of the afterlife, death is not to be feared.'

Ann pours our tea, which is a little on the strong side, but the shortbread is crisp and buttery. She gives Pinky some milk in a saucer, and a corner of biscuit, and after we've drunk two cups each and I've heard some more about her Scottish holiday, which sounds rather boring to me, she says she'll just clear away the tea things and why don't I continue my rest while she unpacks.

I must have dozed off, but you know how it is when you're half asleep, you're aware of movement and noise, but you can't rouse yourself enough to work out exactly what's happening. Vaguely, sleepily, I suppose it must be Alice coming back from wherever she's been, so I don't bother to open my eyes. When I *do* wake up, someone is sitting on the chair next to the sofa. I'm just getting whoever it is into focus when a familiar voice says, 'Hello Granny'. And here is William, looking very large and grown-up.

'Darling William. How lovely! What a surprise!'

'I just thought I'd come and see you, Granny. Are you feeling better?'

I tell him I'm much better now, and his mother has been very kind. William doesn't look well. He's pale and thin and he has tired eyes. He gets out of the chair and bends down to give me a kiss. I ask him to tell me what he's been doing. He says not a lot because most of his friends have been away on holiday.

Ann Lister comes in with a cup of tea for William, and she says 'We've introduced ourselves now, but I'm afraid I was not very welcoming to your grandson, Mrs Maddison. I didn't know he was expected.'

'I don't think he was. Were you William? But I'm so pleased to see you.'

'Mrs Lister thought I was a tramp or a New-Age traveller.'

Ann glances at William's jeans, which are torn and not terribly clean, and at his hair which could do with a cut. 'Yes, I'm sorry, dearie. I thought you were stopping by to ask for a drink of water. You had your rucksack, and you looked ever so hot.'

There is the sound of a car drawing up outside. 'That must be Alice,' I say, and William gets up and goes out into the hall. Mrs Lister stays behind with me and says, 'When I told him you were having a snooze and his mother was out shopping, he said he'd like to take Emily for a walk. So I had to tell the poor lad his dog had passed on.'

William and Alice are talking in undertones in the hall. It's not possible to catch what they're saying until, suddenly, loud and clear, I hear William's voice. 'You should have *told* me Mum. *Why* didn't you tell me about Emily?'

It seems a good idea for us all to have a little drink together, so Alice opens a bottle of white wine, since I think William is not quite old enough for spirits.

Alice seems puzzled by William's sudden appearance, and was clearly not expecting him. I have a feeling he may have had an upset with Ralph. Perhaps they won't go home tomorrow after all. It would be a shame, now William has come all this way. Then I wouldn't need Ann. She could easily disappear for a few days.

After our supper – spaghetti Bolognese, not the easiest thing to eat – Ann clears away while Alice makes up the bed in the box room for William. William and I have a cup of coffee together in the sitting room, and I remind him of the lovely chats we had over the phone when I was in hospital. 'You cheered me up so during that dreadful time, William darling. I remember we talked about *Great Expectations*. I'm pleased to be able to remember that.'

'Yes,' he says. 'It's one of my A-level books.'

'I used to so love reading, but I find it rather tiring these days.'

William says you can get books on tape, and he'll try and find me some.

I ask about his friend Tim, and he says he doesn't see too much of Tim these days. And most of his other friends have been away on summer holidays. He tells me about the washing-up job he's been doing at a restaurant called Dominics. The chef is not much older than he is and he's taught William to cook duck in orange sauce. 'But you should see the amount of food that gets wasted, Granny. If no-one turns up to eat it, they just throw it away. Marion thinks it's dreadful when there are so many hungry people about.'

'Marion?'

'She's at college with me. She's got a holiday job being a waitress at Dominics.'

Marion. I'm fairly sure that's not the name of the wretched girl who stood him up. The one he took all that trouble to cook lunch for.

'Is Marion nice? Do you like her?'

'She's O.K. Her parents are nice. They're very friendly and they don't fuss. Sometimes I go to her house before work. And her Mum makes us a proper tea with sandwiches and cake. They've got a Broads yacht. Marion's dad says he'll take me sailing some time.'

'They sound a happy family.'

'Well, they aren't *divorced* are they.' William's voice is full of bitterness and resignation. I think, as I often do, how wrong it was of Alice to foist Ralph on her children, and I believe I am right about William turning up here because he's had a row with his stepfather. Cautiously, I ask. 'How are things at home?'

William doesn't answer straight away. Although he keeps a tight hold on himself, I can tell he is seething with anger.

'Difficult,' he says.

'I'm sorry.' I put a hand out to my grandson's jeans-clad knee. 'You know there's always room for you here, don't you darling.'

'Thanks Granny.'

Suddenly I feel very tired. Alice and Ann are sorting things out in the kitchen, so I ask William to help me upstairs. He takes my arm and as we climb the stairs I tell him I'm so sorry

174

about Emily. I didn't realise his mother hadn't told him. 'But you know it was so sad to see her just dragging herself about. She had a good life. And it's a wonderful thing, to be able to give an animal a quick and painless end. Animals are luckier than we are.'

William doesn't respond. I ask him to run the bath for me while I go into my bedroom to take off my skirt. I've just got my dressing gown on and managed to find my shower cap when William calls, 'the bath's full Granny,' so I come out of my bedroom, and as I walk along the landing, I hear Alice talking on the phone. Her voice sounds weary and cross. 'Yes, Ralph. William *is* here. Of *course* he's perfectly all right. I'm sorry if you didn't know where he was. I'd no idea he was coming myself, until he arrived. We're both rather upset. I was going to tell you when I got home: we've had Emily put to sleep.'

When I'm in the bath, I find I've forgotten the cotton wool I use for cleaning my face. I call to William, who is still hanging about on the landing and ask him to fetch it for me. 'It's in the drawer beside my bed.' He's quite a long time, but eventually he opens the door wide enough to put the roll of cotton wool on the chair that always stands there. 'Thank you William,' I call. 'You're a dear boy.'

Something wakes me. It's very dark. I fumble for the light switch. Finally my fingers brush against it. The comforting light shows me my familiar bedroom, and when I find my spectacles, I see that it's only three o'clock. Far too wide awake, I find I cannot help thinking about Emily passing so easily into that final sleep.

My hand moves, as if commanded, to the chest beside my bed. I slide open the top drawer, and take out the euthanasia book. At first, my mind does not process the meaning of the black printed words on the white page, but after a while, a particular paragraph leaps out at me:

'I do not believe we should strive to keep a human being alive against his own will, when he has lost all dignity, and

175

all meaning to the word "life" is gone. We would not force our pet dog to endure such an unbearable existence.'

Precisely. But it doesn't do to keep reading about death. I won't any more. It gives me a funny feeling. I just wish I could stop *thinking* about it: about the slow decline into – what?

It's still very dark outside. Everything seems worse at night. My bladder is uncomfortable. I'll certainly not be able to get back to sleep unless I relieve it. I swing my legs out of bed, slip my feet into my slippers which Ann has kindly placed within easy reach of the bed. I try very hard to open the door quietly. I get safely along to the bathroom but somehow I manage to knock over the chair just behind the door. I hope I haven't woken them all, but as I come out of the bathroom, I see that the other bedroom doors are open. William, looking tousled and sleepy, is on the landing, 'I thought I heard a crash,' he says.

'Oh dear, I'm so sorry to wake you all up,' I say as William comes into the bathroom, picks up the chair and puts it back where it belongs. Alice puts her arm round me and asks if I'm O.K.

Ann is buttoning her blue dressing gown. 'Don't worry,' she says. 'You go back to bed, dearie, I'll see to your mother.' And she takes over from Alice and guides me to my bedroom. I do feel a little shaky. She settles me into bed, and then she picks up the euthanasia book, which is lying face down on the chest of drawers where I left it. Her eyes scan the page, but she doesn't comment.

'I know it's gloomy reading,' I say. 'But when I woke up, I couldn't stop thinking about Emily. I'm very frightened of having another heart attack and being carted off to hospital. I'd rather anything than that.'

'Mrs Bunting felt just the same.'

'My family say they won't let it happen. But I'm not sure I can trust them.'

'Everyone wants to do the best for their loved ones,' she says, closing the book, and putting it down. 'Now Mrs Maddison, dear, don't you think you should be getting back to sleep and not worrying yourself silly.'

176

'I'll try,' I say. 'But I want you to promise me something, Ann.'

Ann sits down on the side of the bed, leans forward, and takes my hand gently in hers. I look through the lens of her glasses at her pale eyes, and I say, as steadily as possible, 'I want you to promise me you won't let them put me back in hospital.'

Alice

William is being unusually truculent and uncooperative. He is quite rude to me when I tell him he ought to have let Ralph know he was coming here, and he pulls a face of total disbelief when I say, 'Ralph was worried: he was afraid something might have happened to you.' And now William is making a fuss about going home. He says he's come all this way to see his grandmother and why can't we stay on for a few days. Unfortunately, he hasn't taken to Ann Lister. 'We could send the grey woman away,' he says. 'I'll help you look after Granny.'

Ann *was* rather tactless when William arrived. I know he looked scruffy, but it was pretty dim of the woman to mistake him for a tramp or a New-Age traveller. And it didn't help William's view of her that Ann had to be the person who told him about Emily. I should have told him myself. But I'd planned to do it in person, when I got home.

I do wonder why William suddenly took it into his head to come here? He was probably bored. He's made a point of telling me, frequently, that *all* his friends are away on holiday. Mother thinks he's had a row with Ralph. Mother, of course, has been trying to persuade us to stay on. 'I'm sure Ann Lister won't mind going home for a few days,' she says.

In the end I have to be quite firm with William and Mother. I tell Mother that Mrs Lister has been engaged to come and look after her and we can't just tell the poor woman she's no longer wanted. She might be annoyed and not come back again, and then where would we be? I tell William that there are things I need to do at home. I confess that it's quite hard work looking after his grandmother. And I could do with a break.

After breakfast, I ask him to help me stack up the car and while we're doing that, William suddenly says, 'Do you believe in euthanasia, Mum?'

'*Voluntary* euthanasia. Yes I do. But it's illegal in this country.'

'Do you really think humans should be killed when they're past it?'

'I think we would all wish for a peaceful and painless end. That's what I was able to give Emily.'

'But do you have to have a lethal injection to give you a peaceful death? Can't a natural death be peaceful?'

'Of course, but there's no guarantee.'

I think of my mother's fear of slipping into senility. The only guarantee of avoiding that is to go ahead of time.

William puts Emily's empty basket into the back of the car. 'Mum, do you want Granny to die?'

I am shocked at the baldness of his question, the measured evenness of his tone. 'Of course not William. I love your grandmother. But she is very afraid of losing her senses, of losing bodily control, of suffering pain. I would like to be able to save her from the distress and the indignity of that.'

By the time we've stacked the car and William has helped Mother organise her diary and select programmes worth watching from the current issue of the *TV Times*, it's nearly lunchtime. Ann says we must have something to eat before driving all that way, so she makes a ham salad and we all sit down together to eat it. Mother is looking gloomy and picking at her food, but Ann says quietly to me in the kitchen, 'You mustn't worry, dear. She'll be fine when you've gone. Your mother and I get on ever so well.'

William is not very good company. He falls asleep as soon as we get through the Dartford tunnel. Within minutes of our arrival home, he shoots off. He says he's going to see a friend and he might not be back for supper. He must be missing Emily. He adored Emily and from the time when he was a small boy and she a tiny puppy, they were companions. That could be another reason why he didn't want to come home.

179

Because there will be no old yellow dog lying in her basket in the kitchen, hauling herself out of it to hobble after us. I understand how William feels. I would not have believed I could grieve so deeply for a dog. I must have dreamed about her every night since she died.

The first thing I do, on reclaiming my house, is remove all traces of Emily: her basket, her feeding dish, her collar and lead, the old shoe she used to carry around with her, her brush and comb, still full of stiff yellow hairs. I put them all out with the dustbins, which are full of empty wine bottles.

The house is tidier than it usually is when I've been away. For once, Ralph has eaten most of the food I left him. There is only one yoghurt left in the fridge along with half a carton of orange juice, a few dingy-looking tomatoes, a fresh lettuce and half a pound of a brand of low-fat spread I never buy. The honey jar is empty and he's even washed it out. Two unattractive ferns sit complacently on the sideboard. My house feels different: antagonistic, as if it is punishing me for leaving it.

In the bedroom, I switch on the clock radio to listen to *Kaleidoscope*. I take my jeans and my one dress out of my case and hang them in the wardrobe. A pair of Ralph's cotton trousers hangs over the back of a chair along with one of his ties which, as usual, he's pulled over his head without untying. I take my nightie out and put it on my pillow. Ralph's pyjamas lie, neatly folded, beneath his. I pick up the edge of the duvet to give it a shake, and as I do so, a balled-up something pops out of the end. I kneel down to pick it up and, when I straighten it out, I see that it is a small, nylon foot sock. The sort of thing a woman wears inside summer shoes. Disbelief. Shock. Still as stone, in the middle of my bedroom, I hold in the fingers of one hand a garment belonging to another woman: the sort of garment I would never possess. I start to shake: a whole-body kind of shaking. This is what an ague is, I think. The shaking that starts inside. Right in the very kernel of you and spreads outwards in an uncontrollable fluttering. This is why my house feels alien. This other presence; this other female presence is stamped upon it. Has washed up a honey jar, bought half a pound of Clover Light. Left a foot sock in my bed. The whole of my being is focused on the spin-off from that scrap of nylon. I straighten it, stretch it between my fingers, sniff it and retch. I drop it, for it scorches my fingers. In my mind sprout obscene visions of Ralph and Judith Page – *it must be Judith Page* – coming together in my bed. Doing what Ralph and I do together – so intimate, so private, so central to our relationship. I gave him the deepest and most secret part of myself. And I thought he gave me an equal part of himself. I used never to doubt the power of his feeling for me. Whether that feeling was love, suddenly, now, I question.

Love – real love – *mutual selfless love* – is each of you caring enough about the other to value their well-being more highly than your own. Doing nothing to mortally wound that other person. Which is not the same thing as rushing about trying to please people, so they won't be nasty to you. The thing I spend so much time fruitlessly doing. Perhaps neither I nor Ralph is capable of mature, mutual love?

After weeks of uneasy, untested suspicions, I am faced with the incontrovertible evidence of Ralph's infidelity. I now know that suspecting your husband of having an affair is not the same as *knowing* it. I am overwhelmed by a sense of betrayal. I feel violated. I am desolate: shocked that he could rate our bond so lightly, that he would reveal himself in all his intimate nakedness to another woman. It calls into question the authenticity of his declared love for me: neither long-lasting enough nor of sufficient power to keep faith. Perhaps – and I am filled with sadness – perhaps his so-called love was always a sham? How long has it been going on? When did Ralph commission Judith Page to design furniture? Around the time Mother had her heart attack, so it must have been April. It is now the beginning of September. I should have had it out with Ralph ages ago. Now everything is ruined. Our so-called commitment to each other shot to pieces.

I fling away the duvet and examine the bottom sheet. There is a whitish stain in the centre. I bend close. Do I detect a faintly sweet, musky female odour?

I comb the house for traces of this woman who has been in my home with my husband. I look under the bed, for tissues, for handkerchiefs, for jewellery, for clothing: search the bathroom for her deodorant, her moisturiser. Pacing distractedly

181

from room to room, fingers fumbling, heart thumping, I throw cushions off the sofa, check the kitchen for more alien food. There is a limpness in my armpits and at the joints of my wrists and my knees, as if a line maintaining the framework of my body has gone slack. I find no more evidence of Judith Page. But now, the washed-out honey jar, the low-fat spread in the fridge and the ugly plants on the sideboard have a horrible significance. In the end I have to stop. I ease the cork from the opened bottle of red wine on the sideboard, and pour a glass full. The trembling eases. I ache all through my body. Ralph cares too little for me to resist temptation. He has betrayed me. Even as I experience this sense of loss, I am also faced by a blinding comprehension of the unknowableness of another human being. Six months ago, if anyone had asked me if Ralph could be unfaithful, I would have said no. The shock of grasping, in one mind-blowing moment that I have been wrong about him is almost the worst thing about it. Like a Christian suddenly losing his faith. Like being told there is no Father Christmas when you are five. I have been wrong about Ralph: certainty, solid as a tumour, grows inside me. The signs have all been there: the physical withdrawal, the continual fault-finding, the complaints that if I put my mother, my children before him, I must take the consequences. Guilt. Justification.

I will have to confront him now.

Or perhaps I'll just go? Leave a note. Go where? Back to Mother? For whom I have sacrificed my marriage? If Mother had died when she had her heart attack, this might never have happened.

I am filled with sudden rage towards my frail, invincible mother, who is so afraid of senility, of a lingering death. I've walked along pavements holding her scrawny arm and watched a double-decker thundering towards us. It would only take a split second to release her arm, give her a gentle shove, and do both of us a favour. Jonquil's elderly parents died instantly in a car crash. She says herself what a blessing it was that they went together and were saved the infirmity of extreme old age. An accident would be the kindest thing. *Any* kind of accident.

I drink more wine. My head throbs. What do I do about

182

William? I can't run away and leave William with Ralph. I'll have to have it out with Ralph. He's not going to get away with this. I'll *make* him tell me.

I cannot bear to suffer so. I've always been a reasonably confident, self-assured person. I am frightened of snakes, heights and tidal waves, but not of the dark or of being alone. I get on fine with most people. I'm bright enough to hold my own with people cleverer than me. Once I shed what mother called my 'puppy fat', when I was about sixteen, I discovered I was attractive to men.

Now, in one fell swoop, all this, this sense of worth, is torn from me. My belief in myself, built over the years, stripped away, like bark from a tree, exposing the naked stem to the wind and the rain and to animals with claws.

I tip the dregs of Ralph's red wine into my glass and knock it back. In my unsteady hand the glass clinks against my front teeth.

I don't know what time it is when I hear Ralph's key in the latch. I remain sitting at the kitchen table. I hear him walk along the hall. There is the familiar sound of him putting down his briefcase. He comes into the kitchen. I don't look up. The feel of his arm laid round my shoulders turns me cold. I brace myself against his hand as it moves down the back of my head, slipping down my hair and resting in the nape of my neck. 'I'm sorry about Emily,' he says. 'The poor old dog.'

I cannot control the shudder that jars my whole body, as he kisses the top of my head. He picks up the empty wine bottle and takes it over to the sink. 'I'll open another,' he says, and goes off to fetch a bottle of wine from the cellar. I let him open the bottle and pour us both a glass and then I take from my pocket Judith Page's revolting foot sock. I push it under his nose.

'What have you got there?'

'What do you think it is?' I drop it onto the table. He picks it up and says, 'I've no idea.'

'It was in our *bed*, Ralph.' I am watching him very carefully. He is looking down at the object in his hand. His face is expressionless. 'You're having an affair, aren't you?' I am on fire.

183

'No,' he says. 'I am *not* having an affair.'

'I don't believe you. Look at me Ralph.' I force him to lift his head and look me in the eye. He's trying hard. His eyes remain almost expressionless, but I *know* he is lying. I hold him with my eyes. 'You owe me the truth.'

And now, his eyes slither away from mine. 'All right. Yes,' he says quietly.

I cannot stop myself. I jerk to my feet. The chair falls back. I come at Ralph with both fists, beating into his chest. He fends me off, gripping my wrists. 'How *could* you, Ralph. How *could* you do this to me?'

'You left me alone. What did you expect might happen?'

'It's that design person isn't it? That Judith Page.'

He doesn't answer.

'I hate you, I hate you,' I'm yelling like a child.

'You've never been hurt before. Now you know what it's like.'

'You're glad!'

'You don't really care for me.' His voice is cold and hard. 'It's just a blow to your pride.'

'I've always cared for you Ralph. But you never cared for me because the only person *you* care about is yourself. You're so stuffed full of your own feelings, your own desires, your own needs you've got room for nothing else.'

'I've done everything for you. But it's been one-way traffic. I've never come first with you, have I Alice? You've always let me down. You and your bloody family.'

'Oh God Ralph no-one can come first all the time. We all have different needs at different times – love in different ways. You don't understand. It's like I have this basket of fruit and I give you the big shiny red apple but it's not enough – you want the orange and the banana and the pineapple and the strawberry as well.'

'I don't know what you're on about.'

'I'm telling you about love – all kinds of love. You can only tell me about your need to come first. But you didn't put *me* first did you? You're the one whose always on about pair bonding. You're the one who's broken that trust.'

'I don't love her,' he says. 'I love you.'

'You can't. You don't.'

184

'I'm sorry,' he says. 'It's over really. I'll finish it.'

'Do you expect me to believe that?'

'Alice. You're the love of my life, Alice. Please forgive me.'

'You *bastard*!' I throw my wine at him. Red dribbles down his face.

There is a sudden clatter. I whip round. William is standing at the open door. I catch a glimpse of his horrified eyes and then he bends to pick something up from the floor and dis-appears.

28 October 1996

William watched the man with the bald head, Granny's solicitor, put down his empty glass, shake David by the hand and thread his way through the press of people to the door.

William stared at Rosamund and he knew they were both trying to imagine what it might mean if their mother were to inherit Hunter's Moon.

'I loved staying at Hunter's Moon with Granny and Grandpa, but I've got so accustomed to our cousins being there I've almost forgotten what it used to be like,' said Rosamund. 'Mum loves the place and it would be somewhere for her to go.'

'What, and let Ralph have *our* house?' said William. 'I don't want to live in Kent. I want to stay at home.'

'Rosamund!' Their mother was battling towards them. 'Come and help make coffee.'

'O.K.' Rosamund shrugged her shoulders at William and reluctantly followed their mother in the direction of the kitchen.

William poured himself some more whisky. His life was being turned upside down and none of it was his doing. Now Rosamund had disappeared, there was no-one to talk to. Observing June and Arthur moving relentlessly towards him, he hurriedly tipped more whisky into his glass and shot into the downstairs cloakroom. The familiar sight and smell of his grandmother's anoraks and mackintoshes and rubber boots made him feel odd. He gulped whisky, stood his glass on the shelf above the washbasin, pissed into the toilet, flushed it, closed the lid and sat down. If only Marion were here.

Marion became his friend the night he found out about Catherine. He was walking home early, after a slow evening at Dominics. Marion was on the opposite side of the road with a group of people from college. She called to him, came over and persuaded him to join them. 'There's a band at the Golden Star,' she said. He remembered feeling very large and clumsy striding along beside her, taking one step to her two. As they approached the Golden Star, they saw the coloured lights flashing and heard the music pounding out of the sound system. They went inside, swallowed by the noise, dizzied by the lights. Marion said, 'Will you get the drinks – here's some dosh,' and it crossed his mind that, like Tim, she'd only asked him to come because he looked old enough to buy alcohol. But when he returned from the bar with a lager for himself and a rum and coke for her, she stayed by his side. They shouted at each other above the noise and agreed that the summer holidays were often a let-down. They watched the band for a while and then, tired of trying to make themselves heard, they went outside to the scruffy piece of ground behind the pub. There were several figures standing around on the thin grass under the dark trees, smoking. He could smell that unmistakeable sweetish smell.

Catherine was there. William heard her laugh, saw her hair gleaming in the darkness. Saw her kissing Tim, her bare arms wrapped round Tim's neck. Last time William was here, those arms were twined round his own neck. William's face caught fire. For a moment he couldn't move.

'I've got to go.' He blundered towards the street.

'Wait.' Marion was following.

He was out in the street, raging inside. Marion trotting behind. 'Come and have a coffee.' He hardly heard her but found himself walking through the door of Pizza Express, and sitting down at a small table opposite Marion. Marion ordered two cappuccinos. 'I'd no idea *they'd* be there,' she said. 'And I didn't realise you were keen on Catherine.'

'I thought *you* were keen on Tim. You always go around with him.'

'Tim's good fun, but you can't trust him. You must know that.'

'Catherine's your friend.'

187

'Cathy doesn't live in this world. She just goes along with anything, not thinking. But she doesn't mean any harm.'

Tim does, thought William. *Why did Catherine say she'd love to come to lunch and then just not turn up?* William wanted to punch Tim hard right in his stupid mouth.

After a while, Marion said, 'Those two aren't worth worrying about you know. You shouldn't get upset over people like Tim and Catherine.' Her brown eyes looked into his, serious and steady, and her small hand came out and lightly brushed the back of his.

William stared down at his grandmother's narrow red rubber boots and up at her dark blue anorak with its hanging hood. He knew Granny had not been ready to die. He'd discussed it with Marion. He wished Marion was here.

Someone rapped on the cloakroom door.

William picked up his glass of whisky, unbolted the door, pushed it open and was elbowed out of the way by a burly old codger clutching his fly.

William stood unsteadily in the hall. He looked round, searching for a fresh retreat. Then, fixing his eyes on their target, he made for the door, dodged out of the room and climbed the stairs.

William entered his grandmother's bedroom and closed the door. It was very still and quiet. It felt as if Granny was not far away. James inhaled a trace of her left-over scent, like stale flowers.

Muffled sounds floated up the stairs, blocked by the closed door: the hum of conversation, rising in pitch, laughter. It sounded like an ordinary party. He felt very remote from all that, as if he was existing in a different time-span, miles away. He looked around him. It was just the same, except Granny's old person's underclothes and her jumpers and scarves and woolly hats, which were usually spilling out of the half-open drawers of the two chests, had been tidied away. The photographs of the family, the books and magazines still stood around on the small tables. The dressing table still held her bottles and jars and tubes of make-up, but the spilled pink powder had been dusted away. The little china ornaments and

188

the silver-topped glass jars were grouped, as usual, in front of the small swing mirror.

The single bed in the middle of the room was made up as if his grandmother would be sleeping in it. Clean white pillow cases on the three pillows, the blue blankets folded down beneath the white top sheet. On top of the bedside cabinet stood the the small kettle Granny used for making her early morning tea. Beside the kettle, Granny's medicines were ranged in a neat row. He examined the bottles one by one. They all contained small white pills. He paused over the one labelled 'for animal use only'.

Furtively, he opened the top drawer of the cabinet. Last time he'd opened that drawer it was to look for a roll of cotton wool to take to his grandmother in the bathroom. His mouth, tingling from the taste of the whisky, went dry.

The book had been hidden beneath the cotton wool.

He picked up the roll of cotton wool and his fingers brushed against the book's hard cover. He put down the cotton wool and, once again, he took in his hand, *Euthanasia – the Gentle Ending*. With a wave of nausea, he opened it and read once more: 'If the patient has requested it, I believe it is our solemn duty to help him towards an easy death.' And then, his eyes racing down the page: 'Death opens unknown doors. It is most good to die.' Now he felt dizzy. He snapped the book shut, returned it to the drawer, closed the drawer and went over to the window. William could not imagine how it could ever be good to die. He stared out of the window. Cars were parked all the way down the crescent. The elderly Mercedes and middle-aged BMWs, the green Jaguar and the ancient Rolls. As he watched, the vicar came out of the house accompanied by his mother. They shook hands and the vicar, who was wearing an ordinary suit with his white dog-collar, got into a battered Volvo estate and drove away. William's mother waved and then stood for a while staring after the departing car. When she turned round William could see a sad, lost expression on her face, as if she didn't know where she was. She waited a moment or two before walking up the gravel path, slowly, as if she was very tired. It felt like he was spying. He thought of all the things you do when you believe no-one is watching. You don't need to hide how you feel, for one thing. It's like being mentally naked. As she reached the front door; he saw her cover her face with her hands as if she could not bear to see any more. Then, she dropped her hands, straightened her spine, shook back her hair and her lips moved as if she was saying something important. He could not tell if she was speaking out loud, for the window was closed, but he felt sure she would not have wished anyone to hear.

This is my mother, he thought. Just because she's my mother doesn't stop me thinking terrible things about her.

William was so absorbed in watching his mother, the sudden small sound took him by surprise. He jumped nervously and whirled round. 'Granny?' he gasped, feeling her presence so strongly. The black cat, Pinky, had materialised from somewhere. It stood watching William with glass-green eyes, tail held high, straight as a flag-pole, trembling at the tip.

'Hullo Pinky,' His voice sounded strange.

The cat stared disdainfully at him, with all the power of a panther. Then, it jumped onto his grandmother's bed, sinuous and sleek, and daintily placing its paws, trod the topmost pillow before slowly dropping into a graceful curve, its alien eyes still fixed upon William.

William returned the feral glare. '*You* know what happened don't you,' he burst out, making a wild grab for Pinky. '*Tell* me what happened.'

Pinky hissed and shot out his claws, dragging them down the length of William's right hand. Beads of blood welled up and dripped on to the clean white sheet. The sickness in William's stomach swelled. His head spun. Suddenly, the door opened and Mrs Curtis appeared. 'Just looking for Pinky. My word William what's happened to your hand? Was that you, you wicked cat? We'd better run that hand under the tap and I'll see if I can find some TCP.'

William got to his feet and abruptly had to sit down again on the bed. Mrs Curtis took hold of his hand and examined it. 'That *does* look nasty, and you've gone ever so pale William. Best stay sitting down and I'll fetch a bowl of water.' She went off and came back with a small bowl of water and a bottle of TCP.

'Put your hand right in while I bathe it for you. I'm afraid

Pinky's not been himself since your Gran went. Hardly moves out of her bedroom. I've been coming in to feed him. I keep an eye on the little chap for her sake, and he's happy here, so I don't like to take him home with me. Your grandmother doted on that cat. She was such a lovely lady. I'll really miss her.' Mrs Curtis took William's hand out of the bowl and blotted it dry with a towel. There were tears running down her face. 'And it was so sudden. I never thought she'd go, just like that.'

William tried to halt the whirling in his head in order to focus his eyes on Mrs Curtis's round pink face and her orange hair which was escaping from it's knot on the back of her head and floating round her face in wisps. 'I don't know what happened,' he said, with difficulty, for his tongue had grown too large for his mouth. 'I don't know how Granny died.'

'They *said* she died in her sleep. They *said* it was very peaceful.' Mrs Curtis dropped William's hand and blew her nose. 'I came in as usual, the morning after she went. I wanted to take a last look, so I crept quietly up here, on my own, just to say goodbye. She was lying in the bed in her pink nightie. Her face was very white, of course – you'd expect that – but there were some funny marks near her eyes. If you want to know what I think, I think she didn't look peaceful at all.'

The whirling inside William's head speeded up, like an out of control merry-go-round, and the contents of his stomach started to rise, like the big dipper. He made a desperate lunge for the bathroom.

September 1996

Hilda

I feel very sad as I watch Alice and darling William drive away. They were here for such a short time and I wonder when I shall see them again. And what about dearest Rosamund? Alice says she is still in Turkey but she should be back in a couple of weeks. I hope she will be allowed to come and stay with me before she returns to Edinburgh. But my daughter is terribly possessive over her children. For instance, I know William didn't want to go home at all, but Alice insisted.

Ann is very kind: she understands. 'You've a lovely family, Mrs Maddison dear. Don't fret. They'll soon be here again.' She makes a pot of tea and we sit down and have a nice chat. She says I'm lucky to have a good daughter and what a helpful lad William is. Her childless state has always been a great sadness to her, and you feel it just as much when you get older.

When I wake from my rest, I find Ann in the kitchen, making quite a pleasant-looking fish pie for our supper. It *is* rather nice to have someone doing the cooking. I've never been keen on the domestic side. Fortunately Clive enjoyed plain food, so I seldom had to bother with puddings or exotic sauces. He was very fond of fish. I can see him so clearly, standing in the porch at Hunter's Moon, just before driving to the office. He'd say something like, 'Dover sole would be nice for supper tonight dear,' as he kissed me goodbye. I always had the table laid, so when he got home in the evening, it looked as if dinner was nearly ready. We'd sit down for a quiet drink, gin for me, whisky for him. Clive was of the generation

192

that didn't help in the kitchen, unlike the new generation of young men, or so I'm led to believe. But he was good at practical things like timing the vegetables. I was always so delighted when he got home, I'd sometimes forget I was supposed to be cooking. He'd look at his watch and say, 'I think it's about time you put the sprouts on, dear,' or, 'The potatoes are almost ready to be mashed'. Darling Clive: I do miss him.

I watch Ann sliding the fish pie into the oven and I tell her my husband used to be very fond of fish. While it's cooking, we each have a large gin and I begin to feel more cheerful.

After supper, since Alice hasn't called to say she and William are home, I telephone her myself. The phone rings for a long time and just as I'm beginning to worry, the receiver at the other end is picked up and William says hello. I tell him I'm only ringing to check he and his mother got home safely. William says they're all right. He's out of breath, and his voice does not have its usual even-tempered tone. I ask him if he's *sure* he's all right and he insists he's fine but he had to run for the phone.

I ask to speak to his mother, but he says, in a strange voice, that she's a bit busy at the moment. I'm just beginning to feel that things are actually *not* all right, when suddenly, in the background, I hear Alice and then Ralph. I can't make out what either of them are saying, but both their voices are raised and angry.

'What's going on there, William?'

'I don't know, Granny. I don't know what's going on. I'll ask Mum to telephone. Goodbye Granny.'

Ann comes in as I'm putting down the receiver. 'Is something wrong, Mrs Maddison? You look worried.'

'I'm not sure Ann. I'm really not sure. But it sounds as if my daughter and son-in-law are having an almighty row.'

Ann says she's sorry to hear that but we all have our ups and downs don't we. I explain about Alice's two marriages and I tell Ann exactly how I feel about Ralph.

Although I don't approve of divorce, I wonder if Alice might be about to come to her senses. The silly girl doesn't seem to be much good at choosing husbands, and it might be best for everyone if Alice finishes with Ralph. I hope she's all right. I'd like to telephone again, just to hear her voice. But

Ann says I shouldn't upset myself and why not wait until morning.

I must speak to someone, so I telephone my son. Jonquil answers. She says David is away for the night. Her voice is cool: I know she resented me coming home when I had that tummy upset. I try to think of a way to talk about Alice without making it seem that is my only reason for calling. I ask after the girls and Jonquil says they're all very busy getting things ready for going back to school and Helen has grown out of her winter uniform, and blazers are incredibly expensive. Then, luckily, she asks if Mrs Lister is there. I tell her Ann arrived yesterday and Alice and William drove back to Norwich after lunch today. Jonquil says, 'I didn't know William had been with you'. I explain that William turned up unexpectedly and I rather think he'd had a row with Ralph. 'Actually, Jonquil,' I say, 'I'm worried about the situation there. When I telephoned this evening, I didn't speak to Alice. William said she was busy. He sounded very upset. I think Alice and Ralph were having words. Ralph was shouting. I don't know, Jonquil. Do you think Ralph might harm Alice? Maybe she and William should come back here.'

There is a silence at the other end of the phone and then Jonquil says, 'Mother you mustn't interfere between married people. I know you've never got on with Ralph, but Alice chose him and I'm sure she's perfectly capable of sorting out any little problems. Why don't you ask Mrs Lister to run you a nice hot bath, and then she can make you a cup of Horlicks to drink in bed.'

After I've put down the receiver, Ann fetches the whisky and pours one for me and one for her.

In the morning, Alice telephones. She says she's sorry she wasn't able to speak to me yesterday; she was so tired she went to bed really early. I can tell from her voice, things are very wrong, but she's obviously not going to talk about it. I mention Ralph and she says Ralph has gone away on business. My heart leaps a little. Perhaps Ralph has left her. I tell Alice how lovely it was to see her and William. 'Come back again soon,' I say.

When I go into the kitchen to give Pinky his breakfast saucer of bread and milk, Mrs Curtis is washing up. She grunts a reply to my usual 'Good morning', and bangs the saucepans about in the sink. I say, 'Steady on', and ask her if she's feeling all right. 'If you really want to know, Mrs Maddison, I've enough to do cleaning the house, without washing up supper dishes. And I think your nurse has a lot of cheek – complaining. It wasn't me caught the bottom of the saucepan.'

Poor Mrs Curtis. I try to soothe her. Her nose is out of joint on account of Ann Lister. Mrs Curtis has been coming to me ever since I moved here, and I'm really very fond of her. I'll speak to Ann. She must be more tactful.

After breakfast, Ann says she thinks a little outing might stop me worrying about my family. She says she's very fond of picnics and why don't we go and have a look at the sea. When I ask her how we'll get there, she says, 'I've had a driving license for twenty-five years, Mrs Maddison, I'm sure I can handle your Rover. It will do the motor good to have a bit of a run. So long as it's insured for me to drive.'

I imagine it is. Rosamund drove us around while she was staying here. So I tell Ann it's an excellent idea and I'd love to see the sea.

Ann disappears into the kitchen: I hear her telling Mrs Curtis she's going to pack up a picnic and can Mrs Curtis lay her hands on a thermos. After a while Mrs Curtis comes out of the kitchen, looking displeased. I explain that Ann and I are going out for a little trip, and I'd be very grateful if she would feed Pinky for me before she leaves. I tell her I know I can rely on her to see Pinky is all right. That brings a smile to her face. She says she'll just pop up and make my bed. It's about time the sheets were changed, and she knows exactly how I like it done. Then, while Ann is organising the food in the kitchen, Mrs Curtis helps me find my light anorak, my Liberty silk scarf, because it's bound to be windy by the sea and I do so hate my hair blowing about, and my lace-up shoes.

I tell Ann *I* will back the Rover out of the garage, since it's rather a tricky manoeuvre. She nods her head. It's a pleasure to sit behind the wheel of my car again. I turn the key and the engine starts sweetly. Reverse has always been stiff, but I manage it, and then it's no trouble at all to back gently out and turn into the crescent. I shall definitely have another go

195

at getting my licence renewed. Dr Robson *must* realise I'm perfectly safe on the road. It's nearly six months since my heart trouble; and no problems since then.

'I've had a driving licence since I was seventeen,' I tell Ann, as I hand over the wheel.

When we drive off, I realise Ann's gear change could do with improving, but I say nothing.

I've always been very fond of Folkestone. Ann parks the car and we get out and walk along the Leas. I'd forgotten how refreshing a sea breeze can be. I breathe it deep into my lungs. It's a beautiful day. I am surrounded by blue: blue sky, almost perfectly clear today and down below the darker blue sea. Blue is my favourite colour. There are blue delphiniums growing in the ornamental flower beds.

Ann takes my arm, which makes me feel quite safe. I can look around without the fear of tripping. We walk on the grass, past the Leas Cliff Hall, where there used to be concerts and dances in my youth, and the bandstand where, as I tell Ann, the Band of the Royal Marines played after the war. She says she loves a brass band. Standing next to each other, the huge old hotels, the Metropole and the Grand, look rundown and forlorn: lifeless ghosts. In their heyday, before the war, I tell Ann, they were palaces, full of light and colour, music and dancing: bursting with people enjoying themselves. It looks as if the bulk of them have been turned into flats now. We agree that modern package holidays to Spain have put paid to our seaside hotels. Ann says she thinks it's a great shame English people don't have holidays in their own country; there's so much to see here. Queueing for hours in crowded airports in order to lie about on a hot beach getting sunstroke and eating indigestible foreign food isn't her idea of having a good time.

Ann has brought our picnic along and we find a shelter in which to sit and eat it. We sit side by side on a wooden seat, protected from the wind. I have to say, it's not quite what I'm used to, but it makes a change. Unfortunately, there seem to be several elderly people doing exactly the same thing. They plant themselves in deckchairs or on wooden seats, and they get out their sandwiches and their thermoses and they turn up their old faces and stretch out their bare white legs to the sun.

196

No doubt, like me, they are remembering more vital times of their lives. But they seem relaxed, contented.

We gaze out at the busy shipping lanes, and a sudden haze obscures the horizon as I remember the sinister rumble of the German guns from the other side of the English channel. I tell Ann I believe one of them was called Big Bertha.

We eat the sausage rolls that Ann made this morning. Very tasty, though it's a shame she forgot the mustard. We have egg sandwiches and a piece of fruit cake. Then Ann kindly peels me an apple and pours coffee from the thermos.

The soft wind strokes my face, the sound of the sea soothes me. I close my eyes. When I open them again, Ann looks up from her magazine and says, 'You *did* have a nice little nap Mrs Maddison. I'm sure it's done you good.' She has packed our picnic things neatly back into the large striped bag. She gets to her feet and says, 'How about another stroll before we go home.'

We walk slowly along the Leas in the direction of the harbour. We decide not to take the zigzag path to the beach, but stand on the cliff looking down at the banks of grey shingle and the breaking waves. I am glad of the feel of Ann's firm hand on my arm. Heights hold a horrible fascination for me; they give me vertigo.

I doze in the car on the way home. 'It's the sea air,' says Ann. 'I feel quite tired myself.'

But when night comes, I can't fall sleep. I swallow one of my pills which doesn't work, so I take another. I worry about Alice. I've thought for some time things are not right, and now I know it. I love my Alice: I want her to be happy. If she and Ralph separate, where will she go? What will she do? I wonder, have I been quite fair to my daughter? I know how strongly she feels about Hunter's Moon. I could change my will and leave our family home to Alice. I'd have to put things right with David. He and Jonquil wouldn't like it, but they *have* assumed rather a lot.

I shall ask Alan Sheppard to come and see me. As well as being our family solicitor, Alan is a very old friend and he's always given me good advice. There are several things that need tidying up in connection with my affairs. I definitely want to leave Mrs Curtis a small legacy and I still haven't decided exactly how to sort out my jewellery. I'll telephone Alan in the morning. Yes: planning to do something about my worries is calming me down. Pinky's familiar weight nudges my feet. A night breeze sways my bedroom curtains. I close my eyes and sink my head into the soft pillow. Sleep welcomes me.

Alan says he'd be very pleased to come and talk to me about my Will, so I ask him to lunch on Thursday. Ann can make us a quiche.

I suppose I should brave up and do what they call 'my autumn spring cleaning', so when I'm gone, there won't be an awful muddle for the children to deal with. Happily, Rosamund and Ann between them have organised most of my clothes. I've already given a great many away – to Mrs Curtis and to the church jumble sale. I'm afraid there are masses of papers that need sorting out: bank statements, share certificates, receipts, but David will have to give me a hand with those. It's too tiring a job to manage on my own. I shall write Alice a note and ask her to take care of my precious letters. I cannot bear to destroy them, but I wouldn't want just anyone reading my Clive's letters.

While Ann is in the kitchen organising our supper, I get out my jewel case, and the list I made earlier in the year. I lay my best pieces of jewellery on my dressing table. I hardly have occasion to put them on now. Most days, simply out of habit, I wear my gold long-guard chain, doubled round my neck, and in my ears, the pearl stud earrings. Now, I pick up my engagement ring, and ease it carefully over the enlarged knuckle of the third finger of my left hand, next to my wedding ring. I was so proud to wear Clive's ring. He chose it for me and slipped it on my finger the first time himself. It is an oval ruby, of a very beautiful translucent rose, in a gold setting encircled by tiny diamonds. My Alice shall have my engagement ring. With a bit of an effort I just manage to place my sapphire eternity ring next to it. Clive presented me with me this ring when David was born. It is fitting that Jonquil should inherit it, and she does have very pretty hands.

The first time I wore my beautiful pearl choker was on my

fiftieth birthday, when Clive laid it gently round my neck. The last time I wore it was at my seventy-sixth birthday party. I do love it. I take the lustrous thing in my knobbly old fingers, lift it to my neck and fasten its diamond clasp. I stare at myself in the mirror. The four rows of pearls glow with an inner life. They are kind to my shrivelled throat. Alice would never wear this; it's just not her style. Jonquil covets it, I know. Perhaps I should leave it to Rosamund. She is my eldest granddaughter. But would she truly value it for itself and not for the huge amount of cash it could bring her? I have already noted that darling Rosamund shall have the emerald necklet and matching drop earrings, exactly right with her green eyes and fair hair. I take my pearl studs out of my ears and replace them with the emerald drops. The brilliant green looks quite well with the pearls. Louisa shall have the antique garnet brooch which belonged to my mother. I pin it to my dress. On the thin summer fabric it looks heavy and incongruous. But it's a fine piece and will suit Louisa with her milky skin and dark eyes. The gold bangles are for Helen: too gaudy now for my age-spotted arms.

I tip onto my dressing table the rest of my jewellery, the less valuable pieces. These they can divide among themselves. There are several gold chains, a topaz ring, a chased silver bangle, a thin gold locket, an enamel brooch, jade earrings, a necklace of semi-precious stones, a heap of costume jewellery, and some silvery, gilded junk bought on foreign holidays. They tantalise me with memories of the past. I sit at my dressing table and stare at myself, decked out in my jewels. I don't think I look too bad for an old girl. My face is thin but my thick white hair frames it nicely. My eyes are too deep set, but there is a good spark of life left in them. My back is straight, my chin high, my mouth firm.

There is a knock on the bedroom door. I call, 'Come in, Ann.'

'My goodness,' says Ann. 'You do look a picture! Where's the party?'

I laugh and say, 'I wish there was one: I love a party.' I can tell Ann is very impressed with my jewellery. The only thing I ever see her wearing is a rather plain silver locket. I tell her it's not easy, deciding who to leave one's precious things to.

And I'd hate to upset my family. Ann says well you can only do your best to be as fair as possible, and you certainly do have some lovely things. Since she's clearly interested, I remove each piece and show it to her. She loves my ruby engagement ring. She says her husband gave her a very pretty amethyst ring, but the stone fell out at a dance. They had it replaced, but it was never quite the same. She loves my earrings, but since her ears aren't pierced, she's never bothered much with earrings. Best of all she admires my pearl choker. 'You look just like the photos of old Queen Mary,' she says. I tell Ann I'm in a bit of a muddle about my pearl choker. 'You see, I want to leave it to someone who will really appreciate it.' Ann strokes the luminous pearls and says she's never seen anything so beautiful in her life.

Alice

I wake from a dreamless sleep and aim for the light like a diver rising to the surface. I find I am in bed in our spare room, and the awful realisation of what has happened floods over me. I might have been anaesthetised last night, I lost consciousness with such ease. Ralph is standing in front of me. I notice that his nose to mouth lines are deeply etched and his eyes seem to have moved back into his head. 'I'm going now,' he says. 'I told you last night, but I'm not sure you took it in. I have to see Herb Lurie. He's not happy with the finish on the last lot of wine tables. I'm hoping to find a craftsman out there who can put them right. If not I'll have to send him a polisher. I can't afford to replace the whole consignment.'

'You're going to New York.'

'New York and then North Carolina to see some people who may take our stuff.'

'Don't bother to come back.'

'Alice.' He puts a hand on my head. I shrink away and shut my eyes.

'Alice I'm sorry. We've too much to lose. Try to understand.'

I remain absolutely still.

'Goodbye Alice,' he says. His fingers are smoothing my hair. 'I'll phone.'

I am glad Ralph has gone.

William is back at college and some evenings he is out working at Dominics, so I have a lot of time to myself. The hours seem to dissolve, leaving no trace of things done. And yet, the inside of my head is like an overwound clock, ticking too fast. The empty house challenges me with uncompleted tasks. The washing machine waits to be emptied of its clean load; the Hoover stands lifeless in the hall; there is no milk and no butter in the fridge. The vegetable rack holds a few limp beans and flabby potatoes.

My mother knows something is wrong: she telephoned in the middle of our bust-up. When I feel strong enough to talk to her, I fob her off with excuses. But she still pursues me. Often I don't answer the phone.

William studies me earnestly and asks, 'Are you all right Mum?' I explain that Ralph and I are going through a difficult time, which of course he knows. William knows too much. I can see from his measured expression and the deliberate set of his shoulders when he comes across reminders of Ralph – Ralph's jacket slung over the back of a chair, Ralph's glossy furniture catalogue displayed on the sideboard, the peaked hat Ralph wears when he plays a rare game of golf – that William is hoping Ralph will never come back.

When he isn't washing up at Dominics in the evenings, William takes charge of our abandoned vegetables and roots about in the freezer for some kind of meat, and makes supper for us. Struggling to swallow, I watch him wolfing down a plateful and when I thank him for cooking, he says, 'I'm hungry Mum – go on, eat some, it's nice.' I am touched by his concern.

This evening, he makes a stir fry, with chicken and broccoli and peas and noodles. If I take small mouthfuls and chew properly, I can swallow. William is talking about college. He's telling me in a roundabout way he's thinking of giving up French. I summon enough energy to remark *that* would be a shame; everyone should be able to speak one foreign language, and maybe I should come and have a word with his teacher. William says there's no point me doing that, his teacher is a wally. I tell him I'd prefer to judge that for myself. William says he'd rather I didn't, and if I really want him to, he'll carry on with the French.

William is finishing up the butterscotch ice cream and I'm drinking a cup of black coffee when the phone rings. William answers it before I can stop him. 'It's for you,' he says, handing me the hand set.

'I've been trying to get through for ages.' Ralph's voice comes clearly down the line. 'Has the phone contracted a virus?'

I don't bother to reply.

'Alice are you there? Can you hear me?'

'I can hear you.'

'I thought I'd let you know the plane didn't crash. How are you?'

Flippant bastard. 'I'm fine thank you Ralph. William has just cooked a delicious supper. Don't bother to call again. I'll be watching the news.'

I replace the handset. A few minutes later it rings again. 'Don't answer it,' I say to William. It stops ringing and after a few moments, rings again. 'It might be for me.' William picks up the handset, and speaks into it. 'Hello. Yes, oh hello Granny. Are you all right?'

I signal to William that I don't wish to speak with my mother. He pulls a face at me and says, 'I'm sorry Granny, I'm not sure where she is right now. Yes, I'm fine. How is Pinky? And the grey – er – and er – Mrs Lister?' There is a pause while he listens. Then he says, cautiously, 'No, he's not.' She's asking if Ralph is here. William walks a little way off with the handset, not saying anything, just listening to Mother, who will be complaining about Ralph. William scratches the back of his head and scuffs his toes on the carpet. Eventually, he says, 'Yes Granny; I know Granny. I hope so too Granny. I'll tell Mum to ring.'

'Poor Granny,' he says. 'You ought to speak to her. She's worried about you.'

When I don't reply, he says, 'I think it's morbid to think about dying just because you're old. Marion says her Granny still helms her sailing cruiser on Wroxham Broad. I bet she doesn't think about dying.'

'Marion's Granny is probably younger than your Granny, William. Tell me about Marion?'

William says Marion is in his English class at college. And she works at Dominics some nights as a waitress.

Marion must be the friend William keeps shooting off to see. I think he sometimes has tea at her home before going to Dominics. That's one good thing to be happy about. If

203

William is friendly with Marion, it means he's got over that other wretched girl. Poor young things. They've all got so much to learn.

'Why don't you bring Marion here for supper one night?' I suggest.

William looks steadily at me and says he'll see.

Judith Page weaves her way through my mind. I am haunted by her blue eyes, so calculatedly echoed by the blue flowers in that blouse, by her hair which must owe its corn colour to the bottle, by her flat face, her soft monotonous voice, her white skin. Her *youth*.' I want to have it out with her, face to face. I want to ring Trudy and ask for Judith Page's number. I'll tell her Ralph phoned with a message for the designer of his new range.

What lies has Ralph told Judith Page about our marriage? '*My wife doesn't care for me*.'

I imagine myself confronting Judith Page. I imagine myself marching into her house (*what sort of house does she live in? Has Ralph made love to her there? slept in her bed?*). I will say, with icy control, 'I understand you're having an affair with my husband. Perhaps you'd like to tell me exactly what's going on?' Too demeaning.

Ralph told me he didn't love her. He said it was over. He said '*I'll finish it*'.

Ralph is in New York. He hasn't had time to finish it. He asked me to forgive him.

I think about forgiveness: the word lies in my mind, heavy with Christian allusions. I'm not sure I'm capable of forgiveness. Perhaps I know myself as little as I know Ralph. I shall never forget. '*Try to understand*'. My imagination helps me understand. I can understand that, left alone, a man with Ralph's temperament, with Ralph's insecurities, might fall prey to temptation. I can understand that. But can I accept it? I believe you need to reach acceptance before you can learn to forgive. Infidelity is not a crime, even if it feels like one. But for Ralph and me, nothing will ever be the same again.

Trying to rationalise, I know our marriage was far from ideal, but how many couples *do* actually achieve perfect harmony? Is it therefore reasonable to wipe out ten years of intimacy on account of one sexual transgression? But how can you be objective about love and broken trust?

Ralph is a passionate man. Do those powerful feelings, by their very strength, burn themselves out? *'You're the love of my life.'* Maybe he thinks he means it. Probably he doesn't know what he does feel for me, even as now I question my own feelings. In his absence, I cannot define him. A confusion of Ralphs spins inside my head. The physical impact of Ralph when I first met him, Ralph being loving, Ralph being cruel, Ralph being funny. Ralph my friend – Ralph my enemy. You live with someone for ten years, and still you don't know him. I wish I had never met him.

It is the middle of the afternoon and I am lying on my bed, fighting off a headache, when I hear Ralph's car turn into the gate. I don't want him to see me laid out like this so I get up, brush my hair, pinch some colour into my cheeks, and walk downstairs. I arrive in the hall, just as he opens the front door. He looks white and tired.

'Have a good trip?' I ask in a neutral tone.

He puts down his small black suitcase and his brown leather attaché case and says, 'I found a polisher for Herb. Carolina was good. There's a lot of interest. I've firm orders for partner's desks, dining tables and long sets of chairs, and I think they'll take a walnut bureau.'

We stand looking at each other and Ralph asks, gently, 'Are you all right darling? You know I've been phoning. I'm sorry you wouldn't speak to me.'

'There was no point. I didn't know what to say.' (*'Darling'. How can he call me 'darling'?*)

'We need to talk, but I'll have to lie down first, Alice. I'm absolutely beat.' He heads for the stairs, suitcase in hand, leaving his attaché case in the hall.

William arrives home while Ralph is upstairs. Through the dining-room window, I watch my son swing off his bike. I cannot miss his expression of dismay at the sight of Ralph's car standing there. He fixes the padlock to the rear wheel of his bike and then I hear his key in the front door. I call hello and go into the hall to meet him. William glowers at Ralph's

205

brown attaché case. 'Hello Mum.' He regards me with disillusioned eyes and says, 'He's back then'.

I am silenced by my son's disapprobation.

William slides his rucksack off his shoulders and heads for his attic. Miserably, I go into the kitchen and open the fridge. There are two bottles of white wine, a packet of sliced ham, some liver sausage, and a box of unripe Brie. In the salad compartment, there is a fresh lettuce and some tomatoes, which Marion's mother gave to William: she grew them.

When William comes down, I ask if he'd like some supper and he says no, he has to be at Dominics early tonight and he'll get something to eat there.

I go into the kitchen and wash the lettuce and cut up the tomatoes. I make a salad dressing with the remains of the olive oil and some balsamic vinegar someone gave me for Christmas. I put the ham and the liver sausage on a plate and I take the Brie out of its box. Then, I find myself glancing automatically towards the corner where Emily's basket used to stand. She would be watching me preparing the food, her chin resting on the rim of the basket, hoping a few scraps might come her way. I feel her absence so sharply, tears sting my eyes.

I take a bottle of wine out of the fridge, open it, pour myself a glass, and wait tensely for Ralph. I still don't know what to do. What I want . . . is for time to reel itself in, to go backwards. What I want is for my mother never to have had her heart attack. My mother's heart attack has damaged my own heart.

When Ralph comes down, he still looks exhausted. I'd feel sorry for him if I didn't hate him for what he's done to me. He pours a drink. We look at each other, not speaking. And then, Ralph says, 'Well, I suppose we've got to eat,' and helps himself to slices of ham. He rejects the cheese after poking it, and takes some of Marion's mother's crisp lettuce and her firm ripe tomatoes.

After a while, I say, 'What do you want to do Ralph?'

He looks at me and I believe there is sincerity in his eyes. 'I don't want us to split up. I love you.'

'What about *her*?'

'I told you, I never loved her. It's over.'

'That's not the point. If you loved me, you wouldn't have betrayed me.'

206

'Don't say that word. It's a terrible word. In my heart I never betrayed you.'

'How did it happen then? You can't pretend she seduced you. She must be half your age.'

'You have to bear some responsibility for getting us into this mess.'

'I don't believe you really said that.' All the slow-burning guilt I've felt about not being able to please Ralph, not being able to please Mother ignites. I take off like a rocket. 'You bastard!'

'You left me alone. You didn't care for me.'

'You're not a child, Ralph.'

'I'm sorry.'

'It's not enough.'

'What do you want? Blood?'

'I want to know how it happened. I want to know how you feel.'

'Don't make me, Alice. I'm ashamed. It's over.'

'So what do we do now? Pretend nothing's happened?'

'Give me a chance, Alice. Couldn't we try again?'

'I don't know if I can trust you. I don't know if I can believe a word you're saying. It's like I don't know you any more. It's like I never knew you.'

'I love you, Alice. I need you.'

I look at Ralph, sitting at the kitchen table, still as stone, all the blue brilliance gone from his eyes. Perhaps he does care. I imagine leaving this house, packing up, dividing ten years of sharing. I know I'll never feel the same about anyone else. I imagine telling Mother I'm heading for another divorce. I think of David and Jonquil and I envy their complacent security.

William and Rosamund would approve. We three could live together. But soon they will leave me, to get on with their own lives. Rosamund has almost left. It won't be long before William goes. I'm not afraid of being alone. I think sadly of the companionship of shared sleep. 'I don't know. I don't know how we can live together now.'

'Please can we try? I want to go on living with you.'

The emotion in his voice touches my heart. Maybe I've too much to lose. Maybe I should give him another chance.

Hilda

Alan Sheppard is coming to lunch today. After breakfast, Ann cooks a mushroom quiche and prepares a bowl of green salad. She says men always enjoy a sweet, so she also makes a sticky treacle tart, which won't suit my bottom plate. She lays the table for two and when Alan arrives promptly at twelve-thirty, she opens one of the bottles of Portuguese white we bought at Waitrose when they were on offer. She accepts my invitation to join Alan and me for a drink and then she says she must pop into Maidstone as she has an appointment with the hairdresser. Dear Ann is very tactful. I tell her to take the car, which could do with a run.

Alan's father, old Johnny Sheppard, was a great friend of Clive's. They died the same year. Johnny was such a good-looking man, and a wonderful golfer. I believe he played off four. Alan doesn't play. His wife has horses. Alan is discreet and conservative, just like his father, which suits me fine. He took on a partner when Johnny retired, but there are still only two of them in the partnership. Clive always said that is one of the reasons we get such good service. It's the same with doctors; in those big practices, you're always getting passed on to someone else.

We talk about old times while we eat Ann's quiche, which Alan says is delicious. I tell him I'm afraid I don't cook any more myself; I'm a lazy old girl these days, but my family insist on my having a keeper and Ann really does quite nicely. Alan says at my age I've earned a bit of a rest, and eats two slices of treacle tart.

Ann has left the coffee pot, milk jug, the sugar bowl and the

208

cups all ready on a tray. The Gold Blend stands beside the filled kettle. Alan insists on making our coffee, and brings the tray through to the sitting room. He is a kind man. I open a box of Bendicks bitter-mints, which Alan says are his favourites and we have two each. Then, Alan gets out a copy of my current Will, and we go through it together. We discuss the legacies and I tell him how I want to leave my valuable jewellery. He is pleased I have decided to take his advice.

When we get on to the subject of my property, he cannot quite conceal his surprise to learn that I'm having second thoughts about who shall inherit Hunter's Moon. He is too professional to ask why I'm thinking of changing my mind, but since he is an old family friend, I confide my concern for Alice. I tell him I'm not sure exactly what's going on between her and Ralph, but I don't believe that the marriage will last, and I wonder how she will manage on her own. She has a secretarial training, Clive and I saw to that. But she has no job at present, and what sort of work is available to someone like Alice at this stage in her life? Alan says he's sorry to hear she has troubles. He's known Alice since they were both teen-agers. I think Alan has rather a soft spot for Alice. I point out that David is in a very good position, and Jonquil does quite well with her paintings. They certainly have no money worries.

Alan says the only piece of advice he will give me is to say that it is not a good idea to leave family property in joint names. It always causes trouble.

Jonquil arrives, just as Alan is preparing to leave. She has brought me a basket of strawberries. I wish she wouldn't. I've told her strawberries are bad for my arthritis: they're far too acid. Alan asks after David and the girls and Jonquil asks after Alan's wife and his girls. Alan says his wife has spent all summer in the horse-box driving the girls and their horses to events. Jonquil says she's been driving *her* girls round to events, only in their case it's tennis. Alan says he'd better get back to the office so we say goodbye once more, and he steps into his large, shiny car and drives away.

Jonquil's eyes follow the car and she says, 'What a nice surprise! Alan is such a sweet man. Exactly the kind of person

209

you want for a family solicitor. I'm sure he's been very helpful to you, Mother.'

Jonquil is dying to know why I've had Alan round here. She bristles with curiosity. I say, casually, 'I just wanted to tidy up a few things.'

Jonquil says, 'Of course. And you must let us know if there's anything we can help you with.'

'Well, I *do* need to have a word with David, but he's always so busy, poor love.'

'I'll ask him to give you a call.' Jonquil takes my arm and we go inside. 'Where's Mrs Lister?' she asks, staring at the uncleared remains of lunch. I explain that Ann is having her hair done. Jonquil very kindly washes up while I rest on the sofa for a few minutes. Too much thinking makes my head swirl. She's just making us a cup of tea when Ann arrives back. I can see Jonquil is surprised to see Ann driving my car, but she says nothing.

Ann's hair has certainly been 'done' and her face is very red. I suppose it's the dryer. She thanks Jonquil for washing up and says really she shouldn't have bothered, and she admires the strawberries and says we'll have some for supper: luckily, there's cream in the fridge.

We all sit down and drink tea. My stomach feels distended it's so full of liquid. I tell Ann how much Alan Sheppard enjoyed her quiche and the treacle tart and Ann says it's been really nice for me to have company and she's so pleased Jonquil has popped in. I need cheering up. Jonquil's blue eyes sharpen, but she doesn't ask why I need cheering up. Ann gives Jonquil a confidential look and says, 'Mrs Maddison does have a few little worries at present,' and she picks up the tea tray and disappears into the kitchen.

Jonquil says, 'You're not still worrying about Alice, are you?'

I tell her I simply can't help it. Alice pretends she's all right, but I know she isn't, and half the time she won't even speak to me on the phone. 'You see, Jonquil, whatever happens, you and David have each other, and you have financial security. Poor Alice can't rely on Ralph. They're getting on very badly at present, and if he leaves her, I wonder how she'll manage. That house is probably in his name. Alice and the children

210

could well find themselves without a home! Alice hasn't had a job for some time, and anyway how is she going to earn enough to support them all? I don't suppose Ralph will feel like helping Rosamund and William.'

'Mother,' says Jonquil. 'I'm sure you're getting this right out of proportion. Alice and Ralph have always had their little quarrels. It's just the way they are together. They love each other, really they do. I'm sure Ralph would never leave Alice.'

'William thinks he will.'

'William's only sixteen. He doesn't understand. And he's always resented Ralph, even though Ralph has been a much better father to him than Richard ever was.'

'You're suddenly very pro Ralph,' I remark in what I've been told is my frosty voice. I really can't have my daughter-in-law presuming to understand my daughter's situation better than I do, and I don't see why I should listen to her defending my son-in-law when I know perfectly well she and David never thought he fitted in.

'Look Mother,' says Jonquil, soothingly, 'I'm only trying to help. It upsets me to see you working yourself up into a state like this, when there's really no reason for it.'

'I just want to see Alice. I wish she'd come and stay. She could bring William with her, and maybe Rosamund, if she's back from Turkey.'

'Please forgive me if I say I don't think that's a very practical idea, Mother. But I tell you what. If you like, I'll go and see Alice myself. I could get there and back in the day, if I start early, and it might put your mind at rest.' Jonquil smiles happily, as if she's waved a magic wand.

'That's very good of you, dear. Perhaps I'll come too.'

Jonquil looks thoughtful and then she says. 'Do you really think you're up to spending all that time in the car, Mother? And we'll have to leave at six.'

I think about crowded motorways, the limited capacity of my bladder, the uncomfortable seats in Jonquil's sporty little car and I say, 'Perhaps you're right. I don't want to push my luck.'

Alice

Ralph brings me roses. He helps with the washing up. He takes me out to dinner at Black's which serves exquisitely prepared and presented French food: he orders expensive wine. His efforts to win me over are traditional and unimaginative. I wonder, would I be more receptive if he whisked me off to Prague for the weekend? Or wrote me a poem?

I can see Ralph is trying to be tolerant of William. I watch him biting his tongue when I would expect him to be ordering William to turn down the volume on his music system booming down from the attic, to switch off the lights up there, to clear up the mess he's made in the kitchen, to brush his hair. William watches Ralph carefully and doubles his efforts to be irritating. I think of all the time William was in this house with Ralph while I was away. William knows too much. Does he know things I don't know?

I have no-one I trust well enough to confide in. My friends are our friends, couples like Ralph and me: some of them have had problems in their own marriages. We haven't seen many of our friends this summer, because of holidays and because I've been looking after Mother. If I tell anyone about my troubles, they will be sympathetic and supportive, but they will *know*. Talking about something makes it real. Friends, wanting to help, will give me advice. I'm not ready for advice and sympathy. I need to face this alone.

During the day I switch off the phone. In the evening I make Ralph or William answer it. I cannot always avoid talking to Mother. I know she worries about me, but I cannot suppress my anger with her for being the unwitting cause of my marriage breakdown.

One sultry end-of-summer afternoon, Rosamund arrives back from Turkey with her friend Jake, whom I have heard about, but not met before. Jake smiles and shakes my hand. I warm to him immediately. He has lively brown eyes and a humorous mouth. Both Rosamund and Jake look incredibly scruffy. Their jeans and tee-shirts are creased and stained and Jake's sun-tanned knees poke through rents in the denim. He is in need of a shave and his dark hair and Rosamund's lovely fair curls are matted from salt water. They've been sleeping on beaches and travelling on Turkish buses and long-distance trains. While they shower and change into clean clothes, I go and buy food for supper. When I come back, they are drinking coffee in the kitchen and sorting out their possessions, which litter the table: their cameras and their rolls of exposed film, foreign coins, picture postcards, sea shells, snorkels, shards of broken pottery, packets of biscuits, a small pile of cotton shirts, and a tightly rolled rug. They tell me this is a prayer rug and they unroll it so that I can admire its rich earth colours. They are easy and affectionate with each other. I thank them for the white shirt with blue embroidery round the neck, and for the box of Turkish delight, which they have brought back for me. I try on the shirt which is loose and comfortable, and we all eat a piece of the rose-scented confectionery.

Rosamund makes more coffee, and while I unpack the plastic bags of food, Jake tells me, in his light Scottish burr, that he enjoys being at Edinburgh, where he is studying modern languages with Rosamund, that his home is in Oban and he has two younger sisters.

William comes home and is introduced to Jake. I leave them in the kitchen and go upstairs. Since I am still occupying the spare room, I make up a bed for Jake in the little attic room next to William's.

I am feeling better. Activity and company have lightened my load of misery. I actually *enjoy* making parsley and thyme stuffing for the extra large free-range chicken I bought for supper. I wind rashers of streaky bacon into neat rolls and I arrange chipolata sausages on a baking tray. I scrub the new

213

potatoes, scrape the carrots and string the runner beans, and while the chicken is in the oven, I make gooseberry fool for our pudding.

When Ralph comes home, he is uncharacteristically affable to Jake. (Usually he ignores Rosamund's and William's friends). While I carve the chicken, he opens a bottle of Chablis.

William helps himself to new potatoes, and says, 'This is nice Mum', generously keeping the surprise out of his voice. Ralph, still on his best behaviour, asks Rosamund and Jake about their travels. They say the Turkish buses are good and they travelled as far east as a place called Kekova, where they stayed in rooms above a little bar. The owner was very friendly and his wife made breakfast and supper for them. A fisherman took them out in his boat and they snorkelled, in crystal clear water, over a sunken city. William says they're jolly lucky, he'd love to go to Turkey. Then Ralph tells Jake about a holiday he and his father had in Oban thirty-five years ago. Ralph's uncle and aunt came along too and they hired a sailing cruiser and sailed over to the Isle of Mull. I never knew about that, I think to myself. It's only a little thing, but Ralph has never told me he even *went* on holiday with his father. I have only ever heard about the times Ralph had to remain at his boarding school in the holidays because there was no-one at home to look after him. Or how he was packed off to relatives who didn't want him.

In the morning, Jake, accompanied by Rosamund, goes to the station to start his journey back to Oban. When she gets back, Rosamund says, 'You look awful Mum. And Ralph's very odd. What's happened?'

I thought I had dissembled well enough. But she will have talked with William. It's wrong to burden your children with your own adult problems. My children are the only people I trust well enough to confide in, but I curb myself and generalise. I tell Rosamund that Ralph and I are having problems, but I do not tell her of Ralph's infidelity. We both know neither she nor William would mourn the loss of Ralph. But Rosamund is sensitive enough to perceive my torn emotions. She sees my dilemma. She says, 'Mum you must do what you want. You must think of yourself.'

214

It is so lovely to have my daughter home again: I cannot bear the thought of being without her. I resolve not to let my misery spoil the short time she has here before going back to Edinburgh. I help her get things ready. We go shopping together and I buy her a navy worsted coat, leather boots, warm trousers and a thick sweater. It will be her second winter in Edinburgh and this time she will be living in a flat with her friends. I give her blankets and a feather duvet, and we pack them, along with a kettle, saucepans and a frying pan in an old school trunk that used to belong to David, and will go by rail to Edinburgh.

Now, I stand on the platform and wave as the train creaks slowly away. Rosamund leans out of the window and waves back. I strain my eyes and watch my daughter's fair head and her waving arm grow smaller as the train gathers speed. Finally I lose sight of her as the long line of carriages curves away from me. Bereft, I walk slowly back along the platform and out of the station. I get into my car and, as I drive home, I think how sad partings are. But Rosamund will come home at Christmas. What will we *do* at Christmas? I remember I promised William he shall go skiing at Christmas, and I remember wondering what my life would be like then. That was before Ralph had confessed. Ralph's face flashes up in my mind's eye. There is a pleading expression in his eyes. He does seem to be doing his best to repair the damage he's done. Can I bear to part from him? Do I really want a final separation? If we stay together, it won't be the same. Will that be better than a life empty of Ralph? Should I tear up this chapter of my life on a matter of principle?

Ralph is at work, William is at college and I am drinking coffee and reading *The Times* in the kitchen when there is a knock on the front door. It's probably those wretched Jehovah's Witnesses, I think to myself as I walk along the hall. But when I open the door, Jonquil is standing on the step. I am so surprised to see her, I don't know what to say. And then I think, she's come to tell me something has happened to Mother. I've been stupid about not answering the phone. She must have seen the fear in my face, because she says immediately, 'Everything's all right, Alice – I just thought I'd call in for a coffee; I've one or two things to do in Norwich.'

I can't imagine what she needs to do in Norwich. I know she has a cousin here, but they seldom meet. I invite her in and I make fresh coffee and get out the biscuit tin which has a few sorry-looking digestives inside it.

Jonquil refuses a biscuit and sips her coffee. 'This is nice,' she says. 'We don't see enough of each other, you know, Alice.'

I let her ask after my children and I tell her William is fine and Rosamund went back to Edinburgh yesterday. I tell Jonquil that Rosamund had a lovely time in Turkey with her friend Jake, whom I like very much. Jonquil tells me it's quite a relief to have her girls back at school; she found the summer holidays exhausting.

I do not want to bring up the subject of Mother. I can't think of anything else to say to Jonquil and I begin to wonder how much longer she plans to sit in my kitchen stopping me from reading the paper. I switch off as she embarks on an account of their current social life. David and Jonquil have a busy time going to dinner parties, and giving them. I can never remember the names of their friends who in any case pass in and out of favour. Jonquil has a soft, monotonous voice. I hear it as if through ear muffs. 'Poor Lizzie was broken-hearted. It was such a shock you see. She had absolutely no idea what was going on. Thought everything was perfectly fine. We all know how much she adores George. She found out from a so-called friend, who bumped into them in Milan. The swine was supposed to be there on business. But there's only one reason you take a sexy-looking redhead to Milan! The friend, who I won't name because I think it was such a rotten thing to do, told Lizzie she saw them strolling around, quite brazenly, hand in hand. Lizzie came to me in floods of tears, poor love, but I managed to calm her down. I knew there was no question of George leaving her and the boys. David says George's wandering eye is common knowledge, but it's never serious. In the end he owned up to Lizzie, when she confronted him. Lied through his teeth to begin with. Said the girl was only his secretary, which Lizzie says makes it even worse. Anyway, she's trying to forgive him,

216

and George has taken her to the Seychelles for a second honeymoon. I believe they'll stay together. David says the affair would have blown over in no time. The sad thing is, there was no need for Lizzie to have *known* about it. But a twenty-year marriage is worth too much to sacrifice on account of a fling. Don't you agree, Alice?'

Since I've only been half listening, I'm not certain what she wants me to agree to, so I grunt something that could be interpreted as yes, and then, before she sets off again in that softly insistent tone, her words start to knock holes in my slack consciousness. Abruptly alert, I wonder why Jonquil is telling me this tale of infidelity.

'Jonquil,' I ask, sneakily. 'What would you do if you dis-covered David was having an affair?'

She appears to deliberate and then she says, 'I honestly don't believe that would happen. I think I can say we have total trust in each other.'

'No doubt that's what your friend Lizzie believed.'

Jonquil looks pious and says, 'Not everyone is fortunate enough to find a soul mate: David and I are very lucky. But we do have our differences. You have to *work* at marriage, don't you Alice. It's no good opting out at the first hint of trouble.'

I ask her acidly whether she thinks Richard and I should have stayed together. She is immediately over-apologetic and says she didn't mean that at all, she was commenting in broad terms on the state of marriage. Rapidly, like a striker aiming for an empty goal, she kicks in with, 'How is dear Ralph?'

'Dear Ralph'! I never remember Jonquil referring to Ralph as *dear* before. I've always had the impression Jonquil and David just tolerate Ralph for my sake. I now realise what all this is leading up to. Jonquil has wind of my problems and she's checking me out. Why?

'Ralph is fine.'

'We haven't seen him for ages,' says Jonquil, forcing a note of regret into her voice. 'It was such a shame he couldn't get to Mother's birthday party. That must have been the last happy time we all had together. Why don't you both come and stay at Hunter's Moon for a weekend? You could go and see Mother, and it would be much more comfortable than squeezing yourselves into her little house.'

217

I tell Jonquil it's a kind thought, but Ralph has too many business commitments to think of getting away just now.

Jonquil is not satisfied. She looks searchingly at me and asks, 'Is everything all right, Alice. You look tired and you've lost weight.'

Jonquil is the last person I would confide in. I smile brightly and say I'm on a diet. I offer her more coffee, which she accepts. As she drinks it, I can feel her seeking openings. She's not yet defeated. I lead her out into the garden to look at my roses, which, though dry and untended, have put on a marvellous show this summer. I ask her advice about pruning the wisteria. That excursion successfully takes care of half an hour.

'Well, Jonquil,' I say, 'I mustn't delay you any longer, since you've got things to do.'

Jonquil looks at her watch, and nods. 'It's been good to see you Alice. Mind you take care of yourself.' She pauses and then she says, casually, 'Mother gets in such a muddle with the phone. We can't really expect her to make many calls. I think it's best if we ring her, don't you? Keep in touch.'

That's it! Mother has been complaining about me to Jonquil. Mother has sent Jonquil here. It's my own fault for not answering the phone.

Jonquil kisses me goodbye and roars off in her little red Japanese sports car. I telephone Mother, who is so delighted to hear my voice, my resolve to tell her off for lumbering me with Jonquil weakens. Mother says she's been worried about me; she knows something is wrong. I tell her, coolly, I'd rather she hadn't sent Jonquil along to snoop. She is immediately defensive. 'Alice dear, if you refuse to talk to me you can't expect me not to be concerned. Jonquil caught me on a bad day. She very kindly offered to come and make sure you were all right. To put my mind at rest.' There is a pause and Mother adds, 'You're not all right are you, Alice? I can tell from your voice. That's why you wouldn't talk to me. I do like to be told what's going on, you know. I'm not a child, Alice.'

Am I angry enough to inform Mother my marriage is cracking up on account of her? I take deep breaths and then I say, 'Things are difficult, but I'm hoping they'll settle down.'

218

'What about Ralph?'

'He's hoping things will settle down too.'

'I see,' says Mother, and then she adds, thoughtfully, 'Don't make yourself miserable, Alice. Whatever happens, you'll be all right you know.'

I'm not sure what she means by that, but I don't want to talk to her any longer, so I say of course I'll be all right and she must stop worrying about me.

We are granted a spell of beautiful October weather. There is dew on the grass in the mornings; webs the spiders have spun overnight sparkle as if strung with glass beads. The holly is loaded with bright red berries and there are fat hips on the musk rose. The garden is full of birds making the most of the glut. In the afternoons the sunlight is deep gold.

I talk to Rosamund in Edinburgh. She and Jake are organising their flat which they will share with friends, a boy and two girls. Rosamund says they each have a room to themselves, so it must be a large flat. Mother tells me over the phone that Alan Sheppard is coming to see her. She says she wants to tie everything up in good time, so she can forget about it. I thought she'd already finalised her Will. I wonder if she's changing anything. She tells me Ann Lister is an excellent needle woman and she's busy making her a winter skirt.

William still regards Ralph with hostility, and makes himself scarce in the evenings.

Ralph is cheerful; business is good. His customer in North Carolina has ordered the special Queen Ann style bureau cabinet, two mahogany break-front bookcases, one partner's desk and two sofa tables.

If I am to save our marriage, I must respond to Ralph's efforts to win me over. But I cannot stop thinking about Judith Page. Judith Page designed a whole new range of furniture for Ralph.

After supper one evening, I ask him outright: 'What's happened to Judith Page? Are her Art Deco pieces completed? Is she still doing work for you?'

Ralph must have been anticipating this question, for without flinching, he says, 'Nearly all the prototypes for the burr oak range are ready, but we added a sideboard. She has to come to the factory from time to time. I still have a business relationship with her, Alice.'

'You're sure that's all?'

Ralph looks at me; his blue eyes blaze with conviction. 'My personal relationship with Judith Page is over. You have to believe me Alice, or you and I are finished.'

We drink a lot of wine, and Ralph lures me out of the spare room and back into our double bed.

21 October 1996

Alice

Maybe everything will be all right, in the end. There are many things more terrible than a husband's infidelity. Life isn't so bad, I decide, bundling clothes into the washing machine. As usual I undo shirt buttons and check pockets. Once I washed a watch. It was in William's jeans pocket. There is something now in the back pocket of Ralph's cotton trousers. Surely he hasn't been stupid enough to forget his credit card? I retrieve it. But it isn't a credit card, it's a photograph. Tadpole head, rudimentary limbs, umbilicus – floating.

I wait in the hall for Ralph. I hear the car. I hear his key in the lock. I watch him put down his attaché case. When he straightens up, I thrust the photograph in his face. I can hardly hold on to it, I am shaking so badly with rage.

The colour drains from his face.

'You don't have to explain what this is.' My voice trembles in time with my shaking body. 'And you didn't even have the guts to tell me. I despise you.'

'I tried to tell you.'

'Oh yes! Coward! Cheat!'

'You don't understand.'

'How can I *not* understand? It's here – staring me in the face.' I jab his chest with the photograph.

'She must have slipped it in my pocket.'

'You're still seeing her.'

'I've been trying to finish it. I wouldn't believe she was pregnant – until the scan. I don't love her.'

'You must be mad.'

221

'Please try to understand.'

'You always wanted a child, didn't you Ralph?'

'I wanted *our* child.'

'So it's my fault is it?'

'It happened.'

I pace the hall, burning with anger. 'All this time you were trying to get back with me, you were still seeing her. You lied to me Ralph. You think because you have power in your working life, you can control people the same way in your private life. You said it was over. But it wasn't. You thought you could get away with it.'

I *told* her it was over.'

'How can it be over with a child?'

'I don't want to live with her.'

As we face each other in the hall, the telephone begins to ring. 'It'll be your mother,' says Ralph.

'I can't talk to her now.'

Acknowledgement lies mute between us like an unexploded bomb. If it wasn't for my mother, we wouldn't be in this mess.

Ralph's eyes plead with mine. 'I want to live with *you*,' he says, 'I love you.'

But now I know that our marriage is over. I feel myself board up its windows, seal every small crack, bolt its thick door and turn my back on it.

'It's no good Ralph. I don't love *you* any more.' I drop the photograph, stride down the hall, and fling open the door of our home.

'*Alice!* where are you going?'

Ralph's anguished voice rings in my ears as I crash the door behind me and make for my car.

Hilda

Ann says we must make the most of these warm autumn days. There may not be many more of them, so we are having a little walk round my garden. David arranged for someone to cut the grass and do the weeding, but I like to keep an eye on things myself. Most gardeners are far too keen on chopping things down: light pruning not being something they are attracted to. Next time the old chap comes, I must remind him not to touch my clematis. Ann cuts yellow roses for the house. I tell her how, when I lived at Hunter's Moon, I used to make *pot-pourri* with rose petals; there were roses of every colour at Hunter's Moon. She tells me she learned how to press flowers when she was at school, and once she made a picture entirely of pressed wild flowers. Before she takes the roses inside, she sets up my lounger on the terrace. 'The fresh air will do you good,' she says. I settle myself down and Pinky jumps softly onto my lap.

Alan Sheppard came again this morning. He brought the final copy of my Will. We asked Arthur to witness my signature. I do believe I have been fair to my family, and now I shall stop worrying about what might happen when I am gone. I don't want to think any more about dying.

I rest my hand on Pinky's warm coat and he starts to purr. It is a very soothing sound. I close my eyes and enjoy the comfortable weight of my limbs.

I am back in our cottage in Loose. I am standing on the flagged floor of the tiny kitchen. The sheltering thatch makes it a dark little cottage. I peer out of the small casement window above the sink. I am waiting for Clive to come home. I leave the kitchen and walk into the main room, which has an open fireplace with a massive oak beam across the top of it. There is grey ash in the grate. I know that a stream runs in front of the house. I know it has clear water flowing over sand and pebbles. I can hear it. The sound increases, but as I listen, our cottage dissolves away, and the sound I am listening to is no longer the sound of water rippling over pebbles, but the rattle of the wind in the trees. When I open my eyes, I am no longer a hopeful young woman, but a cantankerous old one. Pinky has slipped away from my lap, the sun has slunk behind a cloud and the wind is whipping the tremulous leaves of the poplar into a frenzy.

Every now and again, I dream about that dear little cottage where Clive and I started our married life, just as, every now and again, I dream about being back in Hunter's Moon. I ease myself out of my chair and walk carefully over the terrace, back through the glass doors and into the sitting room of my present boring little house, where I find Jonquil and Ann drinking cups of tea. Pinky laps a saucer of milk. Jonquil smiles and says, 'Hello Mother, you looked so peaceful, I didn't like to wake you.' She rises to her feet, puts her arms round me and gives me a kiss. Her long hair sweeps my face. We sit down on the sofa and Ann fetches another cup and pours my tea. Jonquil offers me a macaroon. 'Do have one, Mother, I made them this morning.'

I drink a cup of tea and eat two macaroons, which are marvellously light, and soft in the middle with a crisp outside. Then Ann takes the tea things into the kitchen, tactfully leaving Jonquil and me alone.

There's no need to upset Jonquil by telling her that Alice phoned to complain about her visit. I simply ask, 'How did you find Alice?'

Jonquil tells me, in her cheerful voice, that Alice seems very normal and calm. 'She looks a bit tired, but then, she *has* been dashing about rather a lot hasn't she Mother? I think that might be one of her troubles. I do believe she needs to stay quietly at home and be with Ralph. They are very fond of each other, you know Mother, really they are. We should allow them more space.'

Is Jonquil implying that I've been filling up the space between Alice and Ralph? That Alice has been refusing to talk to me out of resentment? I thought my daughter was trying to protect me. That, misguidedly, she didn't want to worry me with her troubles.

'I think they ought to have a little holiday.'

Jonquil's answer to any problem is a little holiday. It's a lot more complicated than that. I thank my daughter-in-law for driving all the way to Norwich and back, and I let her think she has put my mind at rest.

'So you mustn't worry about Alice any more, Mother. And you mustn't worry about anything else either.' And then Jonquil says, 'It was nice to see Alan Sheppard, last time I was here. He's such a sensible man.'

I don't see why I should tell Jonquil that Alan was here again this morning. My son will be the first person to learn how I've left things. She continues, casually with, 'You wanted to talk to David, didn't you Mother. I'll get him to 'phone you.'

'Oh yes,' I say, equally casually, 'there *are* some changes I need to discuss with him.'

After a while, Jonquil says she ought to be going, the girls will be home from school and she does like to be there for them. She kisses me goodbye, 'Now you mustn't worry about Alice any more, Mother. I'm sure she and Ralph are working things out between themselves, and everything will be fine.'

Ann has made cottage pie for supper, not very exciting, but easy to eat. While it's in the oven, we sit down for our usual apéritif: a pink gin for me and gin and tonic for Ann. We spend so much time together that Ann and I have grown quite close. We talk openly about many things, about life, about our own lives. She tells me she and her husband never discovered why they couldn't have children. 'My husband refused to have tests. He thought it unmanly.'

I tell Ann that children are the greatest joy, but you never stop worrying about them, so she has saved herself much heartache. I say that I'm still unhappy about Alice and I don't think Jonquil is being entirely truthful about the situation there. 'You know Ann, I believe my daughter-in-law is implying Alice and Ralph are having problems because of *me*. I really *can't* believe that. I've always done my best to get along with my son-in-law for my daughter's sake, but he's such an unreasonable man. To tell you the truth, Ann, I'm sure Alice would be better off without Ralph.'

Ann says of course she's never met my son-in-law but Alice is a lovely person. 'And your daughter-in-law does seem fond of you, Mrs Maddison.'

'Jonquil can be very kind but she's a bit of a devious character. And my son David, he's so very clever, I do love him but, you know Ann, sometimes he can be a little pompous.'

We have another gin each and after that, the cottage pie doesn't taste too bad. She's overcooked the beans as usual. After supper, Ann stacks the dishes and then she fetches the whisky for our night cap.

We settle down on the sofa with our drinks. I begin to feel pleasantly drowsy and Ann's face slips out of focus. It's been a long day, I say to her, and I've come to terms with important things. 'I'm glad Alan Sheppard was here. I'm glad I don't have to worry about my Will any more. But you know, Ann, I wish I could stop thinking about what might happen next. Perhaps it would be easier if I was a believer, like you.'

'We are all children of God, Mrs Maddison dear, whether we believe or not.'

Ann's voice is comforting. My eyelids are heavy. I allow them to fall.

Ann's firm hand is on my arm. 'Time for bed, dearie.' She helps me up the stairs and we decide it's too late for my bath, so she helps me undress, and wash and ease my limbs into bed. She brings a glass of water and doles out my pills. I fumble in the drawer beside my bed for a handkerchief, and my fingers brush against the hard cover of the euthanasia book. I've been trying not to think of that, but I realise I have done nothing about making a Living Will. My head swirls: I am swamped by the dread of what might be in store for me. I sway and fall back on the pillow, as I visualise the horror of the hospital. 'Oh Ann!' My tongue has grown thick and clumsy in my dry mouth. 'I'm glad you are here. You will remember your promise won't you.'

Ann's cool hand strokes the hair back from my forehead. I hear her voice, as if from far away. 'Sleep now, Mrs Maddison. There's nothing to fear.'

I am abruptly awake. Something is wrong. I fumble for the light switch and in the sudden glare can see nothing. When the giddy feeling stops, and my sore eyes adjust to the brightness, I'm relieved to find that I'm in my own bed and not at Hunter's Moon, or in that terrifying hospital, but I know what is wrong. Pinky is not asleep at my feet. My head is muzzy. I taste bile. I must find Pinky. Carefully, I slide my legs out of bed and search for my slippers with my toes. I find them and, holding on to the side of the bed, push my feet inside each one and stand up. It's a struggle, but I put on my dressing gown, and clutching it round me, I shuffle towards the door. I believe there is someone in the house with me, but the whirling in my head prevents me from remembering who it is. Alice? Ann? Whoever it is, I will not wake them. I just need to get down the stairs, and go into the kitchen. Perhaps Pinky has been shut in there. If the catflap is locked he might still be in the garden. Alice sometimes locks the catflap to keep Pinky away from Emily. *But Emily isn't here any more.* The banister rail slides smoothly in my hand as, step by step, I go slowly down the stairs. Fortunately, the hall light has been left on, so I am able to see what I'm doing. I open the kitchen door and switch on the light, but there's no sign of Pinky. His catflap is locked. Bloody Alice. Bending down, I try to unlock it but my head spins so wildly I almost fall to the ground. I sit down and rest on a chair. I cannot leave poor Pinky outside all night. It is a while before I am steady enough to turn the key and to pull back the bolts on the kitchen door.

'Pinky!' I call into the blackness, and I remember once he was attacked by a vicious tabby. Or was it another cat – some other time? My head feels as if something is racing round and round inside it. I lurch against the door frame.

'Pinky!' I step cautiously out onto paving stones which are hard and cold beneath my thin slippers. The night air feels dense and heavy as plush curtains. There is no moon nor any stars to pierce the blackness. I spread my hands in front of me and move slowly forward. This is what it is like to be blind. Stepping out from the lighted kitchen, my garden turns strange and unfamiliar. Shadowy shapes shift above my head, as if creatures are flying around up there. 'Pinky!' Now there is grass beneath my feet and a sighing in my ears. Wind? A shudder ripples coldly through my body. 'Pinky, Pinky, puss, puss.' My voice wavers out, weak as a child's. Why did I not bring a torch? I stand still and strain my ears. Blessedly, I hear faint miaows, and in a moment Pinky is rubbing against my legs. Relief washes through me and I bend my stiff back to stroke him. 'Oh Pinky I'm so happy to see you.' His coat is soft as silk beneath my hand. A giddy feeling spirals, starting small and growing large, taking over the whole of my body. My legs fold up, the breath is forced from my lungs and I sink to the ground. Pinky rubs against my aching body. He pats my face with his paw. I know I must not lie here in the cold or I will die. I fight myself to my feet and stumble towards the light spilling into the garden from the kitchen. When I reach the door, I haul myself in and shut it behind me. With tiny steps, I shuffle across the kitchen and into the hall. Clutching the banister rail, I climb the stairs, Pinky by my side. When I finally reach my bedroom, I think I've done pretty well. I kick off my slippers, slip out of my dressing gown and fall into bed. I pull Pinky onto my chest. 'Make me warm, Pinky,' I whisper into his pricked black ear.

Clive holds me in his arms. We are dancing. I am deliriously happy, my head against his chin, his breath in my hair.

'*Some day I'll find you – Moonlight behind you.*' Dancing and dancing. His arms tightly around me. All I want to do for ever and ever. Clive, my young love. Music in my ears. Romantic music. The music swells and fades.

'*I'll see you again*' – another of our songs. Dancing on a terrace now. Starlight. But I'm suddenly alone. '*I'll see you again*' – what comes next? – '*when the sun shines through again*'. No. Not that. Am I asleep or awake? I clutch at something warm and furry. I hear myself calling, 'Clive. Where are you? Clive.'

He comes. There he is, looking down at me. Grey like a

ghost. I see his pale eyes, searching for mine. And his mouth, but where is his moustache? He bends over me. And now, full of happiness, I am standing once more in the starlight with Clive, the scent of flowers in my nostrils. Bluebells, hyacinths. Music in my ears. '*I'll see you again*' – honeysuckle, roses – '*When the spring breaks through again*'. Yes. '*When the spring breaks through again*'.

'*I'll see you again – when the spring breaks through again.*'

The stars are fading. Clive's face glimmers in the dimness that floats in front of my eyes like veils of black gauze.

'Clive.' I reach out my arms to him. 'Clive.'

The veils of gauze part as his face comes down to cover mine. My breath is stopped. I fight to draw air into my lungs. Pain expands like a monstrous plant forcing out its swollen parts inside my narrow chest, cracking my ribs.

'Oh Clive – I didn't think it would be like this.'

28 October 1996

The noise from Hilda's funeral party was abating. It was as if all those present realised simultaneously that this really was to be the last of Hilda. Never again would Hilda's family and friends be gathered together in this house: all of them thinking of Hilda; all of them, at some time during the afternoon, poignantly aware of Hilda's presence. The time was now come when enough whisky and gin had been drunk, enough sandwiches and cake eaten, enough affectionate anecdotes related, for her spirit to be released. Hilda, beloved mother and grandmother, dear friend, had been given a rousing send off. It was fitting that, finally, sobriety should predominate.

I should never have come, thought Ralph. What a macabre ending – if this is to be it – to my uncomfortable ties with this domineering family. I'll just leave now, without saying goodbye. I cannot be expected to put up with another of William's antagonistic glares, with Rosamund's vague rebuffs. If only, Alice had bred pleasing, tractable children. If only my wife had had the sensitivity to see things from my point of view. Never once, in all these years, has she taken my side against Rosamund and William, however reprehensible their behaviour.

If only Alice had been born to a kind and gentle mother. I never planned to make an enemy out of Hilda, he thought with a sliver of guilt. It was just that she expected to have the same status as a husband. And Alice always pandered to her.

Ralph watched his wife (she was still his wife) quietly making sure everything went smoothly, and was consumed with self-hatred. He loathed the weakness of character that had allowed him to answer the invitation in Judith's blue eyes, to fall victim to the pleasures of her firm young body, to abandon himself to the temporary addiction of her enthusiastic love-making. He was already bored with her by the time she announced she was pregnant. Tearfully, she had insisted it wasn't intentional. Ralph contemplated his dismal future. I'll have to do the honourable thing and support Judith, he thought, but do I really have to live with her? For ever? How did Alice allow this happen? Why am I not a better man? Have I really lost the love of my life? He took a last look at her strained face, at her long limbs and her dark shiny hair. And he slipped away from this house where he was not wanted, away from this family who could only condemn him. He shut the door behind him, and thought, I'll be homesick for you, Alice.

There were cups of tea or coffee to be drunk, organised by Alice assisted by Jonquil and Ann Lister, after which Rosamund helped each of her grandmother's elderly friends to find, among the pile in the spare bedroom, the correct dark wool coat or beige mackintosh, their own black Homburg hat and their own polished wooden walking stick.

Alice and David stood side by side at the front door. The old men and the old ladies shook David by the hand and some of them kissed Alice's pale cheek and they thanked the brother and sister for their hospitality and they said, once more, how fond they had been of Hilda and how much they would all miss her. Then they said goodbye and went out of the front door, down the small driveway and into the crescent, which was soon echoing with the raucous sound of engines being revved and gearboxes mishandled. When they had all gone the only people remaining, apart from the immediate family, were Arthur and June, Ann Lister and Mrs Curtis. June and Ann started collecting dirty glasses and plates and cups and saucers and taking them through to the kitchen. Arthur had acquired a cigar from somewhere. Swaying slightly, he said to Alice, 'Your Ma was a good friend and neighbour. We'll miss her.' He took a long puff of the cigar and leaning closer to Alice, he asked, slowly in a slurred voice, 'What's going to happen to her house then?'

Jonquil, who was standing next to Alice said stonily, 'I really don't think *that* is any of your business.'

The colour of Arthur's face deepened to rich plum. 'Hoity toity,' he said.

June, arriving at this point, put down the tray she had been collecting cups on, took hold of Arthur's flabby arm and said, 'Come now Arthur, that's no way to speak to a lady. I'm taking you home right now.' She cast a flustered glance round the room, littered with the debris of food and drink; peopled by Hilda's family, and she said, 'I'm sorry. I'm afraid it's the whisky talking.'

'Thank God they've gone,' said Jonquil after Arthur, angrily towed along by June, had staggered out. 'What ghastly people.'

Ann Lister took two more trays loaded with empty glasses into the kitchen and then she came up to Alice and said, 'I must be away now. My husband is waiting outside in the car.'

Alice said dully, 'Thank you Ann for all you did for my mother, and for coming along today.'

Ann Lister's eyes shone moistly behind her glasses and she said, in her faint North Country accent, 'It was a privilege, my dear'. And she slipped on her grey tweed coat and disappeared through the front door.

Mrs Curtis, who was hovering tearfully, touched Alice's arm and said, 'Can I have a quick word please'.

'Of course.' Alice followed Mrs Curtis into the kitchen. Mrs Curtis said, in an apologetic voice, 'I thought you should know, your William is upstairs and he's not too good. Don't be alarmed, now. Someone's been feeding him whisky, if you ask me. And that Pinky gave him a nasty scratch. I've bathed it, and put a plaster on. But the poor lad's rather upset. I think he needs his mum.'

'Thank you for telling me,' I said Alice. 'I'll go straight up.' And she hurried towards the stairs.

William was stumbling out of the bathroom.. Alice was shocked by his dishevelled state. His hair was on end, his face white as a sheet of paper, his eyes huge and bloodshot. He had a large Elastoplast on one hand and in the other he was holding a book.

'William, what on earth's the matter?' Alice moved forward to help him, for he looked extremely unsteady, as if he might topple face down at any moment. 'Mrs Curtis said Pinky scratched you.' Through the open bedroom door, she could see the horrible creature glaring at her from the top of the bed. 'Are you all right? Let me see.' William shrugged away her hand. 'Look Mum!' He pushed a book into her face. She read, '*Euthanasia – the Gentle Ending.*' 'This was in Granny's bedroom.'

Alice glanced from the book in William's hands back into her mother's bedroom. Her eyes rested for a moment on her mother's empty bed ... on the large black cat curled up on the pillow, staring at her with baleful eyes.

'Is that so very strange, William?'

'Who gave it to her Mum? You can't tell me she went out and bought it herself.'

Clutching the book, William moved unsteadily along the landing and started down the stairs. Everyone glanced up as he entered the sitting room.

William felt all their eyes upon him. At the same time, he felt insulated from those eyes, as if they saw an entirely different world from his. Part of him knew the whisky he had drunk was responsible for his extreme behaviour. At the same time, a core of sound reasoning, still centre of his pounding brain, told him that without the whisky he would not have the courage to express what he felt to be the truth. What must be said.

He stood among them, and he held up the book in his hand. It was hard to talk. It was always hard talking in front of a lot of people, but the words came.

'Granny didn't want to die,' he said. 'But she was frightened of going back to hospital. Where did she get this book?' He waved it about. 'I think someone gave her this book. I think someone made her think she *ought* to die. I think someone *helped* her die.' There was a sudden silence, resonating with soundless shock waves. And then Jonquil said, 'What nonsense the boy is talking. He's drunk. And he's desecrating Mother's funeral.'

233

'She was supposed to have died peacefully in her sleep,' said William, gaining confidence. 'Mrs Curtis saw her in the morning and Mrs Curtis said my grandmother didn't look peaceful at all.'

Everyone's eyes switched to look at Mrs Curtis, who was standing by the kitchen door, holding Pinky in her arms and weeping openly. She bowed her head and nodded.

David, suddenly authoritative, said, 'Alice, take William upstairs. The poor boy is distraught.'

Still grasping the book, William turned his back on them all and climbed the stairs, followed by his mother. He went into the bedroom he always slept in when he stayed here, and sat down heavily on the bed. His mother sat beside him. She put an arm round him, smoothed his hair but said nothing. He felt the warmth of her protective love for him.

Alice smoothed her son's hair and stroked his feverish cheek. After a while he turned and stared at her. Inches away from hers, his eyes were wary. 'Mum,' he said, making an effort to speak, 'The telephone rang and rang that morning, so I had to answer it. It was the grey woman. She asked to talk to you. But you weren't there. And Ralph wasn't there either. She said, "I have some sad news for you all," and then she said, "I'm sorry to tell you, your Granny has passed away".'

'Why weren't you at home Mum? Where *were* you?'

22 October 1996

Alice

I lie flat on my back in bed in my old room at Hunter's Moon. Spills of pale morning light glint between the edges of the heavy drapes. When this was *my* room, the curtains were of faded pink velvet to blend with, but not match, the pink rosebud wallpaper. Everything matches now. Striped yellow and white curtains, striped yellow and white wallpaper, white bedcover, and a soft yellow fitted carpet, which covers the loose floor board that once held my secrets. As the light increases, I see that the ceiling has been replastered. There used to be a crack in the middle almost the shape of a Scottie dog. My hopes and dreams rest here. I did my homework at a table in the corner near the window. In this room my mother helped me dress for my first wedding day. Mother, whom now I cannot forgive for causing my parting from Ralph, helped fasten my white wedding dress, and arrange the long veil with the coronet of orange blossom from the garden. Its botanical name is philadelphus and its perfume is of a dizzying sweetness. Poor Richard. Poor me.

Last night, I was out of my mind with rage and the shock of coming to terms with what Ralph had done. Unable to remain in that house with Ralph for one minute longer, I got into my car and I drove, regardless of the direction I was taking. After a while I realised I was heading down the A12 and I knew I was going to Hunter's Moon. I'd been just sensible enough to grab my handbag before I left; it lay beside me on the passenger seat. I drove automatically, without caution. By the time I remembered to check the petrol gauge, it measured less than a quarter full: not enough to take me to Kent, so I began to look out for petrol stations and eventually I found a twenty-four-hour one. I filled the tank and drove round to the Travel Lodge at the back but the lights were out and there was no-one about. My watch showed midnight. I always thought these bloody places stayed open all night. I turned back onto the trunk road and joined the streams of traffic surging on through the night. Waves of lights swept towards me from the opposite carriageway. My mind seethed with random images, disconnected thoughts. I tried to fix my eyes along the beam of my own headlights, steering through my sea of troubles. Someone flashed, close behind and then, a few feet from my right arm, a long-distance coach, its discreet lighting briefly revealing rows of slumbering heads, steamed past. It happened again, flash, flash. On my tail. This time he hooted. A low-loader filled the carriageway to the near side. I slowed and started to pull in behind it. The overtaking car flashed again and hooted. I caught a glimpse of a turned head, a raised fist. My foot slipped from brake to accelerator. Suddenly, the steel rear of the low-loader filled my windscreen. In the split second when I looked death in the face, instinctive reflex took charge. My right foot found the brake and as I stamped down, the revelation struck – *however broken my life, I don't want it to end.*

I pulled in at the next lay-by, parked the car behind a tree, locked the doors and leaving myself a few inches of air at the top of the front windows, I curled up on the back seat and slept.

I probably only slept for a couple of hours, but it was enough for me to decide I was safe enough to drive and I certainly didn't want to remain cramped on the back seat of my car in a lay-by in which I was now able to make out the long black shape of a stationary juggernaut.

It was still dark when I crossed the huge grey Queen Elizabeth bridge. The lights of the factories and the deserted wharfs glowed brightly underneath me. By the time I got to Hunter's Moon, the heavy sky was growing lighter. Thankfully, I drew to a halt and turned off the engine. I considered just staying out here for a while and not waking them up. But I was suddenly desperate to see my brother; hungry for warmth and comfort and a hot drink. I knocked gently on the front door. A light flicked on and then I heard a bolt drawn back, a key turned and David stood on the threshold in his striped pyjamas, blinking at me. He took a longer look, drew me inside and put his arm round me. 'Alice! What's happened?'

I told him my marriage was over, but I couldn't talk about it. He fed me sweet tea and toast and honey and then he led me up to the spare room, which used to be *my* room, and I slept again.

Now, I continue to watch the light grow stronger and soon I get out of bed and I pull back the curtains. The familiar garden glows in the early sunlight, strangely immaculate these days. After a while, there is a tap on the door. 'Come in,' I call, and Jonquil enters carrying a cup of tea and a plate of biscuits. She is wearing a pink silk dressing gown and her hair is tied back in a pony tail. 'Oh Alice,' she says. 'I'm so *very* sorry.' She lays the cup and the plate of biscuits down on the bedside table, puts an arm round me and gives me a hug. 'When you feel you can talk about it, I do hope we can help. Maybe things are not as black as they seem just now.' I'm unable to cry, which is a blessing really. Jonquil goes on to ask if I would like to borrow any clothes, and she fetches one of her skirts and an armful of shirts. She tells me to come down for breakfast as soon as I feel up to it. The girls will be off to school in half an hour.

I drink the tea and eat two biscuits. And then I have a hot bath in the en-suite bathroom that has been fashioned from about one third of my original bedroom.

I get dressed in the jeans I was wearing yesterday and a green cotton shirt of Jonquil's. David comes up to see me and I thank him for being so kind and understanding. He says don't be silly, he's very glad I'm here. 'Stay as long as you like. Just rest and don't make any decisions. Life may look quite different in a day or two.' He kisses my cheek and says he must go to work now, but he'll see me this evening.

I hear car doors bang: I hear David start up the BMW and then there is the crunch of gravel as he drives away, to drop Louisa and Helen at their school before going to the station to catch the London train. I am about to go down to have breakfast with Jonquil when the telephone rings. I hear Jonquil answer it and talk for a short while in a low voice. I hear her slowly climb the stairs. She comes into my room. Her slightly protuberant eyes are like inverted saucers. 'Alice!' Her voice wobbles, 'Bad news Alice! That was Ann Lister on the telephone. She says Mother died in the night.'

I hear Jonquil sob. All around me everywhere, everything is cold and dark. I turn away from Jonquil, who has collapsed onto the bed and I stare out of the window. I think of all the thousands of times I have gazed out of this window. I would say that I have seen this garden in every season, in every light, at every time of day, in every mood. But never have I looked on it with such desolation in my heart.

Suspecting your husband of having an affair is not the same thing as *knowing* he is having an affair. I learned that very recently. Now I have learned that imagining your mother to be dead is not the same thing as coming to terms with the finality of her death. Often, God help me, I wished her dead. But then I had no conception of what it would be like to experience the final lack of her. My imagination did not prepare me for this overwhelming sense of irredeemable loss.

Blaming Mother for the stresses she laid on my marriage affected my relationship with her. But she could not be held responsible for Ralph's faithlessness. Now it is too late to put things right with her.

I have to go to Mother's house. Jonquil comes with me. Ann Lister is waiting. She steps forward to greet us. She clasps my hand and her colourless eyes gaze soberly at me from behind the lens of her glasses. 'Please accept my sincere condolences,' she says. 'Mrs Maddison was a lovely lady. You will all miss her.' She brings mugs of coffee, and Jonquil and I sit on the sofa with the ghost of my frail mother. I blink back stinging tears. Ann says, 'I took it upon myself to telephone the surgery. The doctor should be here very soon.' We drink our coffee in silence and I nerve myself for the task of going up to see my mother.

Ann says quietly, 'It's what your mother wanted you know: to pass away peacefully in her sleep, at home in her own bed.'

'But not yet,' I say. 'It's too soon. Too sudden. She wasn't ready to die.'

'It's a shock,' says Jonquil, swallowing a sob. 'But she was so very afraid of having another heart attack, of going back to that hospital. Of becoming a vegetable.' She stops and blows her nose.

Ann says, in her quiet voice, 'Mrs Maddison – and all of you – have been spared much pain. I've worked in geriatric wards. I know about that kind of suffering.'

I miss you, Mother. I put my hand in my pocket and touch the crumpled fabric of my handkerchief.

Ann raises her chin and there is an almost rapt expression on her face. 'Your mother is near us,' she says. 'I can feel her, just over the other side.'

I put down my mug and rise to my feet.

Jonquil says, 'Oh Alice – I must phone David. He should be in the office by now.'

Jonquil and I leave Ann in the sitting room and Jonquil goes to the telephone in the hall and slowly, heavily, I climb the stairs.

The curtains are drawn but sunshine filters through the flowered chintz. In the half light, Mother's bedroom looks exactly as it always does, cluttered with all the things Mother could not do without: family photographs, ornaments, trinkets, cosmetics, clothes. The clothes she must have worn yesterday are draped over a chair: her navy pleated skirt and the pink blouse. Her quilted dressing gown lies over the end of the bed. I smell, faintly, her Blue Grass perfume. And now, I make myself look at my mother. She lies on her back in the bed. Her arms are down by her sides. The white sheet rests lightly against her white neck. Her eyes are closed. On her waxen face are a sprinkling of small reddish-blue marks. I bend to kiss her cheek and I am shaken by the cold solidity of it.

I sit down on a chair, with her slippery petticoat and her vest and pants. Soundlessly, I say a prayer. I ask Mother to forgive me and I ask God to look after my mother. I rest

239

quietly here in the half light of this bedroom and I pray for my own peace of mind.

There is a hand on my shoulder and an unfamiliar voice is saying, 'I'm so sorry, my dear.'

He draws back the curtains and the room is flooded with dust-laden sunlight. 'I'm afraid Dr Robson is in France with his family. I'm the locum, Tony Wright.' I shake the hand he offers me. He is thin, with sparse white hair, a dry wrinkled face and a prominent Adam's apple. He looks as if he's been brought out of retirement.

I do not watch while Dr Wright examines my mother. When he has finished, I tell him it's been rather a shock. That really we had not expected this just yet.

'It's a pity,' he says, pensively, looking down at Mother. And then he picks up one of the bottles of pills, and fiddles with the lid before putting it down again. 'But you never know with hearts.'

I say, shakily, that I hope my mother didn't suffer.

Dr Wright says, 'She would have gone quickly, my dear.' He looks carefully at me and he says I should get some rest and he offers me sleeping pills, which I refuse, thinking Dr Wright looks as if he could do with a good night's sleep himself.

We leave the room together. I turn and look back and as I look, a familiar black shadow appears from nowhere, and leaps lightly up onto the bottom of the bed where my mother's body lies.

Downstairs, Jonquil says David will get here as soon as he can. Ann Lister says she has telephoned her husband, and he'll come and fetch her in the car. 'I'll just go up and pack my things,' she says.

Mrs Curtis, who arrived while I was in my mother's bedroom, is weeping in the kitchen. I say goodbye to Dr Wright and tell him that, when Dr Robson comes back from holiday, I would like to thank him for all he did for my mother. Dr Wright presses my arm and says, 'Mind you get some rest now.'

Eventually, only Jonquil and I remain in the house with my mother, until David arrives, looking drawn and sad and begins to put things in motion.

I don't watch while the undertaker's men carry my mother downstairs and take her away from us.

Eventually, we lock up the house, consume a silent, alcoholic lunch in the buffet bar at the Wheat Sheaf, and go back to Hunter's Moon.

Now there are practical things to be done: a date to be fixed for the funeral, friends and relations to be given the sad news, a notice to be put in the paper. I telephone Rosamund in Edinburgh and she says she will come home as soon as she can. I explain that I'm staying at Hunter's Moon and she should come here. She's too upset about her grandmother to ask about anything else, so I don't tell her what has happened between Ralph and me.

I must go home to see William. I remember his distress when he learned about Emily from Ann Lister, and I suddenly realise that he won't know where I am. When I rushed away last night, he was out, washing up at Dominics. Ralph won't know where I am either. *Ralph* might think I've had a car accident. There is no reply when I telephone home.

David and Jonquil persuade me to wait until the next day before driving back to Norwich. I worry about William worrying about me. During the afternoon, David answers the telephone to Ralph. I hear him say, 'Yes Ralph, she *is* here. I'm not sure if she's able to speak to you right now.' I signal that I'll take the phone. David gives me the handset and discreetly slips from the room. Ralph's voice is jagged with emotion. 'Alice, I've been out of my mind with worry. There was no need to rush off like that. Please come home. We have to talk.'

'There's nothing more to say.' I listen with surprise to my own emotionless tone.

'It can't just end like this.'

'It has.'

Silence sighs in my ears. Coolly, I tell him about Mother.

There is a pause and then he is saying, in that rough, splintered voice, 'I'm sorry. I don't know what else I can say except that. But I am truly sorry for you Alice.'

'There is one thing you could do for me Ralph,' I say in my

241

new cool tone. 'Please would you let William know where I am and that I'm all right.'

'I'll do that.'

'But don't tell him about Mother. I'll come back tomorrow, and tell him myself. And I'd rather you weren't there.' I put the phone down.

23 October 1996

Alice

I enter the hall of my house to the monotonous beat of William's music, booming down from the attic. For once, I am pleased to hear it. I call out to him and climb the stairs. The music is so loud, he doesn't hear me. His door is open, and I walk in. William is lounging on his bed, and beside him is a girl. They both look up when they see me. The girl is small and dark, with a pointed leprechaun face. Her thick, straight hair is cut short, and she is wearing black leggings and a loose red shirt.

'Hello Mum. This is Marion.' William and the girl get to their feet. I smile and say, 'Hello Marion – It's good to meet you at last.' She has a curly mouth, sparkly brown eyes and a clear skin.

I don't quite know how to proceed, as I'd expected to find William alone. I suggest we eat the sandwiches and fruit I bought at a filling station on the way home. William turns off his music and we all go down to the kitchen. I unwrap the sandwiches and set them out on a plate. William makes coffee. Marion arranges the fruit. I tell her she must thank her mother for the beautiful salad vegetables, and Marion says her mother loves gardening, and she's busy making green tomato chutney just now.

I search for the right words, for the right moment, to tell William about his grandmother. We sit down at the table and William and Marion each take a chicken sandwich. I help myself to a soggy tuna and cucumber one and I say, 'So Ralph told you where I was then, William.'

William looks up, and says wearily, 'Yes Mum, he told me'.

243

I can't talk about Ralph in front of Marion. Neither can I tell William about his grandmother in front of Marion. I either wait for her to go, or I ask her to excuse me and William, as I have something important to say to him. We munch in silence for a few minutes, and then William puts down his half-eaten sandwich, and gives me the kind of even, measured look that sounds warning bells in my head. He clears his throat. 'Mum.'

I force a lump of tuna sandwich down my throat and watch my son's eyes darken as he says, 'Mum I know about Granny.'

'Oh!' I can't hold back an exclamation of surprise.

'The grey woman told me. She phoned yesterday morning.'

Of course, Ann Lister would naturally have tried to get in touch with me. I wish she'd told me she'd spoken to William.

'I didn't believe her at first.' William stops and looks keenly at me and he says with bewilderment. 'Why did she die? Granny wasn't ready to die.'

'I know. We're all shocked. I'm so sorry William. I came back specially. I wanted to tell you myself.'

'It doesn't matter,' he says. But I can see that it does.

I'm sure he knows I ran away from Ralph but I just tell him that I need to be in Kent at the moment to help David with the funeral arrangements. I tell him that Rosamund is coming down from Edinburgh and we'll all be staying at Hunter's Moon. I shall drive back there tomorrow and he can come with me. William says in his obstinate voice that he doesn't want to go to Hunter's Moon yet, he wants to stay here, until his grandmother's funeral.

I can't believe that he chooses to remain in this house with Ralph. *Will Ralph be here?*

'William,' I say firmly. 'I can't leave you to look after yourself.'

'It's all right Mum,' he says, equally firmly. 'I can stay with Marion.'

Marion nods, looks at me anxiously and says, 'My mum says it's all right with her, as long as it's all right with you.'

William says, 'I don't want to miss college, and there's my washing-up job.'

What can I do? This was fixed before I even got here. I flinch at the thought that Marion must know an awful lot

244

about our family. 'Very well William,' I say, lamenting my loss of authority, and employing the last vestiges of it. 'It's extremely kind of your mother, Marion, but I must talk to her first.'

25 October 1996

Alice

David and Jonquil and I have fixed the day for Mother's funeral and arranged the order of service. In the *Book of Common Prayer*, under the section entitled 'The Burial of the Dead,' I read, *'Man that is born of a woman hath but a short time to live, and is full of misery,'* and I think it a bleak message for those not banking on an afterlife.

This is the end of an era for me. Two deaths. Double grief.

I think how I never really understood the extent of my mother's loneliness. Did I tell her I loved her? I hope that I did. If I had brought her home to live with us, Ralph might not have got involved with Judith Page, and Mother might still be here.

Grief is natural. But regret is futile. When all this is over, I must not look back with longing.

I have made it clear to David and Jonquil that my marriage to Ralph is over, although I do not tell them about the baby. In her own way, Jonquil tries hard to cheer me up. 'Poor Alice, I can see what you're going through and I'm very sad for you, of course I am, but it doesn't do to mope.' I allow myself a wry smile when I see how quickly *'Dear Ralph'* has become someone 'you've always had problems with, Alice. He wasn't very sensitive or understanding. Mother didn't like him and to tell you the truth David and I never thought he fitted in. It'll take time, but I do believe, in the end you'll find you're better off without him.'

She also says it's easy for her to say so when she has her art to occupy her, but perhaps, when everything is sorted out, a 'little job' would help.

246

There are three days to be got through before Mother's funeral: many long hours at Hunter's Moon with Jonquil. I shall not go home, for I cannot face Ralph, who keeps trying to reach me. I won't talk to him when he phones and I tear up his unopened letters. Escaping Jonquil, I drive out in my car and find somewhere to walk. Footpaths, country lanes, common land, I hardly notice my surroundings, but the rhythm of my tramping feet soothes the hurt in my head. I've had enough of so-called love between man and woman. Physical love, romantic love, exclusive love: that is short-term love. Enduring love seems to me now to be finally and faithfully linked to the ties of blood. My mother, my children, my brother.

I visit my mother's house, which is still being cleaned and tidied by Mrs Curtis, who also feeds Pinky. We drink coffee together and mourn the absence of my mother. Soon, I must face the task of going through Mother's things. Papers choke the drawers of her bureau: legal documents, bills and receipts, share certificates, personal letters. David will help me with these. I must sort out, and dispose of, her familiar skirts and blouses, her trousers and pullovers and her mountain of underwear. Jonquil will help me with those. But first we must bid my mother farewell in the proper manner. We must say the prayers, sing the hymns and celebrate her life. Alan Sheppard has been in touch with us. He will bring Mother's Will to Hunter's Moon.

Mrs Curtis says, 'I'm ever so worried about Pinky. He's still up in that bedroom and he won't touch his food. I took him a plate of his favourite fish Whiskas, and he didn't even open his eyes.'

We go up to Mother's room. Pinky is curled on the bed, comatose.

'Poor little chap – he's pining.' Mrs Curtis rubs the back of her hand across her eyes. Pinky's breathing is very slow. When I touch him, his coat feels dry and his flesh slack. I think he's probably on the way out.

'Are you going to take him to the vet?' asks Mrs Curtis.

'It might be the kindest thing.'

Mrs Curtis is shocked. 'You're surely not thinking of having him him put down?'

'Well – I'll have to see what the vet says,' I reply firmly. 'Do you know where my mother kept his travelling basket?'

I carry Pinky, still comatose, in his basket, into Joe Baxter's consulting room.

'Hello Alice,' says Joe. 'How are you? How's your mother?'

'She died – four days ago.' How brutal that sounds: what else can I say?

Joe's warm-coloured face flushes deeper with embarrassment. 'I'm very sorry to hear that. I should have known: I don't always get a local paper.'

'Please don't worry – it doesn't matter.'

Joe turns his attention to Pinky. We undo the basket and Joe lifts Pinky out and lays him on the bench. I don't let myself remember Emily.

'My mother's daily thinks he's pining. He's quite old.'

Joe's hands are moving gently over Pinky's furry body.

'Has he been having his pills?'

'I'm not sure. Since Mother died, Mrs Curtis has been feeding him.'

'Hmmn. We might need to increase the dose. I'll give him an injection now.'

I have to admit to feeling disappointed. I had hoped the problem of my mother's horrible cat would be easily solved. 'I can't look after Pinky myself.'

Joe looks up at me and reads my mind. He says, quite sternly, 'This cat is not on his last legs you know. He'll perk up with medication. You'll probably find someone who will take him in.'

'I'll give him to Mrs Curtis. Mrs Curtis is very fond of Pinky.'

Pinky has his injection and is put back into his basket. Joe consults his watch.

'Come and have a drink. Surgery's finished. If you don't mind meeting me in the pub we went to last time, I'll be along in ten minutes.'

'O.K.'

Is he making a pass at me? Or just being kind? Anyway, it's something to do, I think as I put Pinky back in the car.

I buy a half of cold lager and sit down at one of the round

tables. I suppose I'm free now. And so is Joe Baxter. I can't remember when I last thought in terms of a sexual relationship with someone other than Ralph. I've lost all that. Given it up for ever. Passion. Intensity. Ralph.

Joe Baxter is not like Ralph. Joe is calm and sensible and kind. Joe would make a good friend. As I drink my lager, I think it will be pleasant to have the company of someone other than Jonquil and Mrs Curtis and June and Arthur. June pops over from next door whenever she sees my car. She is kind and sympathetic, and she was terribly upset when I told her about Mother. But I now see exactly why Mother found her so irritating.

Joe walks in, relaxed and smiling. 'Thank you for waiting.' He glances at my half empty glass. 'Can I get you another?'

'Thanks.'

He goes to the bar and returns with another half of lager for me and a tankard of bitter for himself. 'It's nice to see you again,' says Joe. 'Sorry it's not at a happier time. Please accept my sympathy.'

I thank him and we drink our beer. Then Joe says, 'Would you like some lunch? They do the usual stuff here: scampi and chips, cottage pie, lasagne, beef in Guinness. All home cooked but not homemade. Or you could have a sandwich.'

'What are you going to have?'

'Saves me cooking in the evening if I eat lunch. The scampi and chips is just about edible with loads of tartare sauce.'

'That's fine.'

Joe orders our food and says, 'Are you feeling all right? You've gone very pale.'

'I'm having to get my head round a lot of things just now.'

'It takes time to grieve.' There is compassion in his greenish-brown eyes.

'It was so sudden. Death is so final.'

'Was it her heart?'

'She died in her sleep. Suddenly. I feel so guilty, Joe.'

'Why on earth do you feel guilty?'

'For not being there. I should have been with her. A carer was looking after her – quite competently I believe, but you can't be certain. Mother didn't much like having a carer. She called Ann Lister her "keeper". My mother was lonely. She wanted *me* there.'

'You have your own life to lead.'

'She was frightened of becoming senile; of losing control. She talked about euthanasia.'

'As do most of us, occasionally, as we grow older.'

'When I went in to see her, she had little bruises on her face. There were bottles of pills by her bed. None of the lids were screwed down; she has arthritis in her fingers. I saw the doctor pick up one of the bottles and look at it.'

'Do you think she might have taken too many pills?'

'One of the bottles was Pinky's medicine. For his heart. I got them from you.'

'Even if your mother took them, the cat's pills couldn't do her any harm. If they were prescribed for a dog it would be different. You'd give a dog digitalis – same as a human. Overdosing on that could be dangerous. But you can't give digitalis to cats. If that's what's been worrying you – forget it.' There is quiet conviction in his voice.

'Thank you for telling me that.' I can't stop now. 'The little bruises. What could have caused them do you think?'

'Alice, how can I possibly know? I didn't see them. But the doctor saw them. If they worry you, you must ask him.'

A young woman wearing a long white apron over a short black skirt clomps over to our table and dumps down two plates of breaded orange scampi and anaemic looking chips. When she has gone, Joe says, 'Stop torturing yourself, Alice. You can't bring her back.'

'I know what you're saying.'

'You'll feel better when things get back to normal. When you go home. Norwich isn't it?'

'I may not go back to Norwich.'

'Oh!' The monosyllable is loaded with polite enquiry.

'My marriage has just broken up.'

'You poor thing. I'm so sorry.'

'You understand. You've been through it. But now I have two deaths to mourn.'

He touches my hand in friendship. 'Time,' he says, 'I'm afraid it takes a lot of time, but please believe me, in time it won't feel so bad.'

250

I give up trying to eat the rubbery scampi and I lay down my knife and fork. 'I feel I've brought all this on myself, you know. Trying to please Mother, trying to please Ralph, I've ended up losing them both.'

'Alice, don't you think it's time you dumped this load of guilt you've been carting around.'

I remember Joe saying something similar to me, when I lost Emily. I remember knowing then that I needed to change my life. At that time, I believed I was in charge, capable of bringing about my own kind of changes, if I wanted them badly enough. But I never imagined my life could spin right out of control like this.

Joe says, 'Try pleasing yourself'.

'How?'

'That's up to you.'

'I haven't got any hidden talents. I'm no good at anything.'

'I don't believe you. Anyway you don't have to be *good* at anything. Doing what you want isn't about being good at things.'

I have no answer to this. Joe spears a scampi and pushes it round his plate, coating it with tartare sauce. He lays down the fork, looks me in the eye and says, in his stern voice, 'Alice, if you don't think your life is important, no-one else will'.

Joe eats his scampi and orders coffee from the young woman with the short skirt and the long apron.

'Thank you Joe. You've been very kind,' I say. 'And I expect you are right.'

He just smiles.

We drink our coffee and I say I probably ought to take Pinky home and get back to my brother's house. Jonquil will be wondering what has happened to me.

'I'd like to see you again,' says Joe. 'You know where I am. Please get in touch and let me know how you are.'

'I will,' I say, meaning it.

In the early evening, Alan Sheppard calls round at Hunter's Moon. We all have a drink together and Alan says how fond he was of our mother, and how much he admired both our parents. He says he is in possession of Mother's Will and when would we like him to go through it with us?

251

Certainly not now, I think, and I am very relieved when David looks at me and says, 'Shall we wait till after the funeral? Shall we say goodbye to Mother first?'

28 October 1996

Alice was exhausted. Slumped on the bed in Mother's little box room, she tried to take in the significance of her son's words. 'What are you *saying*, William?!' William's grey eyes, usually so calm and clear, were bloodshot and bleary with alcohol. Alice looked into them and she saw confusion, and a trace of something so deeply shocking, so unacceptable to her, that she could not hold his gaze. She thought, this is my son: for nine months I carried him in my belly. I felt the flutter of his first stirrings to life. I have nurtured him, watched him grow, worried for him, celebrated with him. No-one on earth is more dear to me. His words – the way he is looking at me now – strike me with as deep a dread as any of the blows I have ever suffered.

William lowered his gaze and, elbows bent, rested his head in his hands. He couldn't stop now. He had to let loose the venomous creature flapping about in his brain. He said it again, 'Where were *you* Mum? The night Granny died you weren't at home and neither was Ralph. I believe *someone* helped Granny to die.'

He heard her sharp intake of breath followed by silence. And then, she said, as if her heart were breaking, 'Oh William, I can't believe you could think *that* of *me!*'

Touched by the unbearable sadness in her voice, William could not answer her. He looked at her stricken face and was overwhelmed by shame. No. She would never do anything *really bad*. He stared down at the euthanasia book still grasped in his hands, and he thought he was going to be sick again. He squeezed his eyes closed and tried to count his breaths.

Alice saw that she was absolved. She recognised his shame. The distorting mirror he'd held up to her face reverted to normal. Her changeling son cast off his ghastly disguise and returned to her. Poor William, she thought. What a state he must be in. She said, lightly, 'You'd better stop reading the tabloids, William'.

Ralph will have gone to Judith Page that night, she thought bitterly, but I won't let myself dwell on it.

Sorely penitent, William flipped through the pages of the book in his hand. 'Did you know Granny had this book?'

She shook her head.

'This is all about dying, Mum. It was in the drawer beside Granny's bed. I saw it ages ago when I came to stay that time. When the grey woman told me about Emily. While Granny was in the bath, she called to me to fetch her cotton wool. The book was hidden underneath it. Granny told me she thought animals were luckier than us, because *they* can be given a painless death. She had all these *pills*, Mum. And some of them were for Pinky.'

Alice thought, William is echoing my own unease, but she said, 'Pinky's pills couldn't have harmed Granny. I know that for a fact.'

'I still think Granny wasn't ready to die,' said William stubbornly. He thought of Granny enjoying her birthday party, of all those old people having a good time.

Granny would have known Mum and Ralph were having problems. Granny had a way of knowing about things. But the real bust-up came the night she died. All of that happening together had made him imagine all the terrible things people can do to each other.

Alice said, 'I don't think Granny was ready to die either. But at least she was spared what really frightened her.' William's hand stung from the scratches inflicted by Pinky; blood oozed out under the Elastoplast. He thought of Mrs Curtis's wisps of wild orange hair and of the tears in her scared blue eyes. 'Mrs Curtis said there were some funny marks near Granny's eyes. If she died in her sleep, like they said, what could have caused those marks?'

'Maybe the curtains were drawn. Maybe Mrs Curtis imagined she saw something odd,' said Alice, trying not to visualise those disturbing little blemishes on her mother's dead face, and wishing she had asked Dr Wright about them.

'And there's something else, Mum,' said William portentously, thinking of what Rosamund had just told him. 'Jonquil was afraid Granny was going to change her Will and leave Hunter's Moon to you, Mum.'

'I can't imagine why Jonquil should believe your grandmother would do that,' said Alice with surprise, and she thought, Mother knew how much I loved Hunter's Moon, and she knew I was upset when she told me she'd left it to David. She guessed Ralph and I would split up. But she's an old-fashioned traditionalist.

'Louisa told Rosamund she overheard Jonquil and David talking about it. She's afraid they might all have to move out of Hunter's Moon. *Jonquil* would hate that.'

'We don't yet know how your grandmother has left everything, but I'm sure they've no need to worry,' said Alice.

Jonquil wanted my mother dead, she thought – and urgently, if she believed Mother was about to change her Will.

William could no longer bear the touch of the euthanasia book. He pushed it into his mother's hands. 'Do you really think Granny bought this all by herself?'

Alice accepted the weight of the book and was suddenly overwhelmed by a solid wave of grief.

'Well if she didn't buy it, who did? Who would give Granny a book about dying?'

Her head ached. There were pains in her arms and legs, undigested food in her stomach. She longed for the refuge of sleep. 'I'm too tired to worry about all this any more. Granny is dead. Nothing can change that.'

William thought, nothing can change what has happened, but it shouldn't have happened. Mrs Curtis knew something was wrong. 'We can't just leave it, Mum,' he said forcibly, 'We ought to find out who *did* give her that book, and it wasn't any of us, so it must have been David or Jonquil. Or the grey woman.'

After Alice had succeeded in persuading William to rest for a while and to tidy himself up before coming downstairs, she went wearily down herself. They were sitting around glumly, drinking cups of tea, all except David, who had a glass of whisky in his hand. The party debris had been cleared away by Mrs Curtis, helped by Rosamund, Louisa and Helen. By the time Alice got downstairs, Mrs Curtis was preparing to leave.

'How is he feeling?' asked David.

'Upset, but he'll be down in a minute. Poor William, I don't know how he managed to drink so much whisky. It's my fault for not keeping an eye on him.'

Alice sat on the sofa, next to Rosamund and Louisa, and accepted a cup of tea from Jonquil. She was suddenly struck with a longing for Ralph: for the Ralph who was lost for ever. She was all alone now. Here, in this quiet sitting room, marooned in a heaving sea of troubles. After a while, she braced herself and laid the euthanasia book on the table beside the tea-pot. 'William says this book was hidden in the drawer beside Mother's bed,' she said evenly. 'You saw how badly it has upset him. I've never seen it before today. Has anyone else?'

Glancing at his daughters, whose eyes were fixed upon Alice and the book, David said, 'Shall we talk about this some other time?'

Alice looked towards Jonquil who gazed back at her sorrowfully. 'No,' said Jonquil, quietly, 'I think we should get it over with right now. I have to tell you that *I* bought this book with Mother.'

Alice watched an expression of disbelief ripple over her brother's face. Louisa and Helen appeared to have stopped breathing.

Jonquil continued, less steadily, 'We went to a bookshop in Maidstone while Mother was staying at Hunter's Moon.' She paused and when she began to speak again, her voice was trembling and her eyes brimmed with tears. 'Mother and I grew very close while she was staying with us at Hunter's Moon. She was able to really open her heart to me. She was so frightened of the future. Her greatest fear was of being trapped in a living death. We had a little talk about euthanasia. And I told her I thought there was something called a

Living Will in which you could say what you wanted to happen to you if you got too ill to tell people yourself.' Jonquil halted for a moment to blow her nose. 'It's a legal document. This book explains it all. I don't suppose she ever made a Living Will, or we'd know about it. And in the end she didn't need it. Poor Mother.' Jonquil keeled over and laid her head on the arm of the chair. David strode to her side, knelt down and put his arms around her trembling shoulders.

William rinsed out his foul-tasting mouth and drank two glasses of water. Then he washed his hands, splashed his face under the running tap, and replaced the bloody Elastoplast on his hand with a fresh one he found in the bathroom cabinet. He dragged his fingers through his hair and tucked his shirt back inside his trousers. He thought he'd probably been sick enough times not to risk throwing up any more, and he resolved to stay off whisky for a very long time.

He began to wonder what would happen next. Mum couldn't go on staying with David and Jonquil, unless, of course, Hunter's Moon now belonged to her. He tried to imagine himself living in the luxury of Hunter's Moon.

Would they go home to Norwich? He thought of his attic, of all his stuff heaped on his work table, of his music centre and his posters and his collection of pot lids, and he wondered when he'd sleep in his own bed again. As long as Ralph wasn't there, he wouldn't mind going home. He missed his attic, but he liked staying with Marion. Marion made him happy. She was pretty and kind and good fun, and he felt welcome in Marion's easy-going home, where everything was comfortably worn as if they'd done a lot of living there. Nobody minded if you left a light on or stood a mug of coffee on the table. Marion's noisy little sister rushed around with her friends, and her mum made proper meals with roast meat and vegetables and a pudding. Marion's dad always said hullo and asked him how he was and remembered his name. In Marion's bedroom which was still full of the My Little Pony stuff she'd been keen on once, they lay on her bed and played her tapes and he talked to her about Mum and Ralph having a bust up, and about Granny dying so suddenly. She cried. He was touched that she cried on account of him. And when she tried to smile

257

at him, a not quite straight smile, he kissed her. She kissed him back. Kissing Marion gave him a sweet strong feeling that overpowered everything. He wished she was here now.

William got up off the bathroom chair, drank another glass of water and prepared himself to go down and face them all. On his way, past his grandmother's bedroom, he glanced through the open door, and wondered, piercingly, what had really happened in there. He caught a glimpse of luminous eyes glaring out from beneath the bed. Pinky was still on guard.

William walked into the sitting room in the middle of Jonquil's confession. He didn't believe a word of what she was saying about wanting to put Granny's mind at rest. Scaring the wits out of her more likely: devious cow. Then he had to watch while Jonquil made an embarrassing scene, and was comforted by David, overreacting as usual.

'We're all going back to Hunter's Moon for tonight,' said his mother, briskly. Rosamund pulled a face at him, but as she said later, the only alternative would have been staying in Granny's house, and none of them was prepared to do that.

There was homemade mushroom soup and cold chicken and salad for supper, but no-one felt like eating. After that, William watched television with Rosamund and Louisa and Helen, in what Jonquil called 'the children's sitting room', while David and Jonquil and Alice stayed in the drawing room.

Much later Rosamund came and sat on William's bed and they talked for a long time about what had happened, what might have happened and what was likely to happen. As Rosamund said, 'There's not much we can do about anything'. William didn't agree. 'I still think someone helped Granny to die,' he said, soberly. 'We've got to find out who it was.'

29 October 1996

After breakfast, when William enquired about returning to Norwich, his mother said they'd all be driving back after lunch. Right, William thought, so Mum is going home at last. He wondered where Ralph might be, but he didn't ask.

Rosamund said, 'Louisa told me the solicitor is coming to explain the Will. They're still paranoid about Hunter's Moon, you know. If Granny *has* left Hunter's Moon to Mum, they'll probably never speak to us again.'

'I don't much care if they don't,' said William.

At midday, William and Rosamund saw a maroon BMW draw up on the gravel outside Hunter's Moon. The short bald man, who was their grandmother's solicitor, got out carrying a briefcase. They watched while David greeted him at the front door, and they heard David say, 'Thanks for coming, Alan,' and they went into the drawing room, followed by Jonquil and Alice.

'Come on Ros, let's go for a walk,' said William, and he and Rosamund went into the garden, noticed Louisa and Helen hitting balls at each other on the tennis court, and headed down the gravel drive and out into the lane, where they picked and ate a handful of blackberries to pass the time. When they got back, the BMW had disappeared. David and Jonquil and Alice were in the drawing room with the door shut and Louisa and Helen were watching television in their room. Rosamund and William hung around in the hall. Eventually, the drawing-room door opened and David, Jonquil and Alice came out. David looked quietly satisfied, Jonquil looked smug and Alice looked uneasy. Jonquil was saying, 'Dearest Mother. She thought of everything.'

'She tried to be equitable,' said David.

Alice said, 'There *is* one thing I'm not happy about'.

'It *does* seem rather extreme,' said Jonquil.

'Let me think about it,' said David. 'I'm not sure there's much we can do, but we'll discuss it again in a day or two.'

In the car on the way back to Norwich, Rosamund said, 'It's obvious they didn't need to worry about Hunter's Moon. But it's a bit sad. You love Hunter's Moon, don't you Mum.'

'It wouldn't have done for your grandmother to have left it to us, and she's been very fair. I'll explain when we get home.'

There was a note from Ralph on the kitchen table. William watched his mother pick it up and read it without comment.

Rosamund went up to her bedroom. William slowly climbed the stairs to his attic. Everything was as he had left it. He stood by his work table and stared down at the untidy pile of books, at his half completed *King Lear* essay, his piece of driftwood shaped like a bird. What the hell was happening? It suddenly came to him, *I may have to leave my attic.*

Downstairs, Alice read, in Ralph's small, barely legible handwriting, 'Hope you got back safely. Food in fridge. I've put central heating on. Am in London on business. Alice – we *must* talk. I will phone. love R.'

Alice thought, Ralph thinks just because he's bought milk and bread and eggs and apples, everything will get back to normal. The heart has gone out of this house. We can't live here any more. She thought she might make some tea, so she filled the kettle and put it on the cooker. Rosamund and William arrived in the kitchen as the kettle was boiling. They watched solemnly as she put tea leaves into the teapot, poured on boiling water and fetched milk from the fridge.

William said, 'It's about time you told us what's going on, Mum.'

Rosamund poured tea into mugs. 'You're leaving Ralph,' she said. It was more of a statement than a question.

'We can still live *here*, can't we,' said William, feeling homesick already. 'It would be nice here without Ralph.'

'We will have to sell this house,' said Alice, gazing bleakly at the space where Emily's basket used to be, and thinking how unstable life was. She sat down heavily on one of the hard kitchen chairs. 'I'd better tell you about Granny's Will. As you've realised, Hunter's Moon now belongs to David and Jonquil, but Granny has left us quite a lot of money and she's also left us her house.'

'Well you don't *want* it, do you Mum?' said Rosamund. 'It's a horrid little house.'

'We might have to live there for a while,' said Alice. And then, reacting to the glum expressions on her children's faces, she added, 'Just while I'm sorting everything out.'

'What about college?' said William wondering if he'd be able to go on living at Marion's house.

'I don't know, William; we'll try and find a way of staying in Norwich till you finish.'

'What else?' asked Rosamund. 'I heard you tell David there was something in Granny's Will you weren't happy about. I suppose she's left a legacy to Pinky, or some old cats' home.'

'No, she's not done that, but there is one rather odd bequest. Granny has left her pearl choker to Ann Lister.'

'Good God!' said Rosamund. 'That pearl choker's worth thousands. Jonquil told me it was by far the most valuable piece of Granny's jewellery. Grandpa bought it at Asprey's. Granny wore it for her birthday party. It was her favourite thing. Why did Granny go and leave it to Mrs Lister?'

Alice said, 'If the family had known about this, we would have stopped her.'

It felt like a blow to the head. William's hands grew clammy; the skin on the back of his neck prickled. 'The grey woman knew that. That's why she didn't wait. *Now* I know what happened. It was *her*. That creepy grey woman killed my grandmother.' He stared at his mother, aghast. Her eyes met his in silent acknowledgement.

1 November 1996

Ann Lister lived in a semi-detached, 1930s house in a quiet street of similar houses that had seen better days. Some were well maintained, with fresh paint, secure-looking red-tiled roofs and neat front gardens. One or two had rotten wood-work, and greenish damp staining the pebble-dash.

Ann Lister's house was one of the smarter ones, bow-fronted with a circular window beneath the gable. It had pale green walls and black window frames. It's red roof tiles were new, emphasising the dividing line between it and its twin, which was a patchwork of decayed and replacement tiles. Alice pushed open the black wooden gate and walked slowly up the concrete path. Bare brown earth either side sprouted with lines of severely pruned roses. Next door's garden was occupied by a battered yellow Ford Escort and a thin Alsatian dog which barked hoarsely at Alice, before sitting down on its haunches and scratching its ear.

Alice pressed the bell beside Ann Lister's dark green front door. She felt sick. The door opened almost immediately.

'Hello dear. I've been expecting you.'

Alice withdrew her hand quickly from the touch of cool fingers. She had not informed the woman she was coming.

Ann Lister was dressed in a skirt and blouse of her usual greyish colours. Her iron-grey hair sprang in its customary firmly set wave from her pale-powdered forehead. Round her neck hung the silver locket she always wore. Mrs Bunting gave her that locket, thought Alice, with fresh insight. *How did Mrs Bunting die?*

'Come and sit down dear.' Alice was led into the room at

262

the front with the curved bay window. She sat down gingerly on a hard armchair upholstered in a pink material with a scratchy pile.

'The kettle's on the boil. I'll just go and make tea. Back in a tick.' Ann Lister glided away.

Alice looked around her. Northerly light filtering through net curtains defined everything with precision. Bookshelves and a circular table filled the end of the room opposite the window. On the table a collection of glass animals, glass paperweights, and decorative glass bowls gleamed coldly. There were four pictures hanging on the dusty pink walls. Two were landscapes: the purple mountains and blue lochs of Scotland. Another was a picture of a girl on a swing. She had brown ringlets and a dimpled smile and she wore a low-necked high-waisted diaphanous gown, with a beribboned sun-bonnet and in one arm she held a basket of full-blown roses. Over the beige-tiled mantelpiece, in a gold painted plaster frame, hung the largest picture. Jesus, mild eyed, with long hair and beard and golden halo, clad in a white robe, held out his arms, palms uppermost, in blessing. The sandy desert behind him was drenched in golden light. Beneath the picture, Alice read, 'Come unto me, all ye that labour and are heavy laden, and I will give you rest.'

Alice stared down at her feet in their tan moccasins resting on the spiral-patterned beige carpet, and felt sicker. She longed to run away from here. The walls pressed in on her. There was a faint odour of leftover meals, of floral scent and an underlying breath of concealed damp.

A tray set with tea things lay on a low table in front of the sofa: silver jug and sugar bowl with silver sugar tongs, china cups saucers and plates in an old-fashioned design that Alice recognised as 'Indian Tree'; an iced cake decorated with segments of mandarin oranges, on a white china cake stand. She got to her feet and walked over to the bookshelves. Two fat books caught her eye. One of them was called, *Nursing Today* and the other, white title on purple background, *A Study of the Occult*.

'I do enjoy a good book, don't you, my dear.'

Alice couldn't control an involuntary start of surprise as Ann Lister materialised at her elbow. 'I've made Earl Grey. I

263

seem to remember it's your preference.' She stood the silver tea-pot on the low table. 'Just a touch of milk, that's right isn't it.' Alice sat down again in the hard chair and watched Ann Lister pour two cups of tea. Then she cut into the cake, and slid a slice onto a plate. 'Do have a piece. I made it specially, this morning.'

'No thank you.' Alice took a deep breath. 'I've come to tell you about my mother's Will.' She paused, watching closely for Mrs Lister's reaction, and recalling, with a painful stab, the exact wording – '*To my kind friend, Ann Lister, knowing she will appreciate it, I leave my pearl choker*'. Mrs Lister remained quietly inscrutable. Alice continued, with difficulty. 'My mother wanted you to have her pearl choker.'

'I know, dear. Your mother informed me of her intentions. I can't tell you how much I will treasure it. I am deeply honoured by her regard for me.' Ann Lister's smile was calmly complacent. 'Are you sure I can't tempt you to a small slice of cake. Your mother was very fond of my orange cake.'

'No thank you.' Alice felt her stomach tense in revolt. She switched her eyes away from the circle of orange segments, just dampening the white icing on top of the cake, and looked out of the window, through the artfully draped net curtains, at a group of schoolboys sloping past the gate. Next door's Alsatian gave a half-hearted bark. Normal life still goes on out there, Alice thought, with relief. But now, oh my poor mother, I must face up to this hateful task. She opened her handbag, and took out the white envelope addressed to Alan Sheppard. She looked at Ann Lister comfortably at ease on the pink sofa, a smoothly expectant expression on her large face, and she said, handing over the envelope, 'I don't have it with me today, but if you take this to my solicitor, he will get the choker out of his safe and give it to you.'

Mrs Lister nodded. 'I hope you understand, my dear: Mrs Maddison knew I would value her gift. When I saw those pearls round her neck, I told her I'd never seen anything so beautiful in all my life.' She held the envelope for a moment in her square hands and examined the address, before stroking it and laying it gently on the table. 'I shall always remember your mother. She was a fine lady. We had a very happy time together.'

Alice took a gulp of her tea, and then she said, rapidly, 'My mother died very suddenly and rather unexpectedly, Ann. I was too upset at the time to ask you about her final hours. I'd like you to tell me now exactly what happened.'

Behind the lens of her glasses, Ann Lister's eyes stared steadily back at Alice. She swallowed a mouthful of cake and dabbed her coral-lipsticked mouth carefully with a paper table napkin. 'We'd had a lovely evening,' she said. 'I'd made a cottage pie, one of your mother's favourites. And after, we'd reminisced. She loved to tell me about her young days and of course she loved to talk about the family. You're all very dear to her. Then, I saw her into bed, as I always did. In the early hours I heard her calling. I went to her. She was very distressed.'

Watching carefully, Alice caught the gleam of pale eyes which seemed no longer to be focusing on her. 'I knew that her time had come.' The North Country accent was suddenly more pronounced, the tone heightened. 'She was ready to go.'

Hardly breathing, Alice asked quietly, 'Did my mother suffer any pain?'

'No my dear. I saw to that. I helped her.'

'How did you help her?' Alice felt faint.

Ann Lister's voice came as if from a great distance, 'I am a nurse,' she said. 'I know how to ease the way.'

'I see,' said Alice, repulsed by the moist coral lips and grey teeth.

'You mustn't fret for her, my dear.' Those eyes were focusing now, bright with ardour. Ann Lister's powdery face glowed, her voice rang with deadly conviction. 'I have received a message from the other side. Your mother is united with your father. She wants you to know she is happy and at peace.'

The dusty pink wall, the shiny tiled fireplace, the picture of Jesus swayed and bulged towards Alice. She gasped and gripped the arms of her chair, until, gradually, the wall and the fireplace and Jesus's outstretched hands receded.

'Are you all right, dear?'

'I'm glad you told me,' said Alice. 'Now, if you'll excuse me, I really must be going.' She rose clumsily from her chair.

265

Mrs Lister laid a hand on Alice's arm, 'You have your mother's blessing,' she said.

Alice parked behind the garage that still held her mother's Rover. She got out of her car, locked it and walked up the path. As she approached the front door, it was opened by William: she stepped inside, slipped off her jacket and dropped her car keys on the hall table.

Rosamund appeared. 'Poor Mum. You look worn out. Was it awful?'

'Yes.' Followed by her children, Alice walked through to the sitting room and collapsed on the sofa. Rosamund and William stood, looking expectantly at her. She felt the intensity of their gaze and, meeting it, she said gravely, 'I'm afraid you're right, William. She more or less admitted it.'

'Good God!' said Rosamund.

William said, 'What are you going to do Mum?'

'I don't know. I don't know what to do.'

'Mum!' William's, eyes were blazing. 'You *can't* let her get away with this. You've *got* to tell the police. We'll come with you.'

'Yes.' Alice closed her eyes and leaned back against her mother's soft, chintz-covered sofa. She heard the telephone begin to ring. She heard William answer it and say, 'Hello. Oh hello Ralph.' Without opening her eyes, she shook her head.

'My mother isn't here.' Alice imagined, at the other end of the line, the sound of Ralph's insistent voice. 'No. My mother isn't here,' repeated William. 'And even if she was, she wouldn't want to speak to you. Goodbye Ralph.' And he put down the receiver.